Up Dinc-ᴅᴏᴛᴛ

By Mark Hubbard

For Loren and Sophie

The best daughters anyone could wish for. I love you both very much.

Acknowledgements

It seems that some people can sit down and write a book in no time at all, and what they write never needs revision - it's perfect. I can't do that. For a start, my typing leaves a lot to be desired. I often get the correct letters to appear, but they are rarely in the right order, and it takes months to spot some of the errors. I am convinced that someone sneaks into my house at night and rearranges the keys on my keyboard. I think the same individual is responsible for drinking all my wine because it never lasts as long as it should. When my cats were alive, they used to jump onto my desk and revise entire passages while I was making coffee. I miss my cats, Bobble, Bibble and Fluffle, but I certainly don't miss having to find and correct their unsolicited contributions.

In short, it took a very long time to write Up Dinc-Bottom. The first draft was completed in 1997. As I write this, the calendar confirms that it is now February 2023. Aside from mischievous felines, mixed-up keys (or possibly fingers) and a serious quantity of merlot, the primary reason it took so long was that life got in the way. The time to finish this book was never there - something else always took priority. Occasionally, I would find a few evenings to tinker with the manuscript, re-writing passages and deleting others only to save it for another day which was always a long time coming. If it had not been for the tireless encouragement of a few special friends, I am confident that this book would have remained on a hard drive gathering metaphorical dust right up until the moment I gasped my last breath. Fortunately, I listened to those friends, and the book is here for you to read. So, thank you to Kaz Richards, Jane Wharmby, Anita Broadhead and especially Kay Grundon for believing in me more than I believed in myself.

Table of Contents

On The War Path

A small car slowed gently to a halt in the car park of Dinc Valley Primary school. There was a crunch of gears as it moved back and forth until precisely aligned in a parking space marked with a sign reading "Headteacher". Mrs Agnes Braintree was the current holder of this title, and she noted with some displeasure that a second, smaller notice had been appended to the first with the words 'has a fat bum' scratched untidily across it. An identical message had been embossed on the boot of her little Renault the previous week - the same day, an apple core had been stuffed up her tailpipe, and bananas dropped in her fuel tank.

Agnes let out a long sigh and, picking up her handbag, got out of the car. She'd put up with this petty terrorism for most of her teaching career, but lately, her patience had worn thin. It wasn't just the signs or the name-calling, the graffiti in the sports hall, or the tadpoles in the toilet. It was the rudeness and lack of discipline, the ongoing trial of having to be politically correct, the parents shouting at her – never taking responsibility for their own flesh and blood. As far as she was concerned, a creeping, slithering rot had taken hold of society. There were too many people getting paid to sit on their backsides doing nothing, and too many of them had big televisions and satellite dishes – things she couldn't hope to afford. They smoked expensive cigarettes and drove brand-new cars, all at the taxpayers' expense. Most of them had at least eight hungry mouths to feed three times a day on burgers, chips, and deep-fried chocolate.

Agnes was cross. Every term for the past thirty years, she had battled these delinquent, dirty, and often unwanted specimens. It had been easy, to begin with, because she could thrash them with a cane as the need arose or clout them around the head with a substantial encyclopaedia. A well-aimed wastepaper bin often did the trick too. However, in recent years, the threat of prosecution hung over her like a rickety guillotine. The law, it seemed, had swung in the 'vile little sods' favour and didn't show any signs of swinging back again. Worse than this, they knew their rights and could quote them almost as readily as they could wield a can of spray paint or surf the train to Dincsmouth. It was awful, but Agnes knew who was to blame, and she had a plan.

***

Chief Constable Dint was thinking about the boat he would buy when he retired. It was going to be a big one - white with one or even two powerful engines and enough space below to sleep six people in supreme comfort. At least, that was where his daydream started, but

2

the more he thought about it and all the tedious guests his wife would invite on board every weekend, the smaller the vessel became until he ended up with a six-metre launch, an outboard motor, and a hammock. It would do nicely so long as he could store enough fuel on board to get halfway around the world without anyone noticing. It was a lovely dream, but retirement was still years in the future, and the pile of paperwork on his desk kept getting bigger. He'd often considered a transfer to something less desk-bound, but it all seemed much too hazardous whenever he read the small print. He decided he was better off staying out of harm's way in the tranquil backwater that was sunny Dillchurch.

Dillchurch was a moderately sized town in the mostly rural county of Dorkshire. A cluster of Victorian terraces that traced an intricate but haphazard patchwork across the rolling landscape, its form owed more to chance than a coherent plan of any sort. Aside from a prominent county hall and derelict brewery, the most notable structure was the vast, sprawling hospital at its centre. Looking like a converted rollercoaster, it was covered in brightly coloured metalwork and was only bearable when viewed in complete darkness. The idea of a hospital combined with a fairground ride appealed to Dint as he gazed at it from his office. His idle imagination conjured up an elaborate system for moving patients around the outside of the building using rails, vacuum tubes, and steam engines. The idea hadn't gone down well at the Chief Constable's ball, and he'd missed out on all the vol-au-vents.

As he looked through his dusty window, the hospital wasn't the only thing to spoil his view of the countryside beyond. There were countless churches of all shapes and sizes, with spires and towers piercing the skyline in every direction. It was like someone had started a church-building competition and forgotten when to say stop. Competing noisily on Sundays for the few souls still interested in what they had to say, the bells invariably woke Dint up when he was trying his best to have a well-earned snooze.

However, there was one thing about Dillchurch and the county of Dorkshire that Dint was especially fond of: there wasn't an inch of motorway running through it. Dorkshire was completely unspoiled by miles of the triple carriageway, crash barriers, or the nasty blue signs that clashed with the sheep and primroses. It was a genuinely rural county, ideal for the kids on long hot summer holidays, not to mention a blissful haven for a slow-moving, parochial police force. Unfortunately, this deficiency made it extremely difficult to get anywhere quickly, and Dorkshire was near impenetrable throughout the summer months. It was almost impossible to travel at more than a snail's pace, even when you weren't stuck behind a queue of caravans or a big green combine. Road rage was endemic because there was only one place on the main road across the county where overtaking was possible, and the emergency services spent most of August each year sorting out the mess.

People did strange things in cars at the best of times, but in Dorkshire, they drove along railway tracks to get around the queues. They cut across meadows and floated down rivers. Farmers found them in fields, miles from anywhere, trying to catch rabbits because they'd run out of sandwiches days earlier. Every year, thousands of letters arrived at the council offices complaining about the dismal state of the roads, but nothing was ever done. There were too many vested and powerful interests behind the scenes, all intent on keeping things as they were. No one wanted a motorway within a hundred miles of their backyard, and in any case, the congestion gave councillors an excellent excuse to arrive late for their meetings. It was all quite convenient.

The phone rang just as Dint was deciding what to call his boat. Dragging himself reluctantly back to the real world, he lifted the handset and was greeted by the voice of Constable Hewbry, who quickly informed him, "Hay, Mrs Braintree has harrived for her nine-hay em happointment, sir!"

Dint had to hold the receiver some inches from his ear to avoid adding deafness to a growing list of work-related illnesses. Hewbry had a voice that stood to attention all by itself, and he could polish boots with a single glance.

Mrs Braintree was a regular and not particularly welcome visitor to the Chief Constable's office. The only person she went to see as frequently was Councillor Bonditt. In either case, it was always to complain about something. Dint asked Hewbry to show her in, and all too quickly, there was a knock on the door. Hewbry was the station dog handler, and it crossed Dint's mind that this was entirely appropriate because Mrs Braintree had the look of a bulldog about her - that and a touch of Queen Victoria. Plain as a brown paper envelope and plump as a stuffed gooseberry, she tended to dress mostly in black. Apart from her pale white face, the only thing about her that wasn't as dark as the bottom of a mineshaft was her bright green handbag and 'matching' pink shoes. As he watched her barge into his office, Dint wondered if her underwear might compliment the black, the pink, or the green. Then again, perhaps she didn't wear any? He wished he hadn't thought of that and pulled himself together before getting a migraine or something worse. Mrs Braintree wasn't remotely attractive to him, and he couldn't see how she'd fired anyone else's rockets either. She must have 'done it' for someone at least once because she often trailed into the building with her daughter in tow. Dint thought she looked a little too old to have children, but anything was possible these days. If they could land men on the moon and teach parrots to play golf – he was sure he had read about that somewhere – they could certainly get a forty-three-year-old teacher to give birth to something.

On this occasion, Agnes was on her own, and Dint offered her a chair, enquiring if she would like tea or coffee. When she said she wanted neither, he knew he was in for a rough time and glanced around his desktop for the bottle of aspirin he kept for such occasions.

Mrs Braintree got straight to the point. She liked to do this if she could because it caught her opponents off guard. "Now look here, Henry," she said firmly, jabbing a podgy finger in his direction. "I want you to do something about Dinctum Youth Club. It's the worst thing I have ever seen and has an appalling effect on the children going there." Her voice's sharp, clipped tones could have sliced clean through granite.

"Well, I know how you feel about this, Mrs Braintree," said Dint, trying to put things back on a formal footing. He didn't like to be called Henry, not even by his wife, so he certainly wasn't going to encourage Braintree to do it. "As I have often said, Dorkshire County Youth Service is very proud of Dinctum Village Youth Club. They've achieved a great deal with the young people there, and Mr Palmoil says it's a feather in his cap."

Mr Palmoil was the County Youth Officer or 'Head of Service' as he liked to be known and very well paid for it too. He had a lot of feathers in his cap, most of which came from things he'd shot with his twelve-bore.

"I don't want to hear anything about the so-called youth service or that fool Palmoil," replied Mrs Braintree scornfully. "We're here to teach children, not to serve them. I caught a group of them smoking behind the barn at Drubtatt's farm only last week. That Palmoil has a lot to answer for."

Dint reached for the tablets and tried a different tack. "Mrs Braintree, *Agnes*, how do you know those chil... those young people had anything to do with Dinctum Village Youth Club? Unless you catch them at it, in the club, as it were... smoking, drinking, or whatever else you think they do... do you see?" He thought the point was obvious, but he was out of luck. Mrs Braintree was adamant that the youth service, and especially Mr Palmoil, was directly responsible for all the bad behaviour she had seen in children anywhere on the planet - ever.

"I'm afraid that this left-wing, wishy-washy, half-baked nonsense that Palmoil and his cronies perpetrate is ruining the country, and you're not doing anything about it!" The pointing finger was there again. It was a different one this time and even more unpleasant than the last. There was a glint of manic passion in her eyes as well.

"Look, Mrs Braintree, I don't know what you want me to do about it," said Dint, taking the second of the tablets he had tipped from the bottle and leaning back in his chair. "I don't see what I can do to help you. I'm very sorry." He wasn't, and she knew it.

"You could start by having that youth club shut down pending an investigation," she said, feeling sure that there was bound to be something illegal going on if people only took the time to look.

"An investigation into what, and on what grounds? Nothing is going on!" Dint was running out of patience.

"How do you know that? You haven't looked yet!"

"Well, I haven't looked at a lot of things, Mrs Braintree," said the Chief firmly. "There might be a crime taking place just about anywhere and at any time, but I can't go around poking into this or that on the off chance I'll stumble across it. I mean, there could be a crime taking place at your school *as we speak*, but I can't have an officer permanently stationed there 'just in case'. I haven't the staff."

"There bloody well is a crime going on at my school, Henry," responded Agnes, unable to resist the opportunity of moaning about another of her preoccupations. "The toilets are blocked, the window frames are rotten, the roof leaks, and my chair keeps sinking to the floor, which isn't very dignified, I can tell you, especially when you are trying to discipline some little oik who has just attempted to incinerate the caretaker."

Dint looked at her blankly. A lightly roasted caretaker might warrant his attention, but the decaying window frames at Dinc Valley Primary School were another matter. "I'm afraid I can't be held responsible for the failings of the government, Agnes," he ventured.

"What about arresting that Palmoil man?" said Agnes. "He's a bad influence on the children of Dorkshire, Henry. Arrest him!"

"For what?" asked Dint with growing incredulity. "He hasn't done anything!"

"Well, he's got a beard!" snapped Agnes desperately. "You know what men with beards are like." But Dint had had enough and decided to call a halt to the meeting.

"Mrs Braintree," he said heavily, "I note your concerns, but in England," he glanced at a portrait of the queen on the office wall as he spoke, "people are presumed to be innocent until proven guilty - even the ones with beards. Now, if you don't mind, I really do have a lot to get on with." With that, he picked up the phone and called for Hewbry to show Mrs Braintree out.

After she had left, Henry Dint turned in his chair to stare out of the window once more. One day he would be free from people like Agnes Braintree, Palmoil, and all the other petty politicians in Dorkshire. One day life would be simple again and take place mainly in a boat, but he'd have to muddle on in the meantime.

The trouble with Agnes Braintree, thought Dint, *was that she had the ear of some influential people. People like the MP for West Dorkshire, Rear Admiral Plunge-Pithering. You ignored people like that at your peril. She bullies her way around the 'squirachy' until she gets what she wants. It's no good trying to avoid it. I'll have to consider closing that youth club very seriously. Otherwise, I'll find myself back on the beat – without a boat.* It wasn't a pleasant thought at all. He sat in silence for some minutes, considering his options before deciding to give Councillor Bonditt a call and warn him. She was bound to go there next.

As she left the station, Mrs Braintree noticed that some enterprising individual had climbed the wall outside the main entrance and removed the letters P and O from the sign. Chief Constable Dint was now the only officer in Her Majesty's police force in sole charge of a 'LICE Station.' She smiled and thought this was probably an apt description, so she decided not to bring it to anyone's attention - not even the queen.

***

David Faber was on a diet. He wasn't overweight, but his wife, Sally, was always on some sort of, ultimately unsuccessful, drive to get thinner - which meant he was too. He had to show willing. Otherwise, she might 'up sticks' and go back to live with her mother. She'd threatened to leave more than once, which would have been disastrous on his current salary. When they first bought their house - a poky little two-bedroom semi - the interest rates had been lower, and his income alone had just about covered their outgoings. It was too costly now, and they slipped deeper into the overdraft every month. He'd even taken a second job working as a part-time youth leader in Dinctum to help make ends meet. As luck would have it, he enjoyed the work, and the extra money was enough to keep the wolves from the door.

"What are you eating now?" asked David, amazed that Sally could still find room for anything after the takeaway they had just shared.

"Strawberries and cream," answered Sally in a somewhat offended tone. "Why? Do you want some?"

"No," said David, who was pleasantly full of noodles. "Anyway, I thought you were supposed to be on a diet?"

"We are," said Sally pointedly, popping another plump strawberry the size of a golf ball into her mouth. "Don't worry," she said, seeing the look on his face, "it is artificial cream."

"What kind of fish cream?" asked David, looking up momentarily from the magazine he was perusing.

"Oh, go back to sleep," said Sally wearily. "Mother always said you were as thick as a biscuit."

"Well, that's just the sort of thing we'd expect from her, isn't it?" said David as he turned another page. "Your mother's hardly qualified to call anyone names, is she?"

"Shut up!" said Sally, scraping up the cream that had just dripped down the front of her dressing gown. "My mother can't help it if she's out of touch. She is seventy-five, you know."

"Seventy-five per cent Neanderthal if you ask me," said David under his breath, "and I'm not even going to speculate about the other twenty-five!" He switched channels on the TV and then, looking back down at his magazine, muttered, "Amphibian, most likely."

"What? She does very well for her age," said Sally, trying to reach the remote control. "You have to admit that much."

"Well, she still thinks 'get Internet' is something a northerner says to a trout, doesn't she? She thinks 'al fresco' plays the clarinet and that the 'European Union' is something you find on a water pipe. Shall I go on?"

"No, thank you, you're boring me again." She was fishing between her breasts with a spoon, trying to recover a half-eaten strawberry.

But David was on a roll. "What did she ask about that bloke who got the Nobel Peace prize... 'why did he only get a piece of it?'" He screwed up his face as he spoke, attempting an impression of her mother's voice. "And what about the time she got lost on the London Underground? Five days going around the Central Line waiting for Yeovil Junction to turn up! I mean..."

"Give it a rest!" snapped Sally. "And pass me that remote control, please. You can't be reading that silly magazine and watching the TV at the same time." She began her nightly browse through all the channels, and it was a search that inevitably ended in a huff with some comment about there being nothing on again. She settled in her chair and stretched out to rest her legs on the table.

"I see you finally got around to cutting this table down to size," she observed. "It's much more comfortable now. I thought you said it was too valuable to saw off the legs?"

"It is," said David, lifting the magazine to cover his face.

She flicked through a few more channels before stopping to consider his reply. "So... how?" she asked with a look of puzzlement. Looking down at the table, she saw it was at least six inches lower. Then she noticed the folded carpet flaps around the legs and the little piles of sawdust nearby. "What the fuck," she said. "DAVID! What have you done?" Her voice rose to a crescendo.

"Mmmm?" said David, still hiding as best he could.

"You've cut holes in the bloody floor, haven't you? And the sodding carpet." She couldn't believe her own eyes. "I mean. What on earth…." Words failed her.

"It's only chipboard… you know, the floor," he whined defensively. "It won't cost anything to fix it when we sell the place, and no one will want this old carpet, will they? I mean, you can't go around hacking antiques about willy-nilly, can you? It's an heirloom." But Sally wasn't listening anymore. She threw the remote control back at him and stomped up the stairs.

"You off to bed then?" enquired David, but there wasn't an answer, so he decided it would be a good night to sleep on the sofa.

***

Councillor Bonditt sat at his desk in County Hall, looking at his diary, and spotted a two o'clock appointment with Mrs Braintree. "Oh, for goodness' sake," he said, reaching for his phone. He punched a couple of numbers, and the phone on his secretary's desk beeped. "Mrs Clank, I thought I told you I didn't want to see Braintree anymore?"

She explained that Mrs Braintree had phoned before lunch and been very insistent. "She wouldn't take no for an answer. I'm sorry, sir, but she is challenging to deal with. You know what she's like?"

The call from Dint had warned Bonditt that she was on the warpath again. Dint and Bonditt were well acquainted and members of the same clubs, so they tended to keep an eye out for one another.

Things worked like that in Dorkshire. It wasn't what you knew but who and how you shook their hand.

"Get on the phone to her and cancel the meeting, please," said Bonditt. "Tell her I'm ill or something."

It didn't do him any good because, within a few minutes, Mrs Clank was back on the phone again. "I'm very sorry, sir, but it's Mrs Braintree on the phone, and she's insisting that she speaks to you now."

"Can't you tell her I'm out or something?" pleaded Bonditt. He looked as though he was about to cry.

"I tried that," said Mrs Clank, "but she says she has already spoken to Ms Flueflap in planning, and she said you were in your office right now."

Bonditt made a mental note to have words with Ms Flueflap, but he could see there was little point in trying to avoid Braintree any longer. She had more intelligence about his movements than his doctor, and she'd even tracked him down in Kos while he was on one of his frequent town-twinning escapades. Bonditt had surreptitiously twinned Dillchurch with almost every holiday resort in the Mediterranean.

"Oh, very well then, put her on," he said, wiping the sweat from his brow. Suddenly, the room seemed a lot warmer. "Hello, Mrs Braintree," he said in what he hoped was a cheerful tone, "lovely to hear from you again so soon." He thought that was an excellent place to start.

"Now listen to me, Bonditt. Don't come any of that piffle with me. You know why I'm phoning, and I want to know what you've done about it?"

Bonditt had lost track of everything she had called him about over the years and had a hard job trying to think what it might be this time. "Ah yes," he said, searching through the papers on his desk for a clue, "the um… the skateboard park," he said hopefully. It was undoubtedly one of the things that had given her an entire swarm of buzzy things in her bonnet.

"No!" she snapped. "Not the wretched skateboard park! I'm talking about that youth club! The one in Dinc Valley! Why isn't it shut yet?" She knew Bonditt couldn't have her locked away quite as easily as Dint, so she was altogether far less polite.

Bonditt was on thin ice, and he knew it. Mrs Braintree had agreed to support his re-election, on the understanding that he would close the youth club as a priority, but months later, the club was still open. To get as many votes as possible, Bonditt had agreed to almost anything anyone had suggested: the restoration of an old railway that would have meant demolishing a dozen council houses in Tilt, the opening of a brothel in Cold-Waddock, and the banning of all poodles from public places. Closing Dinctum Village Youth Club seemed a relatively trivial challenge compared to that lot. However, once he returned to office, the promises all seemed too difficult to keep – except perhaps the banning of poodles, for which he had overwhelming public support. Mrs Braintree had been on his case about the youth club ever since and wasn't about to give up.

"You promised me you would shut that nasty little club within weeks," she growled menacingly. "You lied to me, and I'm phoning the papers tomorrow to expose you as the useless fool that you are!"

"N… now hold on a minute, Mrs Braintree," said Bonditt. He loosened his collar, which had started to feel too much like a noose for his liking. The vision of journalists beating a trail to his door gave him palpitations. "You must understand that I have many crucial civic duties, Mrs Braintree. I promised you I would shut it, and I will keep that promise. I need a little more time."

"Twaddle!" said Mrs Braintree as she dropped the handset back into place. She didn't have time for Bonditt any longer. Plunge-Pithering would sort things out for her.

It had been her mission in recent years to fight what she saw as the decay in society and restore some respect for authority, to put right the wrongs of what she saw as left-wing and liberal, namby-pamby thinking. Closing the youth club was only the first step in her crusade, and it was an obsession that filled her waking moments and haunted every dream. She had a very satisfying feeling that her time had finally come, especially now that she had wriggled her way into the Right Honourable Plunge-Pithering's good books. It hadn't taken her very long to find the way in either.

***

Gavin kicked his school uniform into the corner of his bedroom and dragged on loose-fitting jeans. They were several sizes too big, and the belt he used to hold them up wasn't exactly tight either. Consequently, they hung down around his ankles or thereabouts. It was a carefully crafted look, popular with his mates, but it had the disadvantage of making it almost impossible to walk, and there was always the risk of indecently exposing himself. Running was a hazardous undertaking to be avoided at all costs, which suited him perfectly.

He looked around the room for a T-shirt to wear. There were probably dozens of the things in there somewhere, but it would have taken a team of highly trained specialists to find one in good time. His room was beyond being simply untidy. It looked like a truck full of rags, and magazines had crashed into the building, closely followed by a plane load of apple cores, empty crisp packets, and coke cans. Finding clean clothing in that room was much worse than finding a needle in a haystack. His mum's cat had been missing for weeks and was probably hidden in there, keeping Lord Lucan company.

Gavin was rushing to change because it was an important day, and he had an urgent appointment with a few of his closest mates up on Paddick Hill. Paddick Hill was his favourite haunt, with its stunning views over the village of Dinctum and the hills beyond. With his friends Peter and Joseph, he'd spent many long summer evenings resting in those pastures drinking lager, smoking roll-ups, and putting the world to rights. However, it wasn't going to be quite as pleasant this time because the sky was overcast, and a fine drizzle filled the air. It was the sort of rain that went everywhere. The only way to get wetter was paddling out to sea and jumping overboard.

Nevertheless, the meeting would go ahead anyway. They had been putting it off for far too long. Word had reached Gavin's ever-attentive ears that Mrs Braintree was causing more trouble again, and something had to be done about it this time. The youth club wasn't exactly on a par with Disneyland, but it was all they had, and life would be almost terminally tedious if she succeeded in shutting the place down.

Dressed to his satisfaction, he grabbed a waterproof jacket and dashed out of the house without a word. He walked briskly along the high street until he got to a gate that led into a field at the north end of the village. From there, a track crossed an old bridge over the river and led him up a steep hillside. The rain had made the grass slippery underfoot, and he lost his footing several times. He wondered if they issued the sheep in these parts with crampons.

Up ahead, Peter and Joseph huddled together under a large green golfing umbrella, sharing a cigarette. Gavin was out of breath and almost completely soaked when he reached them. They had been waiting for him in the usual spot, trying hard not to look like the weather was making them feel cold. Being 'cool' sometimes meant precisely that: freezing cool.

After a short pause to light up another roll-up and complain about being the only one in the whole valley who ever had any smokes, Gavin turned to the matter at hand. "Look," he said, "we need to do something about Brainless." They had many nicknames for Mrs Braintree, but this was their favourite. "My sister works for the council in Dillchurch, and she says Brainless has almost persuaded them to shut the club down. It's only a matter of days, she says."

Peter and Joseph shivered and it wasn't just the cold this time. "What we gonna do then?" asked Joseph, wiping the rain from his face.

"Well," said Gavin, "we've got to find a way of shutting Braintree up once and for all, and I think I know how."

So, they squeezed together even more tightly under the umbrella and made another three roll-ups. The light was fading, and the cigarettes lit up their faces in a way that might have looked scary if you chanced upon them. Like the three witches in Macbeth, they whispered and plotted, carefully conjuring an incredibly convoluted plan.

After an hour and feeling very pleased, they set off back down the hill towards the village. The rain didn't seem to matter very much now.

The Youth Club

If you believed the clock in Dinctum Village Hall, it was five minutes to three. Like many things in the village, it had remained completely stationary for decades – thirty years in this case. Although the village hall committee had often debated the issue, nothing had been done to get it going again. You could predict with complete confidence that the world would grind to a cold and polluted halt at five to three one day in the not-so-distant future. The correct time was half past six, and it was a Friday evening, which meant it was also time for Dinctum Village Junior Youth Club. Already, a collection of pallid, distorted faces pressed against the window of a white PVC door leading into the hall. One was poking out its tongue.

The door, in which the glass looked increasingly insecure, opened directly onto a narrow pavement. David, the club leader, thought it was a miracle that someone hadn't jumped out of the hall straight into the path of a passing tractor. Fortunately, a set of iron railings at the far side of the pavement kept all but the most determined from danger. It wasn't a busy road, but some used it as a racetrack. Once, someone driving a bright red Massey-Ferguson was so keen to beat the record for circumnavigating the village that he ploughed up six hundred yards of tarmac, a water main, and two thousand feet of gas pipe before he could be stopped. It took several weeks to clear up the mess, and for a long time afterwards, the gas board refused to return and repair anything. They had been working on the pipes at the time and didn't appreciate the interruption.

You might have thought that the pavement was a safer place to be, but it hadn't always been so. A strange lady called Jemima Flocks had once lived in the village next to the butchers. Surviving almost exclusively on fish & chips, she caught the evening bus into Dillchurch once a week, where she bought several portions of deep-fried cod and an unreasonably large quantity of chips. She kept the food in her fridge until it was needed. This was extremely hazardous because she kept the fridge switched off, and the door was always left ajar on account of her cat, Sodoff, using the bottom shelf as a place to sleep.

One day Jemima brought home a twenty-seven-foot-long African rock python called Louise, which she decided would make an excellent pet. Sodoff knew trouble when he was looking at it and, to that extent, had a good deal more sense than Jemima. Sodoff quickly vacated the premises and was never seen again. Once a month, Jemima attached a collar and lead to Louise and took her out for a slither. If you believed what Jemima said, Louise wouldn't have hurt a fly. However, many villagers rightly felt that the only safe kind of snake was one with a tail at both ends. Louise came with a large set of spiky fangs and you took your life in your hands if you went within forty feet of them. In the blink of an eye, Louise had swallowed Mr Troutpuddle's poodle. No one complained about one less poodle - except Mr Troutpuddle. However, the various attempts to consume pedestrians led to Ms Flocks and Co. being taken away. Once they were gone, the pavements in Dinctum returned to normal or as near to it as was possible in such a place.

***

With the village hall door about to burst off its hinges, David quickly popped a cola drop into his mouth to calm his nerves. As advertised, it had a 'fizziness that'll make you tingle from tip to toe'. *Much the same as drinking undiluted creosote*, he decided. The time had come to open the door and let the lovely little creatures in.

Working with the senior club members was brilliant, and David loved almost every minute of it, but juniors were an entirely different proposition. It felt like running a kindergarten, and he didn't get paid for it either – only his time with the seniors counted. The trouble was, if you didn't have any contact with the little blighters before they were twelve years old, you hadn't got a hope of taming them as they grew older, and they became set in their mischievous and devious ways.

David walked across the hall, beneath the sagging ceiling, past the damp and smelly orange curtains, towards the entrance. With every step, his legs grew heavier, and his feet became harder to separate from the chewing gum ground into the faded carpet. As the door drew closer, he could see the faces outside. Worse still, they could see him. It was too late to back out, so he placed the key in the lock, turned it slowly, and, without the slightest sign of resistance, the key went snick and click, and the door was unlocked.

'*Hell!*' he thought. "Hello," is what he said.

***

As David was unlocking the hall to let in the juniors, another group of mostly senior members shuffled into the corner of a damp field bordering a gently flowing river. The sound of countless birds echoed across the meadows while sheep and rabbits grazed together on luscious grasses, made fresh and crisp by the previous night's rain. It was a tranquil scene, played out each year for longer than any could recall, and would have been idyllic had it not been for the argument going on.

"Go on, give him another one," said a voice.

"No, he can't have anymore," said another. "He's already nissed as a pewt!"

"You mean he's as pissed as a fart, don't you?" said a third voice.

"No, I don't!" the second protested fiercely. "If I'd wanted to say that I would have done so. So there!"

"No, you wouldn't!" said the third impatiently. "You're scared stiff of swearing, aren't you? You're always saying something pathetic like, 'oh deary me, he's squiffed as a sozzle.' I mean, why can't you say what you mean? SPEAK ENGLISH! You're worse than the flipping queen."

"Yeah, one is too bloody proper for one's own bloody good, isn't one?" said another voice from the back of a crowd.

Then Michael piped up. "I've got one!"

No one spoke, but the words 'Oh God, here we go again' seemed to fill the air. Michael's head was full of absolute garbage, which he was only too pleased to share with anyone who gave him time. None of them did, but he was going to say it anyway. He had very little control over his mouth, which turned out to be the second largest item on his head. His ears held first and second position, and third place belonged to a bright red boil on the end of his nose.

Taking a deep breath, Michael spoke very slowly and carefully. "He's as pickled as a lizard in a jar of extra strong lizard pickling syrup."

There was a moment's silence before someone found an appropriate response. "Michael, you speak complete and utter bollocks sometimes. Now shove off out of here!"

'Little' Michael, as he was known, was only eleven years old. Worse still, he was a member of the 'junior' youth club, and therefore, to most seniors, he was further down the evolutionary tree than you could get with a sharp spade. He dragged himself forlornly across the field and along the path towards the village hall.

After Michael disappeared, the others turned their attention back to the task at hand. This involved getting he who had drawn the shortest straw into the right state of mind for telling Mrs Braintree what they all thought of her. Nobody had the nerve to do it without some assistance. On this occasion, Jamsie, still in possession of a tiny length of straw but very few of his senses, had the help of a seafood pizza and a whole bottle of Uncle Vladivostok's Aromatic Vodka. It was clear to everyone there that he was in no state to drink anymore. They were beginning to get the impression they might have assisted him a bit too much when suddenly, and to everyone's complete surprise, he staggered to his feet and stood swaying like a three-legged giraffe in a force-ten gale. Then, with incredible difficulty, he attempted to focus on something, and after some moments, his eyes met with those of the beautiful Susan. A big cheesy grin washed over Jamsie's spotty little face, and he lurched towards her, hoping for a kiss. Unfortunately, the instant he started to move, he began to feel dizzy and more than a little queasy. It was only a slight sensation at first, but before he got more than three paces, it had become hard to resist. Standing next to Susan, Martin could see exactly what was coming.

"Oh no! Suzy, look out!" he shouted, trying his best to push her out of the way, but he was too late. Susan had a close encounter of the spewy kind.

Not for the last time that evening, Suzy was glued to the spot by a mixture of disbelief, terror, and anchovy sauce. She hoped it was all an appalling dream, but sadly there was no mistaking the horrible smell and inevitable, pervasive dampness. After only the briefest of delays, she executed swift justice on Jamsie, deploying a well-aimed foot firmly between his legs.

Jamsie was beyond feeling any pain and crumpled into a heap again. Having performed to his satisfaction and everyone else's disgust, he settled down for a nice snooze amongst the dandelions and sheep poo.

***

David opened the door, and the first little body to enter the hall belonged to nine-year-old Jennifer. Her ragged clothing and unkempt hair complimented the dirty marks on her cheek – the same marks that were there the previous Friday. She rushed over, clamped herself around David's waist, and, refusing to be dislodged, shouted, "I'm going to be your shadow!"

"I wouldn't want to bet on that," said David, and with some difficulty, he made his way back to the coffee bar dragging Jennifer with him. "Can't you find someone else to hassle?" he asked calmly. David reasoned that if he showed her he was annoyed, she would only do it more. It was just an attention thing.

"No! I'm going to be your shadow!" said Jennifer, as she tightened her grip to the point where David lost communication with his left foot. He tried to remember how long it took for gangrene to set in. He didn't mind going to sleep, it was just that he preferred it when the whole of his body did it at the same time.

Having got as far as the kitchen, he gazed through the serving hatch connecting the room to the main hall. Two beady eyes peered over the counter at him. They belonged to Michael who had finished his walk from the meadows in good time and was pleased that he'd managed to take possession of a genuine five-pound note along the way. He waved it at David, who tried hard to see if it had Monopoly written on it anywhere. The face of the queen staring back reassured him – but not much.

"Three hundred jelly wrigglers and a pint of Guinness, or I'll kick yer friggin teef in!" shouted Michael above the din and then smiled innocently.

David didn't respond straight away. He'd been distracted by the money and wondered why the queen always had the same hairstyle. *Perhaps it was a wig or a cunningly disguised crash helmet for security purposes? Maybe there was a secret satellite communications system built into it?*

He left the queen's hair to one side for the moment and was about to tell Michael precisely what he could do with his five-pound note when a voice from somewhere near his left hip, but higher in pitch than his head, beat him to it.

"Sod off, Michael!" said Jennifer. Then, looking up at David again. "Don't forget I'm going to be your shadow!"

"How could I?" answered David flatly, and with a despairing glance through the kitchen window to the garden next door, he noticed Peter Branigan trying to eat a rose. David sighed, "Oh Christ... mas, here we go again."

He decided to deal with Michael first and started counting the sweets. While this was going on, Jennifer chose to tell him a story about a goat called Nigel.

"Right then," Jennifer began firmly, "Nigel was a goat, and Nigel had a long fink. Goats do that early in the morning when the sun is on its way up from somewhere else. It isn't a perfect time for finking 'cos that's when all the birdies start to tweet at one anover, so Nigel wasn't getting much finking done." Jennifer shook David's leg violently at this point, "You're not listening!"

"No, I'm not really, am I?" said David as he examined the contents of a jam jar.

"Well, anyway," Jennifer continued, "after quite a long time, Nigel wandered over to the woods and stood on his head in the corner of the field. He did this to look closely at the ants, which he found quite interesting. Goats are like that, you see – they're very inquisient."

"Inquisitive," David corrected her, although he didn't know why he was bothering.

"Don't you swear at me!" said Jennifer, trying to sound offended. It was something her mother was good at - swearing and looking offended in any order.

"Whatever," said David.

Jennifer continued, "The ants lived in some tunnels, and sometimes they played cricket when the sun was shining. But before Nigel had time to settle down and watch, he saw an immense grey shape hanging above him. At first, he fought it was a rain cloud, but then he saw that it was an ennetant's bum. 'SODDING HELL,' he said, there's an ennetant's arse in the sky!"

"Oi!" said David crossly. "Don't you dare let me hear you using that sort of language again, especially at your age, and it is elephant, by the way, not ennetant!"

"It's my birfday next month, and I'll be ten. Can I say ennetant then?" she asked mischievously.

"Elephant!" responded David. He gave her a look that left her in no doubt his patience was running out. She took the hint, said sorry, and then, squeezing David's waist until his eyes watered, continued with the story.

"Anyway, the *elephant* couldn't fly, so it dropped out of the sky and squished Nigel dead. Oi! I'm telling you a story!" she shouted, noticing that David's attention had floated back out of the window again to Peter Branigan, who, having consumed the rose bush, had moved on to the dandelions.

Jennifer went on. "The ennet... ELEPHANT had spontin-e-asly matralised in Nigel's field from anover time zone. Only ELEPHANTS can do this because you need to have gigantic ears to time travel properly, but I expect you knew that." She paused briefly before adding, "I suppose it could have been a ginormous fluffy rabbit, but... I digress."

"I wish you'd bloody well digress back to where you came from," said David, immediately regretting his choice of language. "Sorry, but you know what I mean, and what the hell are you going on about anyway? You're being a complete pain. Now shove off somewhere and leave me alone!" It was all getting too much for him, and he couldn't even begin to imagine where a girl her age had learnt 'spontaneously materialised' from, even if she couldn't say it correctly. *That was the internet for you*, he thought.

David had heard enough about Nigel, the goat, for one evening, and besides, he was beginning to get more than a little worried about the almost total absence of foliage in next door's garden. *Young Branigan will be one sick little pigeon before very long, and I expect I will get the blame*, he decided. You didn't get to be a youth worker in these parts without learning how to predict the future accurately. Peter had the sense he was being watched and, seeing David staring at him through the window, dashed out of sight to hide.

Shaking himself free from Jennifer, David turned to face the serving hatch again and all the demands piling through it. A can of Coke, two penny chews, five hundred liquorice laces, and a request to turn up the music. It was already so loud that the speakers moved of their own volition. He calmed himself, knowing that Vicki would arrive soon and make his life tolerable again. Vicki was his assistant at the club and a shining star in his otherwise dull universe.

***

Once the rush for sweets and fizzy drinks had been dealt with, David remembered that he needed to balance an empty crisp packet on top of the clock. An odd thing to do, but according to the latest Area Youth Committee directive, it was vitally important. The AYC, as they liked to be known, was the official body responsible for clubs like the one David and Vicki ran. Their representative, a man with the unlikely name of Humpert Dilling and the improbable title of Area Youth Manager (what, after all, was an area youth, and how could you hope to manage it?), had devised a system of secret signs designed to help one youth leader communicate with another. It was almost as weird as Humpert himself. For example, in Dinctum Youth Club, an empty can of Fanta on the floor was supposed to mean all's well, and a piece of bubble gum stuck next to the main light switch indicated someone had nicked the football. An empty crisp packet on the clock meant 'Branigan's eaten next door's garden again' or, to put it another way, 'expect another visit from plod'.

Even in one club, it was a ridiculously complicated system, but poor old Humpert had twenty-four to manage. He was an intelligent man, educated at Eton, although you wouldn't get anyone there to take responsibility for his current state of mind. Humpert had failed to memorise the eighteen hundred or so secret signs dreamt up by club leaders and refused to write them down just in case they got into the wrong hands. He'd also resisted creating a set of standard signs because it would have made it far too easy for the enemy (club members aged twelve to eighteen) to break the code. Consequently, Humpert could not think clearly about anything and had already travelled nine-tenths of the way down the slippery slope to a nervous breakdown.

It was possible to get into an awful state if you misinterpreted the signs. For example, he tried to have the entire staff and membership of Dillchurch Youth Club arrested for smoking dope based only on a clock hanging upside down in the girls' toilets. Had he been visiting Tilt Village Youth Club, he might have been entirely justified in doing so, but in Dillchurch, it simply meant that they'd run out of Mars Bars.

Nobody could be bothered with these secret signs. It was all far too complicated, and by deliberately inventing so many codes and symbols, the club leaders had succeeded in their undeclared aim of making the whole thing completely unworkable. Unfortunately, they hadn't banked on Humpert's obstinate refusal to accept the blindingly obvious or his unswerving determination to make it succeed. His promotion to Assistant County Youth Officer was riding on it, and all the funny handshakes in the world wouldn't get him there if he cocked up.

David looked around for a crisp packet and found one stuffed down the back of a radiator. According to the label, it was Salt 'n' Vinegar. Cheese 'n' Onion crisps were his favourite, followed by Cod 'n' Parsley sauce – when you could get them. He might even have given Steak 'n' Bluebottle a crack, but nothing on earth would persuade him that Salt 'n' Vinegar was fit for human consumption. He knew it wasn't suitable for hamsters because his example of the species (called Widdle – because that's what it did everywhere) had died shortly after eating a packet.

Getting an empty crisp packet to balance on top of the clock was never easy, and he regretted adopting the sign. However, it was better than some ideas: a dead cow hung on the door to indicate a shortage of milk or a boat on the roof to signal a leaky toilet. Eventually, he got fed up with the empty packet and resorted to wedging it just behind the clock. It might cause a problem if Humpert turned up unannounced, but David decided to take a chance on it.

**

He needn't have worried because Humpert had bitten off more than he could chew at Skittle Lane Youth Centre in Bungbury.

The members of this establishment were in the middle of one of their favourite activities: face painting. It was something the juniors at Dinctum Youth Club also liked to do, making themselves look like all sorts of things you'd see in a zoo: gibbons, lions, rats, and so on. One enterprising soul with an inexplicably large quantity of knitting needles had even managed a realistic porcupine.

Ms Gillian Possit was in charge at Skittle Lane when Humpert arrived and 'GP,' as she was known, was proficient at rendering realistic cuts, black eyes, and broken limbs with minimal effort. This was because she had been a nurse and first aid instructor in a former life. Consequently, when Humpert breezed into the hall on a routine visit, the sight that met his eyes was one of complete carnage. For a moment, he felt very faint. It looked like the scene of a plane crash, but the absence of a large enough hole in the roof convinced him that the Possit woman must have inflicted the injuries. He hadn't been introduced to Gillian Possit before and made the grave mistake of trying to affect a citizen's arrest. The trouble was that GP didn't know who Humpert was either, so when he went to grab her, she smacked him in the mouth with her elbow, knocking him senseless.

On regaining his composure, Humpert should have sacked Ms Possit on the spot or even called for the police, but a seething rage overtook him, and he launched at her. This was his second mistake of the day (third if you counted getting out of bed). Had Humpert taken time to visit the 'Kipper Klub' in Dincsmouth late on a Saturday night, he'd have found Ms Possit earning a bit on the side as a topless mud wrestler. Sadly, he hadn't, so he was blissfully unaware of the tangle about to ensue.

He had the upper hand for a short time, mainly because of his size compared to hers. He was a good twenty-two stone, and eighty per cent of this was located at or near his belly button. Once moving, he was almost impossible to stop – something that the Dillchurch Rugby Club had discovered to their cost in the last county finals. The other reason he had the upper hand was that Ms Possit wasn't used to engaging in combat fully clothed. Realising this to be the case, she quickly stripped to the waist and set about the now completely horrified Dilling with renewed vigour.

Humpert briefly considered adding sexual assault to multiple counts of attempted murder and grievous bodily harm when a sudden darkness overcame him. Gillian Possit was also remarkably well built (that's why she was so popular with the Kipper Klub membership – the 'Kipper Klub Klan') and quickly enveloped Humpert in a sea of soft, sweaty flesh. Humpert kicked, screamed, punched, and chewed whenever he got the chance, but none of it did much good. Possit, who was used to far more aggressive and slippery opponents than this, just sat tight on his chest, grabbing him firmly between the legs whenever she thought he was showing too much resistance. This made him squeal even louder, so she did it some more.

At one point, Humpert managed to free his head, so she swung a breast in its direction – one of her special moves. Weighing as much as two bags of sugar and travelling at some speed, she knocked Humpert clean out of his senses.

When he lay motionless beneath her at last, Possit punched the air high above her head and began her Kipper Klub victory chant. Fortunately, someone had the good sense to send for the police, and they called an ambulance for Dilling, who was now in a critical condition. He had four broken ribs, a dislocated collar bone, and severe internal bleeding owing to the crushing of both testicles. He had probably been given an impromptu vasectomy as well.

The paramedics called in social services, who brought a handful of child psychologists with them, hoping to pull club members back from the brink. They had endured terrible sights that night. Sights that members of the Kipper Klub Klan would have paid good money to see.

So, back at Dinctum village hall, David could have relaxed and stuck his crisp packet wherever he liked, and it wouldn't have made a blind bit of difference.

***

Having arranged things in the hall to his satisfaction, David returned to survey the scene. Everything looked normal. Daniel and Christopher were kicking each other, Trudy and Tracy were pretending to be lesbians, and Arnold Fitzpatrick was smearing jam over Dominic's tee shirt. There was the usual pong of drains blowing in from the house opposite, and the stereo crackled each time a drum thumped. Sometimes, it all got on top of him, but he was in a good mood tonight, and nothing was going to spoil it – not even Jennifer and her silly games. Then he noticed the fish. "Right, who put Coke in the fish tank?" he shouted. The fish – two goldfishes and a handful of other scaly things – were not unaccustomed to Coke but preferred Pepsi.

A quick search revealed that Peter Tamby was the only one in the building drinking Coke, and he also happened to be standing right next to the tank, looking very guilty.

"It wasn't me!" he said unconvincingly.

David wasn't put off that easily. "Don't give me that. Can you see anyone else in the room drinking that stuff?" he asked, pointing at the can in Peter's hand.

Peter looked around desperately, "The fish?"

"Guilty!" said David crossly. "Now, get the water changed, please, and do it properly. I'll be watching you like a hawk."

Peter looked fed up and was about to start on the *'it's always my fault'* and *'I'm fed up with cleaning the fish tank'*, but he saw the expression on David's face and thought better of it.

Jennifer turned up and decided to put her two cents in, "You're a pain in the arse, Peter!"

"Go away," said David. "Stop poking your nose in and STOP swearing."

"That's what you called him last week when he put an ice lolly down Tina's tee shirt, so get off my case, you big bully!"

David decided her memory for detail was far too good. As he turned away, she promptly clamped onto his leg again.

Peter trundled off to fetch a bucket from the storeroom. When he got there, he couldn't see anything, but the smell was quite distinctive. Switching on the light, he saw the room was filled with cigarette smoke and senior youth club members.

"All right then, pimple head?" asked one of them.

"Sod off, jerk," said Peter as he dashed out of the door wearing a bucket, which someone had pushed down over his head. A mop that had learnt how to fly followed him into the corridor.

Senior club members (those aged 12 to 21) weren't allowed into the building until the juniors had left at 7:30 pm. The only exception was in the winter when it seemed to rain almost all the time. However, the weather was fine on this occasion, so Peter knew he could cause some trouble. He ran straight back to David as fast as his little legs would carry him.

"The storeroom's full of senior jerks, and they're all smoking dope! What you gonna do about it?" he demanded loudly.

David looked down at Peter thoughtfully. The white print on his blue tee shirt shouted, CLENCH ALL YOU LIKE, IT'S STILL GOING IN!

"You've got an attitude problem, haven't you mate?" he said and, without waiting for a reply from Peter, walked through to the rear of the hall, dropping Jennifer off by the kitchen door as he went.

She knew when to quit and, with a smile that could disarm the most determined, looked up at David, saying, "I'll wait here if you promise to let me be your shadow when you come back."

"No chance," replied David as he made off into the corridor that led to the storeroom. Partway along, he found Daniel and Oliver taking turns throwing darts at each other. He considered letting them continue until at least one of them was killed but had to give in to his conscience. "Are you two completely stupid, or have you just been practising a lot?" he asked. They both looked at him blankly. "Pack it in and use the dartboard properly," he said, pointing into the other room where the board hung crookedly on the wall.

Daniel was always in trouble. If Peter thought he was persecuted over the fish tank, he didn't know how good he had it. Daniel was harassed by just about everyone, and with good reason. He had learnt to swear before he was off the bottle and got the hang of fighting before he was out of nappies. It was unusual to find so many unpleasant attributes in such a small package – except possibly a hand grenade.

Reluctantly, Daniel and Oliver picked up the darts and wandered off to find something else to do. A dartboard wasn't as much fun as a moving target, so when they got into the main hall, they bullied Kirsty into holding the board above her head while running around in circles.

David choked as he stepped into the storeroom, and his eyes stung. You didn't have to wear a silly hat and smoke a bendy pipe to work out what had been going on. Playing cards were scattered here and there, and cigarette butts lay trodden into the stone floor. All the signs were of a hasty departure, which was very odd. On any other occasion, David would have simply asked the seniors to go outside and smoke. They didn't usually run away. Something strange was going on, and alarm bells should have been ringing. Intuition was worth its weight in gold to a youth club leader, and David could have saved himself a lot of trouble that evening if he'd taken any notice of it. He didn't.

Walking back to the kitchen, he was relieved to see that a) Jennifer had finally lost interest in trying to kill him from the waist down and b) the lovely smiling face of Vicki was looking back at him. David looked into Vicki's eyes and felt them soothing his soul.

Fiddling on the Roof

Vicki was the assistant leader at Dinctum Youth Club. She was twenty-three, cheerful and crucial because, unlike David, she lived in Dinctum and kept him abreast of all the gossip and goings on. Whether David attended the club each Friday out of a love of youth work or his growing love for Vicki was debatable. He knew that her presence in his life each Friday evening was becoming increasingly important with every month that passed. She was a breath of fresh air in a dull life and seemed quite fond of him. There was a chemistry between them that everyone noticed. Unfortunately, Vicki had a steady boyfriend to whom she was now engaged, and David was already married.

"Hi," he said as they hugged each other, "had a good week?"

"Okay, I suppose."

"That didn't sound very convincing."

"More plans for a wedding I don't really want, if you must know. I can't for the life of me see how to stop it – not now, anyway. It's like it's suddenly become everyone else's 'big day', and I would be spoiling their fun if I called it off."

"Oh dear, that's tricky. Have you set the date yet?"

"No, not properly. We've just said in a year 'cos we need to save up for it, but it doesn't stop people from getting carried away with themselves, does it? Mum has already bought a dress!"

"Didn't you say she was trying to lose weight?"

"I know! There's no way it will fit her in a year from now. Her weight's up and down like a tart's knickers."

"That's one way of putting it, I suppose," said David.

Vicki entered the kitchen to serve a group of juniors demanding chocolates, crisps, and dozens of penny lollies between them. They reminded her of newly hatched chicks clamouring for a worm.

"Friday night is the only time they ever get fed, you know," she said to David, who had joined her. But before she got any further, Vicki suddenly remembered something much more important. "Hang on a minute, have you lot paid your subs?" The expression on their faces gave her the answer she was expecting. "Right," she shouted above the din, "no sweets, drinks, or games until you've paid up." Then, picking up the registration book, a tin full of loose change, and a pen that had been stood upright in the sugar bowl, she marched through to the main hall. Once there, she sat on the edge of the stage and began collecting money.

Everyone in the club had to pay their weekly subs, which helped pay for games, outings, discos, and new fish. The money was never given willingly, having to be prized from their sticky little fingers like limpets from a rock pool, but most paid in the end.

The stage in Dinctum village hall ought to have been one of the wonders of the modern world. Made from wooden assemblies of differing sizes to an intricate design that even NASA would have found hard to replicate, it could be folded almost entirely out of sight and yet occupy nearly a quarter of the hall when fully extended. If there was ever a need to perform Shakespeare on the moon, this is the stage astronauts would have taken with them. It was so ingenious that few understood how to make it work, and aside from an occasional disco, the guides' winter pantomime, and the Dinctum WI AGM, it was only ever used by the Dinctum players.

Not widely known for their art, they were a keen group of amateur entertainers who wrote their own plays, composed their own musicals, and juggled their own balls. They worked tirelessly to perfect their skills. Had their talent equalled their enthusiasm, they might have been quite famous. They certainly had a big following, but this was primarily down to a morbid sense of curiosity.

One of their most noteworthy productions was entitled 'The Big Mac', alleged to be Shakespeare's sequel to his Scottish play. In it, Macbeth succeeds in washing out 'that damn spot' with New Daz Ultra and then retires to sell postcards in Brighton. Then there was the intriguingly titled musical 'Gone with the Wind and an Eel in My Pants.' This had to be called off after only one performance, thanks to the mischievous substitution of an electric eel for the stuffed cotton variety used in rehearsals. As a result of that mix-up, they discovered that at least one cast member could do a good can-can, so they did that for their next concert. A few months later, they did a sponsored sword dance which went exceptionally well until the partial castration. A similar show using chainsaws was quickly dropped from the schedule.

The stage had even endured Lady Dinc from Dinctum Manor – a woman possessed - singing *it was only a duck-billed platypus, but it meant so much to me.* She followed up with a tragic rendition of *fetch me a twinkling nutty,* set to a tune by Mahler. It wasn't tragic until she sang it, and the audience had hidden under their seats by the end of the second verse.

As she sat preparing to collect subs, Vicki was either unaware of or had wholly blanked any recollection of these disturbing events. It was usually better that way, and you were less likely to need therapy. A surprisingly large number of people had to be treated for PTSD whenever Lady Dinc sang at them.

Vicky called out names from the register, and members slowly came forward to pay their subscriptions. On the whole, they did this willingly, but one or two always resisted. William was one, and Vicki spotted him lurking by the front door, trying to be both inside and outside the building at the same time. He looked away at a car outside, pretending not to have heard her.

Vicki raised her voice. "OI! PULLIT! Subs or go away!" He gave in.

"Why are you always getting on at me? I always pay up, don't I?" he said, adopting the most hard-done-by expression he could manage.

"Eventually is the word that comes to mind, or better still, not at all if you can avoid it. Twenty-five pence please," she demanded.

The coins seemed to stick to William's fingers before falling slowly into her outstretched palm. They had shared his pocket with a half-eaten toffee he had decided to save for later.

Vicki winced at the sight. "Yuck! You're gross."

"You're a pain in the bottom," shouted Jennifer, who had been watching from across the hall with great interest. She laughed and ran back towards the kitchen, singing at the top of her voice, "I'm going to be your shadow, I'm going to be your shadow!"

Vicki's next task was to try to make the juniors' stay at Dinctum village hall as worthwhile as possible. The trick with juniors was to run the legs off them until they hadn't got the energy left to poison fish, stab the sugar, or set fire to the pool table, and the best way to do this was Plasti-Hoc. It was a sort of indoor hockey played with plastic sticks and was supposed to be less dangerous than the standard version. This was complete nonsense because the risk of injury had nothing to do with the type of stick being used. It was entirely down to the players and how determined they were to cause actual bodily harm, and there were some highly determined individuals in Dinctum Junior Youth Club.

"Two teams please, two teams!" shouted Vicki, trying to make herself heard above the arguments.

"I don't want you on my team, Jack. You didn't play properly last time!"

"I don't like you anyway, Robert Guthrie, so you can shove your team right up it!"

"Tracy's no good at Plasti-Hoc, so you can have her on your team."

"Rupert's too fat to play anything, so he can sit over there and be a goalpost."

Six teams were already forming, and Jason Partimer had kicked Sally Ferkiss in the shins. Vicki had to intervene. "Right, one long line in front of me now, and stop talking, or the Plasti-Hoc gets put away."

After they had been marshalled into something resembling a straight line, Vicki walked along, sending one moaning body after another, first to the left and then to the right until she reached the last face, which also happened to be poking out its tongue. "Daniel! What a surprise to find you here," she observed. "Hoping to avoid paying your subs as well, were you?"

Daniel thought he'd gotten away with it again and looked fed up when he was found out. The problem, and Vicki knew this better than any, was that he hadn't got any money, and neither did his mum, but it just wasn't fair to make all the others pay and keep letting him off. Vicki stepped around this awkward situation by telling him to shell out after the game when she could get him away from the others, who were unaware of his fiscal deficit.

Shortly after the game had begun, Vicki blew the whistle. It was a sign to stop whatever they were doing, stand still, and give the ball to her. She had done this because Jane Small and Jennifer, no longer anyone's shadow, were hacking at each other's ankles with their Plasti-Hoc sticks. Even though they were plastic, a well-aimed blow could easily make the eyes water.

"She hit me first," shouted Jennifer and then sent another blow down on Jane's leg.

Jane was starting to cry. "You're a dirty little toad," she said, swinging for Jennifer's shin.

"Don't you call me a toad, you slimy, worm thingy. My mum says your mum sleeps with the postman and the milkman AND the vicar, so stick that in your pipe and choke on it!"

With that, Jennifer started to swing her stick at Jane's knee, but Vicki caught it just before contact was made. "Cut it out now, both of you!" she said. "Apologise and sit out the rest of this game at the side of the hall!"

Having apologised, Jennifer and Jane reluctantly sloped off to sit on opposite sides of the hall, glaring at each other as best they could.

Vicki signalled for the game to start again, but after only a few minutes of battle, the ice cream van arrived. It parked immediately outside the hall, playing its tinny, distorted tune - Clementine - so loudly that the windows rattled. Before the first verse had finished, the building had completely emptied, leaving only Vicki and David inside.

"He's a blessing in disguise, that ice cream man," said Vicki. "They were just starting to riot again."

Standing behind them, at first unnoticed, Daniel looked dejected again. David was the first to see him and put his arm around his shoulder.

"What's it to be then, a 99 or a Crunchy Nut Surprise Lolly Flop?" he asked and slipped a pound coin into Daniel's hand. Daniel responded with a beaming smile and then shot headlong out of the door to the front of the queue.

The ice cream man - nobody knew his name although Mr Whippy and Oi, seemed to work - liked to sing Puccini while he served his goods. His voice wouldn't win any awards, but he enjoyed the songs and piled the ice cream on each cone as high as he could. His generosity didn't earn him much money, but it seemed that his love of opera and the smiling sea of faces at the side of his van was a far greater reward. He once observed, "when you've sung all the arias and eaten all the ice cream, a mountain of money ain't worth a brass monkey on a boomerang," and who could argue with that?

***

The entire membership of the junior youth club squeezed onto the narrow stretch of pavement between the hall and the van. They reached on tiptoe to exchange their fifty pence pieces and pound coins for a precarious-looking cone that wobbled in their hands. Most had a chocolate stick standing up in the middle, a drizzle of strawberry sauce, and some had a liberal sprinkling of chopped nuts. Daniel had one of those.

David and Vicki sat quietly, enjoying the moment of peace. Each had a small cone overflowing with delicious, white Italian ice cream, melting over their fingers. Vicki was just an inch or two shorter than David. A trim, healthy-looking girl, beautiful to his eyes and always ready with a cheerful smile. Her faded jeans clung tightly to perfect legs, and a white fleece hung loosely around her shoulders, revealing a smooth and slightly tanned neck that he dreamt of kissing one day.

"You look wonderful again," said David. It was a special moment for him - time alone with Vicki. He seemed to grow in her presence, and it felt right to be with her, but it wasn't easy to know what to do for the best. *Should I tell her about the way I feel?* he wondered. *It might make her stay away, and then I wouldn't see her at all. Maybe she feels the same about me… the way she looks at me sometimes.*

Just then, the small but deadly form of Kathy Braintree wandered over. At eleven years and nine months, Kathy Braintree was the brightest member of the junior club by far, and she knew it. "Why are all those seniors *sneaking* around at the back of the scout hut?" she asked, knowing that Vicki was unlikely to have an answer. Kathy enjoyed catching people out. She was her mother's daughter. The scout hut was what some still called the wooden shed at the back of the hall. It was the property of Dinctum Scouts until they disbanded due to a lack of interest. Now it was a store full of games, balls, tables, and chairs.

Vicki took a long look at Kathy and decided that she ought to check things out. You never knew what the seniors might be up to, especially when they were sneaking.

Kathy had come as a surprise to Mrs Braintree. Having just celebrated her forty-third birthday, she was told by her doctor that she was pregnant, and not the result of a few too many dumplings or chronic constipation – both of which she would have preferred. Agnes liked dumplings, and they were often responsible for her slightly turgid demeanour. Teaching young children was all very well, but the thought of giving birth to one of the things horrified her. She never forgave her husband for impregnating her and immediately cut off his limited supply of hanky-panky. He got off lightly because she'd toyed with the idea of cutting off something else.

You had to be careful what you said to Kathy Braintree because it was likely to be taken down and used in evidence against you when the need arose. David could see all too clearly from the look in her eye that Kathy had something quite special this time, but there was no chance of her saying what it was - not until the maximum impact could be guaranteed.

Vicki went to the back of the hall along a short, concrete path that dissected a large patch of grass to reach the wooden hut. It was about the size of a small garage with a gable roof and a door on one side. Gavin and Joseph were standing at the far end of the hut smoking and didn't look surprised to see her. Both said hello in the usual polite manner she had come to expect.

"Hi, you two. Anything going on I should know about?"

"No, not really, nothing special. Why?" responded Gavin.

"Oh... a little bird told me something's going on that shouldn't be, that's all," said Vicki, looking to see if this would provoke a reaction.

A sour look flashed across Joseph's face. "This bird didn't happen to be that nasty little creep Braintree, did it?" He took another drag on the roll-up he was smoking.

Vicki tried to divert the conversation away from Kathy Braintree. "You're not on that cheap stuff again, are you? It's got no filter or anything - looks like an empty toilet roll filled with compost."

"Tastes a bit like it, too!" laughed Joseph. "You never stop trying, do you? I'll give up smoking when I've finished college, and anyway, I can't afford proper fags until next week."

"So, what's going on then? Why all this hushed conversation? Why is everybody hiding behind huts and whispering?" asked Vicki.

"It's Jamsie," volunteered Gavin. "He's out of his tree! Downed all the vodka in Dorkshire! I mean, you wouldn't believe the state the poor sod's in. He threw up all over Suzy. They've taken him to the back of the pub to get some strong coffee."

Vicki looked at them for a few seconds and saw they were telling the truth. "What a jerk. You'd better make sure he doesn't pass out or choke. Has anyone phoned his mum?" They hadn't, of course, so Vicki went back to have a discreet chat with David.

He went pale when he heard the news. "We'll get the blame for this! You see if I'm not right."

"I think they're looking after him, but it might be a good idea if I went and checked. What do you think?"

"Well, why bother?" said David with a shrug. "He hasn't come into the club yet, has he? I mean, we can't be responsible for every immature little fart in Dorkshire, can we?" But even as he said it, he realised that someone would have to go and check. "Oh, all right then. I'll hold the fort. The parents will be here in ten minutes to take this lot home. I ought to be around to meet them, I suppose."

Vicki took a brisk walk towards the Duck and Dinc – the village pub – hoping to find out where Jamsie might be and how he was. Unlike Gavin or Joseph, he was an inexperienced drinker, and she was worried that things might have gone too far, especially if it involved vodka. Partway along the road, Vicki spotted Sarah and Justine hurrying towards her, and they both looked more than a little worried. "What's wrong?" she asked them.

Sarah was the first to catch her breath. "He's… back up… the club somewhere, Vicki! Sorry… but we couldn't stop him!"

"Oh God!" was all Vicki could manage. "The parents will be there any minute!"

She turned and ran as fast as she could. She had to warn David.

***

Jennifer attempted to become a shadow again, but David's patience had run out.

"You're beginning to annoy me, young lady," he said, leaving no doubt about how serious he was. "Now, stop playing a shadow and behave yourself."

"Okay, but can I be your shadow next week instead?"

"No!"

While trying to stop Jennifer's annoying little games, he became aware of the rain running down the window. The weather often changed quickly in the valley, so he wasn't surprised. However, Kathy Braintree was delighted to be the one to point out that it was only raining on one of the windows. At that exact moment, Vicki burst into the hall with a look of utter panic.

"He's on the roof, David!"

"Who is?"

"Father Bloody Christmas! Who the hell do you think? JAMSIE, and he's pissed!"

David felt his heart jump, and a cold sweat broke out on his brow. "Oh hell, the parents will be here soon. We'd better get him down and quickly."

Gavin, Joseph, and a discoloured Susan ran in from the back of the hall, looking equally alarmed.

"Yes, I know, *I know*," said David before they could open their mouths. "Help me get him down. Vicki, you'd better stay here and keep an eye on this lot before they nick all the sweets and set fire to the curtains again."

With that, David, Gavin, and Joseph dashed outside. They ran to the side of the hall and saw Jamsie staggering along the roof, relieving himself all over the side of the building. He had a big smile and was having a wonderful time. When he saw the horrified faces looking up, he shouted to them. "Hello," he said, waving one hand while continuing to 'point Percy' with the other. "Have a pee," and he directed the seemingly endless flow straight at them.

Susan arrived on the scene at that precise moment and got in the way. Her hair, usually long, blonde, and beautifully kept, was already matted with the partially dried remains of a half-digested seafood pizza thoughtfully donated earlier that evening. She stood rigid in horror at the sensation she could feel running down her back and legs and finally dripping around her ankles. The others stood motionless for a moment, unable to believe what was happening. Gavin acted first, grabbing her by the arm and pulling her clear of the flow. She was in shock. At first, she wanted to cry, but her anger took control, and wiping her face dry with a slightly damp sleeve, she ran off towards the back of the building, swearing as she went.

"Okay, Jamsie, it's time to come down now! You've had your bit of fun!" shouted David, hoping he would respond to reason. But Jamsie, was responding to nothing.

"Sod you!" he said and stuck two fingers up at the world. Then, losing his balance, he fell back against the sloping roof and giggled.

Joseph went to fetch the ladders, and then, leaning them up against the wall, he began to climb up, but David stopped him. "It's all right, Joseph. I'll go up in case he pushes you off or something. I don't think anyone had this sort of thing in mind when they wrote the terms of our insurance policy."

Once Joseph was clear, David made his way carefully upwards. He wasn't very good at heights, and the thought of being several metres above the ground in the company of a drunken juvenile didn't make him feel any better. He'd just about reached the top of the ladder when a large house brick sailed over the gable end, bounced off the roof a few feet away, and flew past his shoulder with only inches to spare. A bicycle wheel followed. It seemed to travel in slow motion, and for a moment, it reminded David of the opening scenes of the film 2001: A Space Odyssey. He could almost make out the sound of a Straus Waltz wafting through the trees.

"What the f..." he began and ducked as the wheel spun into the bushes far below. Another brick missed the top of his head by only millimetres this time. He wasn't going to hang around to see how long his luck held out, so he jumped back down the ladder, twisting his ankle as he landed. The others had already taken cover near the wall and watched in disbelief.

Just then, they became aware of a shrieking voice emanating from the same place as the projectiles.

"YOU FILTHY, FILTHY LITTLE SOD JAMES KENDRICK! I WILL KILL YOU!" And with that, another chunk of bicycle launched into the air.

Vicki had heard the shouting too and ran to the back of the hall where she found Susan. There were tears running down her face, which was flushed red with anger - although it could have been tomato purée and she was tearing at the remains of a bicycle, hurling it with incredible strength over the roof.

"I'LL KILL YOU, KENDRICK. I'LL FUCKING KILL YOU, YOU LITTLE SOD!"

Shocked at the complete change in Susan's personality, Vicki pulled her away from the bike. She smelt awful, looked terrible, and was soaking wet from top to toe.

"It's all right now, Sue. It's okay, calm down!" said Vicki, but Susan struggled for a while, still in a rage. Vicki held on to her as best as she could. "You can come home with me and get cleaned up. Leave the bike alone!"

Vicki could easily have Susan looking and smelling as good as new in no time. Her washing machine and dryer had gotten several club members out of trouble at one time or another. It was always a surprise to her that their parents didn't notice how their children often came home much cleaner than when they had left it.

At that moment, Gavin arrived to help. "Jo and David are getting Jamsie off the roof now," he said. "He's fallen asleep."

It didn't matter much to Susan. "I hope he falls off and breaks his nasty little neck," she said bitterly. Then, screaming at the sky again added, "DROP THE LITTLE FUCKING SHIT ON HIS HEAD!"

See You in Court

Jamsie was laid out carefully on the storeroom floor where Gavin could keep an eye on him, and Vicki took Susan into the toilets to clean her up a bit. "You wait here while I get the juniors on their way home," said Vicki. "Then you can come home for a nice hot shower and coffee."

Susan was still shaking with rage but managed a smile. "Thanks, Vicki, you're a star, and I'm sorry about the bike."

Vicki checked in the mirror to ensure she looked half presentable and then went back into the hall. David was by the front door, calmly chatting with the first of the parents to arrive. He had mastered this essential skill: looking completely calm when the world was falling apart. Even if the building was burning down and thick black smoke billowed from a hole in the roof, you still had to be calm and reassuring. "No, I'm sure there's nothing to worry about, Mrs Fridge. It's probably just one of the seniors smoking again."

Susan stood alone in the toilets, looking at herself in the mirror. She wasn't a vain person, and although everyone else said she was gorgeous, she had never considered herself especially attractive. What she saw now made her feel sick. Her hair was starting to dry out and stick together in clumps, unpleasant things were attached to her tee shirt, and there was a cold, damp feeling throughout her body. She began to feel angry again. Looking out of the door across the corridor, she could see Gavin in the storeroom sitting next to the culprit, who was still out cold on the floor. She stood there shivering for a while before an idea wandered into her head. At first, Susan rejected it. She was too well-behaved, too polite, but it kept coming back, and each time it seemed better than before. An eye for an eye. *You can't sink any lower than this,* she thought as she walked towards the storeroom with revenge in her eyes.

Gavin felt a hand on his shoulder. He looked towards it and realised it belonged to a female and the accompanying odour told him which one.

"Do me a favour Gav, go for a walk or something, will you?" said Susan.

Despite her appearance and the overpowering aroma, Gavin still found her attractive, and her wish was his command. "Yeah, I could do with another fag I suppose," he said as he left the room. Then, turning back to Susan, he added, "Don't kill him, will you?" Susan just smiled. Jamsie was going to find out exactly what it felt like to be pissed on from a great height.

Vengeance was sweet, and she felt empowered by it. She left the storeroom and saw Gavin standing just outside the hall. Walking past, Susan paused and spoke in a tone he couldn't ignore. "Play your cards right, mate, and I'll make a man of you tonight."

Gavin's knees began to wobble uncontrollably, and the world suddenly went out of focus. His first reaction was to follow Susan, but curiosity got the better of him, and he decided to check on Jamsie, hoping very much that he wasn't going to discover a crime scene. That would have complicated things rather too much for his liking. The only crime scenes he could cope with were the ones he was responsible for. He carefully pushed open the storeroom door and began to feel dizzy again. JAMSIE HAD GONE!

***

As Susan Taylor went off to calm down in one part of the valley, Agnes Braintree was just about to finish work in another.

"I'm sorry to have kept you so late, Mrs Clifton, this being a Friday and all that, but I had to complete these timetables before the weekend. You know what it's like these days?"

But Mrs Braintree wasn't in the least bit sorry for the late hour. She quite liked to inconvenience Mrs Clifton, partly to remind her who's the boss, but also because she couldn't see why she was the only one who should have to work long hours. It didn't seem to occur to her that she might be an appallingly lousy manager of her own time and could easily have completed her work by mid-afternoon. Being unpleasant wasn't in her job description, but Agnes couldn't help herself. Civility was a thin veil worn to deceive those she needed to impress. Everyone else had better watch out, and her victim on this occasion was the part-time, somewhat muddle-headed school secretary, Mrs Clifton.

"Oh, don't worry at all," said Clifton with a half-hearted smile. "I quite enjoy getting stuck into the work, and it isn't that late." She glanced at the clock as she spoke and realised there was no way she would make her appointment with the hairdresser.

With barely concealed pleasure, Agnes Braintree threw a bombshell at the secretary. "That's very good of you, Nora. I need them photocopied and collated by first thing on Monday morning if you would be so good. And while you're at it, I've drafted another letter to Dint about that confounded youth club. Absolute den of evil, and I'll have it shut down if it's the last thing I do, you mark my words. Mark them well!" She wagged a finger in the air as she spoke. Mrs Clifton imagined a fork of lightning arcing out from it across the room. "I'd like it typed up by Monday, please."

Letter after vitriolic letter had oozed from Braintree's pen about the youth club. Most ended up in the Chief Constable's waste bin, while others were posted to MI5 and Buckingham Palace, dramatically reducing her chances of an MBE.

But as much as Agnes loathed the club, she still found it helpful to let her daughter, Katherine, attend. She was a handy source of intelligence, and Kathy particularly enjoyed how certain titbits made her mother's teeth clench and her face flush with rage. She wasn't beyond embellishing the facts a little to achieve the most satisfying results.

Agnes rose from her desk and reached for her coat. "Now, if you don't mind, I must dash. I have to collect Kathy," she said. "Have a good weekend, and I'll look forward to going through all that paperwork with you on Monday. I'm sure it will be perfect." With that, she was gone.

The only time Agnes ever called Mrs Clifton by her first name was when she was about to inconvenience her, and today was no exception. Staring at the handwritten notes in front of her, Nora knew she would have to spend most of her precious weekend typing, correcting, copying, and stapling. It wasn't time she would ever be paid for, and it wasn't time that could be taken off in lieu either – no chance of that. It was nothing short of theft, of that much she was sure, but jobs were hard to come by in the valley. She didn't have a car, and the buses couldn't be relied on, so she was stuck. Tears welled up in Nora Clifton's eyes. One day, she promised herself, things would be better.

***

Jennifer's mother parked her battered old car outside the youth club and waved at David. The lustful look she gave him, particularly his legs, unnerved him, and he wondered if 'leg clamping' ran in the family. Seeing her drive away with a toot of the horn and her daughter sat beside her was a great relief. Jennifer was pleasant enough, but this shadow phase was beginning to bug him. Come to that, so was Kathy Braintree. She stood in front of him now with a knowing stare on her face. Had she seen Jamsie on the roof or Susan throwing bicycles at the sky? Had she seen the looks he gave Vicki or the kiss they shared last Christmas? Only Kathy Braintree knew, and when she was ready, so would her mother.

Another group of cars pulled up one behind the other, and soon a gaggle of parents stood outside the hall, chatting enthusiastically, waiting to collect the remaining twenty juniors huddled in the doorway.

Presently, Mrs Braintree arrived and, getting out of her tired-looking hatchback, marched over to join them. David took a deep breath. Her lips were nothing more than a thin line drawn under a stubby little nose, and her steely blue eyes were too close together to be of any comfort. She appeared incapable of forcing a smile, and David decided she must be in mourning for something. A sense of humour seemed the most likely candidate.

"Good evening," she said, and it was clear that she didn't expect or want a reply. Then, turning to her daughter, she asked, "Have you enjoyed yourself tonight, dear?"

As she spoke, Agnes raised an eyebrow, increasing the level of 'Spockification' in her expression. David wondered if that was how the Inquisition had started all its interrogations - just before they cooked your feet over an open fire.

Kathy was quick to respond. "Yes, thank you, Mummy! I'll tell you all about it on the way home."

David felt a cold chill run down his spine. As he tried to think of something polite to say, David noticed that the headteacher's attention had passed over his right shoulder. Her eyes widened, and her mouth opened very slowly until her false teeth nearly fell out. David didn't want to look, but turning around slowly, he felt his life flash before him. His heart started missing beats again, and he seriously believed it would stop altogether. On reflection, this might have been the best thing because there, standing in the doorway behind him, was Jamsie, and before David had time to think, he was halfway out across the pavement, staggering towards them like a boy on a storm-tossed deck. He appeared to be finding it difficult to focus on anything at all, and, to his horror, David found himself rooted to the spot, unable to move.

Jamsie crossed the pavement unsteadily to confront Mrs Braintree. He stood before her, swaying back and forth, breathing concentrated vodka fumes all over her disagreeable little fizzog.

"HELLOOO!" he shouted. "Good heveninging Mrs Brainstreams... Mrs..."

Struggling with every word, he attempted to sound both sober and a little posh. "I'd like to take thish oppor, thish opportunit... uoonity, of saying what a luffull... what a luffuly fat arrrrrrse you've got." He frowned, seeming to lose his train of thought. Then, following a loud belch, he continued. "I wonder if you might like to... to ben... end over and ssshow it to heveryonesss?" With that, he collapsed in a heap.

A spontaneous cheer erupted from everyone gathered in the doorway. Even some parents could barely conceal their amusement, but Mrs Braintree failed to see what was funny. Even if he had dressed up like a clown and sung an amusing song while simultaneously balancing a live haddock on his head, she still wouldn't have laughed. Mrs Braintree hadn't seen the funny side of anything since she was in nappies and, for some time, words failed her. She was both intensely livid and, at the same time, mortified with embarrassment.

As people saw the expression on her face, silence descended. The birds stopped singing, cattle froze in mid-chew, and rabbits dashed for cover. There might have been tumbleweeds somewhere.

Agnes seethed like a brooding volcano. Her eyes turned red with rage, and her cheeks flushed as though a terrible fire pushed up from within. David felt sure she would explode and was confident he saw steam coming out of her ears and nostrils. A lifetime of bitterness and hatred boiled up inside. After what felt like an eternity to David, she grabbed her daughter by the hand and stomped off to her car. The engine clattered into life, gears crashed and grated as her temper boiled over. She slammed the car into reverse and screeched backwards, smashing the lights on the car behind. Then, after another brief fight with the gearbox, the vehicle lurched forward until she was alongside David. Winding down the window, she screamed at him, the words gushing from her mouth in a vicious torrent. "I'll see you in court for this, Faber! You mark my words, young man! IN COURT!"

But before David could reply, Jamsie, who had regained consciousness, stuck two fingers in the air and shouted. "UP YOUR BACKSIDE, MRS FAT ARSE!"

The cheers started all over again.

A Great Idea

"Well, I must say I think this is a most serious matter, Mr Chair. We simply can't let it go unpunished," said Dr Function.

Seated in the village hall, he was participating in an extraordinary meeting of the youth club management committee, made necessary by the less-than-exemplary behaviour of young Kendrick (Jamsie) the week before.

Mrs Braintree, unable to express herself adequately at the time, had put pen to paper and written a very stiff letter to 'the idiot in charge' of the youth club. She demanded a full public apology and the complete expulsion of Kendrick from all village activities. The letter was copied to the Chief Constable, Councillor Bonditt, The Rt Hon. Plunge-Pithering MP and HRH the Duke of Edinburgh.

"She's all heart," said David to Vicki when he had finished reading it earlier that day. "Couldn't have happened to a nicer person, could it?"

***

Management committee meetings took place four times a year, and as luck would have it, they were due to have one anyway, so it just meant a change of agenda. Not that any of them took much notice of these things, except perhaps Colonel Fawcett, who fulfilled the role of chairman. Mrs Clifton, The Reverend Pinkle, Lady Dinc, Vicki, and David joined him and Dr Function around the table. Lady Dinc wore a patterned blouse that looked faded. Her black skirt stretched well past her knees, which was quite a good thing because you wouldn't have wanted to come across Lady Dinc's knees without having at least a few minutes to prepare yourself.

Although not visible, her bra must have been enormous, lifting and separating conspicuously. The outfit was finished with a blue silk scarf stuffed untidily into the top of her blouse. With her dark brown Dr Martin's, there was a particular style about the look. Shaped roughly like a telephone box, if you discounted her head, Lady Dinc must have been close to eighteen stone – she wouldn't have approved of kilograms. Her face would have launched a thousand ships - all of them desperately steaming in the opposite direction, and in profile, everything swept back from a large, pointed nose. Her grey 'frizzled' hair gave the appearance of having been styled in a wind tunnel. Her head was almost the ideal shape for breaking the sound barrier. Lady Dinc could have broken any barrier, given a long enough run-up.

She carried a smart black handbag and a matching walking stick. It had an embossed silver device at one end, and she prodded the unsuspecting with it when out and about. She'd been using it since falling off her horse, Plummet, on the way to the bathroom one morning. Dinctum Manor was huge, and she found a horse faster around the corridors than walking. If pushed for time, there was always the motorbike. At seventy years of age, she was still quite active and attended every kind of social occasion, especially if there was a free lunch and booze on offer. Fond of gin, extra strong peppermints, and shooting, she was indisputably mad. Nutty as a fruit cake with peanut icing, walnut stuffing, and Brazil nuts all over the top. Lady Dinc would have been sent to a secure facility if she had not been so wealthy. However, while she had a title and money to spend, she was politely referred to as eccentric - as eccentric as a steam-powered porcupine.

Reverend Pinkle, on the other hand, was a thirty-something lean machine. He didn't have an ounce of fat about him, and there was very little muscle either, a situation entirely due to a partial lack of food. He was a hopeless cook who survived on whatever would fit in his tiny microwave. Most of what he prepared was barely edible, especially the sausages, which nearly always blew to pieces. Often, he would go for days eating nothing but noodles and wine gums. He wore a light brown jacket that closely matched the colour of his hair, and his shoes, which hadn't seen polish in years, were also brown. He looked as though he'd been painted by an impressionist using nothing more than a pot of gravy.

In contrast, Mrs Clifton was a collision of colour that brightened any occasion. Primarily white and puffy, like the body it covered, her dress was decorated with an assortment of red, green, blue, and gold patterns. It wasn't clear what they were supposed to be, but if she'd climbed up a flagpole, someone, somewhere, would have started singing an anthem. Her hair was cunningly styled in the shape of a crash helmet, and the brain it surrounded was in a perpetual state of chaos, interspersed with periods of panic and anxiety. She was a 'cup-half-empty' person and predicted disaster at every turn.

Aside from David and Vicki, that just left Dr Function. He was the complete antithesis of Pinkle, being more than twice his age, well-fed, and dressed in a rather formal but tired-looking suit. As always, he had his bag of tricks with him - a shiny black case in which he kept enough medicines, lotions, and potions to treat almost anything you cared to mention. As he waited for the meeting to start, he busied himself with a bottle of tablets from which he took two pills and placed them neatly on the desk in front of him. He was bound to need them at some point.

Function was always keen to advise on the contents of the club medical kit and often volunteered to teach a strange kind of first aid that involved leeches and moss. The youth club membership loved his unorthodox approach to medicine, and they had endless fun setting him all sorts of challenges like, "What's the first aid for someone who's been bit by an aardvark?" or, "How many times can you break your nose before yer ears fall off?"

**

Mrs Clifton cleared her throat and spoke nervously. "Well, I think it's the parents. They just don't discipline them enough these days. When I was a girl, people got a slap around the legs for behaving like that. And *fancy* doing it to the headmistress of all people! Well, I never! In my view..."

She was about to start on one of her monologues. Dr Function never listened to her for very long. *Like a record stuck in a bloody groove for fifty years,* he had once observed. He picked up the pills from the table and popped them into his mouth. Then, noticing his glass was empty, he reached for the water jug in the centre of the table. Just as he was about to grasp the handle, he caught sight of a goldfish looking back at him. He decided to go without.

Mrs Clifton was still rattling on. "...and if there were more discipline in the home these days, we'd have none of this drinking and smoking and..." she paused with embarrassment. "Well... you know... none of this... um, rumpy..." she fumbled for a polite way to express what she was trying to avoid having to say.

Lady Dinc said it for her. "MATING!" she boomed and then, after a pause, added. "I think the word you're looking for is sex, dear woman, SEX!"

Mrs Clifton and Pinkle blushed in stereo. Colonel Fawcett's ill-fitting hearing aid started squealing due to feedback, and his glasses fell off. He tried to move things over this sticky topic quickly because he didn't like to think about sex. It made him dizzy and conjured up unpleasant visions from a past he cared not to remember.

"I er... think that what, er..." he couldn't remember names very well and shuffled pieces of paper, trying to see the silly woman's name written on something. "I think that er... um, Mrs er...."

"Clifton," said Mrs Clifton helpfully at the same instant as Lady Dinc exclaimed, "Ridiculous!"

Colonel Fawcett's overworked hearing aid muddled the two words. "Yes, er... thank you. I think what Mrs Clitoris is trying to say is that she thinks we should make an example of this young man and... um." Fawcett lost his train of thought just long enough for Lady Dinc to jump in with both feet, two legs, and a handbag.

"I think what Mrs CLIFTON is trying to say is a load of bunkum, Mr Chair, bunkum!" She emphasised the name Clifton hoping that Fawcett might hear it correctly this time.

Mrs Clifton wasn't sure what 'bunkum' meant and made a note to look it up when she got home. It didn't sound very complimentary, but she decided not to argue. Besides, the committee was used to Lady Dinc's outspoken views, which she aired whenever she could stay awake long enough to make them. Often, she would sit in her chair at meetings and take a snooze. With one hand resting on her handbag and the other holding the top of her upright walking stick, her head would tilt slowly backwards, her jaw would drop open, and the snoring would start. It had not gone unnoticed that she snored most loudly whenever Mrs Clifton was talking.

The conversation around the table had stalled momentarily. Lady Dinc was scratching around in the depths of her handbag for a peppermint. Doctor Function was fiddling with the cap on yet another bottle of tablets. Colonel Fawcett was suffering from feedback again, and Pinkle had just beaten himself at noughts and crosses for the third time.

David decided it was time to make some progress. "I hate to say this," he ventured, "but I don't think we should be held responsible for the actions of everyone under twenty-one in Dorkshire. I mean, I know Jamsie walked out of the club to engage Mrs Braintree in... um, conversation, but he wasn't invited into it in the first place. The rules are very clear about drunkenness, and I don't think Mrs Braintree should be allowed to put us in this position."

It was going better than he expected. Mrs Clifton had usually interrupted by this stage, so he decided to keep going. "I need hardly remind the committee of her long-standing opposition to youth work and her many attempts in the past to have us closed down." He was pleased with that bit. It sounded like something Councillor Bonditt might have said.

Lady Dinc, still rummaging around in her bag, appeared to be ignoring the conversation. Eventually, she came across half a mint wrapped in a paper hanky and was delighted with the discovery. A great beaming smile appeared beneath her pointy red nose, and without looking up from her bag or the mint, she chipped in with, "I quite agree, Mr Chair. That woman's nothing but trouble, even when she minds her own business. I think we... that is, Mrs Clifton should write to her, on our behalf, telling her to stop being so bloody silly and shut up." Then, turning to address Mrs Clifton directly, she said. "Tell her to sell up and sod off!" With great satisfaction, she popped the mint into her mouth and appeared to withdraw mentally from the proceedings. It didn't bother her that the mint was still partially covered in tissue.

Colonel Fawcett's hearing aid was particularly troublesome, and the piercing feedback made him twitch again. After a moment spent repositioning the device in his ear, he turned back to the proceedings. His first instinct would have been to declare war on Braintree, but her growing connection to Plunge-Pithering bothered him. 'PP' was a powerful man, and you ignored him at your peril, so Fawcett decided that a moderate approach was needed. He adopted the closest thing to a diplomatic tone he could manage. "May I suggest that while Lady Dinc's feelings are, shall we say, understandable, I think, as a committee, we would perhaps be a little unwise to minute her proposals?" He peered at Mrs Clifton over the rim of his half-round spectacles and she blushed with embarrassment, realising that she hadn't recorded anything yet.

Fawcett continued. "I do, however, think that some written response from Mrs Clit... Mrs Clifton would be appropriate, preferably before this Braintree woman," the name was spat out, "attempts to inflame the situation still further."

He pushed his reading glasses back up the bridge of his nose, which meant he had to bend his head forward to look over them again. In doing so, the glasses slid back down his nose, prompting an involuntary reflex to push them back up. This performance attracted the attention of Lady Dinc, who was getting agitated by it. She looked at him with ever-widening eyes. He seemed stuck in an endless loop, and after she had watched him adjust his glasses for the sixth time in a row, she couldn't stand it any longer. Spitting the half-sucked mint back into her handbag, she cried out. "Oh, for God's sake! Leave them ALONE!" Colonel Fawcett did as he was told. At that moment, Vicki saw one of the club members waving frantically at her from outside the hall. She made her apologies and left the meeting.

Mrs Clifton was in a terrible plight. The thought of writing a 'stiff' letter to her boss at the school troubled her greatly. She had to make a decision, and she didn't like that. Choosing the colour of her toilet paper often made her feel queasy.

As was usual, Pinkle had said very little up to this point, but having given up the noughts and crosses, he became aware that people around the table were looking to him for advice. Colonel Fawcett was tired of watching the man daydream and addressed him directly. "You know the woman, Pickle," he said, "can't you have a word with her or something, calm her down a bit?"

Pinkle slowly drew himself up from a slouch and pulled his eyes away from a hole he'd seen at the foot of the wall behind Lady Dinc. It seemed to be staring back at him. "Well," he said. "I suppose I do know her a little, although I wouldn't say I see her very.... perhaps once a month, except on Thanksgiving... when she gives us a lot of er... you know... with the arrangements and lends us Mrs... um... to play the organ now and... well, she's not very good at it, of course, but then... where can you..."

"For heaven's sake," bellowed Lady Dinc giving him a baleful glance. "I've never listened to so many dithering idiots in all my life!"

But before she could get any further, Vicki returned to the room, clutching a copy of the Dorkshire Herald. David noticed the look of panic on her beautiful face.

"Braintree's gone public!"

***

They each took turns to read the paper, and a very gloomy cloud full of extremely dark things, all painted black for extra effect, gathered over them.

In Letters to the Editor, amongst the complaints about a new one-way system in Bungbury that led everyone into the mayor's back garden was an extensive essay by Mrs Braintree. It practically accused the youth club of being a den of utter wickedness, a booze house, and a brothel. She lost not a single opportunity to distort facts and exaggerate events. She had drawn heavily on what her dearest little daughter had told her to spice it all up. The result was enough to get the average youth worker locked up for decades.

David's heart sank lower than the soles of his boots. He was beginning to wish that Humpert Dilling was well enough to come to his aid, but poor old Humpert was strapped into a complicated apparatus that held his legs as far apart as possible. This was to allow room for his painfully enlarged testicles, now heavily bandaged, to heal. The hope was that one day, someone might be able to repair them. If not, dear old Humpert would have to start calling himself Mrs.

Everyone sat in silence, trying to digest what they had just read. Under the table, Vicki placed a comforting hand on David's knee, but it didn't help very much, and he was starting to think it was all a horrible nightmare. *One night a week, I do this job,* he thought. *Just one bloody night and some silly old sod, who stopped paying attention to the modern world when the only things flying in the sky had feathers, is trying to ruin it all for me.*

Vicki had an idea. "It seems that Mrs Braintree is out to cause as much trouble as possible. She always has been, and I think the only thing we can do is prove her wrong. We've got to do something positive that everyone can see. Something that she can't possibly get away with criticising - not without making herself look like a fool."

"Hear, hear!" shouted Lady Dinc.

"Hear, hear," echoed Mrs Clifton hesitantly. She often followed Lady Dinc's lead without really knowing why.

"Silly moose," muttered Lady Dinc in a quiet voice directed at her handbag.

Colonel Fawcett could see the beginnings of an initiative and decided to take command, just in case it proved to be a good one. "Right, well, that's it then!" he exclaimed. "There we have it. A public relations exercise it is! Jolly good. Do I have your support?"

He looked around the table for a response. Only Pinkle seemed uneasy. For him, membership of the management committee had been a relatively painless and peaceful experience up until now. He didn't even have to attend all the meetings, let alone do anything. The phrase 'public relations exercise' seemed to indicate that work would be necessary, and a feeling of apprehension overtook him.

"Couldn't we write and apologise or... you know... less trouble... I mean, we could sort of..."

"Nonsense, man!" cried Lady Dinc. "Hell will freeze over before that woman accepts an apology. The young lady is right, we must prove her wrong by our deeds and shout it from the rooftops." Lady Dinc had some experience of shouting from high places when she got stuck up a pylon one summer in the late sixties while flying a giant kite made from bits of a yacht.

Doctor Function had been watching the fish swimming around in the water jug. *Strange that nobody else has seen it,* he thought while he listened to the discussion. He remembered winning a goldfish at a summer fête by throwing a dart into a card. He'd never been much good at darts, mainly because he didn't like the beer they served in pubs. Consequently, he didn't play the game very well. Besides, if he wanted to stick sharp objects into things, he could always inject someone at his morning surgery. Function had been fond of his little fishy and kept it in his shed for years before it expired and floated to the top of its murky habitat. He promised himself he would get another, but it had been ten years since the previous summer fête, so the chance hadn't come along. He certainly wasn't going to buy one because that would mean a trip to the pet shop in Bungbury. You didn't get much for your money there because the store owner was never keen to part with any of his stock. He was far too attached to the little creatures and marked up the prices to put off potential customers. As a result, there were things still alive in the back of that shop that had become extinct everywhere else on the planet. Someone claimed to have seen a live pterodactyl in a bedroom window. However, the same individual also claimed to have seen it driving a taxi in Dincsmouth, so the news wasn't taken very seriously.

Then, the idea came to him, and he didn't even wait for a break in the conversation, blurting it out excitedly. "Why don't we hold a village fête? You know, like they did years ago, only get the youth club to organise it?"

There was a pause in conversation as the words sunk in. David was the first to respond. "That's a brilliant idea," he said. "We could use it to raise money for the club at the same time. I mean, there must be loads of things we could do to attract people from all over the valley! Three-legged races, hot dogs, beer tents, ferret racing, bouncy castles, palm reading, you name it!" His mind was racing.

"Duck juggling," said Lady Dinc with equal enthusiasm, instantly bringing the conversation to a halt again. Was she serious, or did she throw it in to be mischievous? Was there even such a thing? Did the ducks have to be trained, and did they need to wear crash helmets? They carefully glossed over the proposal – if that's what it was. Within a short time, the idea of a fête had evolved into a full-blown Village Fun Day. They were all very excited about it.

"My cousin in Cornwall used to be a fire juggler and sword swallower," said Mrs Clifton. "He made a fortune at shows and fêtes and that sort of thing."

"Couldn't we invite him along then?" enquired David. "I'm sure he'd be an excellent attraction."

"Well," said Mrs Clifton, staring at the papers on the desk in front of her. "I'm afraid he's no longer with us. He mixed the two things up one day and swallowed a lighted taper. Exploded himself all over the town hall. It was an awful mess, and they'd only just had it painted." The image was horrifying, and they were left speechless again.

Vicki tried to move past this by asking which of the local dignitaries they should consider inviting. Pinkle said he wanted to ask Plunge-Pithering, but the Colonel wouldn't hear of it, although the worsening feedback in his left ear prevented him from hearing much of anything. Lady Dinc wanted to invite the Queen, and Mrs Clifton agreed. "She likes a bit of a flutter, doesn't she? Perhaps we could give her some good tips for the ferret races... you know?"

At length, and much to David's relief, it was agreed that the Queen would not be invited and that a sub-committee would be set up to plan the event in more detail.

"I hate to put a damper on things, but we still have this letter business to sort out," said Vicki, trying to address the immediate problem. "I'm afraid Mrs Braintree won't easily forget about the incident now that she has her teeth into it, and there's Kendrick to consider as well. We're not to blame for his drunkenness, but he's made the club look very bad."

While Vicki spoke, David followed Pinkle's gaze into the corner of the room, towards the hole in the skirting. His eyesight was keener than Pinkle's, and he could see someone looking through from the other side. He also saw a small cable trailing from the hole and under the carpet toward the table. The wire alarmed him, and he decided to find out where it went. So, doing his best to make knocking his pen off the table look like an accident, David ducked out of sight and looked around. For a moment, he was distracted by Vicki's bare legs. She usually wore jeans but had chosen a short skirt on this occasion. He wondered what her reaction would be if he kissed her thigh and whether Mrs Clifton would minute it. Turning his attention back to the cable, he was horrified to see that it wound its way up through a small hole in the carpet and disappeared underneath Lady Dinc's chair like a brown beanstalk.

"Christ!" he said out loud, bumping his head on the underside of the table. He had a horrible feeling he knew what the cable was plugged into, and as he got back into his seat, the expression on Lady Dinc's face and the faint smell of burning confirmed his suspicions. Making a vague excuse, he dashed out of the room to find the other end of the cable. He quickly located the wire leading to a mains socket on the wall, which was still sizzling in an overloaded way. After unplugging it, he returned to see if Lady Dinc was all right.

Doctor Function was rooting about behind her, trying to locate the source of the burning smell and soon, he emerged with the wire in his hand. "Good God," he said, unable to believe it. "The little monsters tried to electrocute her."

"They bloody well succeeded, you silly arse!" said Lady Dinc, whose hair looked even more frizzled than usual.

Colonel Fawcett was at once outraged and fearful for his safety. "I think you need to have a very serious talk with the members of this youth club, young man! If word of this gets out, that Braintree woman will have the lot of them in jail before you can say FART!" He started to beep and twitch again as if to emphasise his words.

Function gave Lady Dinc a glass of water containing a fish. She stared at it briefly and fainted. So did the fish.

***

After that, there was little point in continuing with the meeting. No one wanted to hang around any longer than necessary, just in case another surprise awaited them. Pinkle edged across the carpet towards the door, trying to feel for hidden trip switches. Function eyed the ceiling, sure that it had been rigged to collapse. He'd given Lady Dinc a strong dose of smelling salts to revive her. On recovering consciousness, she grabbed the small green bottle he was waving under her nose and emptied its contents into her open mouth before he could stop her.

They all went on their less-than-merry way, leaving David and Vicki to shut up shop. Fawcett was the last committee member to leave, but only after he had taken David to one side to have a word.

The Duck & Dinc

Later that evening, David and Vicki sat together in the Duck and Dinc, trying to make sense of the past week.

"Thanks for being there tonight, Vicki."

"It's okay," she said. "I wouldn't have missed it for the world. And don't worry, it will be fine, but we'll have to do more than a fun day to stop Braintree from closing the club."

He knew she was right. "We didn't get anything sorted about dear Mrs Braintree, did we?" he said. "The attempted execution saw to that."

Gavin wandered over with a pint glass and pulled up a chair.

"All right then?" he asked with a cheerful look.

David overlooked the fact that Gavin wasn't quite old enough to be in a pub boozing. He was much more interested in getting to the bottom of the evening's main event.

"So, which bright spark decided to light Lady Dinc up like a Christmas tree?" he asked.

Gavin shrugged it off. "Nothing to do with me, and anyway, she probably feels better for it." He tried hard not to let too much of a smile creep across his face.

"You're a bloody fool," said Vicki. "Someone could have killed her! She's a very old lady now, and her heart might have been... well, you know. It was a stupid and silly thing to do!"

But Gavin was doing his best to play the whole thing down. "Oh, don't worry. The power wasn't on long enough to do any harm. They just wanted to wake her up a bit. At least, that's what I was told. Anyway, it wasn't me."

"On and off quickly!" said David. "The power was still on when I went to the storeroom, and it took me bloody ages to get there. The plug was nearly on fire, for heaven's sake!"

"So was Lady Dinc from what I hear," quipped Gavin, but he could tell they didn't see things quite the same way. "Look, it wasn't me! I just heard what was happening, that's all, and anyway, she's okay. Nobody meant any harm, and it would take more than thirty amps to knock that old fart off."

Gavin might have been telling the truth, but the cable and plug had to have come from somewhere, and he was just the person to acquire them. He was intelligent, inventive, and always up to pranks and jokes. He took great delight in moving the bird seed onto the Muesli shelves at the supermarket, hoping that some poor soul would sit down to a bowl of Trill for their breakfast one morning.

Vicki decided to draw a line under the matter. "You had better not let anything like that ever happen again," she said firmly.

"All right, I promise," said Gavin. "Anyone want another drink?"

"I'll get them," said David. "But you will have lemonade. We're in enough trouble already."

"Oi, I'm nearly eighteen," said Gavin indignantly, "I'm allowed to drive a car and get married - and be a dad if I want, but I can't buy a sodding pint! Bloody daft, this country!"

While David was at the bar, Vicki grabbed Gavin's hand. "You're a complete twit. You nearly got us all in serious trouble – blue flashing lights trouble - just for a silly laugh! I thought you had more sense, especially after Jamsie's little pantomime!"

"I said I'm sorry," pleaded Gavin. "It wasn't just me, honest. We thought it might spice the place up a bit, and it has, hasn't it? We're going to have a fun day, a fight with Brainless, and a few resignations from the management committee with any luck. Result!"

"Her name is Braintree. Mrs Braintree to you unless you want even more trouble," said Vicki. She was beginning to suspect that there was more to all of this than met the eye. Empowering young people might have been one of the club's objectives, but this was ridiculous. "Was Jamsie's performance part of this too?" she enquired, without expecting an answer. She didn't get one.

***

When David returned with the drinks, he told them about the lecture Fawcett had given him after the meeting. "The Colonel says I've got to do something about discipline in the club. 'Get the blighters out on manoeuvres and run them into the ground' were his precise instructions. He thinks we should also start a 'community project' to show the village we're all nice people. Of course, that may not be possible in some cases," he added, giving Gavin a sideways glance.

"Don't look at me," protested Gavin. "I am a nice person. Vicki said so, didn't you?"

"Yes, I remember it well. You gave me a Christmas card six years ago. You were nice then."

Gavin took that as his cue to leave the table and wander off to the toilets.

"So, what else can we do to show everyone in the village that the youth club is full of model citizens?" asked David.

Vicki looked puzzled. "I thought that was the whole idea of this fun day?"

"It is," said David, "but that won't be for a couple of months yet. Fawcett wants us to start something now, and what about these manoeuvres? How are we going to do that?"

They sat in silence, trying to think, but someone was having a birthday bash in the other bar, and the noise was making it hard to concentrate.

"I think I'll make this my last drink. Otherwise, I'm going to be completely wazzed," said David. "I'll have to order a taxi as it is 'cos there's no way I'm going to drive anywhere now. You can see the headlines: Alcoholic youth leader crashes into the river after trying to murder Lady Dinc."

Vicki smiled. "It isn't quite as bad as that... and don't keep blaming yourself. That's what Brainless... sorry, Mrs Braintree wants. Anyway, you can stay at my place if you want."

"Thanks, but I think Sally's got something cooking ready for when I get home." He felt his heart sink as he said the words. In truth, home with Sally was probably one of the last places he wanted to be. She was grumpy about the youth club and especially about Vicki, and she spent a lot of nights out with 'friends' too. David found her quite evasive whenever he asked who they were.

Vicki reached out and put her hand on his. "Look, don't worry, I'll compose a letter to the Herald telling everyone that the youth club isn't as bad as old Braintree makes out. We'll sort it all out, you'll see. It'll be all right."

David was grateful. He knew he couldn't run the club without her and needed her now more than ever. They stared into each other's eyes, but the moment was interrupted by Gavin returning with three full glasses of beer and a great big smile.

"I've just thought about that project," he said. "You know, the one slaphead wants us to do?" Slaphead was a name Fawcett had suffered for many years on account of his baldness. "Why don't we repair all those vandalised benches? The ones down each side of the main road. Paint 'em up nice and new and then put little signs saying that it was us who did it!" He sat back in his seat, looking especially pleased.

"Brilliant!" said Vicki enthusiastically.

"Bloody hell Gavin, that's the best idea I've heard in ages," said David. He'd considered admonishing Gavin for buying alcohol again but decided it was a lost cause. "Well done! Come to think of it, we need a member's representative on the management committee. How about it?"

"Yeah, right… and have some nasty little sod electrocute me too? I don't think so! Anyway, none of them would listen to me, would they? They're all too far up their own backsides that lot."

"No, they're not," said David. "They'd listen, especially if you kept coming up with ideas like that… and anyway, I've already told slap… Colonel Fawcett that we need some club members on the committee. He'd probably feel a lot safer too. Less likely to be vaporised, don't you think?"

"You'd be great on the committee," said Vicki. "Go on, give it a go."

But Gavin was worried and wouldn't commit to anything right away. "I'll think about it. Consult me mates and all that," he offered. "Don't want to be losing my cool, do I?"

***

Feeling much better, they sat and enjoyed the remains of the evening. David bought everyone crisps, and they talked about the letters Vicki would write.

"We still haven't decided what to do about the other things Fawcett wanted," said David, conscious that he would have to report progress in the coming weeks. "I need some sort of a plan to keep him happy."

"What do you think he wants?" asked Vicki.

"Well, it sounded like he wanted to turn the youth club into a boot camp. You know… exercises, runs, and parades. He's completely bonkers."

Gavin was suddenly very excited. "Excellent! You mean we could go out on exercise with guns, grenades, and stuff like that?"

"No," said David, horrified at the notion. "I think even Fawcett would think twice about heavily armed teenagers patrolling the valley, and the Ministry of Defence might have something to say about it as well."

Then Vicki had an idea. "Why not take them all out for a cross-country run?"

"Go on, Dave, that would be a laugh!" added Gavin, winking at Vicki.

"Now, hold on a flaming minute," said David. "I've never run more than five yards in my life! How the hell can I take anyone for a run around this countryside? I mean... there's hills... and cows!"

"You can do it," said Vicky. "Work up to it. Do a little at a time. You'll be fine, and Fawcett will be off your back for good."

"Why don't *you* do it?" asked David, who was beginning to feel like he'd drawn the shortest straw again. "I notice *you're* not rushing to volunteer."

The response he'd hoped for didn't come, so he decided to call it a night. Getting up to put on his jacket, he said goodbye to Vicki and asked Gavin what had made him think of repairing the broken benches.

Gavin looked down at the table. "Well, I might have had something to do with the state they are in now... you know."

To The Queen

Mrs Agnes A Braintree

Dandelions

Dinctum

Dorkshire

Dear Mrs, Your Royal Highness,

I am writing as your humble servant to bring to your attention news of a creeping, festering rot currently oozing through the fabric of the land. It targets our once-great academic institutions and will, in the fullness of time, bring this glorious country to its knees! It perverts and muddles the young mind and degrades moral standards for future generations. It leaves our teachers, the brave souls tasked with improving these young wretches, without the tools, the cane, the belt, the catapult, and the thumbscrew, so desperately needed to hammer knowledge and discipline into the modern youth.

I am referring to the ill-considered, ineffective, <u>snivelling</u> excuses for policies enacted by liberal and left-wing politicians these past few lamentable decades. They have slithered unchecked through the abhorrent pigpen that is parliament and undermined the very foundations of academia. They enforce ideas that leave the most enlightened of us battling fully against the odds. We are left to fight these malodorous, wilfully disobedient, knuckle-dragging misfits – I refer, of course, to students - with our hands tied behind our backs. Believe me, Ma'am, I know what I am talking about, having been a proud member of the teaching profession for almost thirty long, hard years. I know these little cretins inside out, and a jolly good thrashing is what they require! Pain and suffering are the foundations of proper education. Unquestioning obedience and rigid self-discipline are what we need from these felonious, greasy little oiks. Only then, perhaps, can we restore order from the mess that wishy-washy, kowtowing, left-wing dogma has given us.

I know you will be gravely concerned about this terrible situation and thought it best to write since my phone calls to you have so far gone unanswered. However, I also know that you are a busy Highness, so I'm not yet disappointed, nor have I given up hope that you will show much-needed leadership in this critical matter.

I offer you my service and trust that you will consider it carefully. With your support and given complete control of the relevant government departments, I am sure I can lead the fight and have everything restored to order very quickly.

With this in mind, I will start by proposing that the 'so-called' Youth Service (in particular the one in Dorkshire) is closed immediately and that all its staff are sent away for 'reorientation'. It is a matter I have tried discussing with local politicians, but frankly, Ma'am, they're all a bunch of self-serving buffoons.

Ma'am, it is the wonder of our times and England's jolly good luck that you have found me and that I have found you.

I remain, Ma'am, your faithful servant,

Agnes Adolfina Braintree,

Headteacher

Dinc Valley Primary School

PS. Best wishes to the family and the Corgis.

***

Agnes was delighted with this final draft and took another large gulp of Brandy from an already half-empty bottle on her desk. She was especially pleased with the quote paraphrased in the last few lines, even though she couldn't remember where it came from. Composed on her word processor, Agnes had carefully removed the spelling mistakes (including one where an 'auto-correction feature' had her living in the county of Dogshite) before copying it out in a flowing and graceful hand. It would do for now, even though she was still a little troubled by her use of the phrase 'wishy-washy kowtowing'. It had the look of a Chinese laundry about it. All that remained was to purchase a first-class stamp, post the letter, and then wait for the Queen's response.

Agnes had put off writing to the Queen for some weeks, but the embarrassment of being mocked by a drunken, disgusting adolescent was just too much to bear. Besides, she'd heard rumours about a 'fun day' of some sort and seen a very annoying response to her letter published in the Herald a few days earlier. She knew she would have to act fast and seize the initiative to triumph over the forces she was now at war with. Her time had come, and plans would have to be accelerated. The Rt Hon Plunge-Pithering would have to be brought to heel sooner than anticipated, and with that in mind, she picked up the phone to call him.

A Bowl of Fruit

High up on Paddick Hill, Peter, and Joseph watched the sun slip slowly down a reddening sky to meet the pale horizon, half expecting it to bounce like a giant crimson balloon. As the cool evening air gathered in a mist above the river, Peter watched the creatures going about their business in the pastures below. Fox cubs chased each other beneath an Oak tree. A badger poked around the edge of some brambles, snuffling so loudly that he could hear it quite clearly as he sat puffing on a roll-up. Further up the hillside and nearer to him, he could see several rabbits busily filling up on whatever they could find to eat thereabouts.

"See those things down there?" said Peter.

"The rabbits?" asked Joseph, following Peter's gaze.

"Yeah," continued Peter. "Ever wondered where they came from?"

"Holes?" ventured Joseph.

"No," said Peter. "What did they evolve from… like, originally?"

"Can't say I've ever lost sleep over it," said Joseph.

"Well, what's got big ears?" asked Peter.

"Mary Flatsap in year ten," replied Joseph.

"Well… all right," said Peter, "but apart from Mary Flatsap. What else?"

"Don't know," said Joseph, who wasn't particularly interested.

"Bats, that's what," said Peter. "Bats have got big ears."

"And?" asked Joseph, who wasn't following Peter's train of thought.

"What hops a lot?" asked Peter.

"Mary Flatsap!" insisted Joseph.

"No!" said Peter.

"She did when she twisted her ankle," said Joseph, who remembered the occasion clearly because Mary threw his skateboard into the river just after he ran it over her foot.

"Look, forget about Mary sodding Flatsap," said Peter. "What else?"

"Buggered if I know. Grasshoppers? Frogs?" Joseph was getting fed up with this game.

"None of the above," said Joseph with satisfaction. "Kangaroos, that's what. Kangaroos hop, and bats has got big ears. Facti tutti. Those things down there must have evolved from Bats and Kangaroos. They ain't rabbits at all. They're Kangabats!

There was a lengthy pause.

"Bollocks," said Joseph, shaking his head.

"No," said Peter. "It's Darwinianism, that's what it is."

"Nope, it's definitely bollocks," said Joseph. "I've never heard David Attenborough say a word about Kangabats, so it must be bollocks."

There was another long pause.

Joseph had seen Gavin coming up the slope towards them and was relieved to have found a way of ending the discussion about Kangabats.

"Hi Gavin, any news?" he asked.

Gavin sat beside them and took out a piece of paper on which he'd made a few notes. He had just come from a meeting of the Youth Club Management Committee, Sub-Committee for the Fun Day Committee - or something like that. It was a grand title for such a small group, but they liked it. Mrs Clifton had thought it up and couldn't decide when to call it quits with the 'committees' bit.

"Yeah, looks like it's gonna be a good laugh," said Gavin. "Anyone got a spare fag?"

Peter had some tobacco and a few crumpled papers, so they paused to lash something together. Gavin choked on the smoke, which tasted like it was made from cow dung. Peter was into cheap French Tobacco, and even before being lit, there was something of the farmyard about it.

"Right," said Gavin, once he had stopped coughing, "First off, David and Vicki had to go to County Hall and explain things to some bod there... the big boss, I think. They got a right ticking off about Brainless and letting drunks into the club - that sort of stuff. Vicki says we've been cut some slack, providing there are no more drunks or any bad press. If there is, we get some new pain-in-the-arsenumpty in charge who'll have us singing hymns around a campfire and worrying more about the next life than this one."

"Shit!" said Peter.

"Bloody hell," added Joseph, echoing Peter's sentiment, "Can they do that? I mean, that's horrible. Hymns around a campfire? I'd rather have me nob drop off."

"I'm afraid so," replied Gavin. "Total effing disaster. But look on the bright side. We're not going to let it happen, are we?

They all agreed, so Gavin told them about plans for the fun day. "As things stand, the day will start at ten with the first of the races: the one hundred metre blindfold hurdles..."

"Blindfold hurdles?" interrupted Peter.

"Yep… that was my idea," said Gavin proudly. "Neat init? Then there'll be a tug of war, a bouncy castle, tractor pulling, some boot throwing, the ferret racing, and booze at twelve when the bar opens. There's also a barbeque at twelve-thirty, followed by a firefighting competition between Bungbury and Dillchurch Fire crews. Oh, and we've also got a palm reader." He was pleased with the plans and waited for the other two to react.

"Sounds great, but who's the palm reader?" asked Joseph. His worst fears were confirmed when Gavin told him.

"Myrtle Gurt."

***

Myrtle Gurt was a witch, or at least she looked the part. Living in a tumbledown cottage in a tangled wood east of Dinctum Splashit, she did her best to do the things witches do. If you went out in the woods at night, you were sure of a big surprise because Myrtle could often be found crashing from one clearing to the next astride a tatty broomstick. She was trying to fly. Sadly, she had as much chance of getting airborne as a bat with clipped wings and a brick tied to its neck, but that didn't stop her from giving it a go. People tended to give her a wide birth because of the rumours about lizards, newts, entrails, and so on, but if you ignored all that, and Gavin did, she was quite approachable, always willing to sit in a tent, reading palms or gazing at crystal balls. Her fees were quite reasonable, but it had to be cash.

No one knew anything about Myrtle. Estimates of her age ranged from seventy-something to one hundred and ninety. She always wore black and walked with a stoop, a limp, and a wobble to the right every few paces. Her nose was long and punctuated with a prominent wart. Thick, grey hair was bound into a ponytail by what looked like a leather bootlace, although it could have been a bit of snake. Unusually long, bony fingers complimented her surprisingly large feet and, wearing a crooked, pointy hat, Myrtle Gurt was the second most alarming thing you could meet in the valley at night. First place belonged to Lady Dinc.

***

"She's a bit weird that one, isn't she?" said Peter, accepting that this might add to the occasion. Many would turn up to see if she was as ugly as they had heard. They discussed who she might be persuaded to turn into a toad. Brainless was top of their list, followed by Fawcett and then several of the teachers at college.

94

Soon, their attention turned back to the fun day and what they might be required to do. There were bound to be jobs floating around, and the trick was to volunteer for the best before you got lumbered with something awful like entertaining Fawcett's wife.

"Well, there are raffle tickets to sell, burgers to cook, drinks to serve, and all sorts of other stalls and games to organise," said Gavin. "Oh, we need some long pipes for the ferret racing too. I mean, *really* long!"

"Why?" asked Peter.

Gavin offered him an explanation. "You put a load of ferrets in the ends of a load of pipes and wait to see which one comes out the other end first. If you placed your money on the one that comes out first - you win! It's simple."

"But how do you tell which ferret is which?" asked Peter, who still found the sport confusing.

"They've all got names, haven't they?" said Gavin. "You catch the first one out of the pipe and ask it who it is, don't you?"

"Shove off!" said Peter when he realised he was being taken for a ride and he made a mental note not to ask any more questions about ferret racing. Nevertheless, he managed to establish that the ferrets were each fitted with a brightly coloured collar before being set loose in a pipe. Suitably colour-coded, the winner was easy to identify.

Joseph thought about the pipes for a minute and had an idea. "I think I know where we can get some… well, nick 'em anyway," he said. "How soon do you want them?"

"If you're going to nick them, we ought to get them as soon as possible and then keep them out of sight for a few weeks until the heat dies down," said Gavin.

Peter looked at Joseph, and they both said the same name simultaneously, "Why don't we ask Jamsie to do it?"

Gavin knew Jamsie could be talked into almost anything but sounded a note of caution. "You want to be careful with him at the moment. He's trying to live down the last mess we got him into, and they're watching him good and proper. Home to bed at eight and all that, no fags, booze, and no lollipops either! Fawcett's got him doing hard labour up Dinc-Bottom as well." Dinc-Bottom was the Fawcett family seat, a grand-looking house close to the centre of Dinctum, and Jamsie had been working there on various chores every Saturday morning since his run-in with Mrs Braintree.

Whilst all this talk of pipes was interesting, Peter was keen to hear more about the firefighting competition. He liked fires and had a lot of experience starting them all over the valley, but Gavin couldn't supply much detail. "It isn't confirmed yet," he said. "They asked Clifton to sort it out, so it might not happen at all... you know how she is when it comes to organising anything. Basically, they set fire to a couple of old cars and then have a race to put them out."

"Brill!" said Peter, who was starting to get quite animated. "Do we get to test them with different sorts of fires?" he asked. "I mean, we could challenge them, couldn't we? Bet you can't put this bastard out - that sort of thing!" He might have been joking about this, but you could never tell.

They talked excitedly about the coming event. What had seemed like it might be a tedious affair had suddenly turned into something very exciting. They could have sat there on the hillside all night, but it was getting late.

"We'd better take a wander back down and see what we can do about those pipes," said Peter. "You coming?" he asked, and Joseph said he was.

***

Now that the sun had set, the smell of damp grass filled the air and the mist thickened in the meadows alongside the river far below. An owl called out in the woods by Dinctum Splashit, and some deer edged out from a thicket to the north of the village.

Gavin's little spot on the hillside was an excellent place to meditate and put the world to rights. It was almost like floating above the valley, particularly at night when hazy lights shone up from the gloom below. He spent many hours on this hill, watching the comings and goings with interest. It was surprising how much you could see from that vantage point and, if the wind was in the right direction, what you could hear too.

The devious plans to put Mrs Braintree in her place were coming along quite nicely, so he sat back and made himself comfortable. He would be on that hill for a bit longer because one bungalow in Dinctum currently had his undivided attention. It belonged to Mrs Braintree, and every Thursday evening, Gavin made sure he was in his favourite spot on the hill to watch the comings and goings. Nothing much happened in that bungalow for most of the week, but on a Thursday evening… He was very intrigued and lit another roll-up.

***

Oblivious of the watching eyes on Paddick Hill, Agnes Braintree sat quietly in her lounge, eyeing the fruit bowl on a table across the room. It was overflowing with various exotic produce, some of which looked like it ought to be crawling around the bottom of a sea somewhere.

It hadn't gone unnoticed that Agnes had a thing about fruit. A supermarket chain had certainly spotted it because she was in their Dillchurch branch every Wednesday, without fail, emptying their well-stocked and carefully arranged shelves. Her husband had noticed too, and it puzzled him. He knew it was supposed to be good to eat the stuff, but he didn't much care for the side effects. Pineapple brought him out in spots, bananas gave him nightmares, and his alimentary tract had what could only be described as a catastrophic reaction to grapes. He knew that his daughter, Kathy, only ever ate an apple a day and that these came from an entirely different source, in another part of the house. So, the puzzle was this: why had all the fruit gone by Friday morning? Not a single grape, orange, or plum to be seen anywhere. Not a solitary pip.

He eventually plucked up the courage to quiz Agnes about it – you didn't do that sort of thing lightly – and discovered, amidst the acerbic and verbose response, that it was all down to Plunge-Pithering. He visited the house every Thursday night to plan tactics, and according to Agnes, the man had a penchant for fresh fruit.

"If a member of parliament wants a bowl full of fruit, he jolly well gets it, Henry!" she said. Henry got it. Unfortunately, his subsequent quip about bananas and the Houses of Parliament being full of howling gibbons went down like a lead balloon attached to an anchor. The matter was never discussed again.

Braintree's mind focused on the evening ahead as she gazed at the wooden bowl on the table. She was expecting Plunge-Pithering to arrive at any moment for his weekly 'chat' and had given the whole house an extra special dusting. She'd even polished the freshly cut display of pansies that decorated the sideboard.

Agnes had been courting the MP's attention for quite some time and was almost at the point where he would agree to anything she asked. Closing down Dinctum Youth Club was undoubtedly one of those things, but it was only the beginning. An act of parliament prohibiting everyone under the age of twenty-one from gathering in groups of more than one was another objective. So was national service, although, on this point, Pithering was less enthusiastic. As a retired naval officer, he wasn't keen on having a load of half-stoned delinquents drafted aboard his battleships. And then there were the unions, full-time firefighters, police officers under six feet tall, anyone from Scotland, anyone with a beard, people who wore white socks with sandals - all of these and more were on Agnes Braintree's hit list. Come the revolution, she would have all of them locked away for the rest of eternity - not that revolution was a term she felt comfortable with. It had an air of communism about it. The phrase 'military coup' suited her better.

She had reason to feel the way she did. You didn't get to be a headteacher without having to endure the most terrible things: the graffiti and the name-calling, the fireworks in her toilet, or the round of applause the day she fell off her scooter. She had seen the dark side of humanity, and it came in the shape of a twelve-year-old with a can of spray paint, a skateboard, and a head full of liberal or left-wing nonsense. It was high time something was done about it, and having alerted the Queen, the next phase of her campaign was to get Plunge-Pithering into gear.

Her thoughts were interrupted by a car pulling up in the driveway. She knew the sound of that engine and those tyres on the gravel. It was Pithering, and he was on time as usual. A joint of pork was roasting in the kitchen, and the smell permeated every room in the house. Henry was out for the evening with her daughter. Everything was set. As she left the lounge, Agnes looked back at the fruit bowl.

That will do nicely, she thought.

The Ascent of Dinctum Down

Dressed in bright white shorts and a golden yellow tee shirt, David looked like he was auditioning for the part of a daisy in Gardeners World. He had reluctantly agreed to take the senior members out for a long run in the countryside after Colonel Fawcett told him to "get the buggers off their lazy backsides". A run around the valley seemed like it would fit the bill perfectly and placate Fawcett into the bargain. However, David had been uneasy about the whole thing. The trouble with a run in a valley was this: unless you went around in tiny circles, it would inevitably mean going uphill at some point. He hadn't been running for at least sixteen years, and the thought made his legs turn to jelly. He was sure to get stitch, cramps, or worse. Despite these reservations, he convinced himself that a bit of modest exercise couldn't do him any harm. This was the same optimistic and misguided reasoning that led Lady Dinc to ride a pogo stick around the lanes a year earlier. It didn't go well, and the fields were littered with cars and irate motorists who had driven through hedges to avoid having their bonnets impaled by a member of the landed gentry.

To make the idea of a run more appealing, David had suggested they finish it with an overnight camp in Slaptatchit woods, which overlooked Dinctum Splashit. Nights out in the woods were always popular with the club members because there wasn't much they could do in Dinctum that they hadn't done at least a dozen times before. You either stayed in the valley trying to dream up something new, which often meant something illegal, or you went somewhere else, and the trouble with somewhere else was getting to it. Buses were infrequent and often unpredictable. You were stuck unless you had a moped, a bike, or parents with a lot of spare time and deep pockets.

There was great excitement about the camp. So, on the chosen date, Vicki borrowed a tractor and trailer and went ahead with Gavin, taking everyone's overnight packs with them. They bounced off happily into the countryside, crossing the ford at Shit Creek and heading across the fields. The sky was clear, and the forecast was good. It was going to be a memorable night.

***

Aside from the short and potholed lane to Dinctum Splashit, there was only one road through the valley. It passed through Lower Dinctum in the south and Winterbourne Dinctum in the north before making its way to Bungbury and Tilt. Jogging along this route would have been monotonous and probably quite dangerous, given the speed of some tractors thereabouts. Fortunately, the hillsides were traversed by countless old and rarely used farm tracks. Most were dirt paths, barely wide enough for a cart. Some were bordered with hedges, others with old, moss-covered stone walls. In places, huge beech trees had grown in lines, reaching skywards from the top of the walls, their roots binding the stones tightly together. Between these tangled roots, mysterious holes went back between rocks to places only the smallest of creatures could venture. Rabbits, voles, stoats, and mice inhabited those dark recesses. Some thought there were pixies too. There had to be pixies in a place like that. If you were keen on exploring or keeping fit, these old tracks provided a perfect alternative to the tarmac and high velocity combines. David and his club members were keen on neither exercise nor exploration, but they were trudging along all the same.

***

Two miles into the run and facing yet another hill, people were beginning to drop behind.

"Catch up, Joseph. You can do it," shouted David. Joseph was constantly out of breath and beginning to think that smoking wasn't such a good idea after all. He replied to David using only a single finger.

Peter was struggling with the pace as well. "Why the hell are we doing this?" he pleaded between gasps. "If God had meant us to run all over the soddin' place, he'd have made everything closer together, wouldn't he?" But before he could continue with this theme, they turned a sharp bend in the track and were confronted with yet another, even steeper incline.

"Anyone brought a fucking rope and crampons?" enquired Pamela breathlessly. The hill seemed almost vertical to her. "That's the biggest fucking obstacle I've ever fucking seen! If you think I'm running up that bastard, you can piss right off." A chorus of voices supported this opinion, and since David was also feeling utterly shattered, they were allowed to drop into a brisk walk until they reached the summit.

David decided to tackle Pamela about her language. "Look," he said, "I know everyone swears a bit now and then, but it always seems worse when it comes from a girl. Why don't you try to cut down a bit? Act a bit more lady-like."

"I don't swear that often," she insisted. "Only when some mental fart tries to run me up the face of a fucking mountain. And anyway, why can't girls swear as much as boys? That's just fucking racist, that is."

"Sexist," corrected someone from the back of the group.

"Yeah, that as well. Init?" said Pamela indignantly.

David decided he was on a hiding to nothing and turned his attention to Emily, who had just jumped over a gate and run out of sight into an adjacent field.

"Oi, where are you going?" he shouted, anxious not to lose anyone. The paperwork would have been endless.

"I'm going for a PEE," said a desperate voice behind the hedge.

A loud cheer went up from all the male members of the party, and Joseph started searching in his backpack as quickly as he could. Even

104

though she couldn't see him, Emily was wise to his tricks. "You can shove off with those binoculars, Joe," she shouted, throwing what looked like a startled rabbit over the hedge towards him.

When they finally reached the top of the hill, they had a superb view of the Dinc valley with its gracefully rolling fields, and ancient woodland stretched beneath them. Threading through this glorious patchwork of green and gold, the river Dinc wound silently in and out of view. Larks, unseen in the clear blue sky, filled the air with their song, and the fragrance of flowers growing wild in the pastures wafted up on the same thermals that kept the buzzards aloft. Crows called as they flew across fields of corn and wood pigeons flapped noisily through the branches of nearby trees. There was a timeless, quintessentially English feel about this scene. If you listened very carefully, you could almost hear the music of Vaughan Williams or Elgar oozing from the landscape. Then again, it might have been the cows singing. They did a lot of that.

Glad of the opportunity to rest, they sat on a grassy slope and took it all in.

"David. Has Peter ever told you about Kangabats?" asked Joseph. "Tell him about the Kangabats, Peter. Go on."

But David had already listened to that instalment of Peter's strange little world. "You haven't been up to the Manor reading more of Olaf von Dinc's books, have you?" he asked. Olaf was a distant ancestor of the present Lady Dinc and, by all accounts, just as unhinged. "I reckon that's where all those weird ideas come from. You know, Kangabats, Nigel the goat and all that. Perhaps he's a long-lost relation?"

Peter didn't like the sound of that. The thought of being related to old Dinky disturbed him greatly, but everyone else found the prospect quite amusing, and Joseph decided to poke fun. Putting on a very posh accent, he turned to Peter and spoke. "Um, I wonder if one would like to dine with one at the manor tonight or perhaps pop in for tiffin tomorrow?" His impression was a good one, and even Peter had to laugh. Peter was always irritated by posh accents and would often vent his opinions about them. He felt driven to do again. "I mean, what's with this *one* business? What the friggin' hell do they think they're on about?" he asked. "*One* will go to this, or *one* will do that. Oh, golly gosh, I'm so sorry. *One* appears to have farted. How silly of *one*. What the flaming hell is that all about?" he asked. "I hate England."

David was familiar with Peter's views, having heard them many times before. "Oh, come on now, Peter, you can't sit here surrounded by this beautiful countryside and tell us that you hate England, can you?"

"Well, all right, but I hate the people," he said. "So screwed up about class and stuff. I mean, what sort of civilised country still runs trains with first-class carriages, eh? All of them with empty seats while the rest of us have to stand up for hours because there's no bloody room in the few *bloody* carriages that ain't first friggin class! What's that all about then?"

David stared thoughtfully at Peter. He knew for sure that Peter had never been on a train, and he also knew his father was a shop steward and card-carrying member of the Dillchurch Communist Party. Nevertheless, he had a point. However, this somewhat one-sided debate had distracted David's attention from the others in the group who, he now noticed, were huddled against a hole in the hedge behind him.

"What's up with that lot?" he asked.

"I think Pamela and Mickey are in the field doing the I'll show you mine if you show me yours, thing," someone replied. "They've probably got to the I'll stick it in and wiggle it about stage by now."

David sighed and told them all to get back on track immediately. "I wish Vicki was here. She would sort them out."

"Ah, now that's a name to conjure with, isn't it?" said Peter, with a knowing grin. "Got a bit of a thing for her haven't you mate?" He waited for a reaction, but David refused to rise to the bait.

***

Soon, it was time to go on again and make their way around the hills to the camp at Slaptatchit wood. The route took them three miles along a rough, dusty track that ran along a ridge between fields. It was easy-going compared to the steep ground they had come across, and everyone seemed to be in much better spirits.

"I hope it's going to be like this on the fun day," said Mickey looking up at the blue sky.

"I hope so too," said David. "Not long to go now, is it? Does everyone know what they're doing?" No one answered, and David wasn't going to ask again, so he changed the subject. "Anyone know when Gavin's going to start repairing the benches in the village?"

Peter scratched his head. "I don't think he's managed to nick the wood and paint yet."

David's heart sank. "Well, if you see him before I do, please tell him not to nick anything. I'd rather he didn't bother fixing them if that's what it takes." But he knew his words were falling on deaf ears. If Gavin thought he could get away with it, he'd filch all the necessary materials. Despite being very good at making money, Gavin was exceptionally reluctant to part with any of it. Not even the manager at Bincley's Bank in Dillchurch could get his hands on it, and he was known to be as persuasive as a loaded puff adder.

***

It was early evening by the time they got to Slaptatchit woods. It loomed over the downs east of the valley, stretching away into the landscape beyond. The only more extensive woodland was the huge Waddock forest to the west. People venturing into those woods tended to get lost for days, so Slaptatchit was a much better option for camping. Besides, the Waddock forest came very close to Dinctum Manor in one place, which meant you ran the risk of bumping into Lady Dinc. You really didn't want to do that. Not without a comprehensive risk assessment.

They found Vicky and Gavin waiting for them in a small clearing. Once everyone was accounted for, Vicki set them to work, gathering all the dead wood they could find to build a fire for the coming night. Fortunately, plenty was lying around, and soon a large pile was ready for use. Peter and Joseph had to be talked out of felling an entire tree with a couple of axes they'd brought along "just in case". They said they had always wanted to "chop one of the big buggers down," and the fact it would have taken them weeks, given their current rate of progress, didn't seem to be putting them off. As the evening set in, a few stayed near the clearing with David and Vicki, helping to tend to the fire and heat some soup, but most vanished on a range of highly secret missions.

The camp was idyllic, stretched out on the side of a hill facing west. A gap in the canopy of branches above gave them a beautiful view of the full moon floating in a cloudless, star-studded sky. The earth beneath them was dry, soft and warm to the touch. It made a comfortable surface on which to sit or sleep.

The fire was blazing now, and a red glow danced across the smiling faces. David had been reading the Hobbit for the umpteenth time, and the scene put him in mind of certain passages therein. For a moment, he was sure he had seen a troll somewhere beyond the firelight but realised it was much more likely to have been Jamsie. The fire would keep them warm well into the night, and David sat as close to it as he could, holding his knees against his chest. Aside from the sound of crackling, spitting logs, and the occasional screams when someone launched an ambush out in the darkness, there was a magical silence in those woods.

Soon, the mouth-watering smell of sausages sizzling in a pan filled the air. Vicki brought over some coffee and sat down close to David, her face only a short distance from his. For a moment, he forgot the coffee and stared deeply into her eyes. They were both transfixed, unable to look away, but a sudden shout interrupted this perfect moment. "Jamsie's stuck up a tree!"

If anyone was going to get stuck up a tree, it was bound to be Jamsie, and he was likely to make an excellent job of it too.

Fortunately, David had brought along a powerful torch, and they soon found him thirty feet up an old oak tree, hanging upside down by his feet. Gavin was waiting nearby and was still laughing when they arrived.

David didn't want to believe his eyes. "I suppose this is a silly question, but what the hell was he doing up there like that?' he asked.

"Owls," was all Gavin could manage.

"Owls?" asked David.

"He was pretending to be an owl or something," said Gavin. "Trying to scare the girls, I think, and he must have slipped. Looks more like a bloody bat now, doesn't he?"

David considered leaving Jamsie where he was. The benefits of having him stuck up a tree for the night were not inconsiderable. However, that wasn't really an option. "I suppose we'd better get him down. I mean, what's the *matter* with him, for crying out loud? Why can't he join another club or something?"

At that moment, Vicki put a comforting hand on his shoulder. "Well, my old friend," she laughed, "it looks like you're in for a spot of tree climbing, doesn't it!'

"Yeah, I had a feeling that was coming," replied David grumpily. He wandered around the trunk for ten minutes, trying to find the safest way up and it took almost another hour to get Jamsie down. The dangers of falling head-first from that height didn't seem to have occurred to him. David thought it might have knocked some sense into him.

***

By the time they returned to the fire, everyone was tired. It must have been well past two in the morning, and they tried to get some sleep, lying near enough to the fire to keep warm but not so close as to combust. The ground under David, although soft, was uneven, so he searched for a better spot. He decided not to tempt fate and made a point of lying on the opposite side of the fire from Vicki. They were woken several times in the night by various comings and goings, but eventually, everyone settled down enough to get some proper rest.

The dawn chorus and cool air put pay to any ideas they had of a lie in. David sat up slowly and looked over the top of the fire with his eyes still full of sleep and a back so stiff he could hardly move. Coincidentally, Vicki did the same, and all things being equal, their eyes should have met in a romantic gaze over the dying embers, but it was not to be. Instead, they found themselves looking at a dead and very well-basted pig hanging from a wire over a raging inferno. David didn't believe his eyes, but his nose backed them up. There was an overwhelming smell of bacon hanging in the woods, and now he knew why. He didn't like to swear in front of the club members, but sometimes there was no avoiding it. This was one of those times. "Oh, for fuck's sake! Please tell me that's a large rabbit."

Gavin sat stoking the flames with a long stick, looking very pleased with himself. "No. It was going oink, so it must be a pig. Only a small one, mind you. Lovely fire, isn't it? You could roast an elephant over that, no trouble."

David thanked his lucky stars that elephants, or something like them, had left the Dinc valley thousands of years earlier. Had they still been at large, there was no doubt he would have been looking at one right now.

"I'm beginning to think there's something wrong with you lot," he ventured, still too sleepy to rant. "Anyone else would have been pleased enough to catch a rabbit or something. A duck would have been a novelty, but a flaming pig, for heaven's sake! I mean, where the hell did it come from?" He was sure they would be arrested the minute they left the woods. The police were probably out there now, waiting for him. David could see the headlines: 'PORK SNATCHINGS IN DINCTUM - thieves on the trot'. He listened carefully for the sound of sirens or barking police dogs.

Gavin didn't seem bothered and produced two bottles of ketchup and three loaves of fresh bread from his rucksack. "There we are," he said proudly. "Bacon sandwiches with tomato sauce and a nice cup of tea to wash it down. What more could you want?"

"An alibi?" David suggested.

Gavin ignored him and pulled out a small brown bottle from his coat pocket. "Worcester sauce, anyone? Lovely with bacon sandwiches. Almost legendary!"

"I hope you've got a spade in that sack of yours," said David, "because you'll need to bury the evidence before we leave. Come to think of it, don't bother with the pig! Bury me! I reckon that's my best option right now."

"Oh, don't be so gloomy," said Vicki. "We'll be okay. No one's going to miss the odd pig around here. They go absent all the time, believe me."

David did, especially with Gavin lurking in the corner of farmyards like a starving wolf. He wondered what was "odd" about this pig as opposed to any other and whether it was safe to eat. Besides, it is one thing when your bacon comes neatly packaged from your local supermarket, but quite another when it's hanging there, snout and trotters, over your breakfast table. He made a note to stick to cornflakes in the future.

What he didn't know, and no one was going to tell him, was that Gavin had picked up the pig from his uncle at the butchers long before anyone else was awake. There weren't any police or dogs - not yet anyway.

When breakfast was finished and the camp cleared, they set off towards Dinctum. Vicky had returned the tractor and trailer, so they had to carry their packs, but it was all downhill and less of an effort than it might have been. Even so, not everyone was happy. Jessica wanted her boyfriend, Sam, to swap packs with her. His was considerably lighter than hers, but he was having none of it. She tried the "if you *really* loved me" approach first, but when that didn't work, she resorted to beating him violently with a piece of tree. Vicky had to intervene before bones were broken.

By midday, they stood outside the village hall, saying their goodbyes. Everyone, except Jessica, was smiling and still high on the excitement of the night's activities.

"That went much better than I had expected," said David, "and it looks like we got away with the pig rustling as well."

Vicki smiled. She thought about telling him the pig hadn't been stolen but decided it would be more fun to say nothing. "They all seemed to enjoy it. We should do it again soon."

"Maybe," said David. "Just the overnight bit. No running and no pigs!"

Thorn of the Night

A solitary, pale light glowed dimly at the back of a large Victorian building in Dillchurch. It was Dillchurch and West Dorkshire 'lice' Station, and the office belonged to DS Thorn and his assistant, DC Drivel.

Much to Drivel's annoyance, Thorn liked to work nights, principally because it meant he didn't have to hang around the house while his wife, Rose, was in residence. Their marriage had gotten off to a bad start because of her new surname. Somehow, it hadn't mattered before their engagement, but when she saw it written in the register, she knew she would be a laughingstock at the Dillchurch women's coffee club.

There were many things about DS Thorn that didn't seem to matter before the wedding, but it all felt very different once the vows were taken. The ease with which he forgot her birthday was one thing. The pungent smell of his feet was another. The smell was bad enough for her dog to leave home, the budgie fell off its perch and died, and no amount of tasty lettuce could entice the tortoise out of its shell.

Then there was his appetite. He'd think nothing of sitting quietly in his chair after tea, engrossed in a newspaper while munching his way through a packet of savoury biscuits, half a pound of cheese, and a jar of pickled onions. For a nightcap, he'd crack open a bottle of stout, which he drank with even more cheese. All of this guaranteed he'd enjoy a flatulent night and then wake the following morning with breath smelling like the drain in a neglected zoo.

Rose soon voted with her feet, pillow, and bed covers by moving into the spare room and then, when the noise and smell found her again, to the shed. The arguments started shortly after this, followed by threats of a messy divorce. You didn't get to be a Chief Constable without a wife by your side in Dorkshire, so Thorn decided that he would have to turn over a new leaf. It wouldn't have made much difference if he'd turned over the entire compost heap - her mind was made up. So, he went on a diet, cleaned up his act, and even agreed to consider a double-barrelled surname to appease the poor woman. Sadly, her maiden name was Sharp, so the idea went nowhere. Not even the wife of a Chief Constable wanted to be known as Rose Sharp-Thorn, and she certainly wasn't going to be a Smythe this or a Farquharson that.

Predictably, Thorn hadn't been able to keep to his new regime, and he found it was easier to volunteer for all the night duty he could get. It quickly earned him the title 'Thorn of the Night', and he was very fond of it too - a bit like 'Slipper of the Yard' or 'Don of the Kebabs'. It was a relatively comfortable existence because nothing much happened in West Dorkshire at night - nothing that couldn't be left for the day shift to sort out. So, seated at his desk, the most taxing thing in Thorn's life at that moment was finding a clear space amongst the paperwork for a cup of coffee. Covered in forms, claims, and empty crisp packets, his desktop resembled a landfill site that had suffered an airstrike, so he gave up and plonked the cup on top of it all.

"Do you know what, Drivel?" he said, without looking up from his copy of the 'Dillchurch Times'. "I'm utterly sick and tired of all this flaming paperwork."

Drivel grunted and then swore under his breath as his typewriter jammed again. "I wish the Chief would put his hands in his pockets and get me a proper word processor, guv. I mean, this thing must have been here for years. I bet Noah typed out his boarding passes on this useless heap of scrap."

Thorn continued his monologue. "They promised me when I was promoted to detective sergeant that I wouldn't have any of this stuff to do. I mean, you never see Morse or Kojak filling in ruddy forms every time they want to take a pee, do you?" He picked up his coffee to take a sip. A travel claim stuck to the bottom of the cup.

"Sod it!" exclaimed Drivel as he snatched another crumpled sheet from the roller and threw it in the direction of the waste bin across the room. His aim wasn't good.

Thorn turned a page on his newspaper. "They promised me an office of my own, an assistant, *and* a proper covert police car, too, you know? And I believed them." He shook his head and let his mind wander. "To think I turned down the offer of a secondment to

117

the NYPD. The bloody NYPD!" He took another sip of coffee. It was his second cup of the evening, and by the time the night was through, he'd have drunk his way through another ten. All the pastries in the canteen cupboard would be gone as well.

Drivel ripped out more paper from the typewriter. "I don't know what it is about this sodding thing, guv, but I can't get the 's' and the 'd' to work independently, even if I *bash* the keys down. Arrgghh!" He jammed a finger into the machine.

"The bloody NYPD," Thorn echoed distantly. "They'd have given me a proper gun, you know… with bullets, and I could have shot someone with it."

Drivel trailed over to the first aid kit carrying the typewriter with him, his finger still wedged tightly in the keys. "I don't know who's in charge of health and safety around here, guv, but this flaming machine can't be legal." He put the typewriter down on the floor, placed one foot on top of it, and, with a scream, jerked his hand free. His search through the first aid box yielded only the smallest plaster and an empty packet of condoms, so he pulled a paper tissue from his pocket and bandaged his wounds.

"I'd love to shoot someone you know," said Thorn wistfully. "Just once… just a little bit. I've got a list of targets as long as your bleeding arm, Drivel. He held up his hand to point an imaginary pistol at the window and squeezed a notional trigger. "Pull the trigger. BANG! Then, halt, armed police, and Bob's your uncle. Crime wave sorted and no more frigging paperwork either."

His attention slipped back to the office and down to his empty plate. "Fancy another pasty?"

When he finally got a civil response, Thorn left for the canteen while Drivel reassembled the typewriter. By the time he'd returned, Thorn had already eaten half of his food. "Marvellous these things, you know, lots of meat in them. I might have another later. You sure you don't want one?"

Drivel was still focused on his report and appeared not to hear. "How about this, guv?" he asked, handing Thorn a crumpled paper. Thorn tried to read it.

On the morning of the 14th of March at approximately ten thirty-five, I hasd occasdion to call on Msd Funnelpit to enquire about her continuesd refusdal to pay a parking fine. Whilsdt attensding her property I obsdervesd approximately ten chickensd roaming her roughly cut lawn. My sdusdpicionsd were arousdesd on noticing that, without exception, the chickensd were all coloured blue. I wasd able to confirm that sdaisd chickensd hasd, in fact, been paintesd thisd colour in orsder to conceal the fact that they were the white light SDusdsdex chickensd nickesd from Mr Clagginsd farm earlier that morning (sdee sdeparate report).

"That's as far as I've got at the moment, Guv. What do you think?"

"Poetry, Drivel, pure poetry," said Thorn, still trying to decide if the phrase 'aroused suspicions' - however it was spelt - was suitable for inclusion in a police report. He might have given Drivel a lecture at any other time, but he was in a good mood tonight because the canteen had been restocked, and there was an ample supply of pasties, sausage rolls, and pork pies to keep him nicely replete throughout the coming hours.

***

At roughly the same time as Drivel was fighting with his typewriter, Mrs Clifton was getting into a bit of a dither. She knew she wasn't much good at taking responsibility for anything and was trying to work up enough courage to call the fire brigade about the firefighting competition. She recalled the fire officer's name began with a B, but that was about it. So, she conducted a lengthy search of the telephone directory, trying to find a 'B' who put out fires for a living. Unsurprisingly, she drew a blank, so after a lot of 'oh dear-ing' and 'goodness me-ing', she eventually dialled 999.

"Emergency services - who do you require?"

The operator answered so quickly that Mrs Clifton didn't even get a chance to think about what she would say, and she fell silent.

The voice on the line became more insistent now. "Hello, emergency services. Who do you require, caller?"

Mrs Clifton felt one of her hot flushes coming on. The voice was pushing her for a response again, and she could feel beads of sweat forming on her brow. "Er... I want to speak to... to speak to the fireman, please," she squeaked.

There was a click and a buzzing noise on the line. "Fire service. What's your emergency, caller?" It was a different voice now but just as urgent.

"Oh, there isn't a fire yet, my dear! N-no, we won't be starting it for another few weeks yet. At least when I say we haven't started it yet, I mean them, of course... at the village hall on a fun day." She began to fiddle absent-mindedly with her bra at this point. It was a comfort thing, and there was certainly plenty of it to fiddle with.

On the other end of the line, the telephonist leant over to a colleague. "Pam, I think we've got an arsonist on the line. Can you patch it through for a trace, love? She's going to set fire to a village hall on Sunday or something."

By this time, Mrs Clifton had disengaged her brain and put her mouth on autopilot. If you told her that pigs were green and very good at knitting, she would have ordered a pork cardigan for lunch. "Of course, the little terrors might not let us, you know," she blurted.

The telephonist tried to make the best of a bad line and, turning once more to her colleague, continued to express her concerns. "I think she says she's a terrorist, Pam. Hurry up."

While the first operator tried to keep Mrs C talking, Pam pressed a few keys on the workstation in front of her, and up popped an address.

"Now, I'm sure you don't really want to start a fire, do you, Miss... er, what did you say your name was?"

But it wasn't any good. Mrs Clifton wasn't listening anymore. She'd fiddled with her bra so much that everything was in a tangle, and she was beginning to regret ever having agreed to make the call in the first place. The glass of brandy she had poured herself earlier was empty for the third time, and she was starting to babble uncontrollably. "They tried to electrocute us, you know! Two hundred and forty volts up her backside! Two hundred and..." But it was no good trying to continue. She wasn't making sense, so she put the phone down and started to sob. "You're a complete failure,

Nora Clifton," she blubbed. "Fancy getting in such a state, you silly old muddlehead. I'll have to try again tomorrow."

With that, she decided to make herself a nice drink of hot chocolate and retire to bed. She wasn't very good at drinking brandy. Her legs felt like jelly, and there would be a headache in the morning. So, she picked up the bottle of aspirin and trailed up the stairs to sleep it off.

***

Elsewhere in the valley, Peter and Joseph had been in the middle of their pipe-hunting expedition when suddenly, they saw the flashing lights of several police cars and vans further along the lane. They were travelling at great speed and were soon upon them, leaving very little time to slip out of sight behind a wooden gate in the hedgerow. As the vehicles flew past, Peter and Joseph wondered what could have happened to warrant the urgent attention of the local fuzz. The last time police cars sped through the lanes like this was when Lady Dinc had weeded her lawn with dynamite. However, they would have to wait for the answer because there was a more urgent matter to attend to. As soon as the coast was clear, they slipped onto the road and ran off towards Lower Dinctum, where the gas board had been working. Stacked neatly along the side of the road, next to a deep, square-sided trench, surrounded by day-glow tape and yellow flashing lights, were twenty long yellow pipes. Happily, on the opposite side of the road was a short hedge, beyond which they could make out a meadow sloping gently down towards the river.

They picked up the nearest pipe as quickly as possible and hauled it unsteadily over the hedge. It was heavier than expected, but once dropped into the field, it rolled quickly into the river and sunk out of sight. The river wasn't especially deep at that point, but the thick weed growing in it would make even the brightest yellow pipe hard to see from just a few paces away.

"Result!" said Peter feeling very pleased with the achievement.

***

Mrs Clifton got as far as the bedroom door when there was a loud screech of tyres on the road outside and a sound akin to a werewolf barking loudly in the front garden. A loud crash startled her only a few seconds later as the front door flew off its hinges and burst into a thousand splinters. Looking down from the landing, Mrs Clifton was confronted by an armed response unit at the foot of her stairs, and they were pointing automatic weapons at her. As was usual in stressful circumstances, Mrs Clifton passed out.

***

Before Peter and Joseph could cross the road to get a third pipe, the sight of blue flashing lights coming back along the lane interrupted them. They barely had time to jump into a grubby ditch before two police cars passed, returning towards Dillchurch. As they went by, Joseph saw a figure in the back seat of the first car. There was no mistaking the hairstyle silhouetted by the lights of the second vehicle.

"They've nicked Clifton! FUCKING HELL, THEY'VE NICKED CLIFTON!" he shouted, jumping up and down on the spot like a four-year-old.

"What the Fuck?" said Peter, dazzled by the headlights. "We'd better go and tell Gavin. Quick!"

They found him in the Duck and Dinc talking to the barman. It took some time to attract his attention, but eventually, he spotted them waving frantically through a window, and he picked up his pint and put it on a shelf behind the bar for safekeeping. "Be back in a minute, Bob," he said and wandered out discreetly to see what all the fuss was about.

"They've nicked Nora Clifton! The police! Taken the dithering old fool away in a car... and there's a bunch of them at her house right now! Come and see!" The words spilt out in a torrent, leaving Peter utterly breathless.

"It's true!" shouted Joseph, jumping around with excitement. "Come and see for yourself! There are loads of them crawling all over the place... with dogs as well... and guns!" He was on a high and hadn't had this much fun since he'd sneaked into the changing rooms at school while the girls were in the showers and nicked all their clothes. He'd hidden them in a truck full of offal bound for Bristol. It took days to sort that mess out.

"It's okay! Calm down, I believe you," said Gavin, who wasn't sure he did. Then again, he hadn't seen them this excited for a long time, so something dramatic must be going down. Clifton was the last person you'd expect to see in custody. Try as they might, none of them could think of a suitable scenario. Peter wondered if she was a secret drug dealer. Joseph suggested she might be a KGB spy, but it was quickly discounted because she couldn't remember anything important for more than a few minutes.

"Yeah, but that might just be a front," explained Joseph, anxious not to have his theory discarded quite so quickly.

"Listen, mate," said Gavin. "The only front she's got is the one supported by a double Z cup, and I wouldn't want to get involved with that even if you paid me. I doubt the police would either."

Gavin asked about the pipes for the ferret racing, and they told him they could only get one. He decided it was too risky to go back for another now and said one would be okay. With that, Peter and Joseph went off to spy on the police still hanging around Clifton's house, leaving Gavin to his beer.

Sat unnoticed inside the pub throughout all of this was Vicki. She had watched Gavin, Peter, and Joseph through the window with great interest. Although she couldn't hear what they were saying, the animated nature of their discussion suggested that something unusual had occurred. She'd seen the police cars too, so when Gavin came back into the bar, Vicki went quickly across to speak to him.

"What was all that about then, Gavin?"

"Kangabats."

"Kangabats?"

"Yeah, Kangabats," confirmed Gavin.

***

As all this was going on, Agnes Braintree heard a soft tapping on the back door. Plunge-Pithering had found his way to the kitchen. It was odd because his car was at the front of the house where anyone could see it. Why he felt the need to sneak around to the back of the property was anyone's guess, but it didn't matter much to Agnes. Her husband and daughter were always out on a Thursday night and rarely turned up again until nearly midnight – sometimes later. She opened the door and welcomed him in.

In the early days, Agnes would offer Pithering tea or coffee when he arrived, but more recently, a large glass of red was always his preference. Pithering was never very far from a bottle of red if he could help it. He often joked that a good one always matched the colour of his nose. At times, especially when he laughed or coughed - both tended to coincide thanks to the cigars he'd smoked all his adult life - his whole face lit up like an over-ripe tomato. Any half-decent GP would have told him he was living too close to the edge. He was walking the tightrope of life wearing roller skates. However, Pithering was too obstinate to believe that anything as inconsequential as a few thousand Havana cigars and hundreds of gallons of Shiraz might kill him one day.

"I thought it might be nice to have dinner tonight, Pippy, rather than sit around talking politics," said Agnes in a purring tone that even her husband, Henry, hadn't ever witnessed.

Pippy is what she called Pithering now that they had gotten to know one another. It had been almost two years since their first meeting, and Pippy now looked forward to his weekly rendezvous with a woman of Mrs Braintree's appeal immensely. Compared to Mrs PP, Braintree was an absolute boffin and very well built, too: an excellent keel, nicely rounded stern, and a couple of outstanding funnels. An excellent set of portholes as well, he'd observed. In contrast, Mrs PP was an alarmingly dull 'horsy' type. She lived and breathed horses, and judging from her appearance, Pithering thought it highly likely that one of her ancestors had been crossed with a Shire or a Clydesdale. Pithering loathed horses almost as much as he detested his wife. The only benefit to being married to her was that it gave him somewhere to park his submarine once or twice a year.

Soon, they were both seated at the table, tucking into a delicious roast with perfectly served wine. It was, as always, a delightful occasion and everything Agnes had hoped for. They seemed to have so much in common and laughed more loudly with every glass. Soon, the main course was finished, and Agnes glowed as she gazed at her guest across the candlelit table.

"How was the pork tonight, Pippy?"

"Delicious Agnes. Absolutely delicious. Thank you!"

"Oh good," she said, relieved that he hadn't noticed the overcooked peas. "I got it from Waitrose, you know. Much better quality, I always think."

"Indeed!" said Pithering as he raised a wine glass to his lips. It was full to the brim with the deepest blood-red Merlot, and although not the best he had ever tasted, it was certainly better than nothing. Dinner without wine for Pithering was like strawberries without cream, bangers without mash, and sex without melons.

"Would you like some... dessert?" asked Agnes provocatively.

The glass in Plunge-Pithering's hand began to shake, and he gulped a mouthful quickly before replying. "Er... yes," he said, clearing his throat nervously. "Yes, please. Um… a little… f-fruit perhaps?" The glass was trembling quite a lot now.

"Yes, of course," said Agnes, smiling with relief.

Not for the first time that evening, Plunge-Pithering noticed her heaving breasts pushing out towards him from inside her pale cream blouse. It was unbuttoned just far enough to remind him he'd left his blood pressure pills at home. "Please… and… and you?" he asked with a quivering voice.

Braintree leant a little closer, filling his view with her ample curves, and answered him in the most seductive voice she could contrive. "Oh, I expect I'll be… *having a banana.*"

The wine glass in Pithering's hand snapped in two.

Clifton's Passage

There were now several lights shining brightly at Dillchurch nick, and to add to DS Thorn's annoyance, dozens of armed police were helping themselves to his pasties. Consequently, Thorn wasn't in the best of moods when he sat down in the detention room or dungeon, as he liked to call it, to interview 'The Dinctum Terrorist'. To make matters worse, he had been bitten by one of the police dogs as he walked along the corridor. It had taken quite a dislike to Thorn because he refused to give it any of his sausage rolls one day, and it lunged at him every time he got within range.

Thorn sat down opposite Mrs Clifton and took a deep breath, which he then let out as slowly as he could while reading some documents on the table in front of him. He was making it clear that he was fed up with all of this and not in any mood for polite conversation.

"Now," he asked. "Why do you think you have been brought here under armed guard, Mrs err...Clifton? Hazard a guess."

Mrs Clifton was in a desperate state. They'd had to stop twice on the way to Dillchurch for her to be sick in the bushes. She was never that good in the back seat of a car, and her head was spinning wildly. She couldn't understand what might have justified her sudden removal to Dillchurch nick.

"Is it about that thing with the traffic warden last month?" she inquired. "I'd only been there ten minutes, you know." Then she started blubbing again. "I'm a respectable property owner, a member of the W.I. I mean... what do you want with me? There must be some mistake?"

"All in good time, madam, all in good time," said Thorn. "But why don't you tell me about this firebombing first?"

Mrs Clifton was distraught and couldn't put a coherent sentence together for some time afterwards, so Thorn left her alone.

Outside the detention room, DC Drivel was looking worried. "She's obviously innocent, guv. I mean, look at the poor woman. I can't believe she's a threat to the public. I bet she doesn't even frighten mice. Shouldn't we let her go now?"

"Bog off, Drivel. She's not getting away with it that easy," said Thorn, who was now in a foul mood. His quiet night was turning into something quite the opposite. 'That vicious dog' had bitten him again, his mountain of paperwork was about to get substantially taller, and all his snacks were rapidly disappearing.

"Get away with what, guv? As far as I can tell, her story checks out. She's done naff all that we can book her for."

"Try membership of a subversive organisation for a start," said Thorn. By admitting to being a member of Dinctum W.I., Mrs Clifton was unquestionably guilty of terrorism in DS Thorn's eyes. He viewed the organisation with the utmost suspicion, especially since his wife had joined, and he'd tried several times to have their meetings secretly recorded. His patience was running out. "You see, it's like this Drivel. She gets me up out of me nice comfortable chair, gets me bitten by that rabid hound, and makes threatening phone calls to boot. On top of that, I've got a station full of pasty-eating firearms officers. In my book, that makes her as guilty as a cat in a spuggie's nest. She's in for the duration, or I'll eat me boots."

Drivel despaired. "Well, I'll go and get the salt and pepper then, shall I, 'cos you can't keep her locked up just for being a pain in the backside, can you guv?"

Thorn thought he could.

***

Drivel tried talking sense into Thorn as they walked back to their office, but it wasn't any use. Thorn sat down at his desk and picked up the evening newspaper, taking one final bite from a pork pie he'd saved for emergencies.

"Bollocks Drivel! Get back in there and organise a full search of her person for weapons, drugs, and anything else dodgy like knitting needles, Polos, or mothballs, and do it now! She'll think twice before she starts causing trouble again."

Drivel knew that there was little point in arguing. Not unless he wanted a Christmas full of extra duties, so he went back down the corridor again to get the forms and call in some help.

Thorn shouted after him as he left the room. "And see if they've found anything at her house! She's bound to be up to something if we look hard enough."

His attention returned to the newspaper. The pages began slipping apart, and he dropped some on the floor. "Why the hell don't they put staples in these flaming things?" he said irritably.

Once he'd reassembled the pages into order, he reached for a packet of biscuits hidden at the back of a drawer and settled down to do the crossword. He wasn't very good at crosswords, but they passed the hours nicely and it all went well until twelve across and four down had him completely stumped. Nothing seemed to work, and even a quick browse through a dictionary failed to inspire him. He gave up and threw the paper down. All the activity that night had left him feeling out of sorts and unable to concentrate. There were too many distractions, and it dawned on him that almost two hours had passed since he'd sat down. *What was Drivel doing?* he wondered, and putting down his pen, he set off to the detention room.

What he found shocked him. To look at Mrs Clifton, you might have been forgiven for thinking she had been dragged through a hedge backwards, forwards, and then sideways just for luck. Her make-up had run, and her stockings had enough ladders to scale the Eiffel Tower, starting at the ferry terminal in Dover. Her hair looked as though it was home to a flock of puffins.

"What the bloody hell...?" mouthed Thorn.

Constable Hewbry, the dog handler, turned up with the answer straining at the end of a thick chrome chain, its fiery eyes fixed on Thorn's precious little pinkies.

"Sorry about this, guv. It was Fang," said Hewbry, pointing at the dog. "He got a bit miffed with her making that blubbing noise and had a go while I was in the bog. You've got to admit she was going on a bit, wasn't she?"

Thorn knew a lawsuit when he looked at one and suffered a massive sense of humour failure. "Get that ruddy monster out of my face Hewbry, or you'll feel my boot up your backside!"

Fang was one of the few dogs that seemed capable of smiling, especially when it had you pinned against a wall without hope of escape. The animal was coaxed away with the promise of fresh meat elsewhere, leaving Thorn to usher Mrs Clifton to a waiting police car. He'd given Drivel orders to call off the search at her house and was going to drive her home as quickly as possible. He still thought she was as guilty as hell, but things had gone too far, too quickly.

***

When they finally left the station, Thorn looked at Clifton in the passenger seat beside him and noticed how badly torn her dress was. It wasn't a cheap dress either. *Brilliant, just bloody brilliant*, he thought. *I suppose I ought to apologise*, but it took him a long time to say anything. He could see the Chief's face when a claim for damages and wrongful arrest arrived on his desk, not to mention assault with a deadly dog. He'd been annoyed with the woman for sure and wanted to teach her a lesson, but this was ridiculous. Eventually, he put his worries aside and, half-heartedly, tried to make conversation. "Err... Mrs Clifton. I feel I must apologise for the inconvenience you have been put to, but I'm sure you'll agree that we must take our job very seriously. We were only trying to protect the public and..."

Mrs Clifton lost it. "How dare you! How bloody dare you... you *stupid* little man!" she screamed. "I AM the bloody public! I've been abducted from my home, mauled by some monstrous bloody dog, and had some filthy, filthy, FILTHY WPC putting her hands up my... my bottoms in the middle of the night! How dare you tell me..." Mrs Clifton started to cry again.

Thorn knew that the time had come to shut up and switched on his blue light so that he could put his boot down.

***

The scene at Mrs Clifton's home was worse than he could have imagined. Not one inch of the house had been left untouched, and they'd even taken the walls apart in some places because a sniffer dog had indicated something was hidden behind them. It turned out to be nothing more than a dead sparrow, but the wall was in bits by the time they found it. You didn't have to be an architect to realise that most of the property would need to be rebuilt, and there was no way she could stay there overnight, what with the missing front door and everything. Thorn almost cried.

"Is there anywhere you could stay until we get this mess sorted out, Mrs Clifton?" he asked, hoping she might have calmed down enough to deal with the situation rationally, but Mrs Clifton wasn't thinking at all. She was completely numb, and it had started to rain, adding to her misery. Thorn looked in the garage to see if she might be able to spend the night there, but there was no heating, the lights didn't work, and one of the squad cars had run into the door, twisting it so far out of shape, that it couldn't be shut properly.

"What about a relative or a friend? Perhaps you have a..." he was about to say lover but decided it wouldn't be constructive. It didn't seem very plausible either, come to that. "I could arrange a hotel room in Dillchurch if you like?"

"Look!" shouted Mrs Clifton. "Why don't you just go away and leave me alone, you nasty little man? Just GO AWAY!"

She meant it, and DS Thorn gratefully took this as his cue to leave. He was in his car and off faster than you could strike a match. It hadn't been one of his best days, and he had a feeling that the Chief Constable was going to make it worse.

The Shot Gun

It had been an entire month since Jamsie had stood in front of the village hall and entertained the crowds at Mrs Braintree's expense. It had been a difficult month, too: he was grounded without any pocket money, absolutely no sweets or chocolate, and a hangover that took almost a week to shake off. On top of that, he was on fatigues 'up Dinc-Bottom' and completely loathed every minute of it.

The colonel had him turning up at eight o'clock on the dot every Saturday morning to be assigned his day's work around the expansive residence. Sometimes it was painting or washing up, sweeping floors, or polishing brasses, but today, gardening was on the agenda. Colonel Fawcett was a reluctant gardener and found it hard to tell one plant from another. Consequently, whenever he ventured into the garden, his wife, armed with an air rifle and binoculars, sat on a rickety first-floor balcony that overlooked the entire estate. From this vantage point, she observed his every move.

If he so much as looked as though he was going to dig up, cut down or prune something that wasn't a weed, she fired a warning shot past one of his ears.

For this reason, Jamsie did his best to avoid the garden, but sooner or later, he knew his luck would run out. Fawcett presented him with a list of chores, and Jamsie was horrified to see that the first task was 'Back Garden, long grass, strimmer, cutting for the use of.' So, he collected the enormous implement from a shed at the side of the house and, trembling uncontrollably, shuffled out in full view of the balcony and Mrs Fawcett. She was seated in a rocking chair, rolling slowly back and forth, trying to look as though she was fast asleep. He could see the binoculars on her lap, a Pimm's on the table, and the gun beside her within easy reach. He strained his eyes to check that it was only the air rifle and not the double-barrelled, twelve-bore she kept in the bedroom just behind her.

Jamsie liked guns, so he had admired the twelve-bore while cleaning brasses one weekend. It was kept in a large glass case, set into the dark oak panels that lined the bedroom, and it took pride of place amongst an assortment of pikes, longbows, spears, and the pickled head of an unfortunate pygmy.

Cutting the lawn would have been easier. The grass was already short and well-kept, and it was obvious where it started and stopped. There was no danger of cutting down the wrong thing. However, the long grass was an entirely different matter, and he was apprehensive about it because the strimmer was an ageing, petrol-driven gadget that was very difficult to start and incredibly awkward to control. It could wreak havoc in just a few seconds if you weren't extremely careful.

Oh well... this is it then... might as well get it over with, thought Jamsie as he tugged on the cord that was supposed to start the wretched thing. *You might as well stick your head between your legs and kiss your arse goodbye.*

He pulled the cord repeatedly, but nothing happened. He checked that there was fuel and fiddled with various levers and valves. *This is bloody silly,* he thought. *Why am I bothering? That loony on the balcony will shoot me the first chance she gets anyway.* But he kept trying. Then, just as he began to feel his arm would drop off, the machine burst into life. It made a terrible noise, sounding like a thirty-five-foot hornet, and created a smoke screen that only Mrs Fawcett's tireless gaze could penetrate. As he struggled to hold it steady, he glanced up at the balcony and saw her reaching for the gun. He was only slightly relieved to see that she was merely placing it in her lap, so he did his best to keep the machine away from anything that looked either expensive or just plain flowery.

Things went well for a while, and the grass cut quickly. Much to his relief, the strimmer didn't seem capable of felling trees, and he discovered how to stop it from swinging around behind his head whenever he blipped the throttle. As his confidence grew, he ventured into the deeper grass just past the fishpond. Suddenly, he heard a loud shriek, and a ball of gingery-white hair shot into the air. The tortured shape tumbled back to the ground and then ran at full pelt between his legs and across the lawn, leaving a trail of fur behind it.

Mrs Fawcett leapt to her feet in disbelief. "He's strimmed the cat! HE'S STRIMMED THE BLOODY CAT!' she shouted and darted back into the bedroom towards the gun locker, stumbling over the table as she went.

Jamsie guessed precisely where she was going and quickly developed a sudden urge to be elsewhere. It was time to leave the premises, and he ran for all he was worth, casting the strimmer to one side as he went. Gasping for breath, he could still hear Fawcett screaming at the top of her voice. Then, as he leapt over the rose beds, dragging his feet through the uppermost blooms, the ground behind him erupted, showering him with dirt. Mrs Fawcett had emptied both barrels at him, and she wasn't far off target.

The sound of the gun hit his ears only fractions of a second later, and he fell face-first onto the ground in front of him. Fawcett was shouting something about 'Pudkins' and 'REVENGE'. Pudkins must have been the fluffy thing's name, but Jamsie didn't care. With one titanic effort, he scaled the garden wall, dragged himself over it, and dropped painfully to the pavement six feet below. As he lay there beside the road shaking uncontrollably, bricks exploded all around him when the second volley hit the top of the wall. Jamsie covered his head as best he could, trying to fend off the torrent of mortar and dust. Fear paralysed him, but he knew he couldn't stay where he was, just in case the gun appeared over the wall. So, keeping as low as possible and staying hard against the ivy-covered brickwork that marked the boundary between the pavement and Fawcett's property, Jamsie set off. He was in shock and decided to hide somewhere just in case the *'mad bitch'* decided to give chase. He needn't have worried. The balcony, rotten to its core, had collapsed with a dull crunch leaving Mrs Fawcett dazed and confused. She'd shoot the little bugger at some point, but it would have to wait.

***

Not far up the road and just beyond the village border, an old yew tree hung across the river Dinc. Jamsie often retreated to the safety and comfort of its lower branches when he was in trouble. *It's at times like this when you begin to think life's out to get you*, he thought as he made his way across the road towards the river.

After only a short distance, he saw Peter and Joseph running towards him, both looking very alarmed. "What the hell was all that shooting about?" asked Peter. "You shot Fawcett, have you? Blown his tiny little brain out from between his ears?"

"Yeah, shot his balls off, have you?" asked Joseph hopefully, but quickly saw that Jamsie was extremely upset. He was as white as a sheet and still shaking all over, and tears washed the brick dust from his cheeks. They walked with him to the tree.

"Are you all right, mate?" asked Peter. "What the hell happened?"

Jamsie recounted the events to them in horrific detail.

"The crazy bitch!" said Joseph. "I thought old Dinky was certifiable, but this takes the biscuit. We can't let her get away with it!"

"We ought to give Dinga Bell a shout," said Joseph. Dinga was the name they gave to Constable Bell, the officer responsible for keeping the law thereabouts. "She's a bloody nutcase! I mean, you can't just go around shooting at people, can you? Not even the ones that strim your cat. Even Brainless doesn't shoot people."

"No, she doesn't," said Jamsie distantly. "But I don't want to call Dinga. Gavin wouldn't call Dinga, would he? He'd sort her out himself. He'd have a plan like he has for Brainless, and that's what we should do."

"We could set fire to her pond!" said Peter excitedly.

"Plonker," said Joseph.

"What? Oh… yeah… sorry."

So, they sat for an hour, passing ideas back and forth, but nothing seemed to fit the bill. It was either unrealistic or required too much TNT. They needed Gavin for this kind of thing and were just on the point of going to find him when Jamsie suddenly had a thought. "The cellar," he said. "They've got a big cellar under Dinc-Bottom, and they won't let me near it. I reckon there's some dark secret in there that they don't want me to see."

"I bet it's a monster. A big slithery thing with hairy legs, bulging eyes, and huge… huge… er… projections!" ventured Peter, his imagination failing him when it came to the anatomy of monsters.

"Yeah, or maybe there are dead bodies," exclaimed Joseph. "You know, ex-gardeners who strimmed her cat and didn't escape like you did! I bet there are hundreds of the poor bastards down there. Why not check it out next time you're there, Jamsie?"

"Can't," he replied. "It's locked… and anyway, I reckon she'd shoot me again."

"Oh, yeah, I see what you mean," said Joseph as he rolled another cigarette to share. "I don't suppose you ever want to see that place again, do you?"

"Too right," replied Jamsie. "But... well, I would like to get her back for it, you know... scare seven shades of shit out of her... but not when she's on guard with that bloody gun."

"Right," said Joseph. "That means we've got to sneak in there at night when it's dark, and they're both in the land of nod. All we need is a key to that cellar, and we can look around, find out what it is they're trying to keep secret, and Bob's your strange auntie. Easy."

"But why?" asked Peter, who was still hoping he could start a fire.

"Because we might find something to use against them. Or we could set up a nasty little surprise like Jamsie said and scare them shitless."

"Where are we going to get a key from?" asked Jamsie.

"What about Susan Taylor," said Peter. "Old slaphead has got a soft spot for her, hasn't he? And her mum often cooks for them. I bet she knows where to find one."

Jamsie was highly sceptical. "I can't see her helping me get back at Fawcett in a million years, not after what I did to her, and she'd probably encourage the old cow to shoot me again."

He had a point.

"Hold on, we don't have to tell Susan we're helping you, do we?" said Joseph. "I mean, we could just say the old bag tried to shoot one of us, couldn't we?

It sounded like a good plan. Jamsie said he would lie low for a while, and Joseph would speak to Susan about getting the key.

Jamsie also volunteered to help them recover the ferret racing pipe from the river. It all seemed relatively straightforward. What could possibly go wrong?

***

The day had passed into evening by the time Jamsie felt brave enough to make his way home along the winding lanes. As he walked, he hummed nervously to himself and thought about the idea of getting Susan to help teach the Fawcett woman a lesson. He was deeply worried about it. Susan hadn't spoken a single word to him since he'd ruined her self-respect, her dress, and her new socks. On top of that, he had a dim but bothering memory of being laid on a damp storeroom floor looking up at a side of Susan that hadn't been seen before, not even by her.

The light was fading quickly now, so he accelerated his pace. The sounds he was used to hearing at that time of the day seemed suddenly threatening. Was that Mrs Fawcett out there stepping on twigs in the woods, trying to find the perfect shot? Was it Myrtle Gurt brushing through the leaves while invoking some powerful demon to chase him out of the valley? Was Lady Dinc going to come screaming around the next bend on her beat-up motorbike and attempt to run him over? She had a reputation for colliding with things on that bike and had come very close to hitting him once before. Lady Dinc travelling at speed on a backfiring, oily, and smoke-belching motorbike was enough to terrify even the dead. Her habit of wearing a white porcelain chamber pot on her head instead of a proper crash helmet (a protest of some sort) didn't help to calm the nerves either. Every little rustle and creak, every hoot and grunt sent shivers down his spine, and soon he ran as fast as he could. Home couldn't come quickly enough now.

By the time he stepped in through the front door, he was utterly exhausted and, following a hasty bath, collapsed into his nice warm bed, where he kept his face hidden under the duvet. Sleep wouldn't come quickly that night, but when it did, his dreams were littered with strange images of giant ginger cats, Susan's rear end, and an enormous yellow ferret gun. At one point, the whole lot combined into an appallingly horrific vision that woke him with a start. He managed to drift off again, but only after reassuring himself that, in the unlikely scenario that Susan could accommodate a pipe of that diameter, there was no way on God's earth she could have farted fluffy animals out of the thing.

He slept fitfully and remained in bed for much of the following day.

Pithering's Plunge

Agnes Braintree thought it was all going very well indeed. Time had flown, and another Thursday night was upon her. Henry and Kathy were out, and Plunge-Pithering had called to say he would be arriving on time for "the usual". The house was tidy, the pork sizzled in the oven, and the fruit bowl was packed to the brim. There was just time for Agnes to set two places at the table, open a bottle of red and change into something a little more appropriate. Tonight, was the night. She'd been working up to this moment for months, and now the time was right: PP would agree to all her plans, and Britain would be a better place for everyone. She put on some music by Delius. It seemed fitting.

Soon, the clock on her sideboard chimed, delicately announcing that it was a quarter past eight. The sound of Pithering's car pulling up outside sent a hot flush across her chest, reddening the skin about her neck and breasts. She poured the wine and waited for a gentle knocking on the door. Everything was perfect, and everything was ready.

Jamsie, Gavin, Joseph, and Peter were relaxing again on the soft grass of Paddick Hill, quietly passing a roll-up between them. Two weeks had passed since Jamsie's ordeal at Dinc-Bottom, and he felt like his old self again. As the sun sunk lower, the sound of a dog barking somewhere in the valley below echoed from hill to rolling hill. Swallows dipped back and forth above them, and a duck flapped noisily by the river, complaining loudly about some unexpected danger in the reeds. There were lots of unexpected dangers pursuing ducks in the reeds along that stretch of the Dinc: foxes, mink, and even Mr Wong from the Golden Lotus in Dillchurch. It was a magical place to be on a night like this. None felt like going anywhere, but they were getting a little thirsty, so they sent Jamsie off to get a few cans of lager from Gavin's uncle (one of many) at the pub. He knew Jamsie and was used to having him turn up on one of Gavin's many errands.

"Don't forget the crisps and nuts!" shouted Gavin.

"Pork Scratchings as well, mate!" added Joseph.

Happy to be of use, Jamsie made his way down the hillside. At twelve years old, he was the youngest of the group and hadn't yet joined the senior youth club, but he felt accepted all the same. There was a sense of belonging that, until recently, had been missing from his life. His parents split when he was only six, and he'd grown to realise that he was an unexpected and unwelcome accident. His sister felt the same way, although she had a different father.

Lying on the ground, Peter stared up at the stars. "See that up there?'"

"What? Where?" said the others in unison.

"Up there in the sky. Look, there!" Peter couldn't believe they hadn't seen it.

"What, for fuck's sake?" demanded Joseph.

"That star, there," he said. "Do you realise the light from *that* star might have taken eight billion years to get here? Amazing, isn't it? I mean, how did it know we would be here to see it?'

Silence.

"Eight billion light years is a bloody long way," he continued. "I'd be knackered after going that far, so how come light isn't? They say the universe is expanding because light is shifted red everywhere you look, don't they? Well, I think the light is tired, that's all."

There was still no response from the others, who were now starting to wonder what Peter was smoking.

"And I'll tell you something else as well," he continued. "If I switched on the light in me bedroom at night to read, would the room get brighter when I shut my eyes? You think about that."

None wanted to, but Joseph finally had to say something and immediately wished he hadn't. "Why? Why would the room get brighter, Peter?"

"Obvious init," said Peter. "When I open me eyes, they absorb light, so the room gets a bit darker… there's less of it to go around. See? So, when I close 'em again, the room will get brighter. It stands to reason. Dipsi-facti-tuttus."

"Uh?" said Gavin.

"All right then," said Joseph, trying to make sense of it. "Suppose you shut your eyes, and the room got brighter. How would you know without being able to see it?"

"Ah… that's the crux of it all, isn't it?" said Peter, delighted with the opportunity of expounding his theory. "You'd have to get someone in to look, wouldn't you?"

This seemed a reasonable proposal to Peter, but Joseph disagreed. "Yeah, but they'd use up the light as well, wouldn't they?" he ventured. "Except when they blinked, of course, but you'd never know, would you?"

More silence.

Then it was Gavin's turn. "Sunglasses!" he said proudly.

"What?" said everyone else.

"It's obvious," repeated Gavin. "If the person watching was wearing sunglasses, it would minimise their impact on the experiment… every observer affects the results of an observation by the very process of making the observation," he stated confidently. "It's a well-known fact, isn't it?"

"Shove off with you," said Joseph, who was beginning to get a headache.

"Yeah, that's right, Gav!" said Peter excitedly. "If a gnat was flying at the windscreen of a passing car, it would observe itself hitting the windscreen before it heard itself and, in the process of impacting with the windscreen, automatically rule out the possibility of *ever* hearing itself… even if it used a tape recorder. Olaf's second law: light travels faster than sound, except through soup."

"Shut up about sodding gnats and soup, will you," said Joseph, whose head was now definitely thumping.

They were much mistaken if they thought Peter had finished his philosophical ramblings because he'd thought of something else and was eager to share it.

"What about the light bulb?" he asked. "If the room stayed the same brightness, regardless of whether me eyes were closed or not, then it must be because the bulb emits more light when me eyes are open than when they're shut. Now there's an interesting idea, isn't it?" He smiled maniacally at the other two and took a deep drag on his roll-up.

"What a load of utter bollocks," said Joseph firmly. He was fed up hearing about light bulbs and gnats, not least because several of the latter were starting to eat him. "Where's Jamsie got to with that lager? I'm beginning to get a bit of a dry mouth up here."

"Perhaps he's been hit by Peter's gnat?" said Gavin.

"Yeah, or else he has to keep his eyes closed so that there's enough light to see by," said Joseph.

***

Peter was especially fond of quoting Olaf von Dinc. Olaf published his 'Theory of Juste about Everythinge' in 1821, following a lifetime of experiment, careful observation, and several spells in a home for the bewildered. Written in an almost indecipherable code, it expounded his ideas about the world and how it worked. Aside from several theories about the behaviour of soup and its implications for faster-than-light travel, he'd also written about string: "Tin Nip Ping yap, fer bung-bung tillet. Spat kas apti vertuff nad clakker…" and so on. Hours of work by the brightest minds translated this passage to read: "Any single length of string, when left unattended for more than a few seconds, will inevitably become entangled with itself." Olaf's string theory. Perhaps Olaf wasn't as daft as people thought? Then again, he wrote, "Tis the waving of the branches of ye trees that doeth cause ye winde, and not the reverse."

***

Eventually, just as Peter, Gavin, and Joseph were about to give up hope, Jamsie reappeared, bringing with him all they had asked for and more.

"Looks like it's gonna be a long night," said Gavin, rubbing his hands together as he reached for his first can.

Joseph thought he'd try out some of Peter's theories on Jamsie. "Jamsie mate, Peter wants someone to watch him in bed at night to see if the lights get brighter when he blinks, don't you, Peter?"

"Yeah, but I was thinking of someone with legs up to their armpits, a huge great cuddly bum, and boobs the size of hot air balloons, and I'm afraid, Jamsie, my lad, you don't quite fit the bill."

Jamsie looked very relieved.

"Sounds a bit like something you'd find in a zoo to me," said Gavin, who was thinking about someone altogether more available, and he went on to outline his requirements: "Someone delicate, feminine, kind, considerate, intelligent and witty - with a voice like an angel."

"Mary Poppins?" suggested Joseph, who couldn't think of anyone in the real world who would come close to Gavin's specifications.

"No! Suzy Taylor, you plank!" said Gavin. "She would do me just fine, except we hardly ever see her now. Not since Mr frigging charisma here chucked up all over her!"

"I couldn't help it!" said Jamsie. "It was you lot egging me on to drink all that stuff. I'd have been all right if I hadn't drawn the short straw. I could have died trying to drink that much vodka! Anyway, I don't think she's as much of an angel as you do, Gavin. I could tell you a thing or two about her." But he wasn't going to, because no one would believe it anyway.

***

It was now almost completely dark, and the birds were all but silent. Only the bats whirled overhead, so Peter amused himself, trying to confuse the little creatures by jamming their sonar. He achieved this by sucking air in through tightly pursed lips and, in so doing, made a high-pitched squeaking sound. It seemed to work because the bats dived all over the place, but you could never be sure because their route through the air was always quite unpredictable. Even so, he persevered, hoping for a mid-air collision.

As the night wrapped around them, Jamsie decided to hit the trail. "I'm exhausted," he said, trying not to yawn too widely just in case he swallowed one of Peter's disorientated bats. "I'd better be off home before I fall asleep up here in the grass."

Peter and Joseph said they were tired too and set off in a different direction.

Just before he was out of earshot, Gavin called after Jamsie. "Do me a favour, mate and have a quick nose around Braintree's place, will you?"

"Why?"

"She's up to something, mate," Gavin replied, "and I reckon we ought to find out what."

As he watched them go, Gavin picked up the remaining cans and crisps before moving further up the hill to where he knew a smooth rock stuck out from the ground. It was just the right shape to lean your back against for a snooze, but he didn't intend to do that. He was more interested in seeing what would happen when Jamsie snooped around the Braintree bungalow.

***

Soon Jamsie had reached the riverbank. There were several places to cross at this time of year, so he chose a route that took him towards the Braintree's modest residence. It was a fiddly little bungalow, painted white with light blue window frames. Vines and climbing roses wound their way around a trellis that divided the garden, and a frog croaked from an unseen pond near a strange-looking bush. As he slipped quietly from one shadow to the next, Jamsie could hear odd noises coming from the house - sounds he didn't entirely recognise – and it intrigued him. So, he carefully made his way across the garden until he found a place to hide alongside a shed.

The first thing that Jamsie noticed was that Braintree's car was missing, and a rather expensive-looking vehicle was in its place. Although he wouldn't have known, Mr Braintree and his daughter had gone out in the family car for their regular Thursday evening appointment with the Dillchurch Scrabble & Tiddlywinks Society, commonly abbreviated to DS & TW, the Dillchurch Scribbly Tinkers, or even the 'Dubious Scratch-heads and Terribly Weird Society'. Mr Braintree and his daughter loved the society and never missed an evening 'scrabbling' or 'tiddling'. They loved the secret rituals too: the square-legged squop dance and the triple-triple nose scratch.

The noises from the bungalow were getting louder now, so he decided to move across to the kitchen window, which appeared to be the only room illuminated by a light. He spotted what could have been a privet hedge and was just about to dash towards it when a voice boomed out from the house.

"NO!"

He immediately recognised Mrs Braintree's voice and froze to the spot, wondering how on earth she could have spotted him in the dark. But before he had time to turn and run, another much deeper voice rang out from the same direction.

"YES!"

This was quickly followed by Mrs Braintree's voice again. "NO! NO! Not the blancmange!"

"YES! The blancmange! You can't stop me now, you little she-devil."

The next thing Jamsie heard was the sound of pots and pans crashing to the floor. He thought there was a murder in progress and decided he was better off out of it. He'd already come too close to losing his miserable little life 'up Dinc-Bottom' and decided that he was tempting fate by hanging around the bungalow any longer. But it was Mrs Braintree's next outburst that changed his mind.

"Oh, all right then… you gorgeous sexy beast, I SURRENDER! Do it to me with the blancmange. DO IT TO ME NOW!"

While his experience of potential killers was comparatively limited, Jamsie was pretty sure you didn't call them a sexy beast. In any case, he couldn't quite see how it was possible to kill anyone with a blancmange. Curiosity got the better of him, and he edged carefully along the privet hedge towards the window. As he got closer, he could hear the man's voice again.

"Give it to me. Oh… YES! Give it to me now… you sexy little fiend. GIVE IT TO ME!"

Jamsie carefully stretched up from the hedge and placed his hands against the wall to steady himself. Then, inch by inch, he raised his head until he could see over the window ledge. The bright light hurt his eyes at first, so it took a few seconds for his vision to adjust. Having done so, he wished it hadn't because the sight of Mrs Braintree lying stark naked on the kitchen table, generously covered with pink blancmange, made him distinctly queasy. It wasn't easy to tell which bits belonged to Mrs Braintree and which belonged in a pudding. She didn't have the best of figures, and the application of what appeared to be several buckets of the lumpy pink dessert did nothing to improve it. Nor did the use of two peach halves for a bra and an enormous banana for something Jamsie didn't want to think about. It looked like there had been an explosion in a trifle factory, and facing her, with his back to Jamsie, was an equally naked and rather fat individual with a large brown paper bag over his head. He

154

appeared to have been the main course because he was still dripping from head to toe with gravy and had some peas stuck to the back of his right knee. The paper bag made it difficult for Jamsie to see who it was, but there was no mistaking the voice. He recognised the fog-horn tone of Rear Admiral Plunge-Pithering when he heard it, and this was definitely him. Even though Jamsie hadn't been acquainted with the man's plump and distinctly pale posterior in all its distasteful, spotty detail before now, it was undoubtedly him. Mrs Braintree was pointing a handheld electric mixer at the opposite side of the man and was about to give him the stimulation he'd been asking for, but Jamsie didn't get to see it.

Hard as it was to be distracted from this scene, something was beginning to make him feel quite uneasy. Two small, brightly shining lights were just at the edge of his vision, and something about them drew his attention. He couldn't put off looking at them any longer.

Mrs Braintree liked her garden. She wasn't particularly green-fingered, but it gave her great satisfaction to see the plants growing and looking pretty throughout the summer months. However, it gave her absolutely no pleasure at all to find the flower beds booby-trapped with cat poo. She'd tried cat pepper, poisoned mincemeat, and industrial detergents and was on the point of shopping around for nerve gas when she came across a stuffed but vicious-looking tiger in a junk shop. She thought it might just do the trick. Jamsie was about to come across the tiger too, because the little lights that had bothered him were reflections in the unfortunate creature's glass eyes. Thinking he was staring into the jaws of certain death, Jamsie did it in his pants for the second time that month. Had they been wearing any, Mrs Braintree and her playmate might have done the same because Jamsie let out the loudest scream he had ever managed in his entire life and fell backwards into the fishpond.

In complete panic, Mrs Braintree sat bolt upright, entangling what Plunge-Pithering called his 'pink torpedo' in the mixer on the way up. Then she slid with a squelching noise off the table onto the kitchen floor, quivering helplessly. After that, it would have taken a carefully calibrated instrument to determine whose screams were the loudest: Jamsie's as he stumbled out of the garden, trying to avoid death by tiger, or the man in Mrs Braintree's kitchen, dragging himself across the floor towards a wall socket where he could switch off the mixer. It was on the point of doing irrevocable damage to his manhood, and the chance of his torpedo ever firing again was diminishing by the second.

Gavin couldn't tell which of the screams was louder either, but he thought it was all quite amusing. From his position on the hillside, he could see Jamsie, illuminated by the streetlamps, running up the road as fast as his little legs could carry him, but the other screams puzzled him, so he decided another lager was in order. There would be plenty of time for him to find out what all the fuss was about in the morning.

***

There wasn't any time left for either of the unfortunate souls in the Braintree bungalow. Jamsie's interruption made them lose track of time, and panic took hold when the clock sounded out the chimes for half-past eleven. One was hastily applying antiseptic ointment to his shattered parts while the other was trying to establish where the banana had gone. Both were in a state of absolute terror because Mr Braintree, and his delightful little daughter Kathy, were due back in less than an hour. They ought to have been clearing up by now.

Struggling to her feet, Mrs Braintree rushed around, trying to get the place tidy, but only succeeded in spreading the mess more widely than before.

"Oh, bloody hell. *Bloody hell!*" said Agnes. It wasn't going well.

Pithering, who still had a bag on his head, had run out of ointment. He'd given up trying to find his underpants and was now tugging frantically at his trousers in a desperate effort to pull them on, but the gravy made it extremely difficult. They were halfway up his legs before he realised they were inside out. "Blast it. BLAST IT!' he repeated hysterically. Mrs Braintree, naked as the day she was born, was still darting back and forth, shouting, "Bloody hell!"

Unfortunately, Kathy and her father returned home a little earlier than usual. Mr Braintree was surprised to find another car occupying the space usually reserved for his pride and joy, but nothing could have prepared him for what was to come. As he pushed open the kitchen door, his mouth dropped open, and he froze to the spot. Standing beside him, Kathy did much the same.

"What the F…" Mr Braintree's voice trailed off, partly in disbelief but also because of his daughter. He didn't like to swear in front of her, although quite what difference it would have made at this stage was open to debate.

The paper bag man, trousers still at half-mast, had hastily thrown on a shirt and was now furiously wrestling with the bolt on the door to the back garden. "Blast it. BLAST IT!' he shouted as he tugged at the handle, his spotty behind wobbling disconcertingly.

On seeing her husband, Mrs Braintree turned the same colour as the pudding she was wearing and tried to rationalise. "I can explain, Henry. It's... it's not what it looks like! I can *explain*." But the reappearance of the banana, albeit quite slowly at first, suggested to Henry Braintree that it bloody well was precisely what it looked like and a damn sight worse besides. Kathy, whose eyes had now grown impossibly wide, fainted and hit the floor at roughly the same time as the banana.

Once outside the bungalow, the Rear Admiral couldn't find his car keys. He must have dropped them as he fell out of the back door, so he ripped off the paper bag and began crawling around on his hands and knees, looking for them. Inevitably, Pithering, too, found himself staring into the eyes of Mrs Braintree's tiger. With a scream that echoed around the hills, he leapt backwards, landing with a splash in the fishpond where Jamsie had been only a few minutes earlier. Pithering wasn't a young man, and the whole episode was starting to take its toll. Slowly at first, but then with increasing certainty, he realised that he wasn't going to make it out of that pond. With one last "Blast it!" Rear Admiral Plunge-Pithering dropped anchor for the last time.

Back in the bungalow, Mr Braintree, who no longer gave a damn about anyone else, gathered poor little Kathy in his arms and stormed out, slamming the door behind him. He had no intention of returning.

***

Agnes sagged to the kitchen floor in a trembling heap and sobbed uncontrollably. Everything had been going so well. Plunge-Pithering was going to lobby for her in parliament, Bonditt would have to close the youth club, and Fawcett was punishing Jamsie, but now it was all in ruins. Her miserable little life had suddenly turned into a mess. *Where had she gone wrong,* she wondered.

Agnes sat for some time, staring vacantly at the vinyl tiles, absently pushing a grape through a puddle of custard. It made little tracks as it went that closed after a short delay until, in time, she couldn't tell where the grape had been. *That was it,* she realised. *I need to cover my tracks! Don't give up so quickly, girl! After all, has anything changed? Henry has thrown his toys out of his pram - nothing new there, but I don't need him. He's a waste of space anyway, and I know too much about Plunge-Pithering now for him to back down. He'll come crawling back for his bit on the side, and when he does, how could he resist? You've got to be strong, Agnes. Be strong!*

The strength slowly flowed back into her aching limbs, and she began the somewhat delicate process of peeling herself from the floor. While doing this, she remembered the sound of Plunge-Pithering screaming in the garden and guessed he was still in pain from the earlier mishap. But, as she walked to the bathroom to shower, she noticed his car was still in the drive. She stopped and thought for a moment before returning to the kitchen. *Perhaps he's still waiting for me to give him the all-clear?* She would look.

Opening the back door carefully, she stood for a moment letting her eyes adjust to the darkness. It wasn't long before she caught sight of two size eleven feet protruding from the lily pads, and they certainly didn't belong to a frog. She stifled a shriek and started to shake again. "Bloody hell! BLOODY HELL!"

The next hour was frantic as she rushed back and forth, washing this and wiping that in a desperate effort to hide all evidence of the night's sordid activities. Getting the house clean proved to be the easy bit. After all, she had been covering up these goings-on for months. It was the task of trying to drag Pithering's heavy body out of the pond that defeated her: he couldn't be moved. She briefly considered forgoing a pond and burying him where he lay, but it would have taken days and mountains of soil. *Perhaps the fish would eat him,* she wondered. In the end, there was no choice. She had to call the police and report a dead politician in her pond. This was going to take some explaining.

Under Caution

The interview room at Dillchurch Police station needed sprucing up. The room was so dull that the paint, once a bright shade of lemon, had given up being cheerful and was flaking off the walls to try its luck somewhere else. A single green curtain hung limply down one side of a window that overlooked the car park. If you stood near enough to the glass, you didn't notice the dirt, but from where Agnes Braintree was sitting, she could see every smear, every grubby finger mark, and a liberal splattering of sparrow poo.

The desk was empty apart from a cassette recorder, which appeared to have been styled by a bricklayer. It wasn't switched on because DS Thorn was still reading the file in front of him. He'd also forgotten to bring any tape, so the chance of recording her voice for posterity was slim at best.

"Dear, dear, dear," said Thorn disapprovingly as he read through the paperwork. A few minutes later, he started sucking air through his teeth, which made an irritating squeaking sound. He could feel

Braintree's eyes drilling into him, so just for fun, he took his time and turned to the next page.

"Well, well, well," he remarked, raising his eyebrows as he spoke. "Peas, eh?"

He didn't get an answer from her but wasn't expecting one. She was clearly outraged at being there but equally scared of what might happen. Agnes had never been on this side of the law before and didn't like it.

"Bit of a sorry affair isn't it, Mrs Braintree," said Thorn as he got up from his chair. He wandered purposefully over to the window where he stood, hands in pockets, watching the rain bounce off the cars below. "Dead politician in your pond," he said. "I mean… a dead frog or a newt… even a cat perhaps, but a politician?" He shook his head again. "Dear, oh dear, oh dearie me."

Plunge-Pithering wasn't one of his favourite people, and he certainly wouldn't have voted for the man. Pithering had been rude to Thorn numerous times, so he didn't care whether he was alive or dead, but this pond business was all very intriguing. It excited the sleuth in him, which made a change. Typically, events in Dorkshire only stimulated the sloth in his nature.

He turned away from the window and studied Braintree as she looked miserably down at the table. There were names carved into the wood, some of which belonged to former pupils. A creative verse written in what looked like red ink, but it could have been blood, encouraged the reader to support 'Man City' and 'Kick fuzz in the nuts.'

Thorn thought she looked very pale, a look he'd seen many times before in that room. Jacob Flatty had looked like that following his arrest for the theft of an entire steam train. He denied it, of course, but the fact that he was 'driving' it up the main road to Dincsmouth at the time of his arrest, didn't help his case one jot. The weight of the train and five carriages on the tarmac had carved out a ten-mile trench before it ran out of steam. Lionel Twillet from Cold Waddock had looked like that too, when Thorn charged him with impersonating the Queen. Seeing Twillet for the first time, Thorn had to admit his likeness to Her Majesty was uncanny. Had it not been for his full beard, Twillet might have gotten away with his crime: walking into Dillchurch Post Office and demanding they "gave one all of one's stamps back". It was moments like these that kept Thorn going. Moments like the time Oli Panford tried to rob Bincley's Bank in Splode, wearing only a pair of underpants - on his head. One day Thorn would write a book about it - if he could be bothered.

Returning to his seat, he picked up the file once more. Mrs Braintree had wriggled uncomfortably throughout the last reading of her statement, and he thought it might be fun to put her through it again.

"You claim that Rear Admiral Plunge-Pithering was a dinner guest when all of a sudden, he remembered an important meeting... somewhere," he threw Braintree a glance before continuing. "In his hurry to depart, he tripped over his dinner and then out of the backdoor, only to fall lifeless into the pond." He paused for effect. "That is what happened, is it, Mrs Braintree?"

Agnes appeared to be lost for words. Gathering what was left of her composure, she began to answer the question. "Look, I know it seems unlikely, but..." She didn't get any further because Thorn spoke over her.

"You see, what bothers me, Mrs Braintree, is this." He took a sip of tea. It looked like ditch water, but he liked it that way. "The deceased had his trousers on inside out and halfway down his legs. I know the Member for Parliament was getting on a bit, and perhaps he didn't have all his faculties, but I'm sure he didn't go out to lunch dressed... well, undressed like that, did he?"

Braintree spluttered a defence. "W... well, he did have to use the toilet... you know, and he was in such an awful rush when he realised how late he was."

Thorn stared at her doubtfully. "I see, and I suppose that's how he managed to spill carrots down the *inside* of his shirt as well, is it?"

"Well... yes," said Braintree, realising how ridiculous her response would sound to any right-thinking person. Then again, she was dealing with one of Chief Constable Dint's 'Licemen'.

"Oh, for goodness' sake, Mrs Braintree, what sort of simpleton do you think I am?" exclaimed Thorn, throwing the file down on the table. It made Agnes Braintree jump. On any other occasion, she would have been only too happy to explain how, in her opinion, the average policeman was as dense as a lump of granite and closely related to an amoeba. However, she thought she would save that for another, less stressful day.

Thorn sat looking at her for a moment and then decided to take a different tack. "Let's discuss what your husband had to say about all of this, shall we?" he said, picking the file up again. He couldn't resist a little smile at this point.

"Do we *have* to do this again?" pleaded Agnes. She felt she had gone over things so many times that everyone in the station knew it by heart. Even Constable Hewbrey's wolf could have recited most of it without reference to a script.

Thorn disagreed and said, "Oh yes, how silly of me. We can't read what Mr Braintree has to say, can we? Because we don't know where he is, do we?"

Agnes Braintree leant back in her chair and looked up at the light bulb hanging from the ceiling. She noticed that it wasn't very bright. *A bit like this 'liceman'*, she thought.

"Look," she said, "I don't know where he is or what he's done with my daughter either. How many times do I have to say it? If you were of any use, you'd be out there trying to find them."

"Oh, but we are, Mrs Braintree," said Thorn. "I can assure you that we're looking very carefully indeed. As we sit here, I've got divers searching the bottom of the river Dinc."

"I didn't murder them, you fool!" snapped Agnes, immediately regretting the tone of her outburst.

"Ah, so you admit they're dead!" said Thorn delighted at this breakthrough. "Which particular pond are *they* floating in, or did you dump their bodies at sea?"

Agnes had reached the end of her uncomfortable tether, and her natural tendency to be aggressive and bullying was rising to the surface. "I didn't say that, you stupid man, and I'm getting more than a little fed up with your bloody silly games as well." It was her turn to bang the table and she was better at it than Thorn. "I want to see the Chief Constable NOW!" It was time to start pulling strings. It usually worked for her, although, on this occasion, she might have been better off clutching at straws.

Thorn hesitated. He didn't want the Chief involved, at least not until he extracted a signed confession from her. Things had gone badly for him when the Chief got involved with the Clifton case, and he was quite anxious to avoid repeating the experience.

As luck would have it, a knock on the door saved him from arguing with Agnes over her rights. It was WPC Felony, and Thorn was very grateful when she motioned for him to step outside.

Once in the corridor, Felony thrust a pile of paper into Thorn's unwilling grasp. "It's the coroner's report, sarge," she said. "It says he died of natural causes... a heart attack, although there is something in there about lacerations to the genitals. Definitely died of a heart attack, though."

"Blast it!" exclaimed Thorn, inadvertently echoing Plunge-Pithering's last words. "Just when she was about to crack, too," he said while trying to read the small print on the report.

"Well... quite," said Felony, unsure how she was supposed to take that. "The other thing is we have located her husband and daughter."

Thorn's eyes lit up at this news. "Excellent!" he said. "Strangled or poisoned?"

"Er... well... Intercity, actually," replied Felony.

"What, thrown under a passing train?" enquired Thorn, shocked by the grizzly prospect. He'd have to revise his opinion of Braintree after this news. "Who found the bodies?"

"Well... the ticket inspector, I suppose, but..." said a puzzled Felony. "Look... they're still alive, sarge! We found 'em on their way to Scotland... traced the credit card transactions."

Once more, things were going badly for Thorn, and after taking a moment to digest the facts, he had little alternative but to let Mrs Braintree go free. Natural causes didn't include peas on the knees, even he knew that. It was all very suspicious, and instinct told him there was something fishy about this, and it had nothing to do with the carp they found in Pithering's trouser pocket. However, she had rights, so he returned to the interview room and slumped despondently in his chair. It had been another long day, and the chance of proving himself worthy of promotion had slipped through his fingers once again.

Tempted to tell her to 'sod off out of his sight', he remembered his manners and said, "I think that'll be all, Mrs Braintree. We'll be in touch."

"Will you? Will you indeed?" the words vomited from her mouth. "I'll tell you who *you* will be in touch with, my bloody lawyers, *that's* who, and they'll sue the sodding pants off you and your silly little 'lice' force. With that, Mrs Braintree stomped out. There was a lot to be done.

***

On her way home, Agnes decided to stop off at the school. She needed some space to think things through and plan her next move. The school was deserted during the summer holidays - none of those horrid little bodies rushing around shouting, swearing, and fighting in every corner. She was feeling utterly exhausted. Anyone else would have given up the fight. One dead politician and a broken marriage ought to have been enough, but she was made of stronger stuff. Agnes had come so close to succeeding. She wasn't going to let circumstances defeat her that easily.

Her time with DC Thorn was probably the worst of it. She loathed being polite to such an obviously uneducated, dim-witted "waste of oxygen" like him. He should have been on *her* side in the fight and not sat there clumsily trying his best to catch her out. *A complete fool if ever there was,* she thought. *No wonder the country is in such a state if that's the calibre of "LICEMAN" we have these days.* She spat out the word liceman as sourly as she could manage.

On entering her office, she sat at her desk and fished around in a shopping bag. There were two bottles of her favourite wine in it, and she was in desperate need. Soon, she was gulping it down straight from the bottle, and it hit the spot. She began a conversation with herself.

"What a mess, Agnes, what a bloody mess! Why can't people simply do what they're supposed to?" Another gulp.

"Damn Pithering! He was almost at the point of being useful. A waste of time and a waste of good bananas!" she said in a regretful tone. "Not heard a dicky bird from her majesty either. I mean, what is *wrong* with these people, for goodness' sake? They either ignore you or kick the sodding bucket. So bloody inconsiderate!"

At this point, she retrieved a packet of jam doughnuts from the bag and sat quietly eating them. Agnes needed food to soak up the wine, having already consumed almost two-thirds of the first bottle. That was fast going, even for her, and the effect of the alcohol would hit her like a brick wall at some point. When the doughnuts were finished, she started on a large pork pie covered with lashings of strong mustard. The strain of being a head teacher often necessitated an emergency pork pie, and you couldn't eat one of those without enough mustard to make your toes curl.

As she sat alone opening the second bottle, Agnes stared blankly at the walls around her. They were covered with notice boards of all shapes and sizes, each thick with long out-of-date timetables, exam results, and lists of missing books. There were even reminders about reminders, and some papers had been there long enough to fade and gather cobwebs. It dawned on her that none of it meant anything to her now. There was a time when teaching was almost a religious experience for her, something that excited her when she got up in the mornings and kept her awake long into the night, planning enthusiastically for the next day. She thought that everyone would be as keen to learn and understand as she was, and that children would want to know about everything to better themselves. But the truth had been hard to accept. No one was interested. She'd spent all those years of study and preparation for nothing. A pitiful salary, endless futile changes to the curriculum, and a lifetime of what amounted to guerrilla warfare had left her bitter, profoundly disillusioned, and resentful.

"You need to get things back on track, Agnes. Back on track, my girl, but how?"

She spent a moment tapping her finger anxiously on the desk and drinking more wine before appearing to reach a decision. The wine had started to take effect now, and she was developing a pleasant glow. "Right, I'll shend another letter to the papersh, and then we'll sshee if anyone else wants to help. You can't be do… doinging this on your own, Agnes, my luff… luffely, not anymore. You need some troopsh."

She lurched over to the desk Mrs Clifton used and, firing up the computer, started searching the internet for like-minded souls. In no time, Agnes had signed up with every dubious, extremist, and proscribed organisation she could find. Sitting in a satisfied stupor, her words to the Queen weeks before floated back. "What a goo… ood job you found me your majish… majist… majiwotsit and may I say… may I shay, what bloody… bloody good luck it ish that I'm findin me too… hic." Agnes fell asleep.

***

A little green light flashed on a map in a darkened room in Whitehall. It was a secret map, and the room was secret too, as were the officials who staffed it. From now on, they were going to be keeping an eye on that little green light and the person it belonged to.

Cherry Dumples

"PITHERING'S LAST PLUNGE", shouted the front page of the Dillchurch Tribune, while the Bungbury Star led with "FROGMAN CROAKS!"

"Well, well, well," said David while reading the story with Vicki. "Old Plunge-Pithering's finally pegged it then. How will we ever manage without him? I'd like to know what he was doing lurking outside that house. I think there's more to this than meets the eye."

"What about poor Mrs Braintree?" asked Vicki. "Fancy waking up to find a dead body in your fishpond. No one deserves to have an experience like that, do they? I mean, it must have been awful for her."

"What do you mean, poor Mrs Braintree?" asked David. "It's a shame the old bint didn't wake up to find herself in the fishpond next to him. She'd have done us all a favour."

"Don't be so horrible," replied Vicki. "No one has seen anything of Kathy or her husband. She must be worried sick."

"Yes, that's true, I suppose, but it's all very odd," said David.

They were waiting in the village hall for another management meeting to start. It was time to review the progress on arrangements for the fun day and make sure everyone knew what they were doing.

"I guess it will be a bit subdued tonight, although Fawcett won't be too upset," said David. "I bet he'll be dancing around for joy now that there's a by-election coming up."

Vicki agreed. "Pithering wasn't liked by anyone here. He had a real run-in with Function a few years ago when he was prescribed laxatives, and Function got the dose wrong. Pithering was stuck on the loo for a week, and they had to send in food parcels to keep him alive."

"Wouldn't food have made it worse?" asked David.

"They tried some stodgy stuff at first, full of wheat flour and gelatine to block him up a bit, but that only gave him constipation. So, they had to give him more laxatives, leaving nature to take its course. When he finally recovered, he was too stiff to stand up, so they had to put him in traction, and he wasn't impressed with Function after that."

"No, I don't suppose he was," said David, and then, glancing at his watch, he stood up. "Well… I guess there's no avoiding it. We'd better take our places at the table and get it over with. Mrs Clifton coming, is she?"

"No. I think we've seen the last of her for a while," said Vicki.

**

The committee sat patiently around the table, gossiping about the sudden demise of Plunge-Pithering while they waited for Lady Dinc and Colonel Fawcett to arrive. It was the last full meeting before the fun day, and David had checked for hidden cameras, bombs, booby traps, and other unpleasant surprises, such as super glue on the toilet seats. He had good reason to be wise to that one, and it wasn't an experience he could easily forget. Nor, for that matter, was the barbecue charcoal laced with nitromethane. Everybody had sausages on that occasion.

As they exchanged pleasantries and adjusted their papers, the sound of an engine revved to within a few revolutions of disintegration penetrated the building. David hurried to the front door to see what all the commotion was. Pinkle dashed over to join him. "It's coming from over there just beyond the um... you know..." he said, pointing his finger and nodding his head toward Upper Dinctum.

Before too long, they could make out the shape of a pale-coloured chamber pot streaking between the hedgerows bordering the lane. It seemed to be getting faster by the second, leaving a trail of blue smoke behind it.

'It' was Lady Dinc on her almost prehistoric motorbike, and she had undoubtedly exceeded every speed limit in the land by the time she drew level with the hall. She had left it until that precise moment to apply the brakes. Brakes, parachutes, anchors, and even reverse thrust wouldn't have stopped her within half a mile, so it was some time before she strolled into the meeting. Colonel Fawcett slipped in behind her almost undetected. He was a master of turning up late to meetings and somehow appearing to have been there from the very start.

Lady Dinc's belated arrival brought all activity in the hall to a standstill. She was still wearing the chamber pot on her head, and smoke was coming from the soles of her boots.

"What ho!" she shouted. "Have to get those bloody brakes fixed! Not a blind bit of bloody good! Pardon?" She slapped Function on his back to emphasise her point, causing the pills he had just taken to jump clean out of his mouth and bounce across the table.

Once settled in her chair, Dinc became aware of the staring silence that had descended. "What?" she shouted. "Stop gawking, damn it! Get *on* with it!" She put the chamber pot on the floor beside her, placed an opened handbag on her lap, and pulled out a toothpick. Outside, the motorbike fell over and backfired loudly, causing Colonel Fawcett's hearing aid to squeal painfully.

"Bloody bike farts as loud as old Fawcett here, eh?" she laughed. "I see Pithering's buggered off to meet his maker then, Fawcett? Bet you're as happy as a pig in rat's poo now, eh?"

Fawcett shuffled the papers in front of him. "Well... um, sad news... sad news..."

"Nonsense, man! Best thing that could have happened to the old sprat and long overdue if you ask me, eh? Fellow was a waste of rations and an awful bore." She sat back and busied herself with the toothpick, carefully removing the remains of a moth from her teeth. That was the trouble with riding a motorbike along a country lane at close to the speed of sound, wearing only a big grin on your face. However, it didn't seem to bother Lady Dinc. Very little did.

The meeting was much as David had feared. Function popped pills, Lady Dinc fell asleep, Pinkle played noughts and crosses, and the colonel twitched while he gave a speech that no one listened to.

At length, they turned their attention to the fun day, and David was able to bring them up to date on the preparations. "So... it all seems to be coming together very well," he explained. "Gavin, one of our senior members, has booked the fire brigade, which is splendid news, I'm sure you'd all agree?" Colonel Fawcett grunted, Function coughed, Pinkle sniffed, and Lady Dinc snored. *This is a bit like holding a convention in a farmyard*, thought David.

Suddenly, Lady Dinc jerked in her chair, opened her eyes widely, and started to speak. "Yes, I'm glad you asked because I was going to suggest it myself. What?"

Silence.

Lady Dinc often followed a comment with a random 'what' or 'pardon'. A look of bewilderment accompanied the words, her eyes darting around as though the room was full of threatening ghosts.

"Er...suggest what, Lady Dinc?" said Fawcett.

She shut her mouth momentarily and glanced at him obliquely. "Buffoon!"

"I beg your pardon, madam?" said Fawcett. He fiddled with his earpiece again, just in case it had misinformed him.

Lady Dinc leant closer to the colonel. "A buffet," she shouted. "I said a BUFFET, you silly old fool!"

Colonel Fawcett didn't get the 'silly old fool' because the 'BUFFET' bit had overloaded his amplifier, and it seemed to everyone that his earpiece was on fire. Jumping up, he grabbed the jug of water from the centre of the table and poured its contents, including the ever-present goldfish, over the side of his head. The meeting had to be abandoned for half an hour while Vicki plied everyone with coffee and Function tried to administer first aid to the fish. Gavin thought it was the best laugh he'd had in a long time.

When they eventually got going again, Fawcett was still looking pale and couldn't hear very much at all. *Situation normal* thought David when Fawcett asked everyone to speak up a bit.

"I think you were about to make a suggestion, Lady Dinc?" said David politely and was pleased not to have his head bitten off when she continued.

"Quite so," she said calmly. "I was about to say," and then, turning towards Fawcett. "I WAS ABOUT TO SAY that I've been discussing the fun day with cook and have decided to put on a little buffet. You know, a few bits and bobs to soak up the gin, that sort of thing! Eh?"

She bent almost double at this point, buried her face deep inside the handbag on her lap, and rummaged around for something. After a short time, she surfaced again, clutching a wad of papers that she handed to Dr Function. "Take one and pass the rest on, man. Hurry up!" she barked when Function appeared to hesitate.

"Right," continued Lady Dinc. "Cook has drawn up a menu which I've copied for you. FOR YOU, FAWCETT – A MENU! M... E... NU! Read and approve if you please," she said, looking very

176

pleased with herself. She popped an extra strong mint into her mouth and stared at the ceiling. No one could tell where she went on these occasions, but it made her chuckle. She'd been known to pass her time at meetings, pulling faces at people.

Once Function had distributed the papers, everyone read them in silence. Then they read them again just in case the first time had been a trick of the light.

Menu for the Youth Club Fun Day
200 ~ portions of flayed bananas with a mint crundle
200 ~ portions of smashed potatoes and cheese fits
60 ~ bowls of grilled peas and hollow parsings
23 ~ pints of ground lemon sneeps with a dash of fervent twyne
200 ~ custard and raspberry fringes with an iced loader
330 ~ sausage duvets with bread rolls and dingle butters
140 ~ hot fungal fries embellished with frapps and clotchy doos
130 ~ oiled yarbs in a cranberry lick
100 ~ green lentil fondles
26 - pints of homemade cherry dumple

"Yes... er very nice," ventured Vicki, trying to sound as though she meant it. "I'm sure it will be lovely. Thank you."

Lady Dinc's attention returned to the meeting. "That's quite all right, my dear. Mustn't let the little beggars go hungry, must we?"

Everyone agreed without understanding how anything on the menu was fit for human consumption.

David decided it was time to get on with his report. "OK, let me see," he said, fiddling with some notes in front of him. "We'll be kicking off the fun day at ten a.m. with all sorts of sideshows and stalls: roll-a-penny, coconut shies, unicycle races, wellie throwing competitions, that kind of thing. The barbecue will commence at twelve, followed by the tug-o-war competition, and the tractor pulls across the river Dinc. In the afternoon, there will be the firefighting competition, a police dog handling show, and the blindfold hurdles. Then we should be able to present prizes at around three thirty, and we'll finish off with a football match, the youth club versus the village. Oh, ferret racing too," he added before stopping to see what the response would be.

Fawcett nodded in approval, still nursing his ear, but the others were delighted. It was the best programme of events they'd seen for many a year, and they talked amongst themselves for quite some time. It was all very exciting.

Lady Dinc was excited too and offered to do a bit of stunt riding on her bike. "I could ride through hoops of fire and jump the river Dinc," she said, but they managed to persuade her that the generous offer of a magnificent buffet was more than enough.

***

Later that evening, when everyone had finished their third cup of coffee and eaten all the ginger biscuits, David locked the hall and walked with Vicki to the Duck and Dinc. It was a sort of auxiliary committee room, and they had a favourite spot in a quiet corner of the bar where they could chat without interruption.

"What on earth was that menu about?" asked David, baffled by what he had read. "I'm not sure any of it is safe to eat."

"Your guess is as good as mine, but she means well, doesn't she?" said Vicki. "Anyway, her cook always makes good food. She does the catering for the W.I. meetings, and most of them are still alive. I wouldn't worry about it if I were you."

But David couldn't help it. There was just something about clotchy doos which bothered him deeply. "I hope you're right because I wouldn't want to get the blame for poisoning the entire community, that's for sure. Do you think old Dinc is as daft as she makes out?"

"Who knows?" replied Vicki. "If she weren't mad, she'd have to be at least nine parts insane to act that way… if you see what I mean. Anyway, it runs in her family. They've been completely bonkers for generations."

She gazed thoughtfully into the bottom of her glass, which seemed to have developed a leak. David took the hint and went to the bar to get another round. "Pint and a half of Best and two packets of mint crundles, please,"

"You sure you haven't had enough already, Dave?" asked the barman. He sold most of the popular snacks, but mint crundles weren't something he'd had much call for.

"Crisps," said David. "Sorry, Joe, I was miles away. You know how it is."

Joe knew all too well. He'd seen people in all states late on a Saturday evening. It was incredible what a mess ten pints of bitter could make of the human mind.

"I've been thinking," said Vicki when David returned to his seat. "What about getting a brass band?"

"What?" replied David, almost choking on his beer.

"Well, you can't have a village fun day without a proper brass band, can you? I mean, it's all part of the spectacle, isn't it?"

"I hope you're joking," said David, who loathed the things. "What do we need a band for? A brass band is… well, take away all that plumbing, and it would sound like a load of people farting in close harmony, wouldn't it? I mean… who in their right mind… all that spittle too? Yuk!"

"You're such a misery at times, David! Just leave it to me. There's a Salvation Army band in Dillchurch that would love to come and play, and I bet you any money you like that everyone would enjoy it too."

***

As the evening wore on and glasses emptied, the conversation slowed, and tiredness set in. For what seemed like an age, there was silence between them, and Vicki stared intently at David. He was turning a beer mat over in his hands and seemed very far away in his thoughts.

"Are you going to stay with me tonight?" she asked, hardly believing the words coming from her mouth.

David looked up and felt his head spin. He was sure he had gone bright red, but a familiar figure approached before he could think of anything to say.

"Having a nice party, are we? Getting ourselves well and truly anaesthapickled ready for the youth club tomorrow night?" Gavin stood at the table, balancing three pints of beer and a large packet of salted nuts on a tray. He also had a great big grin on his face.

"I hope none of that is for me?" said Vicki staring at the beer, which was just a little out of focus. "I've had far too much already."

"Nonsense, mate," he replied, placing a glass in front of her. "You're still standing... well, sitting... and anyway, I've bought them now."

"Where did you disappear to so quickly after that meeting?" asked David. "I thought you were going to walk down here with us?"

"Ah... I had a little checking up to do, and I think we've got a slight hitch with this fun day thing."

David started to feel a panic attack coming on. "I knew it," he cried. "I said I'd got a bad feeling about this whole thing, didn't I? What's gone wrong now?"

"Don't worry too much," said Gavin, trying to calm things down. "It's the blindfold hurdles race. We can't get any hurdles. Well, not legally, anyway."

"That's never stopped you before, has it?" observed Vicki.

"This is true," said Gavin, "but I can't even find any to nick. However, it don't really matter, do it?"

"Why *doesn't* it matter?" said David, trying to correct Gavin's English.

"Yeah, what's the point of a hurdles race without hurdles?" added Vicki.

"Ah, but that's *exactly* the point, isn't it?" said Gavin. "It's not a hurdles race, is it? It's a *blindfold* hurdles race, so it *doesn't* matter if there's no hurdles, does it?"

"What, you mean... they wouldn't be able to see the hurdles even if we had them?" said Vicki trying hard to understand Gavin's explanation.

"Prexactly!" said Gavin, delighted that someone was keeping up. "We put some marks on the track to show where the hurdles *would* have been, and then, we just shout 'jump' each time someone goes near them. Piece of cake!"

"A sort of virtual reality hurdles?" asked David.

"Yep," said Gavin with a smile.

The conversation stalled as Vicki and David tried to think through the proposal, but thanks to the alcohol, it was becoming increasingly tricky. After three pints of beer and a long, stressful meeting, virtual reality hurdles made sense – sort of. David's mind stumbled through to the other events they had planned, and he wondered what else might be in danger of becoming virtual. "I take it we've got a real rope for the tug of war, have we? I mean, you can't exactly 'make believe' that one, can you?" But even as he spoke, he thought it entirely possible that Gavin might try.

"Don't worry about the rope, mate. I know just where to put me hands on one," said Gavin, obviously confident he could deliver.

Vicki had known Gavin a long time and was two or three light years ahead of David. She looked Gavin squarely in the eyes. "This rope wouldn't happen to have one end attached to the ferry in Dincsmouth harbour, would it?"

Gavin blushed with guilt. "Anyone fancy more peanuts?" he said and wandered off towards the bar.

Vicki looked back at David. She could see what he was thinking and put his thoughts into words. "We've created a monster."

"We have," he replied. "Look, I'd better get going now. It's very late, and I'll be in a lot of trouble if I don't get home in time to eat supper."

Vicki looked up at David. "Listen, I'm sorry I said that earlier. I... I should have known better. I'm sorry."

"Don't be," replied David. Leaning across the table, he kissed her on the cheek. "Smile. I love you too. Loads."

***

As she watched David walk away, her heart thumped loudly in her chest. Did he *really* say that to her? Her head was spinning, and it seemed like she would melt. There had been a powerful attraction between them since they first met, and the feelings growing inside her were hard to ignore. Now, it seemed, he felt the same way too, and that changed everything.

Gavin returned, placing a gin and tonic on the table in front of her. "You looked as though you could do with something a bit stronger. What you going to do then?" he asked.

Vicki was halfway between laughing and crying when she looked at him. "I don't know. I've got a fiancé, and David's married."

"No," said Gavin. "You've got a fiancé *you don't love*, and David's married *to a wife who doesn't want him*. Life's too short to carry on like that, mate."

"I guess I'll have to get on with things and try not to think about it," said Vicki.

"You can't just ignore it. You're in love with one another. It's as obvious as a cow in a wheelbarrow."

Vicki laughed. "So, which bit of a cow or wheelbarrow do I remind you of, or would you like to take another run at that one?"

"Ha ha ha. You know what I mean."

"Yes, I suppose I do."

Choir Practice

The big day came closer, and there was a buzz in the valley as everyone began to get excited, gossiping eagerly about the coming event. Imaginations ran riot, and in no time, rumours of a circus with tigers, flying elephants, and transparent wombats were doing the rounds. Some said they would dig up the playing fields and build a roller-coaster. Others were confident of an air show with stealth bombers and a wing-walking nudist. A few had it that the Pope was coming to breakdance, and the publication of an official programme did nothing to scotch the rumour. People were desperate for a dancing Pope.

As the activity gained momentum, Agnes Braintree spied on them all. She wasn't having as much fun these days. The sudden departure of her pudding partner threw a big sock in her sorbet, and she hadn't been seen very much around the valley. When the bell rang to mark the end of lessons, she scuttled from her office, straight into her car, and then raced the short distance home as quickly as she dared.

Someone was posting packets of Blancmange and pictures of fruit to her. Paranoia had set in. Worried that her phone and computer were bugged, she was forced to adopt new tactics and purchased a ham radio kit powerful enough to send signals all over the solar system.

Every night, hidden in a cupboard under her stairs, she "breaker-breakered" and "CQ-CQ'd" until the early hours. People from the darkest depths of society would rise in revolt, and she would lead them. "No more liberal piffle! No more useless, self-serving politicians! In fact, no more politicians! No more poodles or youth clubs, and none of that skate park rubbish, either! Your time is coming, Agnes," she said to herself. But there remained a nagging doubt at the back of her impatient mind. Those packets and postcards, delivered once or twice a week with the usual collection of bills and junk mail, were worrying. Someone in the village was playing games with her, and she didn't like it at all. So, when she wasn't on her radio organising her troops, Agnes spent her time concealed behind the net curtains waiting to see who was leaving her these little gifts. She waited very patiently, but she waited in vain.

Sadly, Agnes didn't know the worst of it: the people she was talking to on the radio each night were mostly undercover agents from MI5, the CIA, MOSSAD, or the KGB. Worse still, they didn't know the others were covert operatives either. Consequently, each thought they were on to the biggest conspiracy of all time. They were zealously egging each other on in a spiralling web of entrapment that might consume the entire planet if left unchecked. Something horrible was going to happen.

***

While an increasingly obsessed Braintree plotted and brooded in her lair, Gavin lay back on his favourite patch of hillside, watching his handiwork unfold in the valley below. The discovery of Braintree's penchant for fruit and puddings was a bonus and one that he would put to good use when the time was right. However, the top priority now was the pipe for the ferret racing. It had to be recovered from the river and hidden behind the clubhouse on the playing fields. To this end, Jamsie agreed to help while Peter and Joseph created a suitable diversion. Plans were made, watches were synchronised, and chuckles were chuckled. It was time for them to do a spot of cattle rustling.

The following day, Mabel Juthry was on her way to choir practice, trundling along the lanes at no more than twenty miles an hour. Her rusty little Fiat might have been capable of going faster, but she wasn't a confident driver, especially along the country lanes. Besides, it was a lovely afternoon. The sun was shining, the birds were tweeting, and some ponies were playing hopscotch in the meadow. Why rush?

At a mere four foot five, Mabel's height, or the lack of it, hadn't gone unnoticed, especially by Lady Dinc. Never one to be backward at coming forward or any other way, Lady Dinc had once crossed the main road through Dillchurch to reach Mabel, who was doing a spot of window shopping on the opposite side. A large blue sign in the bank's window had caught her eye: 'Bincley's Banks are Better Banks, says Bob the Bincley's Bear'. Standing next to the sign was a giant cartoon bear with red flashing eyes and an off-putting toothy grin. Mabel couldn't decide if it was smiling at her or considering what flavour she might be. Her daydream was interrupted by someone shouting from across the road.

"Excuse me!" It was Lady Dinc, her voice booming over the noise of the traffic. She held her folded umbrella in the air like a sword and charged across the road, causing an oncoming cement mixer to screech to a halt. It was the driver's turn to start shouting now, and what he had to say wasn't for the faint-hearted, but it made no difference. Lady Dinc kept marching onwards. "I say, EXCUSE ME! You there!"

By the time she had reached the other side of the road, six cars had run into the back of the truck and were now permanently fixed to one another.

"Ah, there you are," said Lady Dinc, trying to catch her breath as she approached a wide-eyed Mabel. "I couldn't help noticing how short you were, and I wondered if you might have time to come and look under my ass? I'm too old to bend down that far, but you're already at the right level, aren't you? What?"

Lady Dinc spent some time at the police station after that, trying to explain to the "bloody silly man with the numbers on his shoulders" that she thought Mrs Juthry was just the right height to see under her Donkey, which she feared, might have an infection of some sort.

All of this was a distant memory to Mabel as she motored onwards at a leisurely pace singing 'Hark the Herald Angels' at the top of her voice. Christmas was still months away, but as she always said, practice makes perfect - except it didn't. Even a series of complicated head transplants couldn't have improved the sound made by the Dinc Valley Choir. Only Doris from the bakery had a voice worth hearing. She had once given a sublime rendition of 'In the Bleak Midwinter' only to have it ruined by the organist, who was playing 'The Holly and the Ivy'. They were into the second verse before a well-aimed prayer book sorted things out.

Mabel was getting on a bit but still hoped for a promotion within the choir. She'd been a stalwart member for years, rising from the lowly ranks of Tea Maker, through Choir Master's Baton and all the way to Soprano in Chief. One day, she might reach the highest level of all: Arch General of the Pithel, a position few had ever achieved or thought necessary.

The hierarchy within the Dinc Valley Choir was highly original and entirely the creation of Colonel Fawcett. His idle military mind had invented a rank structure that, as well as being a complete waste of time, was understood by no one. Nevertheless, it was adopted and had endured for many years, becoming something of a tradition, as were the medals he awarded from time to time. Recruits could be a Tea Maker to the Baton or a Boot Boy to the Pedal Stops. After that came Under Frock to the Music Stand, Long Sergeant at Psalms, Chief Tenor at C, Choir Master's Baton, and finally, in the non-commissioned ranks, Quarter Master of the Font. Commissioned ranks included: Second Major Bass, Flute Lieutenant, Soprano in Chief, and, right at the top, Arch General of the Pithel. The Pithel was a dark, smelly, withered-looking thing that Fawcett had liberated from a dead witch doctor. Only he knew what it was or why it was called the Pithel. He probably knew why the witch doctor had died as well, but he never told anyone. In any case, Fawcett had convinced people that it was an extremely significant relic and should be treated with great reverence.

Today, Mabel was in good voice and kept in tune for roughly half the time. She was pleased about that. As she pulled into the church car park, she could see the other choristers making their way slowly through to the nave. They always started with a round of tea and biscuits courtesy of Mrs 'TMB' (Tea Maker to the Baton) Splatterin. Mabel looked forward to the gossip that always accompanied these occasions. The soaps on television were picked over in the same way that vultures might have tackled a dead giraffe. They'd also discuss the baker's daughter and, not to put too finer point on it, the ins and outs of what the butcher's cousin had been doing to her. Then there was the latest news on the strange and very dead Bishop Titlock, who had left his entire estate to a one-armed chicken strangler in Canterbury - if the rumours were true.

The call to arms eventually came from Reverend Pinkle, and they quickly took their places, ready to begin start. The organist had to be woken up partway through the first attempt at 'While Shepherds Washed their Socks', but things went quite well after that. It was during the final verse of 'Good King Thingy' that all hell broke loose, but with her back to the door, Mabel Juthry didn't know anything about it.

It was only a little thing at first, like the whisper of wheat waving softly in a summer breeze, but then it became a very big thing indeed: a herd of cattle closely followed by a massive bull burst in through the old oak doors sending splinters in every direction. The earth shook, candles on the altar blew out, and the organist fell off her stool.

Staring wide-eyed at the horror unfolding before him, Pinkle was sure Armageddon had finally begun. He fully expected a winged beast to fly down from his belfry and pestilence to creep up his vestment. The sight of his beloved church suddenly filling up with livestock was too much for him, and he fainted. Two Boot Boys to the Pedal Stops tried to climb to the top of the organ pipes but slid back down. They landed on the Chief Tenor at C, who was coming up behind them. The CTC had often intimated that he'd like to be coming up behind a boot boy one day, but this wasn't exactly what he had in mind.

Just across the aisle, an Under Frock to the Music Stand had made a mess in a silver chalice, and nearby, poor old Mabel Juthry was about to have a close encounter with an Aberdeen Angus named Cromwell. Cromwell thought Christmas had come early, but not because of Juthry or her colleagues and what they were trying to sing. He had his beady eyes on the twenty Friesian cows huddled together under a painting of a dove with bits of a tree in its beak. The sight of the cows cornered in front of him, with no apparent means of escape, filled Cromwell with sheer delight and a sense of purpose that was plain for all to see. Having regained consciousness, Pinkle saw Cromwell and let out the loudest scream before passing out again. The Twinkin sisters hid under some prayer cushions and did the same. For no good reason, the organist decided to climb back on her stool and play 'I lost my heart to a starship trooper'. It didn't help.

Amidst all this mayhem, somebody found a phone and called the police. No one noticed Peter and Joseph slink away from the scene looking very pleased with themselves indeed.

***

When he arrived at the church, the view that met Constable Bell would return to haunt him for many years. By that stage, most cows had found their way into the graveyard and were eating all the flowers. None of them paid much attention as he picked his way along the path. Entering the church, he spotted Pinkle right away. He was up and about and still screaming. However, Bell couldn't see anyone else. Except for some maniac ringing the bell, they were all too well hidden. The organist must have been alive because the instrument was still blasting out tunes at a frantic pace. It was only a movement in the prayer cushions that led to the discovery of others. Then he noticed that some of the gargoyles adorning the arches overhead were either crying or blowing their noses. It was all very troubling, but his priority was not to become the focus of Cromwell's undivided attention. He quietly slipped back outside the church to call for backup. Cromwell and Pinkle could spend the time getting better acquainted.

"What?" said Thorn. "He's got what in the church?"

Drivel repeated Bell's message. "We'd better get up there quickly before anyone gets hurt."

Thorn had only just come on duty and his first instinct was to get back to his pie and chips. "If you ask me, Drivel, any fool that thinks he can preach to a herd of ruddy cows and baptise an effing bull deserves all that's coming to him." But there was no escaping it. He was going to have to do something. "Right," he said, throwing his chips to one side, "let's get it over with, shall we? Find a farmer - any bloody farmer - and tell him to get his arse down there now. I'm not going to be the one chasing those ruddy things all over the countryside, that's for sure."

Picking up his coat, Thorn took his time walking down to the station car park. He never did anything quickly while on duty, not unless a specific police dog was in hot pursuit.

Back at the church, Bell was in something of a dilemma. The cows seemed quite happy where they were, but Cromwell was still at large and, judging by the shouting, about to send Pinkle to meet his maker. He had to get the creature to a safe place - but where? Sneaking inside the church, he spotted a doorway leading off to one side and remembered that it led down to the crypt. "That will do nicely," he said and dashed across the narrow gap, hoping not to be seen, but by the time he'd reached the doorway and forced it open, Cromwell was on to him. Suddenly, Bell started to feel a little like Pinkle must have done only moments earlier. Fortunately, he had better self-control and managed to hold things together just long enough to get down the spiral stairs and into the darkness. It wasn't an easy path to tread at speed, but the sound of thundering hooves and snorting breath behind him provided all the motivation necessary. Reaching the bottom of the stairs, he doubled back and hid in a small space under the last few steps. Cromwell raced past into the gloom, giving Bell just enough time to dash back unnoticed. He shut the door behind him, trapping Cromwell under the building.

***

"I see the honeysuckle is out now," said Thorn as he travelled along the lanes. The last time he came this way, he was driving, and Mrs Clifton was in the passenger seat, blubbing uncontrollably. It wasn't one of his favourite moments, nor was the predictable audience he had had with the Chief Constable very soon thereafter. Today, Drivel was at the wheel, and Thorn had time to admire the view. It took his mind off Clifton, the Chief, and a load of bible-bashing cows. For his part, Drivel couldn't have cared less about the hedgerow, or the cartwheeling sheep Thorn had claimed to have seen a few miles back. He was enjoying time out of the office and being allowed to drive the 'company car' – a privilege generally reserved for Thorn and no other.

Soon, they arrived at the church and were just in time to see Eddie Graves, Cromwell's proud owner, arrive on his tractor with a large trailer in tow. It was a sight that made Thorn feel a lot less anxious, and they followed him towards the church, where they found Pinkle and Bell. Pinkle was still in shock and looked very ill, so Bell took a few moments to brief them on the situation.

"Well, you're a bloody twit then," said Graves when Bell told him where Cromwell was. "If you think I'm going down there to get him, you're very much mistaken." And with that, Graves walked over to

194

the only upright pew, sat down, and fiddled with his pipe, trying to get it alight.

Thorn took a deep breath and counted to ten before walking over to the farmer. "So, Mr Graves," he said as politely as possible. "Perhaps you can suggest how we might get him out of there? You being the expert and everything."

Graves continued puffing on his pipe and took his time answering. "Well...(puff) what you need to do...(puff) is...(puff) entice the bugger out...(puff) don't you?" he offered, stopping to tamp down his tobacco.

Thorn was now highly irritated. "Yes, that *is* stating the bleeding obvious, isn't it, Mr Graves?" He looked around for support from the others, but there wasn't any, so he tried again. "How... Mr Graves?" he asked. "How do we entice 'the bugger' out... pray tell?"

Graves was still giving most of his attention to the pipe. It never stayed alight for long, but that was all part of the ritual, and each bowl of tobacco was a voyage of inexpressible delight. It had to be arranged according to years of experiment, then lit and puff, puff, puffed in just the right way if it was going to stay alight for more than a few seconds. Eventually, when everything was to his satisfaction, Graves' distracted mind stumbled back to the matter in hand, and he suggested they use one of the cushions the cows had soiled. "They're all on heat, so the minute he gets a whiff, he'll be up them stairs like greased weasel shit," said Graves with a barely concealed chuckle. Then he returned his attention to the pipe, disappearing behind his portable smoke screen.

The three police officers stood staring at one another for a moment, wondering what to do next and who would do it. Thorn considered volunteering one of the other two for 'special duties' but realised it wouldn't look good. He had to lead from the front if he was going to rebuild his tarnished reputation.

"Oh, for crying out loud, I suppose it's going to be me, isn't it?" he said and cast around for a cushion that was damper and smellier than usual. "I only hope this works." Then he trailed off to the crypt. "This is a bloody silly idea," he said to himself when he reached the top of the sandstone staircase. It spiralled down into darkness, and the silence below was troubling. Unless the animal had found another way out, the thing was down there in the gloom, preparing an ambush. He would have much preferred a clue as to its whereabouts.

Odd things come to mind in stressful situations, and Thorn was reminded of the time he and several other officers chased Stanley Sattupon around Dillchurch one cold November night. Sattupon had broken into a Jeweller and then legged it onto the rooftops when the alarm sounded. He spent the night jumping from one building to the next, shouting, "come and get me, you bastards" and "you can't catch me, arseholes" at the officers below. Thorn wondered if yelling down the staircase might prompt Cromwell to reveal himself. Then again, the idea of shouting "come and get me, you bastard" at tons of living, breathing steak seemed like a daft idea, even to Thorn. He decided against it and started to creep down the steps as quietly as possible.

From his vantage point next to the font, Drivel wondered if they would ever see Thorn again. If he went missing in action, the paperwork would be catastrophic. On the other hand, the benefits were hard to ignore: promotion, his own office, and a well-stocked canteen too. He might even get rid of the archaic and aggressive typewriter, which cheered him up quite a lot.

***

Two hours later, David and Vicky were pottering around the village hall when the unmistakable silhouette of Constable Bell appeared in the doorway.

"Ello, ello, ello. It looks like I timed it right for a cuppa, didn't I?" He seemed unusually cheerful and wasted no time making himself comfortable on one of the less sticky chairs.

"What was all that fuss at the church then?" asked Vicki, beating David to it by only a few syllables. They'd both heard the bells and the sirens too.

Constable Bell told them about the cattle in the church and, with a certain satisfaction, how Cromwell had refused to come out of the crypt until Thorn had inched his way right to the very bottom of the steps. "Nothing was moving down there, and he shouted up, saying as he thought the bull had found another way out." Bell paused to sip his tea. "Well, he were just about to come back up again when there were this almighty bellowing and a clatterin' of 'ooves. Thorn come out of there like a cork from a bottle."

"Oh dear," said Vicki in disbelief. "Was he all right?"

"Well, he climbed right up one of them stone pillars and jumped onto a chandelier. He were all right then," said Bell with a chuckle. "Just like Spiderman, it was. Had to leave him up there for an hour while they took the bull away."

Bell helped himself to a biscuit. "They've taken him down to the hospital for a check-up now, but he were lucky. It could have been much worse."

"I can't think how," said David. "It must have scared the living daylights out of him."

Bell was shaking his head. "Well, he could have been impaled on one of those 'orns. Very nasty business that, very nasty indeed."

"Oh my God!" said Vicki. "I didn't think about that. He's so lucky."

"He is," said David with a frown. "I mean, of all the things you might want up your backside, the front end of a bull certainly isn't one of them."

Constable Bell gave David a long look, and Vicki stared at her trainers, suppressing a grin.

As soon as Bell was gone, she thumped David on the arm. "Of all the things you might want up your backside. I mean, what sort of a daft thing is that to say to a policeman?"

"Well, I'm sorry," he blushed. "It just came out... you know?"

"No, I blooming well don't!" exclaimed Vicki. "I mean, what sort of things would *you* prefer to have up your backside if it isn't a delicate question?"

David was spluttering nonsense, so she left him to it.

***

Sat by the font in his broken church, Pinkle was feeling very miserable indeed. He'd only ever wanted a quiet life, and St Johns in Dinctum seemed to fit the bill perfectly. It was a grand old building that must have seen sizeable congregations in its time, but it was ruined now, and he wondered if it would ever be used again. People didn't go to church these days, not his anyway, and especially not now. He knew his sermons were boring because people fell asleep and dropped off the pews. The sound of their heads hitting the stone floor reminded him of coconuts falling out of trees. Some stayed awake by finding an exposed nail to sit on, while others hit themselves vigorously on the nose with a prayer book. There wasn't much support from the church elders either. Lady Dinc thought he "piffled around like a fart in a trance", and Fawcett thought he was "about as outstanding as a cloud in a fog bank".

On top of that, the church was in a deplorable state, and not just because of the rampaging ruminants. There wasn't the money to pay for its upkeep. Thanks to Constable Bell and his predecessors, the church roof had retained most of its lead, but neither he nor the prayers of the entire valley could stop the rot elsewhere. The joists were home to a thousand creeping things, each with at least six legs. If you listened carefully, you could hear the place being eaten. Stand still by the altar for more than two minutes, and you'd probably disappear under a pile of beetle poo. Most of the prayer cushions had passed through a moth of one sort or another, and the mice had started to chew the bells. It was like walking into a vast stomach -

you were surrounded by digestion. There was even a frog in the font, and the more he thought about it, the more Pinkle realised how lucky he was that anyone came at all. It had almost reached the point where the only bodies he could count on were those already interred in the graveyard.

With its well-cut grass, yew trees, and rows of weathered headstones, the graveyard recorded the passage of time and life in the valley going back as far as 1640. Dincs, Blartyfers, Fawcetts, Tadpillits, and Klattershins were resting deep below the earth in that peaceful corner of the vale. There too, were the graves of the Donk-Dinkles, the Dinc-Donkles, and the Dinc-Donk-Dinkle-Donks, each of the latter having a larger number of fingers and toes than was usual. Lord Dinc of Dinc Vale, 1642 to 1687, was buried there after drowning in the river, attempting to prove he could breathe through his ankles. Resting nearby was Professor Olaf von Dinc, 1777 to 1843. Considered a great philosopher and theorist in his day, the inscription on his headstone reads:

Here lies Olaf von Dinc.
1777 to 1843.
Mine is the twinkly, the splot, and the craddle,
Be not sorrowful nor burgled for me,
for I am at play with the cornflobber
and the dillytwitcher, both.
Amen.

Olaf was as much of a puzzle in death as he was in life. A few paces away lay Johann Sebastian Dinc, organist and principal architect to Chief Mbinga Bosoto-Mappato, who ruled a backwater of the Congo during the late nineteenth century. Johann didn't play the organ very much in the jungle but could always be relied upon to design a good mud hut. So far as anyone knows, he wrote the first and only concerto grosso for Alto Kalimba.

Colonel Fawcett's forbears were also present, lined up on parade even in death. The male members of the family had been in military service of one kind or another for centuries, although only one had risen to the rank of brigadier. That honour rested with Sir Charles Fawcett-Bottom, 1865 to 1919, the only Fawcett to be knighted. During the First World War, he proposed using giant propellers mounted on top of the trenches to blow away any gas the Hun directed toward allied lines. In practice, the propellers were of such a size that, where they blew gas, they also blew maps, bicycles, chickens, and copies of The Times. They were not, therefore, very popular. Seeing his mistake, Sir Charles suggested the propellers could be reversed to suck the same items back again, including secret Hun plans and documents. The idea was politely declined, and a veil of secrecy was cast over the entire debacle. Not to be put off, he founded the Dorkshire Battalion of Balloonists. You might be forgiven for thinking this had something to do with surveillance: soldiers hoisted aloft in balloons to spy on the enemy, but this is a Fawcett-Bottom and nothing so simple would have entered his eccentric mind. His idea was to attach small, khaki-coloured balloons to the soldiers' backpacks during route marches, thereby lightening their loads. It worked quite well, to begin with, but as the days went by and rations were consumed, the packs grew lighter until, one damp April morning in 1917, just after breakfast and a trip to the latrine, the entire regiment simply floated away. Fawcett-Bottom was quietly retired on medical grounds.

He returned to the Dinc valley and purchased a desirable and grand-looking property that belonged to the Dinc family. The sale was conditional on him marrying Lady Agatha Dinc (the current Lady Dinc's great aunt). Unfortunately, despite being fabulously wealthy, Agatha Dinc resembled the back end of a baboon, liked to ride camels, and sported an impressive moustache. Selling her with the house was the only way to marry her off, so this is how the Fawcetts and the Dincs became somewhat unenthusiastically related. Agatha Dinc's liking for camels eventually led to the brigadier's death in 1919. Even in those times, Camels were seldom seen as far afield as the southwest of England, so she resorted to stuffing two pillows up the back of his jumper and riding him around the lawn on summer evenings. He endured this for a brief period, as it seemed to entertain Agatha and keep her mind off carnal matters. However, in the last few weeks of his life, she took to swinging a vicious-looking scimitar around her head, shouting something about infidels. One fateful day in July, when the skylarks were at their loudest, and the sun shone directly overhead, she rode him frantically back and forth across the lawn, hacking wildly at the roses and fuchsias. They seemed to be fighting back with remarkable courage, so she fought with equal valour, but in the end, her aim was poor, and her mount less than able. The upshot was that she cut off his head and disembowelled herself in one awkward movement just past the hollyhocks.

A wake took place at Dinctum Manor, where everyone *except* the Fawcett's, who didn't get an invite, got plastered, rendered, and then completely artexed. Fawcett-Bottom was buried without ceremony, and Lady Agatha was parcelled off to Cairo for mummification as was her wish. The memory of that unhappy union lives on in the name of the house they occupied: Dinc-Bottom.

None of this mattered much to Pinkle. He had begun to think he wasn't cut out for the job, and he certainly hadn't anticipated playing tag with fifteen hundred pounds of solid muscle. It was time for a change.

***

Later that same evening, while Pinkle straightened what was left of the pews and tried to make sense of his life, Gavin, Joseph, Peter, and company were sat by a goalpost at the far end of the playing fields, looking very pleased with themselves. The diversion had worked better than expected, and the pipe for the ferret racing was now safely hidden behind the clubhouse, ready for the big day. Peter thought it was the best laugh he'd had for ages, especially the bit where Pinkle's screams could be heard echoing around the hills. "Sounded like his arse was on fire," he said, grinning broadly.

"Yeah... talking of which," added Joseph. "Is this firefighting competition still on? Not been cancelled, has it?"

"Yes, it's definitely still on, mate," replied Gavin. "Don't worry."

"Good. Do you reckon it will be a big fire? You know - like the size of a building or something? I really wanna see something burn."

"Yeah," said Gavin with a smile. "It'll be a big fire, Joseph. I've made certain of that."

The Fun Day Dawns

Jamsie hadn't slept a wink. He'd been allowed to try a cup of coffee the previous evening, and the caffeine coursing through his small frame made him feel as though he could walk on ceilings - quickly. The other reason for his insomnia was the date: the great day was here. It was time for the Dinctum Village Youth Club Fun Day.

As he lay there in the darkness, with only a small bedside light to illuminate the dim corners of his tiny bedroom, he thought about all the games and competitions they would soon be playing. He thought about the secret plans Gavin had dreamt up to keep everyone on their toes, and perhaps best of all, he thought about the race between the Dillchurch and Bungberry fire crews. He was looking forward to that. Gavin had said it would be a blast.

The grey dawn light seeped through his bedroom curtains, and the rain beat loudly against the window. Snuggled up under his duvet, the sound made him feel cosy, and he could have stayed there until late morning, but he had important things to do. So, jumping up out of bed, he looked for something dark and discreet to wear.

He was due to help set up tents and stalls at the playing fields later in the morning, but there was a critical mission to perform before that. An early start was just the ticket.

***

David hadn't slept much either. He'd taken the previous day off work and spent time resting in his car before driving home. After an awkward evening with Sally, who sat in stony silence throughout a boring film, they went to bed and sat up reading. David felt very unsettled about the day ahead and was sure something terrible would happen. Call it intuition or eternal pessimism, but his stomach was knotted, and his back was itching - a sure sign. Luckily, someone had given him a book on fly fishing. He had no interest in the subject whatsoever and had shown his ignorance by asking why anyone would want to fish for flies in the first place. It seemed to him that a swat was a much more efficient way of dealing with things. Even so, he had made it through the first three chapters before his mind drifted back to the fun day and the troubling subject of Dr Function and his rockets.

Years earlier, Dr Function had spent his spare time studying the delicate science of rocketry. It fascinated him, and he built countless scale models in his shed. There were several trial flights too, most of which were reasonably successful. Sadly, one suffered a malfunction and found its way into the rear of a passing horse. By the time they came to rest, the animal and rider were too far from Dorkshire to say with any certainty who was to blame. 'HORSE TORPEDOED' read the headlines in one newspaper, and somewhat predictably, another led with 'BLAZING SADDLES'. It had taken some effort to convince one old lady that she hadn't seen a real live dragon gallop past. She began to doubt her eyes when it was explained that fire was supposed to come out of the other end, but she wasn't convinced. To her certain knowledge, no one else had seen a living dragon, so how could anyone be sure that they weren't fire farting rather than fire breathing? Given what is known about the digestive process, the former was much more likely than the latter.

A few of the rockets he'd launched were set to a deliberately flat trajectory, mainly when he had spotted a passing pheasant. He was very partial to roast pheasant when he could get it, but most of the birds had gone beyond well done by the time they hit the ground. He'd even succeeded in launching a manned rocket. 'Hamstered' would have been a better description because it was one of those fluffy little things, equipped with a crash helmet made from a ping-pong ball, that found itself streaking towards the starry skies one bleak December evening. Despite the setbacks, Dr Function continued with his work, and his enduring ambition was to fly into space before he died. It was highly likely that these two events would coincide.

Earlier the previous day, Function had called to ask David if he might be allowed to display his latest creation at the fun day. He said it was his most elaborate and powerful launch vehicle yet and thought it would be fun to have a competition. "People could try guessing the height or the weight of the thing," he suggested, "or both."

It seemed like an excellent idea at the time of the call, but as David lay in his bed staring at another page full of fish, it suddenly struck him that this rocket might be much bigger than he had first imagined. After all, you only guessed the height of things you couldn't easily measure. True, you couldn't easily measure the size of something very small, either. Sally kept reminding him of this on the few occasions he wanted to have sex with her. No, it had to be very large, and it was a vision that bothered him greatly. It kept him awake long enough to struggle through a less-than-enthralling chapter on selecting the optimum waders.

After another sleepless hour, he decided food was the only option, so he slipped like a slithery thing out of bed and slunk off to the kitchen as quietly as he could. A quick scan of the cupboards led him to the Wheatasnax, which, according to the packet, had zero fat, zero sugar, and no added preservatives or flavourings. *Surprised you can see them*, thought David, as he poured out the milk and, since no one was watching, heaped two teaspoons of sugar into the bowl. According to the clock in the kitchen, it was four o'clock on a Saturday morning. The morning of the youth club fun day - the very day when a good night's sleep would have been almost mandatory. *Typical*, he thought, and having eaten as much as he could, he took the half-empty bowl upstairs with him and hid it by the side of the bed. Sally didn't like him having midnight snacks, so it was as well to conceal the evidence. Then, changing the alarm to wake him at half past eight, he lay down and was fast asleep in seconds.

*****

While David adjusted his alarm, Jamsie walked swiftly down through the village, trying to keep the rain off his hair with a hood that wouldn't stay up. He was feeling very satisfied because, on the way past Agnes Braintree's bungalow, he'd stopped off to carry out a little task designed to get her day off to an excellent start. Then it was Mrs Fawcett's turn. Thanks to Peter, Joseph, and Susan, he was now in possession of a key to the cellar at Dinc-Bottom. It was time to visit revenge upon his would-be assassin. He didn't have a plan, but something was bound to come to him if he could get inside that cellar.

Approaching the garden wall near where he'd been a target weeks before, the memories came flooding back. He was terrified and felt sure that he'd be shot good and proper this time, but he needn't have worried. Both Fawcetts were still snoring contentedly in their separate bedrooms. The snoring was partly to blame for this physical separation, and Colonel Fawcett had evolved it into an art form. Having tried all sorts of inhumane and probably illegal methods of shutting him up, Mrs Fawcett had moved him lock, stock, and bedpan down the corridor to where he was out of earshot. Luckily for him, the twisting corridors also put him out of gunshot because even Mrs Fawcett couldn't shoot around corners.

Jamsie crept across the garden to where overgrown steps led down to a rotten cellar door. He pulled the key from around his neck and pushed it into the lock, and there was a faint, crunching noise suggestive of either rust or something with large eyes and many legs. He felt highly apprehensive, and part of him hoped that the door would be jammed shut, but it wasn't, and it took enormous courage to take the next few steps. *Where's the vodka when you need it*, he wondered. Once inside, he could make out two people snoring in the rooms above. It was definitely two people because one person alone would have died trying to keep up that sort of racket for more than a minute. He decided it was safe to turn on a light and reached behind him towards where he thought a switch should be. A tapestry of intricate, dusty cobwebs adhered to his fingers, and he felt sure he heard the patter of tiny feet marching across the wall. The creepy crawlies in that place had boots on. When he eventually found the switch, he pushed the lever, and the sound of it clicking into place seemed to echo around the cellar like a gunshot. Jamsie felt sure it would have woken even the dead, but there was no change to the steady drone reverberating from above. He pressed onwards.

The cellar was stacked full of junk. There were old bedsteads, rusted through or rotten with woodworm, bits of mouldy carpet and underlay, and a pile of old newspapers that provided a home to a colony of mice. There were plates, paintings, bicycles, and even a dusty cello. At the far end, he could see an old wardrobe leaning at a peculiar angle. There was something odd about it, and the closer he got, the more it began to look like a coffin.

"It is a bloody coffin!" he said loudly, forgetting himself for a minute. He froze to the spot, waiting to see if his outburst had disturbed anyone in the rooms above. It hadn't, and just as he tried to work up the courage to look inside the thing, he became aware of a pungent odour emanating from the gloom to his right. Following his nose, he found a large black pipe coming down through the ceiling. It had barely entered the cellar before it turned through a right angle and left through a wall towards what must have been the front of the house. It had an access plate that appeared to be leaking something.

"Shit," said Jamsie, simultaneously expressing his disgust and correctly identifying the 'something' oozing from the pipe. "That's the drain from all the toilets," he said softly, and a plan crept slowly into his vengeful mind.

He went to work, searching through all the junk for something he could use to remove the plate. After all, a cellar full of sewerage was the least he could do for the loony woman. In no time, he came across an old spade and, with the utmost care, used it to prize off the plate. The rusted bolts that held it in place snapped easily and fell away without much noise. *That will do just nicely*, he thought as he put the spade down and, with his work completed, he decided to leave before his luck ran out.

On his way back up the steps from the cellar, he passed a sizeable green oil tank that fed Fawcett's central heating boiler. A thin copper pipe at the bottom of the tank coiled through a rose bush before disappearing into the wall. "It'd be a shame if that pipe came undone, wouldn't it?" he asked himself. "Yes, it would, mate," he answered, investigating how easy it would be to interrupt Fawcett's oil supply. Surprisingly easy, as it turned out, and soon, he was slipping quietly across the lawn and back over the garden wall to safety.

In the ordinary course of events, the oil would have drained away into the ground, and the cellar would have taken years to fill with effluent, but fate had decided otherwise. The oil flowed into a drain connected to a pipe, and the pipe was connected to another pipe, which led to a missing access plate in Fawcett's cellar. If that wasn't bad enough, there was a hitherto unnoticed blockage in the main sewer running out of Dinctum. Tons of effluent filled the countless miles of ancient sewers running around the valley. The only alternative route was an old Victorian duct connected to a pipe, and the pipe was connected to another pipe, which led to a missing access plate in Fawcett's cellar. It wasn't a good scenario, not for the Fawcetts anyway. Now that the plate was gone and an airlock no longer existed, the backed-up discharge began to flow, slowly at first but with increasing speed until a torrent of the foul-smelling ooze poured forth.

***

David woke up still tired and got off to a memorable start by stepping out of bed and straight into the half-finished bowl of very soggy Wheatasnax, and it squelched up between his toes. "Sod it!" he said.

Just then, the alarm clock seemed to explode into life, so he sent it hurtling across the room, where it bounced off the wall by a painting of a man with a bandage on his ear. He didn't like the picture and vaguely hoped his aim would improve one day.

"What's wrong?" said Sally, still partially asleep. It felt as though she was waking up on a firing range.

David didn't answer and wandered over to the bedroom window, still trying to shake out the cereal from between his toes. It sounded like it was raining, but he hoped it wasn't. The weatherman on the television had said it would rain all day, but he was about as dependable as a wet toilet roll. David drew back the curtains and looked at the sky. It was heavily overcast, and all the clouds seemed closer to the ground than they should have been. Worse still, it was raining cats, dogs, and probably hamsters too. David took one look and decided that he could paddle a dinghy up to cloud base without much difficulty, but he didn't get long to think about it because the sound of a shrill scream and a dog barking suddenly grabbed his attention. He looked down at the road, six feet outside his front door, to see Mrs Tadpillet and her vicious little poodle staring back at him - or at least the part of him which was now indecently exposed.

"Oh, bollocks!" said David, correctly reading Mrs Tadpillet's horrified mind. He jumped backwards, only to land in the cereal bowl again. "That's all I bloody well need! Mrs 'all men are rapists and perverts' Tadpillet on my case at this time of day."

Sally had come round a bit by now. "What's wrong? Who's that screaming outside?" she asked.

"It's that effing Tad-thingy woman and her rat," he said. "In this weather? You'd think she'd have something better to do, wouldn't you? And what about that miserable little dog of hers? The bloody thing will drown without a snorkel!"

Sally tried again. "Yes, but why was she screaming, David?"

David had dropped out of view below the windowsill and was busy trying to get the curtains closed. "Oh, nothing really," he said, attempting to conceal his embarrassment. "I think she might have seen a bit more of me than is healthy for someone of her age."

"I'm surprised she could see anything at all without a telescope," said Sally, unable to resist the opportunity.

"Ha-bloody-ha," said David.

He managed to get one leg into his favourite dark green underpants but completely failed when it came to the second, and he fell sideways into a wardrobe that promptly collapsed around him. A stream of foul language followed.

"Stop swearing," said Sally, watching his pathetic performance with some frustration. She could put up with bad language, but he was overdoing it a bit this time. "You're beginning to sound like one of those foul-mouthed little yobs at your youth club lately."

David struggled out of the debris and brushed himself down. He was getting red in the face and was still complaining about Tadpillet. "I mean, what was she doing looking up into people's bedrooms anyway?" he asked. "Loitering with intent to lurk, that's what! The silly OLD FART!" he shouted, hoping that Tadpillet was still within earshot.

"It's your fault," said Sally. "You can't just stand butt naked in the bedroom window and expect it to go unnoticed. Someone's bound to be looking, and you know what they're like around here. You should be more careful."

But David wasn't interested in a lecture from her. "Now hang on a minute, madam," he said, pointing at her with a sock he was holding. "I remember a certain young lady flashing herself to a well-built young man in a diving suit on the beach last year." David never lost the opportunity of bringing up the matter when it suited him.

"Oh, here we go again," said Sally, rolling her eyes. She swung her legs out from under the duvet to get up and avoided treading on the half-empty carton of rice pudding by her side of the bed. It had been lying around for a few days amongst her magazines. Undocumented life forms inhabited that carton, but disappointingly for David, not Sally's feet.

"As I told you at the time, I was trying to get dry, and my towel fell off, that's all. Now, can we just leave it, please!"

"Of course, my dear," said David as Sally walked through to the toilet. He knew she could still hear him and couldn't resist trying to have the last word. "Most people manage to pick up the towel and cover up quickly. You paraded around stark naked for ages. Poor bloke nearly passed out. It's a good job he had a supply of oxygen strapped to his back."

"You're just so disgusting at times. You really are. My mother said I married beneath me, and I'm beginning to think she was right!" Sally was annoyed that David had brought up the diver incident again. She'd had her eyes (and more) on many young men since they'd been married and hated the thought of David finding out. The incident with the diver (his name was George, and she'd managed to get his phone number) was the closest David had come to stumbling across this other life of hers. She didn't like it and decided it was time for a bit of deflection. "I suppose it's my turn to make the coffee and toast again?" she asked.

"Changing the subject, are we, dear?" said David as he went to the bathroom to clean his teeth and toes. It hadn't been a great start to his day.

***

Vicki lay in her soft, warm bed. She had been listening to the rain on the window but wasn't fazed by it because she was a cup-half-full person, whereas David was more of a 'what-bloody-cup' type. David was never far from her thoughts first thing in the morning, and she was looking forward to seeing him. Sometimes she wanted to phone him but worried about calling him at home because of Sally. However, the rain gave her a good excuse. So, turning to the small bedside table, she picked up her phone, tapped on the screen, and waited for a reply. Sally answered the call.

"Hi Sally, it's me, Vicki," she said. "Sorry to phone so early. Is David still there?"

Sally said he was and called up to him, "David! Telephone!"

When he appeared, she handed him the receiver. "It's your lover, dear," she said, notching up another small victory.

At the other end of the phone, Vicki flushed bright red. "Sorry, David, did I say something I shouldn't have done?" she asked.

"No, don't be silly. She was only trying to wind me up," he replied. "You ready for battle today?"

"Well, that's what I was phoning for, really," said Vicki. "Do you still want to go ahead with things? The rain's heavy here, and it doesn't look like it will let up for a while." She was looking out of her bedroom window at the trees outside. There wasn't too much wind, which was good, but the leaves were heavy with the weight of the water. The sound of the rain outside was lovely and, like David, she was very fond of this kind of weather, especially when you found shelter in a thick wood or a garden shed.

"No. Let's go for it," said David. "They'd all be so disappointed if we called it off now. Anyway, it's only a bit of water."

Setting Up

By the time David had driven to the valley and collected Vicki, the weather had worsened, and the playing field was saturated. Underfoot, the ground squelched in a way that reminded him all too clearly of his encounter with the Wheatasnax earlier that morning. There were puddles everywhere and the river looked alarmingly swollen. Beyond the goalposts and beside a pile of broken bricks, the clubhouse looked in a very sorry state. A wooden affair balanced on a series of short stone columns, it was covered in a slimy green substance that could have been paint but was probably algae. The clubhouse competed with the river for the title of dampest thing in the valley. The committee responsible for its upkeep were builders and decorators and they were stubbornly disinclined to practice their craft in their free time. It leaked like a sieve and boasted the finest collection of moulds for miles around.

Dashing in from the rain, they found the clubhouse in a complete mess. It looked like someone had removed the roof and stirred everything up with a giant spoon. There were ladders, bits of scaffolding, broken plasterboard, half-set bags of cement, dirty spades, and coils of pipe piled up at every angle. It was difficult to move without tripping up, so they started by clearing a path. It took some effort, after which David decided to check the comfort facilities. He peered into a dark chasm that was the bowl of a toilet and wished very much he hadn't bothered. It was disgusting, and he almost threw up.

"Good job we got those 'Porta-Potty' things being delivered. I wouldn't even wish that sight on Braintree, and that's saying something," he said, tipping a bottle of bleach into the pan.

Just then, some damp, smiley faces appeared at the window. Mary, Amanda, Michelle, and about six others had all managed to squeeze under a single umbrella and were waving frantically. "We know what you're doing! We know what you're doing," they sang at the top of their voices.

Vicki blushed.

"We'd better get on with things while we can," said David pointing at a pile of roughly stacked tents. "I'm afraid we'll have to start with those."

Tent erecting was relatively easy with modern equipment, but this stuff had been festering in a county store for decades. All of them looked utterly threadbare, stank to high heaven and came without instructions. David hadn't a clue about tents, but a brief spell in the Girl Guides ensured that Vicki was better prepared, and she had one of the larger examples fully assembled in no time. She stood beside it with a beaming smile and took a bow.

David knew when he was outclassed, so he decided he might be better off trying to mark out a track for the blindfold hurdles. Having located a pot of whitewash and a broken brush, he trailed off into the rain. It didn't go well. He might as well have been painting the river. The grass was soaking wet, and so was he. Paint was running down the side of his trousers, and the biscuits in his pocket had turned to a sort of oatmeal soup. He was thoroughly dejected by the time he returned to the clubhouse.

Following Vicki's example, teams of tent erectors set to work, but they failed to produce anything that would stand up on its own. Alan and Phillip assembled some long poles and used them to prod the girls. Then they picked up a dustbin lid each and started jousting. The girls made a canvas cave and climbed inside to escape the rain.

David watched in disbelief. "It amazes me," he said to Vicki. "The taxpayer spends all this money on trampolines, gymnasiums, and outward-bound centres to keep this lot entertained, but they prefer a mouldy old tent. I don't get it."

Having failed to impale one another, Alan and Philip now turned their attention towards the giggling grotto. They thought it would be fun to 'bomb' the thing and, following a short run-up, jumped in the air and landed right in the middle of it with a thump. Against all odds, no one was injured, and the girls quickly emerged brandishing wooden posts and chased the boys around the field.

"It's nice that they all get on so well, isn't it?" said Vicki.

***

By about ten o'clock, things were looking a little better. The rain had eased to a fine drizzle, the tents were up, and much to David's relief, another group of helping hands had arrived. The gas pipe, so carefully hidden until now, was made ready for the ferret races. Even the rope for the tug of war had appeared on time. Unfortunately, there were still no hurdles.

"Everything seems to be coming together nicely," said David as he surveyed the field. "Blindfold hurdles over there, unicycle races just by those bales of hay, wellie throwing in the far corner, ferret racing next to the car boot sale, and next to that the…the… um."

"The fire engines!" prompted Vicki.

"Ah yes, the fire engines… when they get here. The tug of war is across the river. The barbecue goes next to the clubhouse, and the coconut shy will go by the swings. Perfect."

It was quite a good selection, better than they had hoped for, and he hadn't even bothered to count things like the dart throwing and roll-a-penny stalls, the pogo-stick races, or the inevitable crowd who would turn up to sell homemade cakes and jams to one another. However, something was missing.

"Where are the bogs?" he said. "I mean, weren't they delivered yesterday?"

Vicki stared at a vacant spot at the edge of the field. "Yes. Definitely. They were here yesterday morning, and I had to sign for them," she said. "How weird. We'd better find out where they are and quickly too. There's only that smelly old toilet in the clubhouse now for the whole village!"

They looked everywhere but found nothing. The situation was grave, and David's mind slid down the steep slope towards paranoia. "Better keep a close eye on all the food and drink here today," he said.

"Why?"

"Well, it's obvious, isn't it? The only possible reason for nicking all the Porta-Potties is that you're about to feed the entire village laxatives. Keep your eyes peeled, my love."

"What?" exclaimed Vicki. "They wouldn't do that, would they?" But even as she said it, doubt crept into her mind. "The little shits." She didn't often swear, but it seemed entirely appropriate and was also probably quite prophetic. "Someone's going to have to check everything. You know, taste things, taste everything!"

"Listen, matey," said David, "there's no way I'm going to taste anything on sale here today. I mean, there's all that stuff that Lady Dinc is bringing. God alone knows what that will do to my insides, and then there's all that homemade stuff full of dog hairs, out-of-date ingredients, and worse. No chance!"

"Okay," said Vicki. "But we'd better make sure there's plenty of loo roll. If everyone is going to lose control of their bowels, it's the least we can do."

But David's mind had already doubled back on itself. "No! That's *exactly* why we won't get any extra toilet rolls."

"What?"

"It's obvious, isn't it?" he explained. "If we get extra toilet rolls, people will know we knew about the laxatives and take legal action... see?" He beamed hysterically. "And, if we get extra toilet rolls, the perpetrators of the plot will guess that *we've* guessed and take extra care not to get caught - so we won't catch them." But Vicki was lost somewhere around "they'll know we knew."

"Look," she said, trying to calm him down, "right now, there are two damp toilet rolls in that thunderbox, and there's no way that will be enough for the entire village, not after a Friday night at the pub filling up with Guinness and curry. We must get some more. No one will be suspicious. Stop worrying." Then, changing the subject, "Don't forget about the police dog display, will you? And where are we going to put Lady Dinc's buffet?"

"France, if you want an honest answer," replied David, now worried more than ever about the clotchy doos.

"I don't think you are being very kind to old Dinky," said Vicki.

"I think it all sounds flipping dodgy to me," said David. "Don't blame me if we get done for poisoning everyone. Caroline's dad's a health inspector, and if he takes it into his head to wander down today, we'll be in the cherry dumples for the rest of eternity."

"Stop it," said Vicki firmly. "It'll be okay... and tasty too. Now, I'm going to get out of the rain and sort out the clubhouse. Why don't you check that everyone is doing what they should... and when will I get a kiss?"

"Ah, I was just coming to that," said David with a smile.

***

A battered old truck pulled up as everyone busied themselves with their allotted tasks. It was loaded with two rusty wrecks - a Volvo and what could have been a Ford - that had once been

223

someone's pride and joy. They were for the fire competition and had been donated by Trudy and Janet's father, a scruffy individual who owned a scrap yard in Bungbury. Trudy and Janet were doing a certain amount of mutual backslapping because everyone knew their father was as 'tight as a bowling ball in a snake's backside'. They considered themselves lucky to have been given the cars free of charge. Gavin directed the truck to a precise point marked by a small white cross on the playing field. Once there, one of the cars was carefully lowered to the ground using the truck's hydraulic crane. The other was pushed off the side and fell with a crunch a few yards further down the field. Gavin was quite particular about the location of the first vehicle because he knew the little white cross marked the exact location of some cans he'd buried just below the surface. There were almost fifty gallons of petrol under that turf, and the Bungbury crew was in for a big surprise. They didn't know it yet, but their chances of beating the Dillchurch team were drastically diminished.

Following his adventures 'up Dinc-Bottom' earlier that day, Jamsie now wandered onto the playing field and spotted Dr Function staggering across the road with what might have been an oversized wheelbarrow. Covered by a green tarpaulin, it was cumbersome and loaded with something long and pointed. Jamsie couldn't quite make out what it was. "He's either got some sort of missile on that wheelbarrow or one hell of a massive dick," he said, turning to Rupert, who had followed him onto the field.

Dr Function was in a splendid mood, stopping to wave merrily at the row of damp bodies watching him from a safe distance out on the field. He made his way as quickly as he could to David and Vicki. "Here we are! What do you think of this?" he asked, expecting everyone to be as excited as he was.

"Um... what is it?" asked Vicki, hoping it wasn't what it looked like. Sometimes her mind was on the same wavelength as Jamsie.

"Oh, sorry, I should have introduced you," said Function, reaching down to pull back the tarpaulin with a flourish. "Say hello to Matilda!"

Lying before them was a roughly made rocket, around twelve feet long, with a few spanners and a can of oil. "I thought it would be a great climax to the afternoon if we launched it," he said, hoping they would agree. "I'm sure it will finish things off with a bang!"

All eyes were on David, waiting to see if he would agree. He was trying to remember if the club's public liability insurance covered them for ballistic missiles.

"How high will it go?" he asked as the vision of an airliner falling from the sky flashed before him. "I mean, is it safe? Don't you have to get permission or something from the government or NASA... the Queen?"

"Oh, don't worry, old chap," said the doctor reassuringly. "It's only like a giant firework. They seldom go up more than a couple of thousand feet." He was guessing on this last point because his eyesight wasn't what it used to be. He had tried wearing glasses, but the soot from the rocket engine had rendered them useless. "This is the latest and much-improved model, by the way," he said proudly. "It has a parachute for safer landings."

It didn't matter to David whether it had a parachute or an anchor. There was no way he wanted to risk launching it on an unsuspecting Ministry of Defence. "They'd be down here shooting at us faster than you could mate rabbits," he explained to Vicki when they found space to talk privately. She agreed. So, they set about convincing the doctor that it would be best if he positioned it at the far corner of the field for static display purposes only. Function was disappointed but could see sense in their request. After all, it was impressive to see even if he couldn't get it aloft, and he still wanted to make some modifications. Now that the launch date was postponed, he could do them at his leisure, and he looked forward to that.

Next to arrive were the fire crews from Dillchurch and Bungbury, parking neatly in the allotted spaces. The officer in charge spent some time getting the teams to ensure the engines were clean and that windscreen wipers were all pointed in the same direction. Even the hoses had to be wound correctly, and the ladders were buffed so brightly that anyone trying to climb up the things would have quickly slid back down again. "Very pretty, but sod all use," said one observer.

Then, a white transit van tightly packed with uniformed bodies, trumpets, and trombones bounced onto the field. It had Salvation Army stickers everywhere, and having reached their spot next to the clubhouse, they set about erecting a gazebo to keep themselves nice and dry for the coming hours. Sadly, it wasn't big enough for everyone, so, having drawn the shortest straw, Tubby, the tuba player, had to sit outside. Soon, they were tuning up and 'getting their lips in' with a few bars of the national anthem. The noise drifted across the open ground to David's ears, and he winced at the thought of all that saliva and phlegm congealing in the oily valves. A bad experience in his youth while attempting to play the trombone was the cause of his pain and many subsequent nightmares.

The sight of Tubby puffing away outside the gazebo presented Joseph and Gerald with an opportunity that was too good to miss. Within seconds, they crept out from behind the clubhouse with a garden hose and had a spout of water aimed into Tubby's booming instrument. It wasn't long before he started to gurgle and splutter as the tuba filled up. His wife, Henrietta, blasting away on her trumpet, spotted what was going on, and, in a sudden rage, she chased Joseph and Gerald around the clubhouse, kicking wildly at them as she ran. She accomplished all of this without missing a single note.

***

With everything ready, David was about to make another cup of tea when a policeman they hadn't seen before turned up in a white Land Rover, towing a very long and narrow trailer. The officer unhitched it and then drove off again without speaking to anyone. Whatever it was, David thought it all looked rather complicated and decided that the tea was a higher priority.

Gavin was puzzled by this odd-looking contraption too. It looked interesting and worth investigating. So, with nothing better to do, he wandered across with Jamsie to check it out. There was a car seat mounted on a sort of railway that ran the length of the trailer - a distance of at least twelve metres. The principle of operation seemed to be that a 'victim' would be strapped into the seat at one end of the track. Then, upon some signal that had something to do with one of the brightly coloured levers, the seat, and occupant would trundle down to the other end of the track, where it came to an abrupt halt. The idea was evidently to show people how effective a seatbelt could be in a crash.

"Neat," said Gavin once he had worked it all out. It looked fun, so he pulled a green lever to see what would happen. Electric motors whirred, pumps pumped, and the end of the trailer with the seat lowered down to the ground. "Aha! Must be to help people get on and off," he ventured and tried pulling on the orange lever instead. It had the effect of raising the seat up into the air. "Ah, now I get it," he said. "You make the ramp steeper, so the seat goes faster. Smart!"

Gavin smiled and continued pulling the lever, but the ramp wouldn't go any further - there was a safety cut-out. "Can't see the point in that," he said, wasting no time disabling it. A subsequent test confirmed that a seat on a stationary trailer could easily exceed the national speed limit. Jamsie found a sign identifying the thing as the 'Dorkshire Police Seat Belt Demonstrator.' They put it in a prominent position and added another of their own reading, 'One Pound a Crash'. Jamsie wondered if they should charge extra for broken ribs, but Gavin decided to throw that in for nothing.

⁎

Around this time, Myrtle Gurt 'materialised' with a crystal ball, broomstick, and what looked to be part of a frog dangling from the rim of her crooked but mostly conical headgear. No one could remember seeing how she got there, but she quickly scuttled away into a tent, marked by a sizeable hand-painted notice which read: 'The Amazing Gurt, Palm Reader & Ball Gazer Extraordinaire - Fifty Pence a Go.' It suggested that you could have your palms read and your balls gazed at for less than a quid, so David made them remove it. He doubted anyone would venture within a hundred yards of the tent once they knew who was inside. Some bright spark had erected a windsock nearby just in case Myrtle was planning an impromptu air display.

David was delighted when Albert Thinly-Pip from Dillchurch Rotary Club turned up with a Bouncy Castle and a promise to donate half the takings to the youth club funds.

"Excellent," said David. "I had no idea he was coming, did you?" he asked Vicki, pointing at the trailer with the castle still folded inside.

"Well, kind of," she said, "but I wasn't sure, so I didn't say anything. I didn't want to disappoint you. I know how much you like playing on those things."

David's response went unheard, thanks to a loud bang from the direction of the road. A puff of blue smoke curled above the trees, and soon, a decrepit and somewhat dislocated coach heaved itself into view. Originally painted green and cream, the vehicle now had slogans daubed in thick black paint along the sides, advising people to ban things, stop eating them, or both. A chimney poked out obliquely from the roof, and some of the windows were covered with wooden boards. Much to David's horror, it lurched over to a remote corner of the playing field, where it seemed to expire with another loud bang. A door swung open and fell off, and a group of the most suspicious misfits David had ever seen tumbled out onto the damp grass. They quickly lined up alongside their mobile scrapheap and held up banners before starting to sing.

Vicki's eyesight was better than his, and she was the first to identify one of the figures frantically waving a placard. "Oh my God, David, that's Braintree!"

"Bloody hell," said David. "What does her sign say?"

"Ban the Youth Club & Shoot the Councillors, I think," said Vicki. "She's waving it about too quickly to be sure. Another says, 'Death to Poodles,' and there's one that says, 'Stuff the Pope - Up the Queen!'"

"Charming," said David. "Doesn't that amount to treason?"

"I think you might have the wrong end of the stick," said Vicki, amazed that he could take things so literally. "You don't think she will try anything, do you? You know, sabotage, an attack - that sort of thing?"

"She can't. I mean, how the hell would she get away with it in broad daylight? She wouldn't dare." But David felt worried. Almost overnight, Agnes seemed to have transformed from an upright, albeit unpopular, pillar of society to a crazy hooligan. He'd have to keep an eye on her.

Agnes wasn't in a reasonable frame of mind. A restless night fretting about the day ahead had left her tired and disgruntled. Woken early that morning by the sound of a tuneless klaxon and grinding engine, she had leapt from her bed, thrown on some old clothes, and dashed into the kitchen. She'd intended to collect a packed lunch from the fridge, but a kitchen floor covered in her favourite dessert brought about a sudden and irreversible change of plan. Agnes was on her backside within two paces, sliding into the table and chairs with a crash. Jamsie had done a thorough job while she was asleep, and Agnes was now slithering around hopelessly. Try as she might, she couldn't get to her feet. After pulling down the curtains, smashing several plates, and toppling the Welsh dresser, she managed to swim back to the hall, where a carpet and surer footing helped her recover some dignity.

She ought to have stayed in bed.

***

Soon everything was ready. The ferret racing pipe was in place, bracketed by two small enclosures made from chicken wire, and Lady Dinc's cook had delivered the buffet, which was now spread out neatly in the clubhouse. David had to admit it looked terrific, but he still wasn't going to risk eating anything, at least not until someone else had volunteered – and lived. The fire crews had finished polishing, and a strange smell was coming from Myrtle Gurt's tent.

There was even the obligatory car boot sale. David had often wondered why anyone would want to buy a car boot. He supposed that people with hatchbacks might have a need, but it all seemed a bit odd to his literal mind. Regardless, dozens of cars were lined up neatly along one side of the field, boots full to the brim with utter junk, which they hoped to sell to one another.

Getting there had been a challenge. The signs along the road from Dillchurch were cunningly arranged to lead everyone down a dirt track and into the river, so it wasn't long before several cars were full of trout. Others slipped out of sight beneath the mud, and several fights had broken out. It was chaos, but David was blissfully unaware of it. He looked at his watch.

"Well, if it isn't ready by now, it never will be," he said. "I think it's going to be a good day, after all."

Vicki agreed and kissed him. Neither of them noticed Josephine hiding a cat in the gas pipe.

Blindfold Hurdles

By the time people arrived, in ones and twos at first, the rain had eased enough to make the valley feel a little less unwelcoming. A light wind blew, and although the river Dinc had risen still further, it remained safely contained within its banks.

While they waited, a group of senior club members attempted to master the unicycle. The challenge was to ride it from one bale of hay to another twenty paces away, preferably in a straight line, but this proved to be far harder than it looked. Josephine was the best, but even she couldn't stay on it for more than a few seconds. Someone suggested she might stand a better chance if she removed the saddle, but the idea didn't appeal. "Shove it up your own backside!" she shouted savagely.

David viewed the scene before him. Much to his delight, the crowd was already substantial. The inclement weather hadn't put anyone off, and most had taken the precaution of equipping themselves with an umbrella. The variety of styles and designs gave the damp, grey day a much-needed splash of colour. You could tell a lot about people from the umbrellas they used. Winterbourne Dinctum residents carried designer models that advertised membership of a prestigious club – usually the National Trust. Dinctum inhabitants used your 'filling station specials', some of which were big enough to double as a bus shelter. You could have safely jumped out of a plane holding on to one of those. Then there were the tatty, half-covered frames held aloft by the residents of Lower Dinctum. Most of these were strapped to chimneys receiving the BBC when it wasn't raining. But the ultimate in anti-precipitant accessories came with the wretched figures from Dinctum Splashit. One such had a newspaper tied to his head with bailing twine. A belt made from the same stuff held his oily coat tightly shut. It was difficult to see where this individual stopped and the tractor he was driving started.

***

Soon, the time had come for Colonel Fawcett to do his bit and declare the event open. David was surprised to see Fawcett there because he didn't usually like the rain, saying that it gave him rheumatism, obscured his view, and drained the battery in his hearing aid. Much to David's relief, Fawcett quickly made it clear that he would only be stopping to make a short speech. On a fine day, the Colonel would have droned on interminably, but the inclement weather had saved everyone from enduring that ordeal.

"No sign of Lady Dinc yet," said David, turning to Vicki as he waited for Fawcett to find his notes. "Do you think she'll come?"

"Yes, I'm sure she will," said Vicki. "Dinky loves this sort of thing... any excuse to have fun or celebrate. She gate-crashes weddings if she gets wind of them."

It was common knowledge that Lady Dinc loved a good party. She had even managed to liven up someone's funeral with a couple of crates of vodka. By the time mourners had ploughed through the first nine bottles, they were ready to start digging up the deceased so that he could join in the fun too.

As it happened, Lady Dinc was making a valiant effort to attend the fun day but wasn't having much success. She had spent most of the previous night doing a 'stock check' at the Dinctum Arms and was now so far out of her tree that she couldn't have seen it with a telescope. As she lay in a field full of cows, something in the back of her pickled brain reminded her it was worth going to Dinctum today. So, with some difficulty, she dragged herself slowly back to the manor, filled up on coffee liqueurs, and unpacked the motorbike. As Colonel Fawcett stood in front of the microphone, Lady Dinc saddled up, kicked the bike to life, and set off, leaving a cloud of blue smoke behind her. She was a mile along the lane to Bungbury before realising it was the wrong way.

David checked his watch and told the Colonel it was time to start. The Colonel cleared his throat and began to speak. "Ladies and Gent..." but something was wrong with the PA, and no one could hear him. The PA wasn't working because Gavin had the volume turned down, and now that Fawcett was standing in exactly the right place, he turned it back up again as loud as it would go - and then some.

"LADIES AND G... G... G... G... G... G...'

Cows ran for cover as the Colonel's voice echoed deafeningly around the hillsides. Ducks turned on their backs in the Dinc, and squirrels fell out of trees. No one for miles around could have missed the start of the Colonel's opening address, but none of them was going to hear the end of it because, before he got any further, his hearing aid blew up, and he fell to the ground with smoke coming from the side of his head. The St John's Ambulance crew had to jump into action for the first time that afternoon, and it wouldn't be the last.

***

Lying on a stretcher, Fawcett demanded to be taken home and left alone. So, it fell to David to declare the fun day open, which he did without going near a microphone, just to be on the safe side. Vicki tried to reassure him that Fawcett's exploding ear was just an accident, but David wasn't so sure. He wondered if the care Gavin had taken over the placement of the microphone and speakers earlier in the day had been a simple coincidence.

"You don't think we should sneak off to Bermuda while we're still at liberty to do so?" he asked, but Vicki just gave him another kiss.

"Listen, it's going to be all right. You'll see." But even as the words passed her lips, Vicki could see a bouncy castle floating just above his shoulder in the distance. "Oh, for fuck's sake. What the hell?" she said and, seeing the look on David's face as he followed her gaze, added, "No, you stay here. I'll deal with it!"

She ran to where the castle should have been and found Albert Thin hopping around, shouting something about a "little sod with a gas bottle!" It wasn't the sort of language Vicki had come to expect from an upstanding Rotarian, not even the ones you found at the Dillchurch branch. They both stood helplessly as the thing drifted off across the field, gaining altitude as it went. Albert looked as though he was going to cry. "Some little sod emptied a bottle of helium into the thing! I hadn't even got it off the friggin trailer. Bloody good job, there wasn't anyone on it!"

"Do you want me to get someone to shoot it down?" she asked, immediately regretting it.

"No, I bloody well don't!" exclaimed Albert angrily. "You people have done enough sodding damage already!"

He picked up his box of sandwiches and set off to follow the castle as fast as he could. Shaped like an elephant stuck in a box, the castle was already higher than the hilltops. Vicki thought it would be a long time before Mr Thin and his castle were reunited – if ever.

At that moment, Lady Dinc reached the edge of the playing field and attempted to stop her bike. It was the one aspect of motorcycling that she had never mastered, and it was a miracle that she didn't collide with anyone on her way across the turf. She skidded from one side of the pitch to the other, sliding down a small bank and into the river. Two deep furrows arcing across the grass were the only sign she had been there. People held their breath, waiting anxiously to see if she would get out of the water or sink without a trace, but Lady Dinc wasn't in the mood for drowning. Like a crocodile emerging from a wallow, she dragged herself back up the bank and, with considerable difficulty, stood up, swaying unsteadily. The water turned to steam as it dripped from her sodden jacket onto her leather boots, still piping hot from her attempts to stop the bike. The scorching heat suddenly made itself known to her, and somehow, she managed to jump into the air while simultaneously bending down to take off her boots. This impressive and surprisingly athletic manoeuvre landed her back in the river, generating spontaneous applause from all of those present. Sat up to her waist in the reeds and with her back to the crowd, Lady Dinc responded by sticking two fingers in the air.

***

After that, things seemed to progress smoothly. The rain had almost stopped, and lots more people had arrived. The stalls were doing good business, and no one suffered a 'clotchy doo death' – just one of the many things that had deprived David of sleep that week.

Soon it was time for the ferret racing. Everyone was excited about this, and Dr Function took charge, busily encouraging people of any age to place bets on the animal they thought most likely to win. The money flowed readily, and, in no time, he ordered the teams to "stand by your ferrets".

The ferrets were highly trained creatures in peak condition, having been towed behind a bicycle for a mile or two every day of the preceding month. Each was given a bright and uniquely coloured collar to wear. The first Ferret to race was selected and placed in a holding pen at the entrance to the pipe, ready for the signal to start - a shot from Dr Function's starting pistol. All things being equal, the animal would be released to sprint through the pipe and out into a finishing cage, with the fastest ferret to cover the distance declared the winner. The victorious owner would celebrate, and everyone would get pissed. In the event of a tie, everyone would still get pissed. In fact, the primary objective of ferret racing, it seems, was to get pissed.

When Function fired the pistol, the ferret sat tight, unwilling to go anywhere. There followed a pause in which the animal's owner attempted to reason with the little beasty, but the ferret wasn't having any of it. It could see all too clearly what no one else could: the beady eyes of a vicious moggie halfway up the pipe, and it wasn't at all keen on venturing in to meet it. Only when Dr Function stood immediately behind the poor little thing and fired his gun again did it throw caution to the wind and bolt up the tube as fast as it could manage. Someone started a stopwatch. They needn't have bothered.

Nothing happened for a while. It was the calm before the storm. Suddenly, all hell broke loose. Despite its size and weight, the pipe began to rock, breaking free from the cages at either end. The sound of a cat and ferret in mortal combat, resonating through a giant yellow tube, was unearthly and people backed away in fear. The last time the Dinc Valley had witnessed a similar noise, brachiosaurs were munching the treetops. The ferret's owner, close to tears, dashed from one end of the pipe to the other, frantically trying to establish what was going on. He wasn't about to let his little pride and joy get ripped to shreds, so he tried lifting one end of the pipe and shaking it to see what slid out. Nothing did, so someone suggested pouring a bucket of water down the tube, but that didn't work either. Dr Function called for the Fire Officer, but the only thing he could think of was more water.

"We've already tried pouring buckets of the stuff down there," said Function, pointing at the upper end of the pipe. "It didn't do any good."

"Ah, but we've got more than buckets, haven't we," said the officer with a smile. "We've got high-pressure pumps, and if that don't shift 'em, you'll have to get some dynamite." Even as he said it, the officer found himself strangely attracted to the idea of explosives. However, he suspected that the League Against Cruel Sports might have had something to say about a giant yellow cannon that fired household pets around the valley. So, he dashed off to get a crew ready, and soon they had a hose wedged into one end of the pipe with a bundle of rags to keep it there. The fire engine started, and the pump engaged. Very quickly, the canvas hose filled up and began to bulge. It seemed to take an age before anything happened, but when it did, the officer wondered whether dynamite could have been much worse. The occupants of the pipe shot over a hundred yards across the field and hit Lady Dinc square in the chest. Having just climbed out of the river, she was more than a little surprised to be blown off her feet and back into it again by two large and unidentified hairy objects.

David watched in horror, developing a twitch under his left eye, and he had to sit down to calm his nerves. Even Vicki had to admit that it didn't bode well but decided it could have happened to anyone, and it was just one of those unhappy accidents. She ought to have known better.

With the ferret racing temporarily off the schedule, David brought forward the blindfold hurdles to fill the gap. Several teams had come forward, and it took only a short time to prepare them. The original idea had been to use bandages for the blindfolds, but Vicki discovered that the first aid kit was empty. Someone suggested using supermarket carrier bags. That seemed reasonable until it was pointed out that most of the competitors would be asphyxiated within a few paces. None were particularly fit, and the chances of getting very far in what was likely to be a total vacuum were slim. Then someone recommended that they could run backwards instead of using blindfolds - the effect would be the same.

A reluctant volunteer put this idea to the test and found it almost impossible to jump backwards over anything, especially when you couldn't see where 'it' was. David was on the point of abandoning the event when, at the last minute, a creative mind came up with the idea of using underwear. Consequently, the crowd was treated to the spectacle of twenty competitors wearing an assortment of underpants or knickers on their heads. They were guided to the start line by another twenty assistants, all having trouble taking any of it seriously. Half decided it would be fun to point the competitors in the wrong direction, and David had to step in to restore order. He ought to have saved himself the effort. Vicki inspected the underwear to ensure it performed adequately as a blindfold. Typically, some thought they could get away with using a thong and failed scrutineering.

Soon everyone was ready and waiting to go. All that was left was to hand out whistles to the teams and then find someone to start the race. It was pointless asking Lady Dinc. She was still thrashing around in the river, caught in an altercation with a large eel. Colonel Fawcett would have been the next choice, but he was also 'out of order' and convalescing at home. So, David decided Gavin should have the honour since the whole debacle was his idea. Gavin was delighted to have the privilege.

So, there were now twenty teams, each of two people. One team member was blindfolded, ready to run wherever they were pointed. The other had a whistle to blow each time their teammate approached a virtual hurdle. On hearing the whistle, the blindfolded runner jumped into the air. Judges would keep an eye on things and indicate any foul jumps, requiring the competitor to go back and try again. White lines across the track at ten-metre intervals showed the position of the virtual hurdles. The first to complete the course was the winner. It should have been simple.

When he was ready to get things started, Gavin blew the whistle loudly, but instead of beginning to run, the competitors did what they had been told to do and jumped in the air. Clearly, a different approach was necessary. David used the PA to address the competitors. "On the *first* whistle, you start running. After that, every time you hear it blown, you jump!" It seemed straightforward enough to him.

Very soon, there were blindfolded bodies, with undergarments on their heads, rushing erratically down the track towards the first hurdle. At this stage, a second problem became apparent: all the whistles sounded the same, so no one knew who was supposed to be jumping or at what time. People were leaping into the air at random all over the place. Judges dashed here and there, blowing *their* whistles and shouting "foul" at anyone who missed a hurdle, only to find that the bemused competitor just leapt into the air again. Predictably, this brought forth another blast from the judge's whistle with another cry of "foul jump". To add to the confusion, some cunning little bugger had distributed another twenty whistles amongst the crowd.

Unsurprisingly, no clear leader emerged. With each jump, the participants became ever more disorientated and less able to keep going in a straight line. Some were heading across the playing field and into the meadows beyond. Others bounced towards the clubhouse, bumping into the walls when they got there. Vicki had to chase after the elderly Twinkin sisters, who were progressing rapidly towards the river. They weren't part of the race, nor were they blindfolded, but both thought David's instructions, broadcast over the PA, applied to them as well, so off they went.

Gavin couldn't stand up for giggling. It was every bit as entertaining as he had hoped, but it had to be stopped before someone died - even if it was only from laughter.

"Time for the Tug of War, I think," said David, throwing his carefully crafted timetable into the bin.

***

While chaos surrounded the clubhouse, the scene inside was much tidier than it had been earlier in the day, and the mouldy smell of dampness had disappeared. Lady Dinc's buffet looked much better than it sounded, and people seemed to enjoy the taste. Vicki was helping Alison and Rachel serve cups of tea to an almost endless queue that had formed outside the door. Had they seen the unique ingredients surreptitiously poured into the urn, the queue might have been much shorter. An identical potion had been added with equal secrecy to the barbeque sauce. Given that only one toilet was available, things were likely to get quite complicated at some point in the afternoon.

The Firefight

David took a moment to examine the playing fields and take stock. The band, which had been blasting away resolutely until that point, was having a long overdue rest, and Tubby had fallen asleep during the last verse of All Things Bright and Beautiful. Given the earlier near-drowning experience, his colleagues had elected to leave him be. He had remained relatively motionless for so long that a couple of crows had started to build a nest in his bell end. He was going to get a nasty surprise when he started blowing on his tuba again. So were the crows.

David noted that DS Thorn had arrived and was taking a close interest in the contents of the car boots. Thorn would have laid odds on most of it being nicked and was covertly making a note of number plates. He was there because Constable Bell was on leave, sunning himself on a Costa something or other. Costa-lot, in Thorn's opinion. It had been ten years since he'd had enough spare cash to go on a camping trip to the Ilse of Wight, and it rained the entire week.

Beyond Thorn and tucked into the furthest corner of the field, David could see the wreck of a coach belching black smoke from the chimney on its roof. Agnes Braintree and her band of miserable protesters were still shouting and waving their signs. One made an awful din with a digeridoo and wailed something about tying up kangaroos. David was hoping DS Thorn might do something about this noisy little group, but he hadn't taken the officer's natural propensity for inactivity into account. Thorn had already decided to steer clear of that particular can of worms. Nevertheless, Agnes watched him intently. She was watching everyone. The less-than-ideal start to her day had left her even more paranoid than usual. Someone clearly knew too much and had it in for her. She would have to be on the lookout from now on.

Finally, David's gaze drifted toward the river, where he could make out Lady Dinc lying on her back, holding a large bottle of gin to her mouth. Exhausted from her run-in with the eel, she was resigned to staying wet and making the best of it. David decided he could cope with her lying by the river, providing she stayed there. The world was a safer place when Lady Dinc was recumbent. The time to worry was when she got up and started doing stuff.

As far as he could see, everyone else seemed to be tucking into the food. There were burgers, hot dogs, roast potatoes, cakes, barbequed meats, and, of course, the miscellaneous curios donated by Lady Dinc. David still had reservations about those, but everyone still seemed healthy enough.

Not so bad, after all, thought David as he allowed himself a moment of self-congratulation. He was just about to get a cup of tea when a wisp of smoke spiralling up from a small hole in the top of Myrtle Gurt's tent caught his attention. *She must have a fire going,* he thought and decided that a fire inside a tent was probably a very bad thing, so he hurried over to check. Once inside, he found her toiling over an enormous cauldron and his jaw dropped at the size of it.

"How the hell...?" he started to say. It was a good three feet in diameter, almost as tall, and was suspended precariously over a camping stove that didn't look capable of boiling a tea bag. Even so, the cauldron's contents seemed to be bubbling away nicely.

"Soup?" enquired Myrtle, beaming at him crookedly from under the brim of her pointy hat. "You won't taste none like it nowhere."

He considered her offer but politely refused. He knew the sight of entrails when he saw them and the smell of marijuana too. Myrtle was as high as a kite.

Turning around, David dashed out and back across the field to find Vicki. On the way, he bumped into Gavin. "Listen," he gasped hysterically. "K… keep everyone away… tent. Don't let… anyone… go in, especially PC ruddy plod. Got that?" he said, pointing in the direction of DS Thorn.

"How the firkin hell am I supposed to do that?" asked Gavin, knowing it was an almost impossible task. "Everyone wants to see her… count the warts… you know."

"I don't… use… imagination, disguise… tent… bush… or something," said David breathlessly. "Bloody woman's… stoned! All… get nicked if she starts… sell that stuff… to anyone, and God knows… what's in soup." He ran off, leaving Gavin speechless.

Still gasping for breath, David rushed into the clubhouse with a look of panic on his bright red face.

"What's wrong? What's the matter?" asked Vicki.

Catching his breath, he tried to talk discreetly to her so as not to draw too much attention. "It's that bloody witch!" he hissed, but Vicki still looked puzzled. "The witch! Gurt, for heaven's sake!" he said, shouting in a whisper while hopping from one foot to another. "She's in her bloody tent trying to conjure up God knows what!" He was pointing out of the window while he spoke. "High as a kite on pot, boiling up a horse or something! We got to stop her, Vicki."

"For crying out loud, calm down. Your face is turning bright purple. People will think it's the clotchy doos!"

Eventually, he settled down enough to tell Vicki what was happening and what he had asked Gavin to do about it. Vicki laughed. "You can't just turn a tent in the middle of a playing field into a large bush and expect it to go unnoticed."

He had to admit she was right. "Well, I don't know what else to suggest," he said, hoping something would spring to mind. "What about getting Pinkle in there to perform an exorcism?"

"Pull yourself together," said Vicki. "The chances of anyone going near that tent are remote, and even if they did, the fumes would knock them senseless at twenty paces. Go and get the tug-of-war started. It will keep everyone's attention away from Myrtle, won't it?"

"Oh God, I forgot about that," said David, pausing briefly to grab a doughnut before dashing outside.

He needn't have hurried. The tug of war had started all by itself, and so had the tractor pull. Even Myrtle Gurt's tent was on the move. Gavin had used his imagination and decided that trying to conceal the tent was too much like hard work. Besides, he didn't want to expose himself to the dark arts more than necessary. So, in a flash of inspiration, he attached Gurt's enchanted pavilion to the back of a Massey-Fergusson and was now towing the whole thing into the river. The tent had an integral groundsheet that proved to be water resistant, so instead of sinking below the surface, it remained afloat, bobbing around gently. Myrtle was completely oblivious to this and too far gone to notice the earth moving. She wouldn't have noticed a pink cathedral in her pants, even if the organ had been going full tilt.

Having manoeuvred the tent onto the river, Gavin set it adrift, and it floated away on the current, steam rising from beneath the canvas. Moving gently towards a bend in the river, the tent passed a flotilla of Mallard. One of the unfortunate creatures ventured too near to the tent, and, quick as a flash, a wrinkled, bony hand reached out to grab it. As it left the water, a hollow cackle echoed around the valley, only to be supplanted by Gurt's screams as the remaining ducks flew into the tent, hell-bent on revenge.

***

The tug of war went as well as could be hoped. Nobody drowned, and the teams narrowly avoided fisticuffs. Dillchurch managed to pull the Bungbury fire crew into the Dinc and out the other side – twice. The third round had to be abandoned because one of the participating tractors – it was an unusual tug of war - got stuck in the mud and sank from view.

After a short break for tea and biscuits, the two fire crews assembled for the much-anticipated firefighting competition. It should have been a simple affair: two cars had been prepared and positioned in front of the fire engines, ready to entertain the crowd. The Fire Officer searched to see if anything worth having, such as radios, new tyres, or furry dice, had been overlooked. It was a pointless exercise because the owner of the scrap yard had already been over them with a powerful microscope. Alongside the cars, two dishevelled crews stood facing one another, hoses at the dangle, waiting patiently for the countdown to begin.

After defeat in the tug of war, the Bungbury crew was looking to even up the score, determined to squirt foam as it had never been squirted before. They had meticulously examined every nook and cranny of their rusty Ford and devised a cunning plan: to completely ignore the burning wreck and direct the flow of foam at the Dillchurch team, thereby disabling them. Then, having the advantage, they could turn their attention back to the fire and certain victory. Predictably, the Dillchurch crew had settled on precisely the same strategy. So, when the Fire Officer set the two cars alight and shouted, "Crews, put out your fires!" the two teams turned the hoses on each other and promptly disappeared under a mountain of bubbling, white foam. The cars burned furiously, and the crowd cheered.

While this was happening and the crowd was distracted, Peter stood by the seatbelt demonstrator arguing with DS Thorn. "I can't see how it's anything like a real car crash," he said. "It hasn't even got headlamps."

DS Thorn rose to the bait. Peter knew he would. "I'll have you know that this comes with nothing less than Home Office approval, matey-boy. The Home Secretary herself has sat in that very seat, and it was in all the national papers," said the officer proudly.

"Yeah, but everyone knows the Home Secretary's a bun short of a current," said Peter. "She'd probably jump out of a plane without a parachute if she thought it would win an extra vote or two. I wonder how many times she'd bounce?"

"Depends how high up she was when she jumped, I suppose," replied the detective, forgetting himself for a moment. He didn't think much of the Home Secretary either. "Anyway, are you going to give it a whirl then? Are you brave enough to sit in that seat and feel what a thirty-mile-an-hour impact is like?" Thorn had a look in his eye that made Peter uncomfortable. It was a bit like an executioner showing you his axe and saying, "Feel how sharp it is. Go on, try it."

Peter pretended to be afraid. "Oh, I'm not sure, sir," he said. "Show me what it's like. You do it first. Please, sir."

Thorn had done it so often that it wasn't much fun anymore. However, you shouldn't expect others to do something you wouldn't do yourself. At least, that's what his chemistry teacher had always told him. Then again, his chemistry teacher had dissolved most of his desk while showing them how to handle acid safely.

So, somewhat reluctantly, he gave Peter a quick run-through on the controls and then wandered off to settle in the seat.

"Right, pull the orange lever," said DS Thorn as soon as he was securely strapped in place.

Peter pretended not to hear.

DS Thorn tried again. "PULL THE ORANGE ONE, LAD!"

Peter complied and saw the seat rise into the air. While it was on its way up, he saw Joseph approaching. "All right, mate?" he asked. "I see you managed to talk plod into the hot seat."

"Yeah, neat or what?" replied Peter. "What shall I do with him?" They discussed the options ignoring the shouts from above. Thorn was starting to get worried because the ramp was higher than it should have been and still rising.

"Oi! That's enough!" he shouted. "You can stop now!" But Peter was still looking the other way, talking to Joseph.

The view was quite good from where Thorn was, and it was breezy too, but he didn't like it. "OI! FARTY!" he shouted louder than before. "LET THE BLOODY LEVER GO! OI!" But Peter smiled, gave a friendly wave, and then resumed his conversation with Joseph.

It wasn't long before the ramp was almost vertical and would go no further. Thorn was right at the top, facing downwards and looking very pale. He was still shouting at the top of his voice. "GET ME DOWN, YOU STUPID IDIOT! GET ME DOWN! Unfortunately for Thorn, everyone else on the playing field was thoroughly absorbed in the fire foam fight and completely ignored his cries.

Peter tried to communicate with him. "WHICH LEVER SHOULD I PULL NEXT, SIR? THE YELLOW ONE?" he asked, reaching out to it, knowing precisely what it did. Thorn knew what it did as well, and suddenly became very animated, jerking around in his seat as though he'd discovered a large and especially poisonous viper in his trousers.

"DON'T TOUCH THAT BLOODY LEVER! DON'T TOUCH IT!" he screamed.

"WHAT? PULL THIS ONE?" replied Peter, shaking the yellow lever from side to side. It felt a bit loose, and he liked its effect on the policeman, so he did it some more.

Thorn was panicking. It was a long way down, and he didn't want to cover the distance in a hurry. "LET ME DOWN, YOU VICIOUS LITTLE SOD! PULL THE GREEN LEVER! THE GREEN LEVER!" As he shouted, he tugged wildly at the seatbelt, trying to free himself, but it was too late. Peter had wobbled the yellow lever a bit too much, and the seat was released. Thorn didn't even have time to scream before crashing into the stops at the bottom of the ramp, where he hung motionless. Peter and Joseph were nowhere to be seen.

***

Over at the barbecue, David and Vicki were about to start selling raffle tickets when Jennifer turned up and threw herself around David's leg.

"Don't start this shadow business again, please," said David despairingly. "This isn't the time or place."

"Did I ever tell you about Nigel the Goat?" inquired Jennifer, ignoring his request.

"Yes, you did, several times. Now go away."

"What about Chief Sitting Bull and his brother Creeping Arse?"

"Go away, Jennifer, and don't be silly," said David firmly.

"All right then, but I bet I know something you don't."

"What?"

"They've killed the policeman!" she shouted, and with that little bombshell, she ran off into the clubhouse.

David suddenly became flatulent. It was too unlikely to be a joke. "Oh my God," he cried, looking across at the lifeless body of DS Thorn. "Get a medic, Vicki! CALL A BLOODY AMBULANCE!" He was hoping that he would wake up any second and discover that it was all just a nightmare, but he didn't, and it wasn't.

Vicki ran off to find the medics but hadn't gone more than a few paces when the fuel hidden under the Bungbury Ford went up. It was more of a loud whoosh than an explosion, and by the time she turned to see what had happened, the wreck was some fifty feet higher than it had been a moment earlier and still climbing with a column of bright flame and billowing smoke reaching down behind it. If you substituted NASA for the Ford badge on the boot, you'd have thought it was the shuttle.

Everyone on the field stood rooted to the spot, gazing at the object as it hurtled skywards. As Shakespeare might have written, *'what doth hurtle upwards, eventually cometh back down and landeth on your bonce'*. By rights, they should have been running for cover, but fear and a misplaced sense of curiosity stop the legs from working on occasions like this. Lives flashed before eyes, jaws dropped, and stomachs started to churn - especially those of the people who had drunk the tea or sampled the sausages, which was nearly everyone.

The car seemed to hang in the air for ages as if it was trying to decide where to go next, but then, slowly, it fell back to earth. At this point, legs started to work again. There was blind panic as people ran this way and that, bumping into one another, crashing into tents, tripping over unicycles, and jumping into the river. It was just like the blindfold hurdles all over again, but without the whistles. Thanks to the breeze and some appalling aerodynamics, the smouldering wreck landed with a crunching thud further down the field, right next to Dr Function's rocket, and it didn't take an Einstein to see what was going to happen next.

Some in the crowd thought the flying car was all part of the show, and they began clapping their hands enthusiastically. Lady Dinc, who had run out of gin and risen to her feet, thought the applause was for her, so she took a bow and immediately fell over again. With her face in the grass and bottom in the air, she began to feel rather chilly. Her clothes had soaked up quite a lot of water since arriving at the event, and she decided to do something about it. Looking around for somewhere to get warm and possibly snooze, she spotted the Volvo still burning brightly in the centre of the field. Better still, just beyond it was a shiny red fire engine. "Shperfect," she slurred with a smile.

Lady Dinc liked fire engines with their bells and lights and sirens. All jolly good fun as far as she was concerned. So, on reaching the machine, she climbed into the cab and was delighted to find a spare uniform hanging up behind the seats. No one noticed the vehicle rocking from side to side as she fought to escape her sodden garments, and nobody heard her shouting either. The air in the cab was the same colour as the lights on its roof for a while, but soon she was dressed again and fell sound asleep.

***

If the Bungbury Ford 'shuttle' had failed to reach high altitude, the same could not be said of the next thing to leave the ground in Dinctum that day. A wiser man would have left the fuel out, but Dr Function had brought his rocket to the event intending to launch it, and it was fully loaded.

Even though his designs appeared reasonably sophisticated, Function still fitted his rockets with blue touch paper. None of your electronic starters or "multi-fandangled" computer-controlled countdowns for him. A simple match was all it took, and then you ran like the clappers. If you didn't have a match, a smouldering lump of Ford would do nicely. So, just when people thought they could get back to watching everyone else make complete fools of themselves, the ground under their feet started to shake.

To begin with, it was almost imperceptible, but it quickly gained amplitude until even Lady Dinc regained consciousness. Agnes Braintree and company, who were much nearer the launch site, panicked as they scrambled to get inside the coach for shelter, but the doorway was too narrow. It quickly turned nasty as they beat one another with placards.

Function's rocket accelerated into the air, pinky-white flames blasting out from its base. The unusual colour was due to the odd blend of fuels, which included household sugar, turpentine, and a

256

well-known washing powder. It went up, up, and away, faster and faster towards the rain clouds still threatening overhead.

David stood open-mouthed, his brain refusing to accept what his eyes were seeing. Vicki decided it was time to swear again. "I hope that's just a fucking mirage," she said, reaching out to hold David's hand.

As the rocket disappeared into the cloud, a bright glow remained visible for a short time, but soon, even that had faded, and only the noise remained. It was like an endless roll of thunder reverberating around the valley, and for the second time that day, people were motionless as they gazed upwards. Was that it? Had it left the atmosphere, or would it come down in the river and fizzle out? Perhaps it would go off with a bang like some giant firework, showering the countryside with glittering green and purple sparks.

David was shaking his head. He couldn't process what had just happened. Where in the 'Idiot's Guide to Fun Days' did it say anything about ground-to-air missiles? Then it dawned on him that it was more likely to be the 'ground-to-ground' variety, and it would be coming down soon. He was filled with terror. "Oh God, I hope he didn't fit a warhead to that bloody thing. I bet he did, you know. I bet you anything you like there is enough plutonium in the pointy end of that ruddy thing to vaporise the whole of Dorkshire."

"Don't!" said Vicki. "He wouldn't do anything like that, would he?" But David's words had sown the seeds of doubt in her mind.

"You know what these old quacks are like," he ventured. "No telling what sort of mess all those pills and potions have made of his mind. He could be a complete loony for all we know. Just because he doesn't run around the streets at night stark naked… juggling frozen chickens… you know."

Vicki thought about it. She'd never seen anyone, sane or otherwise, juggling frozen chickens, but it didn't matter much now because the rumbling noise above had spluttered to an end. The rocket was coming down!

***

Someone at the back of the crowd shouted, "TAKE COVER," and everyone started running around in circles again. By that time, the laxative, liberally mixed into the tea and the barbeque sauce was beginning to take effect, making an already desperate situation much worse. Dozens of villagers ran to the clubhouse, hoping to get to the toilet before it was obliterated. Others hid under anything they could find: the tents, bales of straw, and even the unicycle. One man sat on the ground with a large apple cake on his head, and the Twinkin sisters started to sing Jerusalem.

David decided his end was nigh. He turned to face Vicki and, putting his arms around her waist, spoke in a manner she hadn't heard before. "I know I shouldn't be saying this, but… well, whatever happens now, I want you to know that I love you. I love you more than I should, more than anything."

With tears in her eyes, she said, "I know, and I love you too, David."

They held each other tightly and kissed, hearts pounding. What would be, would be.

DEFCON 3

Deep under a snow-covered mountain in the United States of America, a bright red light flashed, and a printer spooled. A man in a highly decorated uniform punched a code into the keypad of a red telephone, which also had a red flashing light. They liked red flashing lights in this part of the world. Within seconds – about the time it took for a signal to bounce around an array of expensive military satellites – another red phone on the opposite side of the Atlantic began to ring.

"Hello, officer of the watch. Captain Plunge-Pithering here, how can I help?"

Heir to the Plunge-Pithering estate and blissfully unaware of his late father's peculiar passion for Agnes Braintree, Rodney Plunge-Pithering had risen exceptionally slowly to the rank of captain in the Royal Navy. Having run a small frigate into the Isle of Wight and then reversed it into one of Her Majesty's nuclear submarines, he was now in command of an entire desk in a dimly lit corner of Whitehall. It was just up the corridor from an even darker, cobweb-filled office where two ninety-year-old retired admirals dreamt up all the military acronyms – even the ones nobody needed.

Rodney PP, as he was known, was the first port of call when the Americans spotted something across the Atlantic that they didn't like the look of. His upper-class accent made it extremely difficult to understand anything he said, which meant that the Americans rarely called. This suited everyone at the Ministry of Defence quite nicely.

"General Babcock, NORAD," snapped a voice. "We got an unscheduled launch showing here, Pillocking. What the hell's going on over there?"

Plunge-Pithering had suffered this name-calling for years. It was either Pillocking or Prattling, and he didn't much care for it. However, he knew you couldn't 'get shirty' with a five-star general, so he opted for a polite correction.

"Now look here, old man, it's Plunge-Pithering," he said. "*Pithering*. Do you see?"

"I don't give a goddamn horse's butt what it is, Pillocking," barked the General. "Who's launching missiles over there?"

"Ah, I see," said Pithering, fumbling for a response. "Well, let's have a little look, shall we?" He cast his eye over an assortment of yellow post-it notes stuck to his desk. "Err… um… well… dashed if I can see a dicky bird… Oh, wait a jiffy old chap. Got a note here about the HMS Argonaut test-firing some torpedoes yesterday. Is that the ticket?"

"Not unless they're pointing the goddamn things at the sky," shouted the general, who thought anything was possible in a navy staffed by people like Pillocking.

"Now you listen to me, Pollock… king," continued Babcock, unable to say anything without yelling it out like an order. His voice was abrasive, and his words were slightly distorted by the almost constant presence of a large cigar in his mouth. "Let me explain this to you in words of one goddamn syllable. Someone over there has just launched a missile. If people don't tell me about things like that, I'll have half the goddamn Air Force over there bombing the shit out of you people faster than you can say dick. Got it?"

Pithering got it and said he would make a few phone calls. He didn't like the Americans, and they didn't like him. Nevertheless, he took "bombing the shit out of you people" seriously. The thought of smoke rising above a pile of rubble where Buckingham Palace had once stood made him feel just a tad anxious.

***

Back in Dinctum, a shadow hung over the playing fields. A giant, multi-coloured parachute deployed as the rocket descended through the clouds. Even from a couple of thousand feet away, onlookers could see that it was made from an assortment of old coats, vests, and two or three king-size duvet covers printed with pictures of Tom and Jerry.

David stared at the missile, which looked to be on a collision course with his nose. The grinning cartoon characters in the sky above gave the whole thing a surreal appearance, and he quickly concluded that now would be an excellent time to vacate the valley.

"We're screwed," he said to Vicki. "There's no way in hell we'll come out of this smelling of roses, not this time. We should sod off now as quickly as we can... while no one's looking."

"I don't know," said Vicki. "We ought to stick around... for the kids... you know. But yes, once this is all over, and if we are still alive. We should just run away together – somewhere far away."

Looking into her eyes, David realised she meant it. The two of them together. Forever. Suddenly, nothing else seemed to matter.

***

Pithering faced an enormous problem: if you believed Babcock, and he did, the American Air Force was on the brink of launching an airborne assault. He was panicking, and a cold sweat had broken across his brow. Grabbing the telephone directory, he frantically turned the pages. Numbers jumbled together, and names dissolved into a sea of meaningless abbreviations and symbols. It was utterly hopeless. Then he remembered 'Puffy' down in Wiltshire. Puffy was an old RAF chum who played with radars and that sort of thing. He was bound to know what to do. Pithering dialled the number from memory and waited as it rang. After what seemed like an age, someone answered, and Pithering breathed a sigh of relief when he recognised the voice. "Puffy!" he exclaimed. "How the blazes are you, old man?"

"What-ho, Pithers!" shouted Puffy into the phone, causing Pithering to jerk his head away from the receiver. "I say, turn up for the books this, isn't it? Haven't heard a peep fwom you in donkey's yonks. Evewything tickety-boo is it, old chap? How's that delightful sis of yours?" Puffy had a soft spot for Anemone Plunge-Pithering. Anemone had a lot of soft spots too, and she liked to squeeze them.

"Oh gosh," answered Pithering. "Silly ass fell off her mount last week chasing that bally fox again. Bruised her behind. Don't think she'll ever catch it, you know. I mean, isn't she supposed to have some hounds, or don't they do it that way these days?"

"Dashed if I know Pithers!" said Puffy, scratching his head. "Last time I went anywhere near a horse, the wotten thing ate my hat. Wouldn't catch me on one of those for all the tea in Aunt Jewemy's pantwy." Puffy had some unusual relatives.

"Absolutely, Puffy, abso-bally-lutely!" said Pithering. He'd forgotten about the dark and mysterious recesses of Aunt Jeremy's pantry and its overpowering smell of ginger, garlic, cannabis, and sprouts. "Now look here, Puffy. Got a bit of a googly at the minute. Seems that someone in dear old Blighty has launched a missile of some sort, and… well, to cut it all short, the Yanks are going to bomb the Queen if we don't tell them what's happening. Don't suppose you know anything about it, old chap?" he asked hopefully.

There was a moment's silence at the other end of the phone while the gears in Puffy's brain clanked. "Good Lord Pithers!" he said at length. "That *is* a twicky one? A missile, you say. Gosh!" He stopped scratching his head and started on his chin. "Awfully careless thing to do if you ask me. Hold on, a tick. Let me give Bimpkiss a shout. See if he knows." With that, he put Pithering on hold.

***

"I *think* it's going to miss the field altogether," said David as he watched the rocket, blown along by the wind, pass overhead. "We might be all right, after all."

"I don't think so," said Vicki. "Dinc-Bottom's over there, and it looks like that's where it's coming down."

They were the only ones to notice. Everyone else was still running around the field, hoping to find better cover and a toilet, and not necessarily in that order.

"I told you someone was up to something with a laxative, didn't I?" said David when he noticed how many people were trying to run with their legs crossed. "How come we're both all right?"

"I don't know, and I don't care to be honest," said Vicki watching the rocket with increasing alarm. "What are we going to do about Dinc-Bottom? The Colonel and his wife will be in the house, won't they? What happens if it hits them?"

"Send 'em a get well soon card?"

"David! They could be killed! We've got to do something!"

"Well, I'm sorry," he said. "That thing will land on them long before anyone can get there to warn them. Are they on the phone? I could try giving them a call, I suppose. You know... 'Hello Colonel Fawcett, look out, there's a... BOOM!' In any case, he wouldn't be able to hear me. His hearing is shot!"

Vicki knew he was right. It was too late to do anything. All they could do was stand and stare.

With chaos everywhere he looked, the bandmaster did what came naturally in such circumstances: he tapped his baton firmly on the flautist's bald head and launched into The Birdie Song. Tubby woke suddenly and immediately tried to do his um-pa-pas but met with a great deal of resistance. Blowing as hard as he could, his face flushed, and his cheeks bulged. Suddenly, with a blast that sounded like the noise made by an enraged elephant, a volley of leaves, sticks, and feathers blew into the air. It brought down one side of the pavilion. Two furious crows immediately launched a retaliatory strike, embarking on a vicious aerial assault. They pecked relentlessly, forcing Tubby off his seat. Once more, his wife, Henrietta, came to his defence. Dashing across, she began flailing about wildly with her trumpet - so the crows attacked her as well. Then, all the crows' buddies, who had been keeping a close eye on events from the trees thereabouts, decided they might as well swoop down to join in the fray. Very soon, more than fifty of them were involved in the brawl, and it became hard to see anything for flying feathers. Attempting to escape, Henrietta and Tubby pushed past the queues for the toilet and dived for cover in the clubhouse. By this time, the crows were having so much fun they set about the crowd. It was like a scene from a Hitchcock movie and a great testament to the band that, throughout the skirmish, they kept playing, even when the laxatives made it almost impossible to sit still. All but the tone-deaf would have noticed the gradual but steady rise in pitch, volume, and tempo as legs were crossed ever more tightly. Soon, the part written for a trombone was being played on an entirely different instrument, one that had never been heard in a musical context, not unless Beethoven had written a nocturne for unaccompanied bottom.

***

"You still there, Pithers?" said Puffy when he returned to the phone.

"Puffy!" said Pithering. "Thought you'd done a bunk for a minute, old man. What's the SP?"

"Nothing to wowy about, old chap," reported Puffy. "Bimpkiss has got it on his scween as we speak. Looks as though it was launched in Dorkshire - the Dinc valley to be pwecise. We see all sorts of stwange things come out of that place. Never amounts to a pod of peas, though. I should tell the yanks to stop fussing if I were you."

"Good heavens! The Dinc valley, you say?" said Pithering. "That used to be in daddy's constituency. He never mentioned anything to me. Some sort of secret research establishment, is it?"

"Oh, lordy no, nothing like that old man," said Puffy, surprised that Pithering didn't know more. "That's where the Dinc woman lives. Batty as a six-legged hamster, that one. Blew up Bungbuwy in the war. Didn't you hear about it?"

Pithering said he hadn't and, saying goodbye to Puffy, decided it was time to call General Babcock with the news. The Queen was safe for a bit longer.

Babcock answered the phone immediately it rang, his voice ricocheting down the line like a gunshot. Pithering only had time to say hello before the General interrupted him. "Pithericks! Where the hell have you been? Now, what's this goddamn missile? I've got the President on hold waiting to hear from me."

266

"I say," said Pithering. "The President? Gosh! Well, would you like me to have a word with him, old man?"

General Babcock didn't need to devote too much time to that suggestion. He suspected Pithering was more than dangerous enough without being given access to the most powerful man in the western hemisphere. "Forget it, Pitherkins. The President's a busy man, and so am I. What's going on, for Christ's sake?"

Pithering adopted the most reassuring voice he could muster - the same one he had used just after driving thousands of tons of warship into a major landmass. "Nothing to worry about, really," he chirped. "Just a teensy-weensy little rocket. Quite harmless. Someone in the west of England launched it, but I'm told it's on its way back to earth now. You can tell your chaps to stand down, have a cup of tea and get back to polishing their planes or... or something." He felt the explanation was a good one and enjoyed having a bit of a dig about their shiny planes, but by this time, Babcock had hung up.

Pithering thought this was a bit discourteous, but he wasn't surprised. In common with most officers holding the Queen's commission, he regarded a five-star American general as being roughly equivalent to a lance corporal in the British Army. He tried calling Babcock back and was told the general was taking a nap. Pithering thought he would do the same.

***

While Pithering was dealing with the Americans, the rocket touched down with a thud in Fawcett's back garden. It made such a loud noise that it woke Mrs Fawcett from her afternoon nap. She opened her eyes and stared out from her bedroom at the smouldering article, trying to determine what it was supposed to be. When the smoke eventually cleared, she could see that it was a rocket of some sort, but it still didn't make any sense. What was a rocket, with or without a fitted duvet, doing in her back garden? Someone would have to be shot, but she postponed that pleasure until she called the fire brigade. A rocket in your garden was one thing, but a rocket on fire was quite another. So, setting her twelve-bore to one side, she gathered up her skirt and hurried across to the telephone. Seconds later, an emergency message was transmitted across Dorkshire instructing the Dillchurch Blue Two fire crew to get over to Dinc-Bottom pronto.

As luck would have it, Blue Two was currently stationed on the playing fields only a mile from the property, but the crews' priorities lay in other directions, and they didn't get the message. Still dripping with foam, they had joined in the frantic hunt for a private place to relieve themselves. Some, who had given up hope of ever reaching a proper toilet, were trying to crawl, with their legs tightly crossed, out to the bushes alongside the field. It was an exercise that proved to be their undoing because, once they were on the floor, there was no way up without uncrossing their legs - a movement that had inevitable consequences. To make matters worse, the crows, now ably assisted by a flock of seagulls and some of the ducks, were attacking anything that moved. It wasn't safe to raise your head more than a few inches off the ground.

So, with the fire crew otherwise engaged, things looked bad for Dinc-Bottom. What a good job then that Lady Dinc was on hand to deal with the matter. Recuperating in the fire engine, the crackling noise of the radio woke her up. She located the microphone and answered the call. "Hello. What? Speak up, you fool, SPEAK UP!' she demanded and, having listened for a while, got the gist of the message. Before putting the handset down, she remembered to shout, "Wilco, over and out!" She was very pleased with that bit, and in no time at all, and with a lot of luck, she had the machine started, sirens blazing, and lights flashing. Gears were crunched, engines were revved, and soon, she was on her way out of the playing field, boot down and full speed ahead towards Dinc-Bottom.

"Hey! Someone's nicked the engine, sir! They've nicked the ruddy engine!" shouted Fireman Ellis, pulling up his trousers as quickly as his tortured bowels would allow. The Fire Officer, also squatting in a roadside ditch, called for the crew to give chase "at the double". Unfortunately, there was only one thing his team could accomplish with any urgency, and it had nothing to do with chasing a pilfered appliance. Lady Dinc was on the road faster than a striking rattlesnake, and there was no way anyone could stop her. Feeling euphoric and thoroughly enjoying this new adventure, she broke into a song. "Dinctum's burning, Dinctum's burning, call the engines, call the engines. Fire, fire..." and so on.

On her way to Dinc-Bottom, she passed two police cars approaching from the opposite direction. One contained the Chief Constable, and she waved to him excitedly. He lifted his hand to wave back but stopped when he realised what he was looking at: a fire engine driven by Lady Dinc in a uniform and wearing a bright yellow helmet. Then he noticed a column of foam-covered firefighters, some with their trousers at half mast, trotting along behind the machine. It was a troubling sight, even for a long-serving police officer who thought he'd seen it all. But there was more: Why were so many villagers squatting in the river? Why were the birds attacking people? What on earth was that tune the band were playing? It was very alarming, and he was on the point of telling his driver to get the hell out of there when something very unexpected happened.

***

Time had finally run out for Dinc-Bottom. The intense heat from the rocket engine set fire to the grass, and the flames spread quickly to a vine. The vine, growing rampantly in every direction, passed it to an old tree, and from there, it spread to a pile of rotten carpet next to the cellar. Thanks to Jamsie's early morning activities, the cellar was brimming with a volatile cocktail of oil and the output from all the toilets for miles around. Big Bang!

A blinding flash lit up the hillsides. Then a powerful shockwave travelled outwards from the epicentre, knocking people to the ground. Birds fell from the sky, fish jumped out of the river, and chimneys toppled from rooftops. Up and down the valley, windows shattered, and Dinc-Bottom rose over two hundred feet into the air. The larger bits seemed to hang motionless for a moment before falling with a crash back to the ground. The rest of the building scattered itself randomly across the surrounding landscape. Finally, a shower of soft, brown, and fetid rain came floating down. It was a bit like snow but nowhere near as much fun.

Silence fell across the valley, and nothing moved except for the river, which continued to meander lazily through the broken landscape. Somehow, Lady Dinc had endured the blast, and she now stood bravely outside what had been the front door of Dinc-Bottom, pointing a flaccid hose at the flames still licking the edge of a vast crater. She was hoping someone would turn on the water.

Great Escalations

As silence gave way to the sound of barking dogs, the Chief Constable's car burst into life. Executing a well-rehearsed manoeuvre, the driver reversed rapidly along the road before spinning the car around to face in the opposite direction. Unfortunately, this was the first time he had tried this on a road lightly lubricated with raw sewage. Consequently, the vehicle spun several times and slipped into a ditch before coming to a crunching halt, catapulting Dint off the back seat and most of the way into the glove box. It wasn't the kind of entrance he was hoping for, and he felt somewhat peeved that several of his staff had witnessed the event. However, the situation was dire. So, gathering his composure, he made a top priority call for urgent military assistance. There was no doubt in his mind that this was a textbook state of emergency, and he knew that firm action was required. DC Thorn must have been right about the terrorists, after all.

Dint struggled out of the car to assess the scene. On the playing field in front of him, mud-covered bodies writhed wherever he looked. Some had made it onto their feet, dazed and disoriented, and wondering what the awful pong was. From where he was standing, it looked like the dead had risen, and just as he was about to run away, he spotted the beat-up coach in the corner of the field. He watched as a rag-tag group of highly suspicious individuals tumbled out of the thing, placards at the ready.

As a rule, Dint wasn't one to jump to conclusions, but given the circumstances, he thought he would make an exception. "Constable McLoonie," he shouted. "Arrest that lot and charge them with something." Years of experience had taught him that people with placards were better off behind bars. It didn't matter whether they were left, right, or any other kind of wing. Communist, fascist, or C of E - in his opinion, they were all guilty of something and needed incarcerating somewhere very far away. Australia would have been his first choice, but only because the moon seemed an unrealistic option.

Unaware of the Chief Constable's interest in them, the motley group resumed their protest. Out came the guitar, the digeridoo, and a nose flute. Up went the placards, and the chanting commenced. However, Agnes was no longer among them. The sight of Dr Function's rocket rising into the clouds had unnerved her, and she decided it was probably time to beat a retreat. Quietly scuttling away to her bungalow and bolting the door behind her, Agnes decided to lie low until things had settled down a bit.

"What the hell are we going to do?" asked David as he got back to his feet. He was hoping that Vicki could think of something quickly, but then he looked at her. Covered from tip to toe in a brown mud-like substance, she looked like a clay model, and the stench was dreadful. "God, you look awful," he said, taking a pace away from her. "Sorry, I mean... well, you know. Are you all right?"

"I'll live," she replied. "You're not looking too hot either! I wouldn't have known it was you if you hadn't spoken."

David started to wipe the muck from his face, but before he got very far, Vicki grabbed his hand and pulled it away.

"Hey, stop!" she shouted. "Don't clean up!"

"What? Why?"

"Well, it's obvious?" she said. "This is perfect. No one can tell it's us, can they? We can slip away to my place, get cleaned up, and then, well... we could be days away from here before they come looking for us."

David looked her in the eye. Had her face been a little cleaner, he could have looked into both of them. *It's now, or never*, he thought. "We're going to get the blame. I mean, someone high up will be looking for someone low down to blame, and that'll be me, won't it?"

"And me, David. We're in this together," said Vicki, reaching out to hold his hand. "Anyway, what about the management committee? Won't they be held responsible? Surely, they'll be in the firing line before us?"

"Who knows? Fawcett's probably pushing up daisies by now, and Function will go into hiding - somewhere out of the solar system with luck. Pinkle can't even look at a milk bottle now without fainting, and Lady Dinc, well…" but all David could do was shake his head.

"Okay, so how about we just go home, get cleaned up, and then see what we can do to sort out this mess?"

David agreed. So, they slipped quickly and quietly past the remnants of stalls littering the field on all sides. They could identify some of it, but the rest looked like a war zone with strange, distorted shapes wherever they looked. Some were moving and must have been people, heavily disguised as zombies. There were pieces of a wall, pipes sticking out of cars, and bits of a tree with a badly twisted trumpet still swinging from a branch. Progress through the debris was slow, and to make matters worse, it was proving extremely difficult to breathe. Neither wanted whatever was in the air, making that smell, to get inside their bodies. A gas mask would have been handy, but they made do with some tissues Vicki found in her pocket.

At the far side of the field, Vicki took David through a gap in the fence and then crossed a small stream using a narrow bridge. It was only a hundred yards from there to a track that led into her house, and they covered the ground quickly. Once inside, Vicki pointed David toward the shower, threw him a towel, and found some of her boyfriend's old clothes for him to use. The shower was wonderful, and the hot water soon broke through the dry, crusted muck in his hair. Vicki used a moisturising shower gel, and as soon as he started washing with it, the smell made him think of her. There was something warm and comforting about it.

When he felt refreshed and thoroughly clean, he washed down the shower and went over to the clothes left for him. At that moment, Vicki walked in. David froze.

"What's wrong, seen a ghost?" she asked as she moved towards him.

"Y... you haven't got any clothes on," said David.

"Neither have you," she replied. "Anyway, I don't wear any in the shower. Should I?"

"Well... no, but... well, I guess it's just..." he was stumbling for his words, surprised at how embarrassed he felt. "I'm not exactly used to seeing you like this, that's all."

"Well, don't look then!"

She was standing so close now that he could feel her body's warmth. Pressing herself against him, Vicki kissed him softly on the mouth. He'd never been kissed with such affection and felt like he was melting into her. It was as though they were becoming one person. After the day's traumatic events, it seemed unreal, and he felt a moment of guilt knowing what was going on outside, but he couldn't stop himself. The moment was perfect, and nothing else seemed to matter. Vicki pressed gently on his shoulders, easing him down to the floor and sat across him.

In time, they were laughing. Vicki pointed at some mud that had transferred from her face to his.

"Mud on *my* face?" he asked. You should look at yourself, mate!"

"Oh God!" she said, remembering she still needed a shower. "I must look awful!"

Vicki jumped up quickly, and then, brandishing a long-handled brush she used to clean the bath, she poked him playfully. "Get out of my bathroom, David Faber! Now! Fancy trying to watch a girl while she's taking a shower! Pervert!"

***

The Chief Constable's call for help was answered quickly, and in what seemed to him like the blink of an eye, Giant green helicopters were skimming over the treetops, their rotors thumping loudly as they arced around the valley, looking for a place to set down. Soon, Gurkhas from the barracks in Dincsmouth and Marines from the camp on Flabtackle Down swarmed all over the hillsides. Camouflaged trucks and Land Rovers careered through the lanes, and Police cars followed behind, with sirens blazing and lights flashing. There was even a vehicle with a nest of missiles in the back, zipping along on clanking tracks. It was a shocking scene for a police officer, and as he watched the deployment unfold, Dint's thoughts returned to the warning about terrorists in Thorn's report. He should have taken it more seriously and decided it was high time Mrs Clifton was taken back into custody, so he sent two officers to find and arrest her.

Oblivious to all of this, DC Thorn lay in the back of an ambulance while a medic treated his injuries. Against all odds, he had survived the best efforts of Dinctum Youth Club to execute him and was now enjoying a second dose of morphine. Life was good when you were mainlining painkillers. The conversation with a native American dressed in the skin of a bison had been enlightening. Then he'd been entertained by a tap-dancing nun wearing only a Wimpole and leather thongs. That took his mind off the pain, but the vision didn't last long. A medic leant into his distorted field of view and began speaking.

"Hi, my name's Kirsty," said the beautiful, smiling face. "You gonna be off work for a few weeks, mate. Broken ribs and a nasty gash on your head. You're lucky to be alive." She ducked out of view to fetch more dressings.

Thorn's attention turned to the carnage outside the ambulance as she wound a seemingly endless bandage around his head and chest. He struggled to understand what he was seeing. He'd been out cold for some time, and none of it made sense to him, so he decided the best course of action would be to lie back and rest. After that, there would be pies, which made him feel a lot better, but just as his head touched the pillow, a familiar sound penetrated his hallucinating mind. It was Drivel, and he seemed indifferent to Thorn's obvious injuries.

"All right, guv?" he asked as he eyed the medics' honed body. "Any idea where Clifton is? The Chief wants her arrested pronto."

It was exciting news, and Thorn sat up far too quickly, crying out in pain as his body fought against the sudden movement. The thought of "that blubbing woman" being in cuffs again delighted him, and he wasn't going to miss it.

Against his better judgement, Drivel helped Thorn out of the ambulance, and soon, they were making their way unsteadily through the debris in search of the Chief. Drivel did his best to explain what had happened, and by the time they found Dint, Thorn was determined to persecute Clifton all the way to the back of the deepest and darkest prison cell he could find.

The Chief Constable was shocked when he saw Thorn approaching. He was barely recognisable under all the bandages and looked like something from a crypt. Thorn begged to be allowed to interrogate Clifton again.

"Please let me do her, guv," he said with clasped hands. "I wanna do her, guv. She's as guilty as fuck, and I'll make her squeal. Please!"

He was almost on his knees, but the Chief was having none of it. Thorn was obviously in pain, and there was the look of a madman about him, especially in his eyes. So, it was a very gloomy Detective Constable who trailed back across the field towards the ambulance with orders to rest and stay out of the way. Under normal circumstances, he would have welcomed the time off duty, but today was different. He'd been right about Clifton all along, and no one had taken him seriously. They all thought he was a fool. Someone else would get all the glory of arresting and charging a terrorist. A Terrorist! In Dorkshire of all places! It was unheard of, and all he had to show for it was a few weeks of sick pay. Thorn wasn't exactly ecstatic about that and fuelled by a potent cocktail of pride and opiates, albeit the legal variety, he decided to disobey orders – entirely. "Sod this for a lark," he said. "I'm gonna show the bastards."

***

Two more fire engines had joined those already on site and were hard at work damping down the remains of Dinc-Bottom and the Volvo, which was still smouldering in the middle of the playing field. This shouldn't have come as a great surprise because, as everyone knows, Volvos tend to go on and on forever, even the charred variety.

Lady Dinc had relinquished control of her hose, but only after the Chief Constable had personally intervened. She looked disheartened and stood staring at the ground like a child whose toys had been taken away. Constable Bradbury was told to escort the "wretched woman" back to Dinctum Manor as fast as possible, so he got in his police car and set off to find her.

When she saw him approaching, Lady Dinc tried to run away, but Bradbury wasn't in the mood for playing games and quickly boxed her in. After a tirade of the foulest language he had ever heard, she reluctantly got in the vehicle and sat sulking in the back seat.

They hadn't gone more than a hundred yards when she prodded Bradbury firmly in the back. "I say! You there! DRIVER!"

PC Bradbury didn't respond, so she grabbed a rolled-up map from the footwell and hit him on the back of his head. "YOU THERE!" she shouted and, having got his attention, gave strict instructions for the blue flashing lights and siren to be switched on "this instant". Bradbury decided it was better to keep the peace inside the car at the expense of everyone outside, so he grudgingly complied.

David and Vicki were dressed and feeling much better now that they were clean again. As they stood in the kitchen making a cup of tea, they tried to decide what to do next. Leaving the valley was still David's preferred option, but their deliberations were interrupted by a loud knocking on the door.

"Oh God!" said David. "Who the hell is that?"

It sounded like the knock a police officer would make, or worse still, an extremely angry and enormous fiancé. He looked desperately around the room for somewhere to hide, but it was too late. Just as he was about to crawl under the carpet, the door opened, and in stepped...

"Gavin!" exclaimed Vicki.

"Hi Vicki, hi David. You Okay then?" he asked.

Gavin seemed perfectly cheerful. If he was worried by the events unfolding outside, he certainly didn't show it. "It's all right," he said, seeing the look on David's face. "Vicki gave me a key ages ago, honest, and I wasn't breaking in or anything. Lovely bang that, wasn't it?" he said, referring to the explosion that obliterated Dinc-Bottom. "They found Fawcett and his misses stuck up an oak tree next to the boneyard. They're both Okay – well, as Okay as they've ever been, I suppose."

David wasn't feeling quite so light-hearted and had a few questions for Gavin. "Tell me," he began, "who was responsible for the laxatives, and why did Dinc-Bottom explode so violently? And while you're at it, who filled the bouncy castle with helium, and who made Fawcett's earpiece blow up and..." but the blank expression on Gavin's face told him he wasn't going to get an answer.

Vicki thought it best to change tack. "Is everyone all right?" she asked. "We ought to go back and help if we can."

Gavin disagreed. He told them the best thing to do was to stay out of the way while the police and army handled things. "If you go out there now, you'll only get nabbed by someone and end up in a pile of kack. Take my word for it."

"We've already been in a pile of kack," said David. "I'll be going down with typhoid any minute now, thanks to you lot." But Gavin insisted.

"Trust me on this," he said. "I'd lie low for an hour or two, honestly."

Vicki took the hint. Gavin clearly knew more than he was letting on and was warning them to stay out of the way. "He's right, David. Let's sit this out for a bit. Please?" David agreed but couldn't help feeling he was missing out on something.

"Cool," said Gavin. "It's for the best. Now, I got to scoot. Things to do, you know. I'll leave you two to, um… get on with it." He winked at them as he left the house.

The beating blades of a helicopter flying low overhead rattled the kitchen windows. There were more of them now, circling the valley like vultures over a carcass.

"Another cuppa?" asked Vicki as she refilled the kettle.

"Why don't we go to bed instead?" said David. "I mean, there isn't anything else to do, is there?"

"No chance, mate," said Vicki firmly. "Not with all this excitement going on outside. I want to see what happens next."

"But..."

"No."

"B..."

"No!"

***

Constable Hewbry was in a state of shock when he got out of his police van and stared at the scene. It was a long time since he'd brought Fang for a tour of the Dinc valley, and he was pretty sure it hadn't looked like this before - he would have noticed. Fang was excited and keen to get out of the vehicle because, amongst all the noxious odours his delicate nose perceived, one stood out in particular: sausage. Fang had an exceptionally well-developed sausage detection organ between his pointy ears, and it was making him dribble quite a lot. There had been a barbeque somewhere in the vicinity, and he was now totally focused on locating it. Once he had made up his mind, there was no stopping him, and he could easily drag Hewbry bodily across the field if he wanted.

While Hewbry struggled to hold back fate, two army Land Rovers pulled up next to the clubhouse. Soldiers jumped out and were hurriedly erecting aerials and banging in posts. A portable generator spluttered into life, filling the air with thick blue, oily fumes. Another squad had just finished putting up a large tent when a Royal Navy helicopter swept low across the field and blew it down. An angry Corporal ran to the back of a nearby truck, looking for a heat-seeking missile to "blow the fucking pansy out of the sky". Fortunately, a Captain stopped him before there was a friendly fire incident, but the Corporal wasn't impressed. "Why's the fucking Navy flying about the fucking sky anyway, sir? They're supposed to be floating in the fucking sea, aren't they?" But his argument didn't win the Captain over. So, denied the opportunity of getting even with the Senior Service, the Corporal shuffled back to the collapsed tent, waving a fist in the air as he went and shouting, "Piss off with you!"

Chief Constable Dint was beginning to feel less anxious and decided to relax a bit. It seemed to him that everything was now under control, and they were in the mopping-up phase. No one was launching missiles. The Army wasn't shooting anyone, and the villagers appeared to be going home. It was all very satisfactory, and he decided to congratulate himself.

"Well done, Chief. I think that was all handled remarkably well. Take the rest of the year off and have a pay rise too."

"Well, that is very generous, I must say. Thank you very much, Chief. How about a cup of tea?"

"Good idea, Chief. Some biscuits as well, I think."

"Indeed."

Unfortunately, there were those in the valley whose plans didn't include the Chief Constable enjoying an afternoon tea – with or without a plate of hobnobs.

Die Dinctum, Die!

Curiosity had finally gotten the better of Agnes Braintree. She'd listened intently to the bangs and crashes, the sirens and helicopters, for long enough. It was time to find out what was going on. Perhaps one of her ham-radio associates had finally come up with the goods? In her opinion, they hadn't been much help, just a lot of talk and no substance. She'd been promised landmines, incendiaries, tanks, and even a couple of thermonuclear warheads, but so far, all she had was a placard.

Wrapping a scarf tightly around her head and donning dark sunglasses to cover her eyes, Agnes slipped stealthily out of her bungalow. Strolling casually towards the noise, she pretended to examine a bush here and a flower there, but her attempts to go unnoticed didn't fool Jamsie. He had been allotted the task of looking out for her and was now watching intently as she ambled along furtively, moving from one side of the road to the other. Once he was confident it was 'Brainless', he dashed to where Peter and

Joseph were hiding. "Braintree's out!" he gasped. "She's coming down the road now with a blue scarf on her head!"

Joseph, now the proud owner of a mobile phone, quickly dialled a number and gave the code words. "Gibbon to dick-splash. Gibbon to dick-splash. The banana has split, and the egg is hatched. Over and out."

***

Mobile phones had shifted the balance of power in the valley, and it was getting increasingly tricky for the police to stay one step ahead. Constable 'Dinga' Bell had noticed how difficult it had become to turn up unannounced and catch the buggers at it. Even his cunningly disguised speed traps were proving less than effective lately. It used to be that getting dressed up as a privet bush and hiding in the hedgerow with his speed camera would always guarantee a result. Now, word got around, and the roads were always empty. The privet outfit was the best he could manage without professional assistance. He'd visited the fancy dress shop in Dillchurch, but the only other outfit they had in his size was a mole suit with realistic paws and an illuminated nose. Hell would freeze over before anyone caught him wearing something like that. To throw people off the scent, he'd taken to leaving a blow-up doll dressed in police uniform at his desk in the local station. If you glanced casually through the window, you'd think he was still in there, diligently writing his reports. When he turned up for an impromptu inspection one morning, the Chief Constable certainly thought so. However, the somewhat stilted conversation and enormous breasts eventually gave the game away - that and the foot pump trailing out from between the 'officers' legs. It had taken many hours of explaining and months of extra duties before the Chief got off Dinga's back. It ruined things for WPC Felony too: she couldn't sit at her desk in Dillchurch nick without the Chief sending someone to check for an airline disappearing up her skirt.

****

There were innumerable buzzards in the Dinc Valley. When they weren't soaring beneath the clouds competing for airspace, you could find them sitting in a field waiting for something small and furry to twitch a whisker. If you were small and furry, it wasn't safe to do anything with your whiskers in the Dinc Valley. If the buzzards didn't get you, one of the several hundred pet cats would.

Thanks to the exploding building, there weren't any buzzards aloft that afternoon, but if there had been, they might have spotted some odd goings on. Behind the Duck and Dinc, outside the toilets, hushed voices discussed the next phase of a convoluted plan. It was anyone's guess whether this was a new plot or an extension of one started earlier that year. Only one or two individuals in the valley could say with certainty, and they were carefully setting up their alibis. Watches were synchronised, and lists were memorised but not eaten - that would have been silly. Then they divided into several assault teams. Becky wasted everyone's time arguing that she wanted to be in a pepper team. "If you can have a salt team," she said, "surely you can have a pepper team as well?"

287

Having agreed that Becky was a complete tit by any measure, they deployed, some making for Dr Function's workshop, others to a barn in Dinctum Splashit. A third group set off to Agnes Braintree's bungalow, and Steven Gosling, dressed in his Army Cadet Force battle fatigues, slunk off towards the Chief constable's car. They moved swiftly, creeping silently along little-used paths, over fences, and under hedges. Even the Special Air Service could have learnt something from this lot. No one noticed them, not even the Buzzards.

***

At about this time, Major Roland Finch, who had just arrived, got out of his Land Rover and marched briskly towards the Chief Constable.

"Are you the senior policeman here?" he enquired in a manner guaranteed to displease Dint.

"I am," replied the Chief, without even looking up from the map he was studying. "And you are?"

"I'm the officer in charge of this incident. Major Finch, Royal Marines. I'm setting up my HQ next to the clubhouse in that field over th..." but he didn't get any further.

The Chief looked up slowly, regarding the Marine with a menacing gaze. "You'll put your bloody HQ where I damn well say so, soldier. This is a civilian incident until I bloody well say otherwise. Now, go away and report back to me at *my* incident control in twenty minutes. Good day to you, sir!"

Finch considered arguing but thought better of it. The last words his CO said to him - "liaise with and assist the civilian authorities" - were still ringing in his ears. He decided to back down and stomped off to play with his radio.

***

Peter, Joseph, and Simon quickly succeeded in penetrating Dr Function's workshop. They were now rooting around in murky corners for anything that appeared to match the items they had memorised a few moments earlier. Soon, they had a barrow full of stuff which they carefully concealed beneath a tarpaulin and bits of a hedge. Then, checking the coast was clear, they trundled back up the road past the police, the soldiers, and the few remaining mud-coloured villagers towards Braintree's bungalow. No one thought twice about a few kids pushing a wheelbarrow full of bush. On arriving at the Braintree residence, they spent several entertaining minutes picking over the spoils they had unearthed.

Elsewhere, John, Carol, and Becky were almost at the end of their journey to Dinctum Splashit. It had taken slightly longer than planned because, thanks to the recent downpour, the river at Shit Creek was higher than usual. Having navigated the obstacle and after running half a mile along a dirt track, they reached a decaying barn surrounded by ancient-looking oak trees. Rusting trailers, tractors, and other oddly shaped farm implements stuck out from the brambles. The barn door hung from its hinges, and they pushed their way through.

Beneath the collapsing roof and hidden behind a pile of empty milk crates stood a copper still, bubbling away over a gentle flame. Comprising of a converted immersion heater and with a mass of coiled pipework, it looked very complicated and ought to have been surrounded by men in white coats. One of the pipes was longer than the others and wound through a hole in the wall to an adjacent outbuilding, where it made its way into a large plastic container. Carol took out some pliers and carefully crimped the pipe flat, sealing it perfectly. At the same time, John and Becky discovered how to turn up the heat. Suddenly, the still was bubbling and creaking quite alarmingly. It was time to leave, so they slipped back along the road into the village and vanished. Behind them, the pressure was building. It wouldn't hold out for long.

***

Once he had made a few notes and briefed a group of rather excitable officers, the Chief Constable decided that he was ready to talk to the military, so he sent for Major Finch and his second in command, Captain Willis. He wasn't going to have them calling the shots and was still highly annoyed by Finch's arrogant manner. Had it been an option, the Chief would have put him on extra duties for months, possibly years. However, the two officers appeared almost immediately, and Dint was quietly impressed, wishing that some of his staff would jump to it that quickly.

Although Dint still had his suspicions about Mrs Clifton and her terrorist activities, he decided it would be best to play them down for the time being.

"Right, gentlemen, listen in and listen carefully," he said, using the most commanding tone he could muster. "As you know, we've had a series of quite unusual events here in Dinctum today, all of which are still under investigation. However, much of it appears to be the result of an unfortunate set of accidents and unhappy coincidence." He paused for a moment, partly for dramatic effect but also to give them time to digest his words. "I know there are some who subscribe to a conspiracy theory - terrorists and all that - but I can assure you that my officers have found nothing whatsoever to support that view at this stage." He paused again to see if there were any questions, and there were none, so he went on. "A press representative has been asking questions about a so-called missile and the alleged use of a chemical weapon, specifically an 'airborne laxative'. I want to make it absolutely clear that I will be the only one dealing with the press. No one else, I repeat, no one is to communicate with them in any way, understood?"

They all agreed.

***

Unfortunately, Jamsie hadn't been invited to the briefing and knew nothing of the Chief Constable's wishes, so he felt free to say what he liked to anyone he chose. To that end, he had the attention of an excited reporter and told him everything he knew about the afternoon's events. Peter and Joseph turned up and were only too happy to corroborate his story. It went something like this: The fun day was all going wonderfully when this missile appeared in the sky, heading straight for the village. Thankfully, a freak gust of wind blew it away from the crowd, but they could make out a message in large red letters along its length saying "DIE DINCTUM, DIE". They told how it blew up Dinc-Bottom and how, as it passed overhead, a shower of fine powder had rained down. Someone was trying to poison the Dinc valley residents. "It was a weapon of mass destruction," they said.

They piled it on as thick as Dorkshire clotted cream, and the reporter lapped it up like a fevered cat. He called his office and told them the story, tripping over his words as they gushed out. "Get a photographer down here fast, Melvin!" he said. "We've got a world exclusive on our hands!" He was quite possibly the most excited person in the western hemisphere.

Unsurprisingly, all the rival news agencies had hacked into each other's telephones. So, before you could say D notice, every major news channel, and broadsheet had its hacks slithering into the valley as fast as they could wriggle. The Chief started to feel more than a little queasy when they began to appear. First, there were the brightly coloured helicopters sprouting cameras with powerful lenses. Then came the press corps motorbikes and cars, breaking every speed limit in the land to get there. Finally, the 'heavy guns' with their truck-mounted satellite dishes appeared. That they mobilised in less than half the time it had taken the Army remained a lifelong mystery to both the Chief Constable and Major Finch.

Doing their best to avoid being noticed, Peter, Joseph, and Simon emerged from Braintree's bungalow, looking very satisfied. They checked their watches before walking smartly off to hide behind the pub. Everything was ready.

Escape and Evasion

Chief Constable Dint felt increasingly alarmed as the valley filled with journalists and camera crews. His stomach was starting to churn, which was never a good sign, and keeping a low profile suddenly became his top priority. Some of the media appeared to be from foreign lands, their trucks and branded clothing bearing strange symbols and unpronounceable names. As any Chief Constable worth his salt knows, international fame can quickly lead to a job back on the beat – or worse – so he started to think about how best to avoid the inevitable interviews and challenging questions. Suddenly it came to him: Finch! He wanted a bit of glory so he could bloody well deal with it.

In a flash, he had an officer despatched to convey the glad tidings to the officer, but Finch was less than impressed with the proposal. He knew a bad hand when he saw it and passed the task like a slippery, wet thing directly to Captain Willis. Willis wasn't entirely joyous either, but he knew he had to get on with at least until some lowly lieutenant arrived. Then he could pass the buck.

Willis did the best he could to calm the clamouring journalists and debunk the rumours, telling them that it was all just an unfortunate accident, but no one wanted to believe him, and who could blame them? How often did a story of this magnitude come along? How many extra papers would it sell the following morning? 'Weapons Of Mass Destruction Hit Rural Village' was a good headline. There was money in a headline like that. So, no longer interested in the truth, they pursued every rumour or theory they could lay their hands on, and the more Captain Willis denied things, the more the press assumed he must be hiding something. The smell of a cover-up hung over this story, and they were going to expose it.

At that moment, the still exploded. A flash and the pressure wave which followed knocked everyone to the ground. Willis shouted, "Take Cover!" but realised everyone except him had already done so.

Shots rang out as soldiers, dug into the hillsides, started firing at the barn in Dinctum Splashit. Others from around the valley joined in, and soon, hundreds of rounds poured into the old building. After surviving centuries of misuse and two world wars, it was quickly reduced to nothing more than a heap of smouldering rubble. Major Finch was quick to act and was on the radio faster than a rat up a rifled drainpipe. "Who the bloody hell was that?" he screamed into the microphone. "Cease-fire! Cease-fire!" But the valley's shape ensured the gunfire echoed from all directions. It was easy to believe someone was out there, hidden in the hedgerows returning fire, so the shooting continued.

The press, some of whom had only ever reported on missing cats, were trying to dig holes with their bare hands. Two satellite trucks raced out of the village, pulling down telegraph poles and miles of cable as they went.

Finch got on the radio again, trying to gain control of his trigger-happy troops. "Hello, all stations, all stations, this is Pip Squeak. Cease-fire. I say again. This is Pip Squeak. CEASE-FIRE!" He stopped to listen, but there were still shots coming from somewhere. Perhaps there was something wrong with the radio, and they couldn't hear him? He decided to find out. "Hello, all stations. This is Pip Squeak, radio check. Over."

After a short delay, the troops started to call in. "Two-one, OK. Over!" said the first.

"Two-two, OK. Over!"

"Two-Three, OK. Over!" and so on until everyone was accounted for.

Then, from out of the ether, a new voice chipped in. "Hello, one! This is another one!"

Finch stared at his radio, wondering if it was just his imagination, but the voice spoke again, "Hello, one! This is another one! I can see you, but you can't see me! Ha ha!"

Finch grabbed angrily at the handset, pressed a button, and bellowed into the microphone. "Who the bloody hell is that? Identify yourself now. Who the hell are you?" he demanded.

There was silence for a few seconds before another transmission broke through the crackling static. It was a female voice this time. "Hello, Pip Squeak. Hello Pip Squeak. This is Mary Poppins. I say again. This is Mary Poppins!" The voice broke into a rendition of 'just a spoonful of sugar' and soon, several other voices had joined in. Finch threw the handset down and stared out at the hills around him. You couldn't conduct a military operation with a ruddy musical going on - he was sure of that and noted with some displeasure that most of the voices now taking part belonged to Gurkhas - the strong Nepali accent gave them away. Next came a rendition of Supercalifragilistic... and so on.

Finch sat in his Land Rover and sulked. He'd volunteered for this mission and was beginning to regret it. His face, accompanied by a badly performed and clearly audible backing track, was about to be broadcast live to an incredulous world. In his professional opinion, nothing good could come of that. His entire afternoon was turning to rat-shit, and it was increasingly likely that his career would go the same way.

***

Once the singing had stopped and the remains of the still had found their way back to the planet, it was time for phase two. Joseph motioned to Jamsie. "Time to go for it, matey," he said. "Enjoy."

They say revenge is the sweetest of things, and for Jamsie, the sight of Dinc-Bottom fully loaded with a brace of Fawcetts hurtling skywards had been very satisfying. Now, it was Braintree's turn, and this would be the icing on his carefully crafted cake. Taking a deep breath, he strolled across to the first important-looking journalist he could find. *Oh, look,* he said to himself in a satisfied tone. *A television crew too. Even better!*

The reporter was in the middle of having his tan re-applied and a few stray hairs glued firmly into place when Jamsie wandered up. "Oi! Matey!" he shouted. "Want to see where the terrorists live?"

An excited crew hastily grabbed their equipment and followed Jamsie along the road to a gate outside Agnes Braintree's home. Jamsie pointed to the front door, which was now wide open. The crew looked inside, and the reporter suddenly developed an embarrassingly damp patch. Every room was stacked full of missiles in various states of disassembly, each covertly transported from Function's workshop a little earlier. There were bottles of coloured liquids and pills, which the reporters decided could only be nerve agents, so they quickly set up cameras to beam pictures to a waiting world. Jamsie showed them a pile of detailed blueprints describing how to build the missiles. He watched with great satisfaction as other news teams began piling through the door and permitted himself a wry smile saying quietly, "Braintree is going to be in it up to her nasty little earrings."

***

Chief Constable Dint hid in the back of his car. The sound of rifle fire and explosions had unnerved him, and he rapidly concluded the situation was better handled by the armed services – in support of the police, of course. He wasn't going to relinquish control that easily. As he listened to the story unfold on the car radio, an officer approached with that 'I've got some bad news' look on his face. Dint wound down the window to hear what he had to say.

"Sir, could you answer your phone, please?" he asked politely. "The Home Secretary has been trying to reach you, and I think she would like a word."

Suddenly, the Chief Constable felt very alone. There were only two reasons a Home Secretary would call someone in his position: a knighthood or deportation. He thought he knew which one it would be and tried to remember if his vaccinations were up to date. Picking up the phone, Dint switched it on and waited only a few seconds before it started to ring. He noted that the caller's number was withheld. *I'd like to bet that's what's going to happen to my bloody pension*, he thought.

"Chief Constable Di..." he said as cheerfully as possible, but that was as far as he got. It was his turn to shut up and listen.

"Ah... there you are," said the Home Secretary in a somewhat irritated tone." I'm hoping you will tell me you already have this maniac Braintree in custody and properly charged?"

Dint swallowed nervously and began fiddling with the buttons on his uniform. "Ah, well... not... not as such, Ma'am," he spluttered. "I... She hasn't been positively linked to any of this yet. She's just a headmistress, you know, and doesn't appear to have... that is to say, she hasn't..." but his voice trailed off. He knew he wasn't making much sense.

"Now, you listen carefully, Chief Constable, or is it to be just plain old Constable from now on?" The politician paused momentarily to give weight to her words. "I've got the PM breathing down my neck over this and every kind of news agency you care to mention phoning my staff. I don't care if that woman's a nun in her spare time and her farts smell of lavender. As I speak, there's enough evidence on the television to keep her banged up for the next twenty-five years. So, Chief Constable, you get your backside into gear, find her, and lock her up. Now!"

"But Ma'am, she might be completely innocent," said the Chief, although he didn't know why he was bothering to stand up for the confounded woman.

"I don't seem to be getting through to you, do I?" snapped the politician. "She isn't innocent anymore. We've got an international incident developing down there, and if we have to lock up one *miserable* little member of the public for all eternity to stop it, that's exactly what we... what YOU will do. As it happens, and you're not really authorised to know this, every security service in NATO has a file as thick as your skull on our dear Mrs Braintree. Arrest her! Good day to you!" She had hung up before Dint had time to answer.

Dint stared into his lap for a few moments and then called over the nearest officer. It was Bradbury, back from his expedition to Dinctum Manor. "I want Agnes Braintree taken into custody on suspicion of perpetrating an act of terrorism - something like that anyway. Find her, put her in chains, and take her away. Do it now."

Bradbury wasn't used to working like this and hesitated until the Chief motioned him away. "Well, get on with it then. Get on with it! And then get someone to bring me a cup of tea. Wait, on second thoughts, get me the tea first." It was turning into a long day.

***

Jamsie still had a TV crew in tow, and promising to lead them to an actual terrorist, made his way back to the playing fields. Having just arrived at the Braintree residence, the police were playing catch up. Any chance of preserving the scene for forensic examination had vanished. The place was full of reporters, photographers, and camera crews poking into every corner. There was an American woman with a face of a thousand lifts, doing a piece to camera in the living room, carelessly waving a rocket motor around while, just around the corner in the hall, a Japanese journalist shouted two hundred words a minute into his portable recorder. It was utter chaos, and no one wanted to leave, no matter what the police did. Half of them claimed not to speak English.

As he approached the playing field, Jamsie could see the lonely, half-hidden figure of Agnes Braintree, looking quietly at the mess everywhere. *It was supposed to be a playing field*, she thought. *Somewhere for the children to play rounders, hockey, and lacrosse on sports afternoons, and now look at it.* "It's that blasted youth club again," she seethed. "Absolute vandals, every last one of them!"

Furious that they still hadn't been taught a well-deserved lesson, she turned around and came face to face with a familiar little shape standing squarely in front of her. It took a moment to recollect where she had seen it before, but her rage found new heights when she did. Several reporters, sound engineers, and a growing collection of expensive, broadcast-quality video cameras were on hand to witness it. Everyone took a pace backwards. Even the cameras seemed to move of their own volition.

With his heart thumping loudly in his chest, Jamsie plucked up enough courage to speak. He was shaking from head to foot and began to wish he'd been plied with vodka. It certainly helped the last time he was looking at the headteacher. With a great effort, he began.

"Good evening, Mrs Brainstreams!" he said, carefully reciting the words he'd rehearsed an hour or two earlier. "I couldn't help noticing what a lovely... a lovely fine day it is, and I wondered if you'd like to *have* this?" he asked, producing the biggest banana anyone had ever seen with a great flourish. "I know you have quite a thing for them, and I'm sure it would fit perfectly."

Agnes looked on in silence for a moment, applying her increasingly dysfunctional mind to the situation. The rage and humiliation building inside grew with every second, making her swell larger than ever before. Jamsie thought she was going to detonate. She rocked slowly back and forth, words piling up one on top of another behind gritted teeth until she could contain herself no longer. "You... YOU... You nasty little SHIT! How dare you speak to me like that! HOW DARE YOU!" her eyes looked ready to burst out of their sockets. "You... ssslither around in that sssmelly little club getting DRUNK, TAKING DRUGS, FORNICATING! DON'T YOU DARE TELL ME I'VE GOT A FAT BOTTOM, DON'T YOU BLOODY WELL DARE!"

Her rage filled the valley, and the clouds seemed to grow darker. The birds fell silent again, and the ducks in the river hid in the reeds. Jamsie kept grinning, and, reasonably sure that none of the cameras was focused on his face, he decided to risk poking his tongue out. It did the trick. Agnes Braintree screamed with anger, clenching her fists tightly by her side. She began to shake. It was a moment Jamsie savoured, mainly because he knew he'd be able to watch it all over again on the News at Ten later that evening. The TV crew and reporters had no idea why Mrs Braintree was shouting about the size of her bottom, but it confirmed their initial impression: the woman was utterly barking. Anyway, it made good viewing.

At that moment, Agnes Braintree spotted two of Dorkshire's most formidable police officers approaching from across the field. She had no idea why they were coming but knew instinctively that it was her that they wanted. She hesitated, glancing this way and that without moving her head. Suddenly, and to the total surprise of everyone watching, Agnes did a runner. She was off like the wind in the opposite direction as fast as she could, and her departure was so rapid that it caught everyone unawares. Slow to give chase, they were all a good twenty yards behind her when, having run out of playing field, Agnes changed direction. For someone of her build, she turned fully about in a flash and ran straight towards the pursuing crowd, causing them to trip over each other and fall in a sprawling heap. Stepping lightly amongst them, Agnes charged with all the force of a locomotive towards the clubhouse. If she could make it to a Land Rover parked there, an escape might be possible.

The two police officers tasked with her arrest started blowing their whistles, but it didn't do any good. Agnes wasn't stopping for anything. Only two things in the valley took notice: the Twinkin sisters, who began jumping up and down again, and Fang.

After consuming approximately fifty barbecued sausages, Fang had been taking a nap when the sound of the whistles woke him. It aroused distant memories in his dark and disturbed mind, and the sight of someone running rang bells too. He got up stiffly and stretched. Constable Hewbry lay beside him, utterly exhausted. Having been dragged against his will to the barbeque by Fang, he refused to go anywhere else and had detached the dog's leash. As far as he was concerned, Fang was free to roam wherever he wanted, and to hell with the consequences.

As Agnes Braintree got closer to her intended means of escape, Fang started to trot toward her. Only half awake, he wasn't sure why he was doing it but decided he would probably remember sooner or later. On an average day, Fang could have overtaken her in seconds and nibbled her backside to see if she squealed. But today, he was replete with cremated bangers and not especially interested in doing anything, so he moved at a more leisurely gait.

Agnes managed to reach the vehicle and get seated safely inside before anyone could stop her. As luck would have it, it was one of the radio vehicles, so the engine was left running to charge the many batteries it carried. She lost no time in engaging a gear, floored the throttle, and sped off towards the road. A smile broke across her face for the first time that afternoon, and she started to think about where she could go. Had she looked in the back of the vehicle, she might have pulled over and climbed a tree because, there between the radios, curled up on a camouflage net, was Fang. He had made one last effort and jumped unseen into the back of the vehicle as it left the playing field. The effort had left him feeling tired again, and since time appeared to be on his side, a nap felt like the best option. He would decide what, if anything, he was going to do with his prey when he woke up.

A Hunting We Shall Go

When she encountered the first roadblock, Agnes Braintree was going too fast to stop, but it didn't matter. She was in a military vehicle, so they mistakenly let her pass. However, radio messages were beaming all over the valley, and by the time she had reached the outskirts of Winterbourne Dinctum, another more substantial obstacle was in place. Overhead, one of the Royal Navy helicopters had caught up and circled loudly just above the treetops, busily sending situation reports to anyone who was listening. This included Agnes Braintree because her Land Rover had one of the most sophisticated military radio systems in NATO. She could hear every word they said and knew the way ahead was blocked. So, at the first opportunity, she turned off the road taking a track to the left. It wasn't the best decision she made that day. In fact, it was probably the worst because, within a short distance, Agnes found herself staring at the imposing entrance to Dinctum Manor. On either side of the gravel drive, enormous granite pillars supported giant cast iron vultures. Agnes felt her blood run cold as she drove beneath their menacing gaze. It was easy to believe they could take flight at any moment. Lady Dinc had very few visitors on account of those threatening artworks. So, as Agnes inched slowly along the serpentine drive, she kept checking the vehicle's mirrors just in case there were a couple of large, slightly rusty birds of prey in hot pursuit.

Some distance ahead, Lady Dinc was filling up on paracetamol. She had a headache that was big enough to give an elephant nausea - probably one of the pink ones she'd entertained in the rose garden the previous evening. On top of that, all the excitement that afternoon had left her completely exhausted and desperate for a nap. So, reclined on a damp and discoloured sofa, she placed large bags of frozen vegetables on either side of her head and prepared to doze off.

Dinctum Manor was full of empty rooms and lengthy corridors. There were secret passages, impossibly deep cellars, countless tunnels, and drafty, cavernous lofts. As a result, all sorts of strange and often disturbing noises reverberated around the building. Most were familiar to her, but as she sprawled there with frost-bitten ears, a new sound started to permeate her addled brain. It wasn't a sound she could easily place, but it was definitely getting louder, and it was starting to irritate her. On and on it went until she could feel the floorboards under her feet vibrating. Pictures rattled on the wall, and ornaments fell to the floor. Nothing in Dinctum Manor had ever sounded like this - not even her electric mangle when it consumed the vacuum cleaner. Her grandfather had once used the snooker room as a grenade range, but even that didn't create as much of a din.

Suddenly, she sat bolt upright. The sprouts fell to the floor, and as her ears began to thaw, she recognised the penetrating whine and thudding vibrations for what they were: some fool was trying to land a helicopter on her roof. In fact, the noise was so loud that she began to think it was already flying around inside the loft. Bats in the belfry was one thing, but a giant, turbine-powered, mechanical dragonfly was beyond the pale. She was going to have stiff words with someone about the wretched thing and leaping to her feet, Lady Dinc crossed the dimly lit room towards a dusty old leather-topped desk where she was sure a phone lurked. A pile of papers, almost a foot deep, covered the antique. As she angrily tossed documents first to one side and then to the other, a cloud of dust enveloped her. "Where's the bloody phone," she demanded. Patience wasn't one of her virtues.

Lady Dinc rarely opened her letters and paid no attention at all to bills, bank statements, or final demands. Dumped in piles around the building, she permitted the family accountants, Godfreys, Skwots & Squertz (deceased), entry once a year to go through her affairs. She didn't like accountants saying they reminded her of lizards, so they were only given half a day to gather up all they could carry. If it hadn't been for the considerable fee they could charge, G S & S (decd.) would have left the work to another firm. However, for that much cash, most of which was in used notes, they would find a way.

Consequently, G S & S (still alive and kicking at this point) had purchased a truck typically used to clear the roadside drains and adapted it for house clearance. They could empty an entire mansion of its paperwork in less time than it took Lady Dinc to clear a public house of its bar stock. They frequently did a good job cleaning the carpets too, and often left the house without a shred of toilet paper. If you were unfortunate enough to be 'powdering your nose' when they evacuated the lavatories, you could easily find yourself with complicated internal injuries. This is what happened to Mr Squertz, who never recovered from the experience.

Finding the phone, Lady Dinc punched in 999. It was the only number she could ever remember, and she found that if she persisted, it usually got her what she wanted. On this occasion, she wanted the Chief Constable and, when told he was unavailable, decided to leave a message. "Right, well, you can tell him that this is Lady Dinc of Dinctum Manor, and if he doesn't do something about Biggles and his bloody flying machine this instant, I'm going to shoot the sodding thing out of the sky! Good day to you!" She threw the phone to one side and set off to the cellars. There was almost certainly an arms cache down there amongst the forgotten relics, deep under the manor.

***

Agnes Braintree was in a lot of trouble. The radio traffic had told her that much, but what was she to do? A cold sweat broke across her brow. The way back was bound to be heavily guarded, and the sight of a helicopter hovering overhead told her that it was pointless trying to sneak out into the surrounding countryside. Open fields surrounded the Manor on three sides, and on the other, dense woodland marked the eastern border of Cold Waddock Forest. It would be almost impossible for anyone to track her in there, but the probability of ever finding her way out again was remote. It wasn't worth the risk – not yet anyway. On the other hand, she wouldn't give up and surrender. Absolutely not! The only option was to take refuge in the Manor even though every fibre of her being told her it was a bad idea. However, there were rumours of a secret tunnel leading from the cellars to an old monastery near Bungbury north of the valley. It was worth a go, and so, with her heart pounding, Agnes pressed onwards.

The Manor House was a vast white building with countless windows and an enormous, covered entrance supported by four magnificent pillars. Even Agnes, in her desperate state of mind, was impressed by the building as she covered the last quarter mile up a shallow rise towards the front doors. She brought the Land Rover to a sudden stop outside the house, catapulting Fang, who was still snoozing, nose-first into the bulkhead behind her. He woke suddenly and found himself in an exceedingly lousy mood. Unaware of her secret passenger, Agnes left the vehicle and hurried into the house, pushing the great wooden doors aside as she went. They were at least three times her height, covered in a thick, gloss black lacquer, and fitted with large brass handles worn smooth from centuries of use. She had to find a way into those tunnels.

Fang, by now a fearsome ball of hairy rage, leapt over the tailgate and followed Agnes into the building. But, after only a short distance, he became acutely aware of an uncomfortable cramp in his abdomen. The feast of sausages earlier that afternoon, and, in particular, the specially prepared barbeque sauce, were beginning to take effect. He'd consumed enough laxative to drain a herd of buffalo, and he was about to have a very difficult time of it. Sooner or later, he would be on the warpath again, but a change of priorities was demanded for the time being.

Agnes dashed out of the vast, oak-panelled entrance hall, past a gigantic marble statue of Lord Dinc, and into the corridors beyond. She calculated that a secret tunnel had, by its very nature, to be underground, which meant going downwards. So, without really knowing where she was headed, she raced onwards, peering into every dark and gloomy corridor, hoping to find some stairs or a lift - anything that looked like it might lead into a cellar and a means of escape.

***

In contrast to Agnes Braintree, Lady Dinc had absolutely no problem finding her way into the vast and byzantine labyrinth concealed beneath her family seat. There were many routes, some hidden behind oak-panelled walls or concealed in the back of wardrobes. In the dusty, cobweb-filled depths, far below Agnes Braintree, Lady Dinc found what she was looking for – a bazooka. That would do nicely, and she picked up a pistol for luck. She wasn't going to have people flying helicopters around her attic willy-nilly. With a satisfied grin and an air of determination, she started the long climb back up, calling into the old boiler room on the way to pick up her spare chamber pot, which she used as a crash helmet. Placing it carefully on her head, she was ready for battle, but by the time she had reached the ground floor, she was quite out of breath. Puffing and sweating profusely, Lady Dinc, with or without a fitted chamber pot, wasn't a sight you wanted to see emerging from a hole in the floor. It was an especially appalling visage here, in Dinctum Manor, where the walls of its dank corridors were decorated with the disembodied heads of creatures large and small.

Feeling slightly dizzy, Lady Dinc surfaced into the passageway and became aware of a figure running towards her. At about the same instant, the figure saw Lady Dinc and let out a piercing scream. It skidded to a standstill, turned around, and then bolted off in the opposite direction. Lady Dinc was trying hard to place the shape. It certainly wasn't one of the many ghosts that haunted the building because they didn't usually run away. Only the living tended to do that.

"What the f..," she began with a look of disbelief, and then, with renewed vigour, she trotted off in the direction it had gone.

***

High above the manor, 'Biggles' got on the radio to let everyone know where Bobcat – the code name given to Agnes - had gone to ground. Police vehicles from all over Dorkshire were already speeding along every road into the valley, and on receiving the news, they made for Winterbourne Dinctum as quickly as they dared. Where the road was wide enough, they tried overtaking one another in a desperate race to get to the scene first. Dorkshire wasn't

311

an exciting place to police, and none wanted to miss out on the action. The chance of finally being able to use a Taser was too good to miss.

Agnes was beginning to panic. She had crossed swords with Lady Dinc on many occasions and knew she was not only as mad as a march hare but probably criminally insane too. Agnes had only a few seconds to see Lady Dinc before taking flight, but the image of what was almost certainly some sort of anti-tank weapon stuck firmly in her mind. Her route into those tunnels was temporarily barred, so Agnes decided to find another way. Perhaps she could outrun her? *Exhaust her and then sneak back,* thought Agnes. *After all, she can't be in peak condition.* It was a plan, so she raced along the corridor as fast as she could.

Soon, Agnes found herself at the double doors leading back into the main entrance hall. She could hide there until Dinc had run past. However, a glance through the doors stopped her dead in her tracks. On the other side and in a terrible mood was a vicious, wolf-like animal the size of a cow, with glistening fangs and eyes that seemed alight with fire. At least, that's how Agnes, in her present state of mind, saw things, and she wasn't about to hang around. A passage that led away to the left seemed like a better choice. So, as quickly as her aching limbs would allow, she carried on. *This is bloody ridiculous,* thought Agnes as she fought to catch her breath. There was a time when charging around like this for hours was easy, but that was a good twenty-five years ago. The strain was beginning to take its toll.

Lady Dinc was starting to struggle too, but she didn't need to exert herself because she had Plummet, and Plummet was only a whistle away. Staggering to a halt, she stuck two fingers in her mouth and blew hard. A long shrill noise echoed endlessly around the hallways, and in no time, the answer came with a distant neighing, followed by the sound of hooves on the floorboards.

Lady Dinc enjoyed riding her horse. It was the only excitement she got when there weren't milkmen or helicopters to shoot at. So, on hearing the creature, her legs parted in anticipation, but she needed to be further off the ground to get mounted, so she clambered awkwardly onto a narrow table wedged against a nearby wall and waited. Plummet came into sight and trotted obediently along the corridor towards her, and after a certain amount of gasping, wheezing, and a good deal of swearing, Lady Dinc was on board and off at a gallop to find her quarry. "Tally ho!" she shouted, wishing there was a bugle to blow.

By this time, Agnes was in a sorry state, trying to run and cry at the same time. The sound of hooves thundering along somewhere behind her was too much to bear, and her ordinarily stalwart constitution was beginning to fail her. *This is insane*, she thought. *No one deserves to be hunted down like a fox. Not even a fox!* Her legs were starting to hurt, her knees felt like they would give way at any moment, and the sweat was beginning to run into her eyes, making it even harder to see in the gloom. Agnes couldn't last much longer, but just as she was about to give in and surrender to whatever fate held in store, she came across a sideboard that looked large enough to hide in.

***

Fang felt he was through the worst of it and decided to venture out in search of someone to attack. He knew the 'nose basher' was still out there because he had spotted her watching him through a crack in the door. That she appeared utterly terrified filled him with pride, and he aimed to ensure she was treated to a severe chewing before the day was done. However, nature had other ideas and was currently reasserting its grasp on his innards. So, he backed reluctantly into the hall again and stood forlornly, hoping for the best but fearing the worst.

Agnes was doing the same as she cowered in her hidey-hole. It was a tight fit, but she squeezed in and closed the doors behind her in the nick of time. Plummet went crashing past, shaking the sideboard violently. It was a terrifying experience, but neither horse nor rider noticed her, and the sound of hooves disappeared around the next corner with a crash. Agnes was thankful, and her spirits revived somewhat. *Aha*, she thought. *You've still got it, haven't you, old girl? I'll make that maniac pay for this. I'll make them all pay*, and with that, she was out and on her way again.

Her first thought was to go back towards the main entrance, but the wolf-cow thing lay in that direction. It was too dangerous, so she decided to trot along behind Dinc and see where it led. She reasoned that Dinc would know where all the exits were and would be checking each for her quarry. Unfortunately, there wasn't anything quite that logical about Lady Dinc, and very soon, Agnes could make out the sound of the horse coming back again. Fear took hold once more. She started to run, her heart straining as the thundering hooves got louder. Lady Dinc was screaming like a banshee. It was worse than being stuck on a railway with a steam train roaring towards you.

Agnes pushed harder, but her body was close to breaking. The sound of crashing plates, paintings, and splintering wood behind petrified her. The corridor was disintegrating as the animal charged through it. Terrified for her life, Agnes staggered on and was just on the point of collapse when a narrow wooden staircase spiralling up into the darkness came into view. She grabbed the handrail and began the climb upwards. There was no way a horse could make it up those stairs, and even if the animal could navigate the tightly winding steps, its weight would have brought the whole thing crashing down. It was another piece of much-needed good luck.

Having reached the top, Agnes fell to her knees, utterly spent. Crawling forward into another dimly lit corridor, she lay gasping for breath on the smelly old carpet. The horse passed by in the passage below without stopping, and Agnes felt suddenly calmed, but she couldn't afford to rest now. So, slowly she got to her feet, and with great care, began to feel her way forward.

As muddled as her mind was, Lady Dinc was starting to think something was amiss. Plummet was fast around these corridors, and she felt sure the wretched intruder should have been overrun by now. It was time to stop and review the situation. Besides, there was a decanter of Bristol Cream sitting on a nearby dresser, and it would have been rude to ignore it. A quick slurp would help focus her thoughts.

In the corridor above, Agnes stumbled. "Damn it," she said, forgetting herself for a moment. She froze, listening for a sign that Lady Dinc was on to her. Silence.

Agnes breathed a sigh of relief, but just as she was getting to her feet, a horrifying sound rose from below.

"Woooooooooo," and then again even louder, "WOOOOOOOO!"

It was Lady Dinc, but it could easily have been the Flying Scotsman, and soon, the sound of the woman chuffing up the staircase filled the air.

For the first time in her life, Agnes nearly wet herself. Utterly terrified, she found the energy to stand up and keep running. Her aching muscles protested, and her joints felt like they might seize completely, but she had to keep going. Then the tears came again, streaming down her cheeks. She was in a living nightmare with no apparent way out.

Somewhere behind them, Fang was still tracking his prey as best as he could, but progress was slow. He'd finally made his way out of the entrance hall, but painful cramps still played havoc with his insides, and in any other circumstance, he would have willingly given up the chase, but revenge drove him doggedly onwards. Then again, given that he had a leg in each corner and barked at cats, 'doggedly' was his only option. Fang's mind was made up. Someone was going to get properly crunched before the day was done.

***

Dinctum Manor was surrounded. An assortment of automatic weapons pointed at the building, and soldiers did their best to blend in with the vegetation. Intelligence reports had it that a well-armed and internationally backed terrorist cell occupied the manor, so the troops were ordered to hold their ground until the SAS arrived. However, standing proudly in the middle of them, and very much against the doctor's orders, was the partially recovered DS Thorn. Sporting the latest in neck collars and with coils of bandage still wrapped around his cracked ribs, he was about to do something which would go down as either exceptionally brave or downright suicidal.

"Oi! Tutankhamen!" shouted a rose bush with a machine gun and three stripes on its arm. "Get yourself into cover before someone shoots your sodding obelisks off!"

Thorn ignored the chuckles that came from other parts of the undergrowth. He was going to show everyone what a good copper he was and put right the mess that had started with the arrest of Nora Clifton. The Chief would give him a commendation, no question – promotion too, with any luck. On the downside, he could get well and truly killed, but at least he'd be given a posthumous award. As things stood, the most he could hope for was a reduction in rank and an expensive divorce.

So, taking a bold pace forward, he shouted to no one in particular and without much conviction, "Cover me!" Then he was off like a scalded cat, running full tilt across the lawn towards the manor house. One of the variegated perennials took his request seriously and let off a few rounds of suppressive fire. Thorn wasn't prepared for this and suffered a severe crisis as he crossed the lawn. His ability to run with his nose in the grass was impressive and fascinating. It was the sort of thing you see a Bloodhound doing, not an officer of the law. Had he been any lower, the moles would have had company.

Reaching the entrance, Thorn took a moment to catch his breath. The impressive doors towered above him, and it took great courage to reach up, turn the handle and slip quietly inside. It was either courage or recklessness, but he did it and then wished to God he hadn't. Thorn immediately found himself gagging for air. The smell of Fang's earlier mishaps hit him square in the nose, and he stared around in disbelief. Only a herd of hippopotami with food poisoning could have achieved something similar – that or an elephant on a centrifuge. He took one of the bandages from his knee and used it to cover his nose and mouth. Turning back now would have made him the laughingstock of the Dorkshire Police Force, and there was no way he would let that happen. So, he made his way anxiously across the hall, taking as much care as someone crossing a minefield. The evidence of incontinence on an industrial scale was all around him.

***

Far above and in a distant wing of the building, Agnes rushed along in near darkness. It was tough going. Obstacles littered the floor, and she tripped several times. Against all odds, Lady Dinc had made it to the top of the stairs and was now on the same floor as her quarry. She could hear Agnes stumbling around somewhere ahead and, in her younger days, would have been off down the corridor like a bison on speed. But age and the steep ascent had drained her strength, so she decided a different, less strenuous approach was necessary. Drawing out the pistol, she let off several rounds into the gloom.

Agnes screamed in terror. "Oh shit! Oh shit," she cried. Some bloody maniac with a potty on her head was trying to kill her! She had to get out, and if that meant giving herself up to the police, then so be it. At least they weren't going to shoot her. Another volley of gunfire rang out, and bullets hit the wall immediately to her right. She dived to the side of the passage, landing against a door, which burst open under her weight. Falling through into a small, empty room, she quickly slammed the door behind her and dashed towards a window, trying frantically to force it open. But no amount of tugging, pushing, or swearing could budge it. Hundreds of years of encrusted paint ensured it wouldn't move an inch. More shots were fired.

"Oh shit. OH SHIT," sobbed Agnes, hopping from one leg to the other while banging hopelessly on the window frame. She was distraught, and realising an escape through the window was impossible, she turned to search for alternatives. Just when she was about to give up all hope of a future, she found a small door that looked more like the entrance to a cupboard, and inside, a flight of stairs led downwards into the darkness. Without hesitation, Agnes took her chance taking the steps as quickly as she dared. She was desperate.

In the corridor outside, Lady Dinc had run out of ammunition but was no longer in a hurry. She knew all about that room and precisely where the hidden staircase led, so she decided to wait. Sooner or later, the "snivelling little intruder" would have to come back up, and she'd be waiting. The pistol might be useless now, but there was still a rocket in the Bazooka, and that would do the trick. Besides, it was long past time for another tipple, and there was bound to be an emergency watering hole somewhere nearby.

Final Confrontation

Go anywhere in Dinctum Manor, and you would never be more than a few paces from one of Lady Dinc's watering holes. These were the places she kept her emergency supplies of liquor - mostly gin - and like a squirrel that buries its nuts, Lady Dinc often forgot where they were. Consequently, she adopted a policy of saturating the place with booze - a bit like carpet bombing, but different. There was now so much gin hidden in Dinctum Manor that it would have burnt for over a century if it had ever caught fire.

Lady Dinc dropped the pistol on the floor and pushed open a nearby door. Stepping into the room, she stood for a while, waiting to see if something jogged her memory. Nothing did, so she decided to have a poke around. The first place to look was the chimney, so she rooted around for something that felt like a bottle. Nothing but soot. She jumped around, testing the floor for loose boards. Not even a squeak. Next, she looked under the table for secret compartments, and then, when that avenue proved fruitless, she checked the radiator for extra taps. Some were topped up with alcohol and quite capable of keeping you just as warm as the standard variety, but not this one. Lady Dinc was getting a bit worried. There was nothing in the light shade, not even a bulb, and the sparsely populated bookshelves were also disappointingly deficient. She was about to start pulling plaster off the walls with her bare hands when she noticed a spider crawling out of a crack in the skirting board. "Aha! The skirting boards," she said gleefully as the first board dropped away to reveal an unopened bottle of London Dry. The next panel fell away effortlessly to uncover another cache. "Bottle number two!" she cried. Almost half of the first bottle was gone in no time. "Bloody thirsty work this hunting business," she said, wiping her mouth on a sleeve before letting out a long and very loud burp. She permitted herself a little giggle and started to hum an unrecognisable tune. It was the sort of noise a badger makes when it finds an especially juicy slug for breakfast.

Already feeling much better, Lady Dinc decided to open the second bottle and consider where the third might be. It was bound to be in there somewhere. As she sat down on the floor with the Bazooka beside her, the intruder faded quickly from her thoughts. Then she remembered dangling a bottle on some string behind each of the curtains. As far as Lady Dinc was concerned, four bottles were just about enough to achieve nirvana, so she settled down for a session. A pack of pork scratchings would have been perfect, but you couldn't have everything.

***

When the shooting started on the floor above, DS Thorn took cover behind Lord Dinc's statue. He wished he was back in the ambulance, connected to a plentiful supply of oxygen. Dreams didn't get any better than the ones you had when breathing that stuff. Even the Drug Squad couldn't improve on it. The statue was made from what appeared to be white marble and looked solid enough to stop an armour-piercing bandicoot. So, crouching as low to the floor as he could without taking off his clothes, Thorn felt less vulnerable. However, his colleagues in the garden were getting quite worried because he'd entered the house alone and without a radio. One of them was sent to find out if he was still alive.

The unfortunate individual ventured hesitantly towards the entrance and stuck his head in the door, but the stench made him step back so quickly that he nearly got whiplash. The sound of bullets flying around was bad enough, but this was biological warfare. He took a deep breath, pinched his nose tightly, and poked his head back inside long enough to shout. "Oi! Sarge! You all right in there?"

Thorn was surprised that anyone was interested and concluded there must be a sweepstake running on the odds of him surviving the day. "Don't worry yourself, Constable," he shouted. "I'm wonderful, thank you very much. You can sod off and tell the Chief that *Detective Sergeant Thorn* has the matter under complete control," Then, for good measure, he added. "Tell him not to worry. I will apprehend the suspect shortly, so get a car ready to take her away."

Thorn's voice echoed around the vast hall most impressively, and he made a note to ask for a larger and more resonant office once all this was over. The reverberation gave his voice a very grand and pleasing timbre. It made him sound just like the master of ceremonies at the annual police pantomime. He'd coveted that role with its magnificent costume, gold chain, and automatic membership of the Dillchurch Freemasons Lodge. Sadly, the honour had yet to pass his way, and he'd had to endure several seasons as the back end of a pantomime camel, which passed as a police horse. In his time, he'd also been a sugar plum fairy, a magic mushroom, and a goblin on a penny farthing. For DS Thorn, rank, it seemed, had no privileges whatsoever.

His voice echoed just far enough along the corridors to reach the ears of a certain police dog, who had no trouble whatsoever in identifying its owner. Given a choice, Fang would always prefer to harass Thorn if he could. So, turning away from the spiral staircase and wearing a doggy-shaped grin, Fang trotted unsteadily back along the corridor.

***

Somewhere under Dinctum Manor, a battered and bruised Agnes Braintree was lying exhausted. Her journey down the stairs hadn't been very graceful, and she'd fallen the last few steps in a rush to evade her pursuer. Lying in an uncomfortable heap, she hadn't realised her legs would bend into such a position before now and wished she'd known about it when Plunge-Pithering was alive. *That would have put a smile on his face*, thought Agnes, detaching herself momentarily from the situation. Struggling to her feet, she began to look around. There were solid stone walls on every side except where the stairs came in. A small hole on the opposite wall was too high to reach. It simply served to light and ventilate the space around her. Underfoot, the floor seemed soft and slippery, and Agnes quickly realised it must be mud or something very like it. She was in a long-forgotten dungeon constructed centuries before to enclose and secure an old well. Lady Dinc occasionally ventured down there to try her hand at fishing and would sit perfectly still for hours in the middle of the chamber, with her line dangling into the void. The only thing she caught was a cold.

Agnes saw the wooden trap door covering the well and wondered if there might be a way out hidden beneath it. The door moved easily to reveal a deep shaft with sheer sides. It was too dark to see into the depths, but judging by the echoes, it must have been extremely deep. Unable to see any steps or ladders, Agnes decided it would be foolhardy to attempt climbing down - not unless you had a lot of rope and a complicated harness that also included a parachute. Turning away, she poked around in the shadows looking for hidden tunnels, loose brickwork, or even a drain - anything that would offer an alternate means of escape. She was desperate to avoid going back up those stairs and wasn't even sure she had the energy to do it.

As she searched, Agnes came across what could only be an old suit of armour, partly buried in the mud. In the dim light, much of it appeared to be rusty, but although she was no expert, it looked more or less complete - enough for her purposes, at any rate. To her surprise and delight, a very unpleasant-looking axe lay beside it. That was it then. If she had to go back up to confront her assailant, she might as well put some armour on and take the weapon for good measure.

Agnes had never worn armour before, not even for her favourite MP, and quickly discovered that putting it on was an immense struggle. This was partly down to inexperience but mainly because the suit was at least a size too small. Eventually, and very reluctantly, she had to discard her clothes and grease her body with slimy mud to slide into the tin cocoon more easily. *Needs must... Queen and country*, she thought, as bits of metal and mail clanked and squeaked around her. It was all very uncomfortable and painfully tight in places. Parts of her body kept oozing out through the gaps and especially over the top of the breastplate. No amount of pushing, pulling, or squeezing yielded a satisfactory result. *It will have to do*, she decided with a sigh.

So, feeling a little less defenceless, Agnes forced a broken helmet over her head, picked up the axe, and with great difficulty, made her way back up the stairs. She looked remarkably like one of Lady Dinc's ancestors, crossed with a robot.

***

Fang felt that he had already suffered more than any dog deserved. His delicate nose was swollen, his backside felt like it had been too close to a blowtorch, and his stomach was tied in the kind of knots only fishermen and boy scouts can undo. He wasn't, therefore, in the best of moods, but the prospect of inserting a canine or two into Thorn's podgy rear lifted his spirits considerably. Moving quickly was out of the question, but it didn't matter because even he, a humble hound, had learnt that you sometimes had to take your time catching monkeys, except that, in his estimation, this one was a complete and utter baboon. Thorn had a big surprise sneaking down the corridor towards him.

***

Lady Dinc had soaked up every drop of the liquor and was now drunkenly pulling lumps of plaster from the laths, convinced there was more booze somewhere. If there was, she had little chance of finding it since she could hardly stand up for more than a few seconds without feeling very giddy and sick. The room spun, first one way and then the other, until unable to focus, she put her back to the wall and slid gently down to the floor. It was, she decided, high time for a snooze.

Sitting there with a crooked smile, Lady Dinc decided that this might be the biggest binge since the late fifties when her Aunt Gladys had hijacked a tanker full of single malt. Gladys had concealed the tanker in a gully behind the manor house and disguised it as a log pile. It had taken the Dincs only a year to consume all the whiskey, after which her aunt spent her weekends hanging upside down in the empty tank, sniffing the fumes. She'd been as high as a spy satellite for months and was subsequently known as Glad the Inhaler. Her picture still hung on a wall somewhere in the manor.

With her eyes just about closed and already snoring contentedly, Lady Dinc became aware of a clattering noise like the sound of several saucepans banging together. She dismissed it at first, but after hearing it for a third and fourth time, she started to sober up. Opening both eyes, she sat perfectly still and listened intently. There was silence for a moment, and then, just when she thought it had gone away, it started again: clank, clank, plunk, bump. It was the sound of footsteps, but they were distant, slow, and oddly metallic. Lady Dinc's heart pounded faster than was good for her, and adrenaline coursed through her body quicker than baked beans travelled through a baby. She reached out slowly to grasp the bazooka and slithered through the door into the gloom beyond as silently as she could manage. The sound was coming from the far end of the corridor, so she took a defensive position on the floor with the weapon held tightly against her shoulder. Whatever it was, it wasn't going to get past her.

Agnes was finding the going much harder than she would have liked. Beaten panels dug into just about every part of her suffering body. She couldn't begin to identify which bit was the most uncomfortable, but the breastplate forced sharply up under her bosom and, causing it to protrude at a most abnormal angle, probably took first prize. The sheer weight of the armour made her sweat copiously, and it had begun to occur to her that it might not be so easy to get the confounded stuff off. Making her way painfully forwards, Agnes tried hard to see what lay in wait for her up ahead, but there wasn't enough light. Lady Dinc could have been on her feet, doing a rain dance, and still been virtually invisible to Agnes, so she kept plodding blindly onwards into the unknown, huffing, puffing, squeaking, and clanking like a geriatric android.

***

DS Thorn was considering his next move. It came down to finding the best way of catching Braintree without getting shot, and no matter how he looked at it, he kept coming to the same conclusion: he was going to die horribly. *I'm going to be extremely pissed off if I end up getting killed in here,* he thought. Without a weapon and having no idea how many rooms there were in the house or where any of the corridors led, the task suddenly seemed hopeless. He didn't even know if Braintree was alone. *What if she had accomplices?* "Oh, for crying out loud," he said as the severity of the situation dawned on him. He'd gotten into some messes, but this was about to cap the lot.

Just then, it crossed his mind that maybe - just possibly - he could save face by tearing his clothes and then stumbling dramatically back outside to collapse on the lawn. He could say that he'd tackled Braintree and that she'd held him at gunpoint, but he'd managed to escape with his life. It seemed like a good plan. There was promotion in a plan like that and a medal too, if he did well. So, as quickly as he could, he started tugging at his shirt and tie. Buttons popped, and sleeves were torn. Then he had a go at his trousers. Luckily the seam on one of the legs was a bit frayed, and it soon gave way. For good measure, he smeared some dirt and dust from the back of the statue over his face.

"This is it, Thorn," he said. "It's time for an award-winning performance."

Stepping out from behind the massive marble statue, he made ready to dash across the hall to the front door, but as he looked ahead, his legs froze to the spot and refused to go any further. Standing between him and his route to safety was Fang, drooling uncontrollably and snarling in a manner calculated to show off every one of his very sharp and enormous teeth. The phrase 'all the better to chew you with' came into Thorn's increasingly terrified mind. The situation had just gone from bad to catastrophic.

"Oh, HELL!" exclaimed Thorn.

***

Lady Dinc was about to wet herself, and it wasn't just the vast quantity of gin inflating her bladder. Even though she couldn't see it clearly, she was utterly convinced the ghost of Sir Lancelot Dinc was making its way up the long, murky corridor towards her. Her grandmother had warned her about this terrible phantom. Lancelot Dinc was one of her most malevolent ancestors. He ruled the west of Olde Dorkshire with an iron fist, a glass eye, and a mouth full of foul-smelling teeth. If you believed legend, he ate live chickens and had his serfs put to death at the drop of a hat, sometimes an apple. He even had them put to deaf by chopping off one or more of their ears. Many myths and stories were associated with this individual, but the one that leapt into Lady Dinc's unhinged brain was this: if you looked his ghost in the eyes, death would visit you within the week, and all your pansies would wilt. Lady Dinc wasn't much of a gardener and couldn't have given a tinker's cuss about the pansies, but "death within a week" was an entirely different matter. She had to act quickly before Sir Lancelot got close enough to zap her with his beady little eyes.

The Bazooka was heavy, and her arms were getting tired, but with great effort, she lifted it a few inches from the floorboards and pointed it toward the noise. Just as she was about to pull the trigger, curiosity got the better of her. She wanted to see if the ghost was as horrific as it was alleged, so she waited, trying to close her eyes enough to avoid certain death yet wide enough to see.

At first, only the sound of the armour came out of the shadows, but soon, there was the glint of a leg and then an arm. As she lay there, perfectly still, Lady Dinc forgot all about the legend and opened her eyes wider and wider as the whole, ghastly spectacle came gradually into view. Not only did Sir Lancelot have breasts almost as large as her own, but the absence of an 'apparatus' between his legs suggested that 'he' might well have been a she. It wasn't a vision that Lady Dinc could endure and definitely not a piece of history she wanted redrafting. The legend of Lancelot Dinc had served the family well for many generations, and it wouldn't do to have the truth exposed to quite the extent that it was now. Without a second thought, she pulled the trigger as hard as possible.

A loud bang was quickly followed by a whoosh as a flaming projectile shot out of the barrel towards Agnes Braintree. It hurtled along the corridor, lighting up the paintings and stuffed heads on either side as it went. Fortunately for Agnes, the rocket was designed to travel many metres before arming itself. So, when it hit her square in the breastplate, the rocket didn't explode. It simply accelerated her back along the corridor and out through the wall at the far end. Agnes emitted a scream that grew in pitch and amplitude with her velocity. A wartime Stuka bomber would have had trouble duplicating the effect.

Lady Dinc saw none of this. The recoil sent her sliding backwards and down the spiral staircase to the corridor below. The sound she made was almost identical to the one uttered by Agnes. Lying at the bottom of the stairs, Lady Dinc made a brief but doomed attempt to stand up before falling to the floor, giggling.

**

Soldiers and police officers, still hiding in the greenery outside, looked on in disbelief as the side of Dinctum manor erupted. Bricks and plaster crashed down around them, and dust filled the air. A vision of incomparable horror unfolded as the semi-naked head teacher, still screaming like a banshee, passed overhead. It would have been a gross understatement to say that they saw her in an entirely different light. Arcing across the sky above them and followed by a trail of dust, she looked like a pornographic meteor, with pink, wobbly bits protruding at all angles. It was surreal and she seemed to be destined for that great 'pudding fest' in the heavens. However, luck, if you can call it that, was on her side. The rocket failed to detonate and simply jettisoned her forcefully into an ornamental lake beyond the azaleas. Only when she hit the water did Agnes stop her screaming. The sound of the splash reminded those who heard it of a depth charge exploding. Steam gathered above the turbulent surface, and fish tried swimming to safety across the lawn. Struggling free from what remained of her armour, Agnes rose to the surface and drifted slowly into the reeds, which is where she was found, talking to a frog.

The whole episode only lasted a matter of seconds, but for those who witnessed it, the trauma would endure for a lifetime.

***

Thorn instinctively dived for cover when he heard the bazooka go off. Fang tried to take advantage by pouncing toward him but fell short, losing his footing and sliding helplessly across the tiled floor. Realising that this was his only chance of escape, Thorn scrambled desperately to his feet and dashed to the front door, repeatedly shouting 'SIT' as he went. He managed to get most of the way out of the building before Fang grabbed him by the ankle and dragged him, screaming, back inside.

"Poor sod," said Constable Hewbry, recognising the sound of his dog. He could hear the growling in between Thorn's screams. Hewbry had lost track of Fang earlier in the day and now knew exactly where the animal was, even if he wasn't quite sure why, or for that matter, how. It crossed his mind to sit tight and let Fang play with Thorn for a while, but he wasn't a vindictive man. So, he rushed out from the cover of a buddleia and sprinted towards the house. As he ran, he blew hard on a whistle that was supposed to bring the dog to heel.

"Aargh! Get him off me. GET HIM OFF ME!" pleaded Thorn to anyone who could hear and then, turning to the dog, shouted 'SIT' again for all he was worth. But Fang was having far too much fun and found Thorn's screams surprisingly therapeutic. All the whistles in Dorkshire wouldn't make him stop. To amuse himself, Fang let Thorn crawl partway out of the doorway before dragging him back in again. It was the sort of thing a cat could get away with doing to a mouse, but not the kind of behaviour you would have wanted from a police dog. Eventually, Hewbry burst through the door to find Thorn face down on the floor, whining pitifully, with Fang sitting triumphantly on his back. The dog was trying to appear as innocent as possible, but Hewbry had seen that look too many times and knew it usually meant he had to call the air ambulance.

"Hold on a minute Sarge," he said as reassuringly as he could. "I'll have him on a chain faster than you can say, Constable Glossop."

Thorn lost it: "I DON'T GIVE A RAT'S ARSE ABOUT CONSTABLE FUCKING GLOSSOP! GET THAT RUDDY MONSTER OUT OF HERE AND SHOOT THE FUCKING THING BECAUSE I CAN PROMISE YOU THIS, MATEY BOY. IF YOU DON'T, THEN I BLOODY WELL WILL!" With that, Thorn passed out. Lady Dinc, exhausted from the day's events, did the same.

***

David and Vicki remained in the front room of her house until the focus of activity moved to Dinctum Manor, further up the valley. They had no idea why most of the troops, police, and press had gone in that direction but assumed it was probably safe to go out and see what, if anything, they could do to help.

The scene before them had a post-apocalyptic feel to it. Green, sodden turf had disappeared under a blanket of dirty brown sludge. Bricks, pipes, and pieces of twisted metal were strewn in every direction. Trees, where they were still standing, were stripped of their leaves, wraithlike against the leaden sky. A thick vapour hung over the river. It was undoubtedly mist, but the troops weren't taking any chances and were now wearing their gas masks. This ought to have spread panic amongst the few villagers still picking their way carefully through the debris, but they were well beyond caring by this time and tramped on regardless.

The Firefighters had given up with what was left of Dinc-Bottom and had resumed their attempts to put out the burning Volvo. Medics, who were by this time feeling a bit surplus to requirements, wandered the field, looking for something to do. They had trained for years for moments like this, and it seemed like a waste not to be putting their undoubted skills to good use. So keen were they to use their new defibrillator, they had mistakenly tried to bring a bit of tree back to life and started a good bonfire in the process. To be fair, it did look a little like someone lying dead under the mud, and some moss-covered bark could pass as a human chest with a bit of imagination - just. Only the Twinkin sisters seemed to be in good spirits. They laughed and sang as they danced in a puddle. Sometimes, living in your own strange version of reality was a blessing.

"It's hard to know where to start," said David as he looked around. "There's devastation everywhere you look."

He was just starting to moan about the very suspicious absence of senior club members when he felt a heavy hand on his shoulder. Turning around, he came face to unpleasant face with Constable McLoonie, who was wearing one of his most severe expressions.

"Mr David Faber?" asked McLoonie in a detached manner that made David run cold.

"Yes, that's me," he replied. Time to face the music, he thought and quickly rehearsed how he would explain the missile.

"Can I ask you where you were between the hours of… shall we say six and eight this morning, Mr Faber?" The Constable glanced at his notebook to confirm the timings.

David was utterly thrown by this and started to mumble. "Er…w… well, this morning?" he spluttered. "Six and eight? Um… in bed, I suppose. Why?

"I see," said McLoonie, wearily. "You weren't standing at your bedroom window exposing yourself to a member of the public then, Mr Faber?" The distasteful expression on McLoonie's face told David that the officer already had the answer to that question. The sound of Mrs Bryant's screams came flooding back.

"Oh, for f…"

Aftermath

The hunt for what had become known as the West Dorkshire Popular Front ended with the capture of Agnes Braintree. Even so, the press still didn't want to believe what Chief Constable Dint had told them all along - that it was all just an unfortunate accident. They searched every corner of the valley, looking for evidence of a cover-up, wasting weeks chasing rumour and gossip before finally packing up their equipment and leaving.

Lady Dinc spent many long and tedious days answering questions about her role in the events surrounding Agnes Braintree's sudden and novel expulsion from Dinctum Manor. You couldn't go around shooting head teachers with a Bazooka just because you felt like it, but she stuck tenaciously to her story about "a terrifying ghost with an axe and big tits". Eventually, the specialist officers from the headquarters in Dincsmouth decided that enough was enough and, acting on the Chief Constable's advice, gave her the benefit of the doubt. In their professional opinion, Lady Dinc was either completely mad, poorly sighted, or suffering from severe alcohol poisoning - probably all three. However, Dint decided it was in his interest to have her released without charge. It wasn't a good idea to lock up the lords, ladies, and knights of West Dorkshire - not unless you wanted to lose your seat on all sorts of prestigious committees. So, much to everyone's surprise, Lady Dinc narrowly avoided spending the rest of her days in jail getting a stripy suntan. She returned to Dinctum Manor as triumphantly as possible, sitting in the Chief Constable's car with the lights flashing, siren blasting, and a flag on the bonnet. Dint had reluctantly agreed to this on the condition that she dropped her demand for outriders.

When the motorcade reached Dinctum Manor, they found a collection of odd-looking vehicles parked around the entrance. Ropes, flippers, gas bottles, and hoses lay scattered around the drive, and bundles of thick cable trailed through the front door into the house. Lady Dinc had a horrible feeling that the plumbing had failed again. It had happened once before and flooded most of the east wing. There was so much water that the plumbers used a dinghy to get around, and a flock of geese took up residence in one of the dining halls.

However, it wasn't the plumbing or even a freak tide this time. After arresting Lady Dinc, DC Drivel, and Constable Hewbry were ordered to conduct a thorough search of the Manor and its grounds. If he was going to release her without charge, the Chief certainly didn't want her sat on an arms dump. He had a feeling that now she had a taste for it, Lady Dinc would be itching to blow someone else through the side of her house, and God forbid, it might even be him.

He made a mental note never to go inside Dinctum Manor again without an armed escort.

For Drivel and Hewbry, the task appeared simple. But they were ignorant of the depths of its cellars or the surprising number of tunnels that led in every direction for miles around. Consequently, they quickly became completely and utterly lost. Several unsuccessful attempts had been made to find them, and it was now the turn of the cave divers.

Days passed without a sign of the unfortunate officers, and Dint was beginning to fear for their lives. He started having nightmares about the press coming back, but just as he was on the point of alerting the Home Secretary, Hewbry and Drivel turned up in a chicken coop a mile west of Dinctum Splashit. Suffering from starvation, they began plucking the first bird they could catch. It wasn't too pleased about any of this on account of still being very much alive and gave the two officers a severe pecking. Soon the entire brood and a dozen geese had joined in, and the officers had to crawl over two hundred yards through a dung-filled meadow before escaping their plight.

During a debrief, the story they told was of an incredible adventure beneath the Dinc Valley through miles of twisting tunnels, hidden caverns, and the skeletons of pirates. No one believed a word of it, especially the bit about Neandertals and Dodos. Somewhat put out, Hewbry and Drivel limped off to freshen up and write a detailed report. When the Chief read it, he had both of them placed on sick leave for an indefinite period pending a psychiatric report.

Also enjoying a spell of extended leave was DS Thorn. Having escaped from the jaws of his least favourite police dog, he spent a week at the hospital in Dillchurch, where doctors treated his injuries. He passed the time designing complicated contraptions that would, had they ever been built, have been perfect for making the nasty creature feel as uncomfortable as he did – hopefully worse. The Inquisition would have awarded him honorary membership and a complimentary thumbscrew for these inventions. The animal was still at large because Hewbry had popped in with the thing in tow one day during visiting hours. The sight of the dog at the foot of his hospital bed sent Thorn into apoplectic convulsions, and it took three of the largest nurses Hewbry had ever seen, armed with a powerful tranquilliser, to sedate him. Hewbry had to make a swift exit and narrowly avoided a lecture about bringing dogs into a hospital. Strapped securely to his bed, Thorn knew his time would come and that he would visit revenge on the vile thing. He would see to it, even if it was the last thing he did.

Pinkle had put in for a transfer. Events at the church left him unable to sleep properly, and when he did eventually doze off, his recurring nightmare was of being chased to the top of the spire by a vast, snorting monster with horns and steam coming from its nostrils. He felt constantly drained and anxious, so he decided to investigate becoming a monk. It couldn't be as bad as people made out, and their brown habits had a certain appeal. He also liked that most of them seemed to tinker in the garden all day - no sermons to write, no decisions to make beyond which kind of fruit to plant and what kind of booze you could make with it.

Unfortunately for him, the bishop was having none of it. Pinkle was sent back to the valley with advice that a diet of only dairy products would "immunise you against this irrational fear of all things bovine". Bishops often have strange ideas. The only thing the diet achieved was to bring Pinkle out in lots of spots. Some said he also looked a bit cow-eyed, and the large brass bell he wore around his neck had a few people worried. For him, life at the church slipped back into the usual mundane and lonely pattern. He told himself it could have been a lot worse, and that the valley would quickly return to normal. Surely nothing so traumatic could ever happen there again.

A peek inside Dr Function's shed would have given him the answer to that question. Spurred on by the rocket's performance, he immediately began work on his largest-ever project. He called it his Saturn Six. Naturally, he regretted the demolition of Fawcett's residence, but sacrifices had to be made for the cause of scientific advancement, and who took any notice of court injunctions these days, anyway? Dr Function was ready to get into orbit and confident that his latest masterpiece would achieve just that. There would be no more flying hamsters. It was his turn to pilot the thing. All he needed was a couple of tons of titanium and a thousand litres of liquid oxygen, but where to get it?

Gavin would have been the obvious choice. He could be relied upon to supply almost anything anyone needed, but Gavin was keeping a very low profile. This was on account of some surreptitious endeavours relating to the gas main. Work on repairing the pipes had come to a halt after the fun day, and it took him no time to take full advantage of the situation. At first, he considered resurrecting plans to connect the water and gas mains to the same pipe. It had to be worth the effort just to see what came out of the fountains in Winterbourne Dinctum. A sheet of flame around a hundred feet high would have been entirely satisfactory. However, he settled for a private and secret extension to the gas main. Suddenly, gas bills were a thing of the past, and he was very pleased with himself. So was his mum.

Jamsie was feeling very pleased with himself too. In partnership with his eldest sister, he'd set up a stall near the post office in Dinctum selling porcelain miniatures of Agnes Braintree sat astride a giant missile. The Dinc Valley became a popular attraction thanks to all the television coverage, and people arrived in droves to point, gawp, and gossip. There was good money to be made from selling them souvenirs, and Jamsie cashed in. Aside from the Braintree rocket, he was also selling bits of brick which he alleged were pieces of Dinc-Bottom and managed to get over a hundred pounds for a toilet seat "sat on by a genuine Fawcett". He was very pleased with that and quietly liberated another ten seats from the public convenience in Dillchurch to meet the obvious demand.

As a listed building, Dinc-Bottom was to be rebuilt from the ground up, and regulations insisted on it looking exactly as it did before the unscheduled demolition. In the weeks that followed his rescue, Fawcett had tried without success to get the insurance company to cough up for a ten-bedroom extension and heated pool.

His wife's plans for a three-hundred-meter rifle range also met with disapproval. So, somewhat disillusioned, they left to spend time with relatives in the south of France. Life, they hoped, would be better for them in France. Only time would tell if it would be better for the French.

Agnes Braintree continued her conversations with the frog. She even wrote them down and pinned them to the walls of her cell. It was a nice cell with soft walls, a fitted pond, and realistic plastic lilies. Special dispensation was given for her to keep her little pet frog, Pithy, with her. Sadly, the frog croaked, but it didn't seem to matter because, by that time, Agnes had made friends with a fly. The Queen never did reply to her letter.

Dinctum Rests

Another Friday evening youth club session came to an end. Thankfully, there hadn't been any significant incidents. No fires, no drunkenness, no eating of gardens, no telling headteachers they had fat behinds, and no arrests. Naturally, Jennifer had clamped herself to David's leg and was playing at being his shadow. Nigel, the goat, had learnt to ski, and someone had stretched cling film over the girls' toilets, which meant everything that was supposed to go down the pan bounced straight out again. But these were all minor irritations compared to what the summer had thrown up. There were some difficult conversations with authorities, and many apologies had to be made. There was also the inevitable witch hunt. Someone had to be blamed for the catastrophic events. It wasn't possible to have a simple accident anymore - people wanted to point a finger, especially if there was a sniff of compensation. So, there were enquiries, hearings, committees, and endless reports. Vicky stood by and defended David steadfastly, hour after hour, day after day. As far as her fiancé was concerned, she'd spent too much time with him and his patience eventually ran out. They had a big bust-up and Vicki told him to take a hike, so he did. He took his tractor too.

In the end, common sense prevailed. David avoided incarceration, but it did give Sally the perfect excuse to pack her bags and run off with her diver friend. She left her wedding ring in the bedside bin. "Probably the size of his oxygen bottle," said David when talking it over with Vicki.

***

Despite everything, the fun day had done some good. David and Vicki made a case for extra funding that the County Youth Officer - still Mr Palmoil, but only by the skin of his teeth - had found difficult to refuse. The unwelcome attention from the national press left him with little option. Hands were shaken, and winks followed nods. Papers were shredded, budgets were quickly revised, and Dinctum Youth Club was now the proud owner of two new pool tables, a suite of computers for their Internet club, and a brand-new disco system with lasers. In the right conditions, it was possible to shine a concentrated beam of light at a tractor on the opposite side of the valley. Lady Dinc had shown them how to do it and managed to ignite two Massey Fergusons before deciding to lay low. David also had enough money to offer Gavin the position of Assistant Leader and pay him the going rate. Gavin was chuffed to bits and appeared to grow two inches taller.

At the end of the evening and with everything packed neatly away, David, Vicki, and Gavin stepped out of the hall and locked the door on another chapter of youth club life. The club would be shut for redecoration now, and they all needed a well-earned break.

"You two coming down the pub?" asked Gavin.

"No thanks, mate," replied Vicki. "It's been a long week, and we're tired. Time for an early night, isn't it, David?" David smiled and nodded in agreement.

"Tired?" asked Gavin sarcastically. "Pull the other one. It's got bells on."

The glint in his eye suggested he knew exactly what sort of early night Vicki had in mind.

***

The sun was setting slowly over Dorkshire, and the light slipped silently from the valley. Bats whirled noiselessly around the hillsides, the cows practised a line dance, and Kangabats nibbled the clover. Summer would soon fade from memory, and the crisp chill of autumn mornings would flush the podgy little faces gazing out from the school bus on its winding way to Dillchurch. The Dinc Valley licked its wounds, lay down in front of a log fire, and snoozed contentedly - until the next time.

The End.
Mark Hubbard
Snowdonia 2023

About the Author

Born in Birmingham, England, Mark grew up in Devon and then Dorset before joining the British Armed Forces. A decade later, he left to work for a local council before founding an electronics company with his brother, where he had a variety of roles, including responsibility for product design, marketing, computer graphics, and health and safety. Thirty years later, and with the company sold, Mark has been able to devote more time to his other interests, which include writing, hiking in the mountains with his best friend, Noah, the dog, and composing orchestral music. Mark is the proud father of two amazing and remarkable daughters, Loren and Sophie, and now lives in Snowdonia, North Wales.

Milton Keynes UK
Ingram Content Group UK Ltd.
UKHW020644010823
426141UK00016B/753